# DOUBLE JEOPARDY

# DOUBLE JEOPARDY

*William Bernhardt*

BALLANTINE BOOKS
NEW YORK

LIBRARY OF CONGRESS CATALOGING-IN-PUBLICATION DATA
Bernhardt, William, 1960–
Double jeopardy / William Bernhardt.
p.    cm.
ISBN: 0-345-38683-3
I. Title.
PS3552.E73147D68 1995
813'.54—dc20                                    94-21909
CIP

Text design by Mary A. Wirth

Manufactured in the United States of America
First Edition: March 1995

10  9  8  7  6  5  4  3  2  1

TO ESTHER PERKINS

*for getting this whole business started*

*It's not what we don't know that hurts.*
*It's what we know that ain't so.*

—WILL ROGERS

*Friends may come and go, but enemies accumulate.*

—THOMAS JONES

# DOUBLE JEOPARDY

# SUNDAY

## *April 14*

**1**

11:55 P.M.

Thomas J. Seacrest, Esq., kicked the sand on the north bank of Lake Palestine. According to the fluorescent-tipped hands on his new Fossil wristwatch, it was almost midnight, the appointed time. He looked all around, but he couldn't see anyone. The night was pitch-black; the moon was hidden behind a dense cloud bank.

Seacrest harbored a terrible, humiliating secret: he was afraid of the dark. He had hated the dark when he was a boy, and he still hated it now, when he was thirty-two. He supposed in some respects boys never grow up, never overcome those primitive fears. Even though he knew of no legitimate cause for alarm, his hands shook and the short hairs on the back of his neck stood erect.

He lit a cigarette. That helped a little. The comfort did not come from the nicotine rush. In fact, Seacrest despised cigarettes almost as much as he despised the dark. The small, cold comfort came from the tiny glow given off by the burning ash.

He didn't want to be here in the first place. If he could have avoided it, he would have. But the man on the phone had been insistent; he possessed information—so he said—that could guarantee Seacrest would win the trial he was scheduled to start the day after tomorrow. Seacrest didn't take the Rules of Professional Conduct any more seriously than necessary, but he couldn't ignore an opportunity to slam-dunk a case for the client he was ethically obligated to "defend zealously."

Seacrest blew smoke into the night sky. Still no sign of anyone. Damn, damn, *damn*. He knew he was in trouble the minute he was transferred to the firm's litigation department. Litigation meant constant bickering, backstabbing, and conflict. He wanted to be a business attorney, pure and simple. That was what he loved—doing deals, analyzing contracts, plotting takeovers. Taking a corporation public—that was as close to heaven as this dirty little profession ever got. Unfortunately, after the recession hit the Southwest, big-bucks business deals became scarce. But everyone wanted to sue somebody. Exit business department, hello litigation.

Bad enough to have to handle civil litigation, but now he'd been appointed to a criminal indigent case as well. As luck would have it, he'd managed to draw the sleaziest slimeball he'd ever met. Personally, he wouldn't cross the street to give this spitwad a dime. And now he was the man's zealous advocate. Thank you, Judge Hagedorn.

Seacrest gazed out at the lake—a black, unreflecting sheet, like a mirror of his own dark soul. It was forbidding, but at the same time strangely compelling. He should spend some spare time out here, he thought. If only he had spare time. Maybe in a few years, after he made partner, after the firm started treating him in the manner that he deserved . . .

"Are you Seacrest?"

The deep voice erupted out of nowhere, shattering the silence. Seacrest leaped half a foot in the air, then landed off balance. The stranger reached out and grabbed his shoulder, preventing him from tumbling into the lake.

"Are you Seacrest?" the man with the deep, gravelly voice repeated.

Seacrest could barely make out the man's features. He was tall and drawn, with a face marked by pocks and craters—disconcerting, especially in the dark. There was something deformed about the left side of his face. A scar, maybe? If so, it was a huge one.

"I'm Seacrest," he answered, careful not to let his voice tremble. "Who are you?"

"You don't need to know my name." The man was standing unnaturally close. Seacrest could feel his hot, fetid breath on his cheek.

"Why did you want to meet?"

"I'm an old pal of your client, Al Moroconi," the man replied. "I hear you've been doin' some investigatin'."

"You mean for the trial? What do you know about it?"

"I'm more interested in what *you* know."

Seacrest tried to step away, but the man's grip on his shoulder remained firm. "The prosecution won't tell me shit. And Moroconi barely grunts. All I know is what little I've been able to figure out on my own."

"You've been pokin' your nose where it ain't wanted. Doin' some . . . corporate research."

"That's kind of my specialty." Why was this stranger interrogating him? He was supposed to give *me* information, Seacrest recalled. Still, something about the man convinced him it would be best not to be difficult. "I haven't worked out all the details, but I've definitely linked a corporate entity to Moroconi. Got the business records from the secretary of state. Got a list of the corporate officers."

"That," the stranger said, "was a big mistake."

"A mistake? No, it was brilliant. See, what I did was—*ahhh!*" Seacrest's speech became a scream as a stabbing pain radiated through his upper left leg.

"Oh, my God! *Oh my*—" Seacrest clutched his leg. "What

was—*ahhh!*" His shriek split the night. Whatever the man had thrust into his leg had been removed. Seacrest could feel his own hot blood gurgling to the surface.

"What—was that?" Seacrest gasped, his head swimming.

"An ice pick," the man replied. "Trite, I know. But I saw somebody use one in a movie once and it looked like fun."

"Oh God. Oh *God*!" The blood oozed through Seacrest's fingers. "Are you going to kill me?"

"Oh no," the man said. He began to smile as he pressed down on Seacrest's shoulder. "Well, not at first, anyway."

Seacrest fell onto the sandy bank of the river. He wanted to run, wanted to flee this brutal madman, but the aching in his limb immobilized him.

Seacrest heard a swishing, splashing sound. "What—what's that?"

"Lighter fluid," the man replied, still smiling. He doused Seacrest's face, then his chest, then his groin.

"Please don't," Seacrest begged him. Tears sprang to his eyes. "I have a wife. I have a little boy."

"That's a goddamned shame." The man vanished, then reappeared a second later. He was holding a blowtorch.

"Please—*no*," Seacrest pleaded. "I'll do anything. I've got some money. Friends in high places. I can get you anything you want. Anything at all."

"'Fraid it's too late for that," the man said cheerily. He pushed a button, and blue flame surged from the nose of the blowtorch. "There'll be a hot time in the old town tonight."

# MONDAY

*April 15*

# 2

## 4:00 P.M.

Travis Byrne leaned against the jury box, established eye contact with each of the jurors, and began his closing argument.

"Ladies and gentlemen of the jury, make no mistake about it. My client is an animal. He is vile. He is less deserving of your sympathy than the lowest vermin, the slimiest snake. He is entitled only to your disgust and your contempt.

"Do you think I enjoy sitting at that table with him? I don't. Being near scum like him makes my skin crawl. Just looking at him sends shivers up my spine. You haven't seen me feigning friendship with the defendant during this trial. For a reason. Because he is not my friend. He is the most revolting man I have ever met. If it were up to me, I'd lock him in a cell with no windows and throw away the key."

Travis took a step back and folded his arms. "But that is not the law, ladies and gentlemen. The law proclaims that every man charged with a crime, even one as horrible as the offense you have heard described today, is entitled to a fair trial before a jury of his peers. If my client is convicted, it must be because you have determined not simply that he is a bad person, but that the evidence has proven beyond a reasonable doubt that he is guilty of the specific crime with which he has been charged."

Maintaining eye contact with the jurors, Travis sidestepped to the prosecutor's table. "Now, what is the charge that Ms. Cavanaugh has leveled against my client? Murdering a federal informant. As the judge will instruct you, that is a very specific, rather unusual crime. Most murders are tried in state, not federal, court. But by latching onto an obscure section of the United States Criminal Code, Ms. Cavanaugh has usurped the state authorities so that she can try this case in federal court and reap all the publicity attendant to a high-profile tragedy."

Out of the corner of his eye, Travis saw Madame Prosecutor squirming. She wanted to object—to interrupt his flow, if for no other reason—but she knew it would irritate the jurors and do her more harm than good.

"What evidence do you have that Sally Schultz, a fourteen-year-old girl, was a federal informant? Very little, I think. Yes, the prosecution has inundated you with evidence that my client knew the girl. They have presented chilling, graphic evidence that he molested her on several occasions. And they have presented circumstantial evidence indicating that—to silence her—he took her life, in a slow, grisly fashion.

"But where is the evidence that Sally Schultz was an informant?" Travis pounded his fist on the prosecution table. "The evidence from the FBI agent, Mr. Banner, was that he had talked to Sally Schultz on one occasion, and that she had not decided whether she would testify. If she had agreed, if she had in fact been part of the FBI plot to ensnare my client at the time of her tragic death, then I would not be standing before you today."

Travis planted himself front and center before the jury. He was a large man—heavy and big-boned, like a linebacker. The extra pounds around his gut were masked by his dark suit. Up close, he had an impressive bearing. "But that is not what happened. There had only been one conversation between Sally and Mr. Banner, and Sally had not made up her mind. If that single inconclusive conversation made Sally a federal informant, then any of us could become federal informants whenever the whim strikes an ambitious prosecutor. Clearly, that was not the intent of the law my client has been charged with violating."

He took a deep breath, then released it slowly. "Ladies and gentlemen of the jury, my client has committed acts that probably horrify you, just as they horrify me. But this court has no jurisdiction over him. I ask you to put aside your personal feelings and remember that this is a court of law, not a court of vengeance. The only question before you today is whether my client is guilty of murdering a federal informant. And the answer is no."

Travis returned to the defendant's table and sat without so much as glancing at his client. Ms. Cavanaugh rose and began her rebuttal argument, but Travis could tell the jury was not listening. They were looking at him, and his client, and considering the question he had put before them.

**3**

**4 : 4 5 P.M.**

Cavanaugh drained her paper cup of coffee. "I don't mean to get personal, Byrne. I don't know you that well. But I have to ask you one question. How do you sleep at night?"

Travis Byrne carefully considered his response.

"You've read the Constitution, Cavanaugh. At least, I hope you have. Every man is entitled to a defense."

The two attorneys were in Judge Charles E. Hagedorn's private chambers in the Dallas County Courthouse, awaiting his return.

"I'm not complaining because you gave your client a defense," Cavanaugh replied. "I'm complaining because you exonerated the filthiest piece of trash I've ever seen!"

"The jury is still out."

"I saw the look in their eyes during your closing. They were mesmerized. Who wouldn't be? You put on a great show. What's more, you gave them the perfect excuse not to convict. They're going to use it."

Here we go again, Travis thought. He poured himself some

more coffee. "So you're saying it's okay for me to defend the man, just so I don't do it very well."

"I'm saying I wish your ethics got as much exercise as your silver tongue."

Travis sighed. He'd confronted this argument a million times before and he didn't feel like rehashing it. Especially not with Cavanaugh. She was a formidable opponent—tall, slender, with jet-black hair restrained in a tight chignon. She could probably be attractive, he mused, if she'd loosen up a bit and act like a human being. "Everybody's got to make a living."

"Yeah, but you don't have to make it by putting child molesters back on the street. Look, Byrne, I understand the issues. I haven't always been a prosecutor. I was a PI for five years—a skip tracer, basically. I hated it. I didn't enjoy rubbing shoulders with the oiliest creeps this side of hell. So I quit. I went to law school and joined the good guys. You could do the same thing."

"I've been with the good guys," Travis said. "It didn't work out."

"Yeah, yeah, I know you're an ex-cop. The fact that you wore a badge for seven years doesn't mean your life has been any tougher than anyone else's."

Travis's face became stone cold. "You don't know what the hell you're talking about, Cavanaugh."

"I think I do."

"You don't know the least thing about me."

"When have I had the chance?"

Travis's head jerked up. "Is that what this is about? Are you yanking my chain because you want to go out with me?"

She brought her hand to her face and stifled a laugh. "My God. Mother *was* right. Men are all alike." She lowered her hand, revealing a broad grin. "I'm not after your body, Byrne. Promise."

Judge Hagedorn poked his head through the door. "Mind if I step into my own chambers? I don't want to intrude."

"Please, Judge," Travis said. "This ethereal banter is making my head hurt. Soon I'll be hearing voices."

"Let me know if one of them sounds like Jiminy Cricket," Hagedorn said. "We've all assumed you'd get a conscience someday."

"Don't you start in on me now. The jury is still out, for God's sake."

"Doesn't matter," Hagedorn replied. He removed his black robe, revealing a casual Western shirt and rattler-skin cowboy boots. When he wasn't on the bench, Hagedorn was a rancher with an expansive spread out in Braddock County. Travis had learned some time ago that he could make more points with Hagedorn talking about cattle than cases. "They're going to acquit."

"How do you know?"

"I've been on the bench for thirty-two years," Hagedorn said, settling himself into a chair beneath a pair of wall-mounted longhorns. "That's how I know."

"Look," Travis said, "it's not my fault Cavanaugh decided to grab some glory by dragging this case into federal court. It should have been tried in state court and we all know it."

"I doubt if Ms. Cavanaugh had much say in that decision," Hagedorn said. "Brad Blaisdell is the U.S. Attorney and he calls the shots for his cadre of assistants. He's been known to purloin a headline or two. Particularly when a seat is about to open up on the federal bench."

"Amen," Cavanaugh said. "And no comment."

Travis resumed his self-defense. "I had an ethical duty to defend my client to the best of my ability."

"You did that, by God," Hagedorn said. "Nothing personal against our learned assistant U.S. attorney, but you whipped her butt. No offense, ma'am."

"None taken."

I'll just bet, Travis thought.

"You're out of law school what—barely a year, Travis?" Hagedorn said. He stretched out in a chair and put his boots up on his desk. "Already you've got the instincts of a first-rate trial attorney. Better than most lawyers who've practiced for decades. I just wonder about some of the . . . choices you've made. Most ex-cops who go to law school end up working for the DA or some other law enforcement agency."

"I'm not most ex-cops," Travis muttered.

"No, you're not. And I can't find fault in your working for Dan Holyfield either. He's a damn fine man. Honest, respectable. I'd just like to see you exercise a little more discretion in selecting your clients."

"Someone's got to represent the scum of the earth."

"Someone's got to pick up the garbage, too, and there'll always be someone willing and able. It doesn't have to be you."

"Thanks, Judge, but I like what I'm doing."

"Fine." Hagedorn shuffled several tall stacks of files on his cluttered desk. "I'm glad to hear you express those noble sentiments, Travis. Because I've got a job for you. Criminal indigent—needs a court-appointed attorney. Normally, I'd feel guilty assigning a case like this, but since you feel so strongly about the rights of the scum of the earth . . ."

Travis didn't care much for the sound of that. "What's the charge?"

"Forcible rape," Hagedorn said, opening a file folder.

Damn. Another sex crime. Travis hated sex crimes.

"Aggravated assault," Hagedorn added. "Several other related charges."

"What happened?"

"A pretty little SMU coed was leaving an off-campus pub. Before she reached her car, she was surrounded by six men—three white, three black. They took her keys, threw her into the trunk of her car, and drove her to a secluded area near White Rock Lake. They took turns at her. In fact, some of them took several extremely brutal turns. And then they tied her to the back of the car and dragged her for about a mile."

Travis closed his eyes. "Did she live?"

"After a fashion. I've heard the phrase *hamburger meat* used at the pretrial hearings."

"And I would represent one of the alleged assailants?"

Hagedorn nodded. "The only one the police have been able to find."

"And how did Brad Blaisdell get this one into federal court?"

"Turns out the parking lot from which she was abducted actually belonged to a nearby VA hospital. She was on federal property."

"That's pretty lame. Surely you're going to dismiss."

Hagedorn spread his arms expansively. "I'll entertain any motion you care to make. But no, I'm not going to dismiss."

Travis maintained his poker face. He couldn't fold now. "All right, I accept. Assuming, of course, that the client has no objection." He saw Cavanaugh's eyes widen in amazement. "Where's the file?"

"It's on Millie's desk."

"I'll send someone to pick it up tomorrow morning."

"I don't think you understand," Hagedorn said. "The trial *begins* tomorrow morning."

"*What?*" Travis's brow protruded from his forehead. "How can that be?"

"This case was originally assigned to Tom Seacrest. You know, the young associate at Rainey and Wright. But he disappeared."

"Disappeared?"

"You heard me. Didn't show up for the pretrial this afternoon. Firm says he hasn't been seen since the day before yesterday."

"Are they looking for him?"

"Of course. But the trial still starts tomorrow morning and his client still needs a lawyer."

"What about someone else at Seacrest's firm?"

"No one else there does criminal work. No, Travis, I offered you the case and you accepted."

"Then I respectfully move for a continuance."

"Denied. I've already granted two continuances to Seacrest. Time to get this show on the road."

"But I can't be ready by tomorrow morning!"

"Why not? The prosecution will take at least three days to present its case. All you have to do is sit around and object periodically. In the meantime, you can prepare your defense."

"Who knows," Cavanaugh interjected, "maybe you can dream up some technicality to get this toad off the hook, too."

Travis ignored her. "I want my request for a continuance and your denial on the record, Judge."

"Suit yourself. We'll do it first thing in the morning."

"If you two will excuse me, I'll collect that file from Millie and get to work."

Travis left chambers and entered the reception area, careful not to let his expression change. His stomach was doing flip-flops, but he couldn't let it show. Millie, Judge Hagedorn's secretary, wasn't in sight, so Travis rummaged around on her desk until he found the file, then tossed it into his briefcase.

My God, he thought. I just hope she isn't a redhead.

# 4

6 : 4 5 P.M.

Harold Satrom loved two things in life: sunsets and fishing. Every chance he got, he'd close the Dallas bait-and-tackle shop he managed, grab his ten-year-old son, Jimmy, and drive to Lake Palestine before the sun faded. They would watch the fiery red light filter across the horizon, find a comfortable spot on the bank, then cast their lines and see what the Corps of Engineers had stocked the lake with this year.

But everything seemed different tonight. Different and wrong. The sky was overcast; ominous clouds were gathering. Worse, the fish didn't seem to be biting, at least not where they were. Harold could see the occasional bass or trout, but he couldn't catch them. They seemed disturbed, skittish. Probably teenagers had been out here last night, drinking beer, causing a commotion, stirring everything up. Damn kids.

Harold left Jimmy with the gear and strolled along the shore, hoping he could find a better location. He'd been walking about half a mile when he came upon a large gray blob that he knew with instant horror was a man. The remains of a man.

He approached slowly, although he realized this desiccated corpse could do him no harm. It appeared to have washed ashore after floating in the lake for some time.

Harold rolled the corpse onto its back—and immediately wished he hadn't. The face was a puffy gray green, swollen and scarred; it had been horribly burned. Thin, translucent skin barely covered the skull. Harold couldn't have identified the man if he'd been his best friend.

Then Harold noticed his legs. The man had been burned from the groin down—horribly so. To make matters worse, his body was riddled with deep, blackened stab wounds. It was grotesque.

Harold wasn't a coroner, but he got the distinct impression that this man had died hard, slowly and painfully, at someone else's hands.

He reached into the corpse's pocket and found a leather wallet. Amazing that it hadn't fallen out in the lake. There were twelve twenty-dollar bills inside. Well, hell, they weren't going to do this stiff any good. But they would buy a mountain bike, and that would give Jimmy a lot of pleasure. And give Harold a lot of peace.

Harold thumbed through the rest of the wallet. A few pictures, a driver's license, and membership cards for various organizations. Several credit cards, but Harold wasn't stupid enough to try to use those. Nothing else of value.

He rolled the corpse back onto its face. A sudden chill swept through his body. He ran into the lake, consumed by the desire to cleanse himself. He ran his hands over his body, scrubbing every inch of exposed skin.

Finally he stepped out of the lake, feeling much better. He started to walk on, then thought of Jimmy, back behind him. Alone.

Harold headed back the way he had come, walking, then jogging, then flat out running, the whole time wondering who the hell Thomas J. Seacrest was and how he got himself into so much trouble.

# 5

8 : 1 0 P.M.

Travis spread the Moroconi file out on his desk. It was all he could do to suppress his growing nausea. He opened the Maalox he kept in his briefcase and drank straight from the bottle. His stomach had been churning all day long.

Most of the trial attorneys he knew suffered from ulcers; some doctors called it *lawyer's elbow*. The tremendous pressure of trial practice was unrelenting. Anyone who handled more than a few trials a year eventually started to feel the cracks in their professional facade.

And this new case was only making matters worse. Travis gazed out his office window at the Dallas skyline. He saw the NCNB Plaza, Dallas's tallest building, trimmed in green argon light. Through the other window, Reunion Tower, with its illuminated geodesic dome, beckoned to him. It was almost enough to make him forget. Almost—but not quite.

He carefully read the case summary in the pretrial order and scrutinized the snapshots the police photographer had so thoughtfully provided. There were several details Judge Hagedorn had neglected to mention. Hideous details. How the rapists broke the woman's rib cage with blows from a tire iron. How they urinated on her and in her mouth. How, when they finished raping her the usual way, they went at her instrumentally, with the tire iron and a Coke bottle. How they abandoned the woman, all but dead, bleeding in a dozen places, naked, facedown in the mud, by the side of the road. How she was in the hospital for weeks, and was forced to undergo a double radical mastectomy as a result of her beating.

Travis's client was Alberto Moroconi. Moroconi had been drinking Scotch and sodas in O'Reilly's, the off-campus bar where the victim, Mary Ann McKenzie, came looking for her roommate. Moroconi admitted being there, and admitted seeing several men leave shortly after she did, but he claimed he played no part in the rape and torture.

As far as Travis could discern from the prosecutor's witness and exhibit lists, there was little concrete evidence disputing Moroconi's testimony. The decision to prosecute him on this rape charge appeared to be based entirely upon Mary Ann's identification. She picked Moroconi out of a lineup, with the help of more than gentle persuasion from the Dallas PD. Given the poor woman's mental state, Travis didn't think it proved anything.

Travis knew the constitutional guidelines for lineups by heart, and he doubted whether those guidelines had been met. Moroconi was the only man in the lineup close to the size, height, and weight description Mary Ann gave for any of her three white assailants. If she was going to identify anyone out of that lineup, it would have to be Moroconi. Travis wondered why Moroconi had been picked up by the police in the first place. They claimed they were acting on a tip from an unnamed informant.

Travis interpreted the facts in the file thus: the police brought in a sucker, pushed the victim for a positive ID, and ran with it to the prosecutor. Which, of course, didn't necessarily mean Moroconi was innocent, but It did give Travis something to dispute during the trial. To his surprise, he saw no indication in the file that Seacrest ever filed a motion to suppress. Amazing. If Travis could get the lineup ID excluded, everything that followed therefrom also would be inadmissible—fruit of the poisonous tree. Perhaps Seacrest considered that type of tactic beneath him. Travis didn't. As a criminal attorney, his job was to exculpate his client, period. If he could do so by means of a legal technicality, he was ethically bound to do so.

"Dinner's here."

Gail, the firm's receptionist and secretary, entered Travis's office with a white Styrofoam container.

"Gail, why on earth are you still here?"

"I'm looking after you, of course. You'd forget to eat altogether, left to yourself. You'd just sit here all night drinking Maalox, wondering why your stomach hurts."

She probably was right. Now that the subject had been broached, Travis realized he was hungry.

Gail tossed the carryout container on his desk. "Here you go. Chow down."

Travis peered inside. It was a salad, of course. Doctor's orders. Dr. Anglis had barely let him squeak by his last insurance-mandated checkup. His blood pressure was too high, his cholesterol count was too high, his ulcer was active, he was twenty-five pounds overweight, and according to Anglis, he was "the most clear-cut Type-A personality" the doctor had seen in his entire career. In short, Travis was a heart attack waiting to happen. The doctor put him on an all-vegetables-and-salads diet and ordered him to get more exercise. As if saying it would make it happen. Travis would've loved to exercise more; he hated the way his body had deteriorated since he quit the police force and joined the relatively sedentary legal world. But when? He barely had time to breathe, much less run laps and do sit-ups.

Unfortunately, Dr. Anglis had repeated his orders to everyone in the office, including Gail. She couldn't make Travis exercise, but she did a thorough job of monitoring his diet.

"Yum, yum," Travis said, licking his chops in cartoonish exaggeration. "Rabbit food—accept no substitutes."

Gail smirked. "This one's a chef salad. Of course, I had them remove all the meats."

"Which leaves what? Lettuce?"

"More or less, yes."

"Great." Travis reached for his wallet. "What do I owe you?"

"My treat."

"No, no, take a fiver."

"Just put your money away, Travis. This is the least I can do, considering all you've done for me."

Travis could see this was important to her, so he relented. Gail had been having problems with an ex-felon ex-husband who had suddenly taken a renewed interest in their eleven-year-old daughter, Susan. Gail was terrified he would involve Susan in his miasma of booze, drugs, and orgies. Travis had drafted airtight custody documents and represented Gail at the hearing that almost totally marginalized her ex. He ended up with radically reduced visitation—one Saturday a month, no overnights, and only under Gail's supervision. After the case was over, Travis tore up the bill, which he knew she could ill afford.

"I'm monitoring the level of your Maalox bottle, too," Gail announced.

"I'm delighted."

Gail was a few years older than Travis, not conventionally pretty, but not unpleasant either. A winning personality easily compensated for crooked teeth in Travis's book.

"You know, Travis, it wouldn't hurt to take a night off."

"I wouldn't know what to do with myself."

She toyed with a lock of his curly black hair. "Well, I could make a few suggestions." She sighed, then walked a dancing step toward the door. "Oh well, maybe in another life."

And a fine life it would be, Travis thought to himself. If only we had several to work with.

"Enjoy your salad."

"Thanks, Gail. I will." Travis returned his attention to the photographs. It was best if he didn't dwell on what he was eating, since there wasn't much of it and what there was was far from appetizing. Soon he was deep in the case. Time passed as Travis compared statements, examined reports, planned cross-examinations, and tried to discern what really happened.

"Travis, have I mentioned that you work too damn hard?"

Travis, engrossed in his research, started. It was Dan Holyfield, his boss. "About a hundred times, Dan. Make that a hundred and one, now."

"Well, then, listen to me for a change. I'm sick and tired of seeing you squirreled away in your office every night." Dan was dressed in his usual manner—brown suit with a bolo tie. Old-guard Dallas, but very classy. "You need to get out more. Visit some friends."

Travis didn't say anything. It was embarrassing to admit that, bottom line, he really didn't have any friends.

"Are you feeling all right?"

"I'm fine. Just a little stomach stress."

"Uh-huh." Dan's voice had just the slightest hint of a Dallas drawl, although Travis suspected it was an accent more cultivated than natural. Dan had always been a master at fitting in. "Have you had anything for dinner? Or did that slip your mind?"

"I ate, in a manner of speaking." Travis pointed to the empty take-out container. "Gail brought me a salad from Sprouts."

Dan chuckled. "Sounds delightful." He picked up the container and tossed it into the trash. "You know, Gail is a fine girl. She's had a tough time of it, raising Susan all by herself. I betcha she'd leap at a dinner invitation from a promising young attorney."

Travis shifted uncomfortably. "No one would want to go out with a tub of lard like me." Travis knew he wasn't *that* overweight, but because he was only five foot seven, every extra pound looked like three.

"You need to get out more," Dan grumbled. "I don't care if it's

Gail, but you hear what I'm saying—it's time to start dating again."

Travis pressed his lips together. "I'm . . . not ready for that yet, Dan."

Dan laid his hand on Travis's shoulder. "I don't mean to seem unsympathetic, Travis, but it's been over four years. When you were in law school, it was understandable—you were busy. You didn't have time to deal with it. But now you have a good job, a steady income. It's time."

"I said I'm not ready. Okay?" Travis hoped he sounded forceful, but not rude. He would never intentionally offend Dan Holyfield, the one bona fide hero he had ever known. Dan had put in thirty-five years as a criminal defense attorney, taking unpopular clients, defending unpopular causes, representing the poor and elderly for free long before it became trendy. Most important, Dan had been there when Travis needed someone—in fact, he was the only person who was. Travis didn't have any living relatives, and he didn't have any inside connections to the rich or powerful. Dan Holyfield made it possible for him to attend law school. When Travis received his J.D. and hit the streets, he was an ex-cop, already in his midthirties, with mediocre grades. Not what most of the blue-chip firms were looking for. Or anyone else for that matter. But Dan Holyfield was willing to give him a chance. That meant something to Travis. That meant a lot.

"All right," Dan said, "have it your way. But don't be surprised if you come in some night and find I've locked you out of your office." He smiled, almost as an afterthought. "I hear you won your trial today."

"Yup. Jury was out less than an hour."

"Talk about turning a sow's ear into a silk purse. Congratulations are in order, I suppose. You've become a mighty fine defense attorney, Travis."

"I learned it all from you."

"That's a crock of bull, but it's nice to hear, anyway. What are you working on now?"

"New case. Forcible rape, aggravated assault. Pretty grisly stuff."

Dan thumbed through the photographs on the desk. "Grisly is an understatement. I thought you were going to take on more civil work."

"Didn't have any choice about this one. Judicial appointment."

"I see. Hagedorn punishing you for having the audacity to win?"

"Something like that. I don't suppose you'd like to second-chair this loser?"

"No thanks, Travis. That's why I hired you, remember? So I wouldn't have to try slop like this. When I said I was retired, I meant it."

"That decision was a monumental loss for the Dallas criminal justice system."

"Travis, if this flattery is your way of campaigning for a Christmas bonus, forget it."

Travis grinned. "Sorry, Dan."

"My retirement was way overdue. I've been staying plenty busy running my parents' food-distribution business since they died. Conrad and Elsie Holyfield may not have been college graduates, but they made a fine little company—and I'm not going to let it go down the tubes."

Actually, Travis was glad Dan had slowed down, though he'd never tell Dan that. Dan was one of the few who deserved retirement; he'd fought the good fight and lived to tell the tale. Looked remarkable for his age, too, which had to be near sixty. The clerks down at the courthouse called him Dorian Gray.

"You'll be impossible to replace in the courtroom, Dan."

"Nonsense." Dan walked to the door. "Don't stay up too late."

"Sorry, but I may have to pull an all-nighter. The trial starts tomorrow morning."

"Tomorrow morning? Man alive, Hagedorn stung you but good."

"Yeah."

"Going straight from one trial to another like this will kill you,

Travis, and that's a certainty. Promise me you'll take a break some-time tonight."

"That I can do. I promised Staci I'd visit."

"I'll let you get back to work then. But seriously, Travis, don't ruin yourself. You've got a loser here, and you're tackling it under extremely adverse circumstances. Every now and then it's all right to let the scum sink."

After Dan left, Travis returned his attention to Exhibit A, the first color photograph of Mary Ann McKenzie taken after her at-tack.

He drew the photo closer to the light. His eyes were drawn to her shattered rib cage, her scraped, bloody face, her bruised breasts. He choked; his eyes began to sting.

"My God," he whispered to himself.

She *was* a redhead. Just like Angela.

# 6

**8 : 4 5 P.M.**

**M**ario sat behind the large oak desk in his downtown office, his hands resting atop a green blotter. A gooseneck lamp illuminated his two visitors, but left Mario in shadow. He liked it that way.

He gazed across the desk at Kramer, Mario's most dependable enforcer, and Donny, Mario's idiot nephew. Mario and his nephew wore sport coats, Ban-Lon shirts, and patent-leather oxfords. Kramer tried to dress like them, but, as always, it didn't quite ring true. And what was that jacket made of anyway—*polyester*, for God's sake? Christ, it wasn't as if the man didn't have enough money. He'd been drawing sizable chunks of change for years.

Mario and Donny both wore gold, too—Donny around his neck and Mario on his pinky. But Kramer put them to shame; he wore three chain necklaces and two nugget-size rings. He even had a gold tooth. That was so like Kramer—always trying to look like a member of the family. Trying too goddamn hard. Mario should've dumped him years ago, and he would've, too—if the man didn't scare him shitless.

Kramer had come in to report. He was pacing alongside Mario's desk. Donny lounged on the sofa by the door, biting his nails like a five-year-old. Jesus T. Christ, Mario thought. Donny wants to be a *made man*, and he sits there biting his nails, barely paying attention. What a worthless piece of crap. Donny would never learn the business. Or anything else.

"You have news to report, Mr. Kramer?" Mario asked.

"Yeah. Matter of fact, I do." Kramer was a thin man—quick, wiry, elusive. Like a snake. His most prominent feature was a long ugly scar that stretched down the left side of his face. "The job was completed accordin' to plan."

"Can you provide a few more details?"

"You really wanna know?"

Mario considered for a moment. "No. I suppose it's best if I don't." It didn't matter how much he worked with Kramer; the man made his skin crawl. Always had, always would. He was so much more than just an enforcer; he was capable of planning, equipping, staffing, and executing an entire operation, from start to finish, no matter how complex or clandestine. He was effective and efficient—he always got the job done. He was creative and innovative—he didn't have to be led by the hand. He had connections everywhere—the press, the police, the government. He could obtain valuable information or plant false information anywhere he wanted. He had countless assistants, all of them willing to do anything, go anywhere.

But he was also a sadist. Most hit men fell into their jobs because there was nothing else they were capable of doing. Not so Kramer. He was in this line of work because he enjoyed it. He was a sociopath who derived inordinate pleasure from cruelty to other people. And his fondness for fire was legendary. Just thinking about it was enough to make Mario grind out his cigarette. Life was safest when Kramer had no access to anything burning, no matter how small.

Donny leaned off the edge of the sofa. His voice was high-pitched and tended to squeal. "Has anyone noticed he's missing yet?"

"Oh yeah," Kramer said. "But they don't know what happened to him."

"Then he hasn't been found. Officially," Mario said.

"No. Not yet. But he will be. That was the plan, wasn't it?"

"Yes. That was the plan."

"You know how stupid cops are," Donny said. "Maybe we should do something to help them along. Leave them a clue, maybe."

By silent agreement, Mario and Kramer jointly ignored Donny. Donny simply had no brains, Mario reflected, not for the first time. Mario loved his sister, but there was no hope for her pitiful progeny.

"I'm glad you put out your cigarette, Uncle Mario. Those cancer-sticks'll kill you. If they haven't already. And I could get lung diseases from the secondhand smoke." Donny coughed. "See? I'm sick already."

"I appreciate your concern, Donny," Mario said slowly. He thought about that for a moment. "In fact, I don't appreciate your concern, Donny. You're a fucking pain in the ass. So sit quietly and speak when you're spoken to."

Donny lowered his head. "Yes, sir."

Just to rub salt in the wound, Kramer snatched a cigarette from Mario's desk case and flicked his lighter. The flame flared out; Kramer's eyes glowed. Eventually, he lit his cigarette.

Mario suppressed a shiver. If Kramer loved anything, it was the red flame that danced before his eyes. "Word is Seacrest will be replaced by some guy named Travis Byrne," Kramer said, breaking out of his trance.

"What do we know about Mr. Byrne?"

"Not much yet. He's a decent attorney—young, but effective. Gets people off. More than that I don't know yet. But I'm workin' on it." He snapped his fingers. "Oh, yeah. He's an ex-cop."

Mario stroked his chin. "That could present a problem. We don't need some law-and-order fanatic on the case. Find out everything you can about him."

"Like I said, I'm workin' on it. I also thought we might try to consider some means of controllin' Mr. Byrne. Maybe screw up his squeaky-clean rep."

"Do you think that's necessary at this time?"

"Nah. But if the time comes, it'll be best if we've already stockpiled our ammo."

"So what did you have in mind?"

Kramer shrugged. "The usual. Unexpected guests. Candid cameras. A few sensational stories that can be leaked to the press on a moment's notice."

Mario waved his hand in the air. "Whatever you think. I leave it to you. It also might not be a bad idea for some sort of . . . incident to occur to Mr. Byrne. Just so he knows where he stands."

"Incident?"

"Something subtle. But not too."

Kramer grinned, obviously relishing the suggestion. "I can handle that."

"You might involve Donny in this," Mario said hesitantly. "He needs . . . experience."

Kramer's displeasure was evident. "I have my own men who—"

"That's not the point." Mario drummed his fingers lightly on his desk. "This is a family venture. It's best if a member of the family is along for the ride. Just send Donny with someone capable of providing the necessary . . . guidance. I would consider it a personal favor."

Kramer frowned. "You're the boss. Anything else?"

"Has Moroconi said anything? About us, I mean."

"Not yet. But we can't rule out the possibility. Especially if he becomes desperate."

"We'll play it by ear. The risk seems slight. A dumb ex-cop plodding in at the last second—how much could he learn?"

"That all depends. Seacrest learned too much."

Mario nodded. It was an unpleasant, but nonetheless accurate, reminder. "Watch Byrne carefully. If you see anything that gives you cause for alarm, act without hesitation. If he gets too close, eliminate him. Just like you eliminated Seacrest. Understood?"

"Understood." Smiling, Kramer headed toward the door. On his way out, he pulled one of Donny's suspenders and popped it against his chest. Just for the hell of it.

# 7

9 : 0 0 P.M.

Travis found Staci at the lighted, outdoor basketball court behind John Neely Bryan Junior High School playing a little two-on-one. A pair of black teenage boys were the two; she was the one.

"Travis!" As soon as she saw him, she tossed the ball to one of her friends, who was at least a foot taller than she was. She ran to meet Travis at his car. "I thought you weren't coming!"

"I was delayed. Sorry. Big new trial."

"*Another* trial? You just finished one."

"I know. Popular, aren't I?"

"You never spend any time with me anymore."

"I'm here, aren't I?"

"You know what I mean." She sat down on the curb, her fists under her chin.

Travis sat beside her. "What's wrong, Staci? Trouble at home?"

"Oh, just the usual. Nobody likes me."

"That's not true, Staci. Your aunt Marnie is crazy about you."

"Aunt Marnie was crazy about my mother. She puts up with me 'cause she thinks she has to."

"That isn't—" He stopped short. No point in offering superficial denials. Staci knew the score. "Look, how's school going?"

"Oh, same old same old."

"Yo, Staci!" It was one of her two friends on the basketball court. "Let's go!"

"You guys play without me for a while," Staci shouted back. "I'm okay." She smiled. "They're worried 'cause you're some big old white guy they don't know. You must look like a suspicious character. Maybe they sense that you used to be a cop. Doc and Jameel aren't too keen on cops."

"Any reason in particular?"

"Well . . . they've been arrested twice for breaking and entering."

"That'll do it." He watched Doc effortlessly toss the basketball into the hoop from half-court. "Well, I'm glad you've made some friends."

"Yeah, Doc and Jameel are okay. They just like me 'cause I'm good on the court. But that's okay. They're way cool."

"Kind of late for basketball, isn't it?"

Staci shrugged. "Gotta stay in practice."

"When I stopped by the house, your aunt was pretty grumpy. Thought you should be at home."

"What else is new?"

"How are your grades?"

"Oh . . ." Staci picked up a rock and threw it across the street. "'Bout the same. A's and B's in art and gym. My grades in English suck."

"Like how bad?"

"C-plus, C-minus."

"That's not so bad," Travis said. Especially for a girl diagnosed with ADD—Attention Deficit Disorder. It caused Staci to have problems with concentration; she was also prone to procrastination and forgetfulness, and she was easily distracted. The doctors weren't sure if the disorder was caused by a malfunction within the inner ear—the most common cause of ADD—or if it was simply an emotional problem stemming from the traumatic loss of her mother.

"You should hear what Aunt Marnie says about me. How stupid I am, how lazy I am. She thinks I'm pond scum." Staci clasped his hand. "Let's go camping, Travis. Like that time last spring at Robbers' Cave."

"You're not listening. I can't go to Robbers' Cave. I've got a new trial. It's going to last at least a week. Maybe longer."

She kicked a tin can. "Figures."

"As soon as this trial is over, we'll do something together. I promise."

"Yeah, sure."

"Aw, cheer up. Wanna see a magic trick?"

"Absolutely not."

"Look, there's something in your ear."

"Oh, Travis, please." He reached behind her ear. "I've seen this trick a million—" She looked down at his opened palm. "It's a charm! For my Disney bracelet!"

She reached out, but just before she got the charm, Travis closed his fists, whirled them around a few times, then extended his opened palms. "Look! It disappeared!"

"Puh-leese, Travis. It didn't disappear. It's up your sleeve." She grabbed his arm, shook it, and caught a tiny gold Goofy.

"That trick fooled everyone back when I was in the third grade."

"That's the problem, Travis. You haven't learned any new tricks since you were in the third grade."

"Oh yeah? How about this one?" He took two large blue marbles from his coat pocket and extended his hands, knuckles up. He swirled his hands around in a confusing blur. "Okay, which hand are the marbles in?"

"Really, Travis, who cares?" She snapped the Goofy figurine

onto her bracelet. "My mom gave me this bracelet," she said quietly.

"I know."

"Aunt Marnie hid my picture of her. She said it was making me all sad and moody. Maybe she was right." She wrapped the bracelet around her wrist. "You're gonna laugh, Travis, but sometimes, late at night, I imagine Mom's talking to me. Not just a word or two. Whole big long conversations." She looked down at her sneakers. "She says a lot of nice stuff. In my head, I mean. Acts like she really likes me or something."

Travis smiled. "She does, sweetheart."

"Yeah, right." Staci hesitated, as if there was something she wanted to say but couldn't. "Travis, this is real stupid. I know it's been four years, but . . . I still miss her."

Travis opened his arms and Staci crawled inside. He felt a cold saltwater sprinkle on his neck. "That's not stupid, honey," he said, hugging her tightly. "I still miss her, too."

# TUESDAY

*April 16*

**8**

7:05 A.M.

Travis sat in the holding cell reviewing the Moroconi file while the guards fetched his client. It was a familiar routine. They insisted that the lawyer be in place first. Maybe they wanted to make the lawyer uncomfortable, Travis speculated. To let him experience a few moments of the foreboding the guards lived with on a daily basis.

The guards made no secret of how much they hated attorney–client conferences, during which they were required by law to afford the defendant and his counselor privacy, if only for a brief period. They seemed convinced lawyers took advantage of the privacy to smuggle weapons or other contraband to their clients. Travis couldn't blame them. Four years ago he knew he would have harbored the same suspicions.

He buried himself in the file, trying to pass the time as profitably and painlessly as possible. It didn't work. He kept staring at the photographs, wondering what kind of monster could do that to another human being.

The cell door abruptly swung open and two uniformed guards

escorted Alberto Moroconi into the cell. Travis was introduced to a medium-sized man with a wispy mustache and a day's stubble. Travis was surprised, although he wasn't sure why. What was he expecting, Frankenstein?

The guards planted Moroconi in his chair and handcuffed him to the table.

"We don't need the bracelets," Travis said. "Please remove them."

The guard closest to him shrugged. "Warden says leave 'em on."

"There are several documents and photographs I need him to examine."

"Ain't that a shame." The guard closed the cell door behind him. "Maybe he can hold them with his nose."

Thanks bunches. Once the guards were out of earshot, Travis addressed his new client. "My name is Travis Byrne. I've been appointed to represent you at the trial today—"

"You're a cop," Moroconi said curtly.

"I'm a lawyer," Travis replied. How on earth— "I used to be a cop."

"Same diff'rence. I knew it was somethin' like that. It shows."

Travis didn't know what that meant, and he didn't plan to kill precious time finding out, either. "I need to ask you a few questions—"

"You ain't one of these cops-and-robbers screwballs with a secret game plan, are you? Like playin' good cop to my face while you're fixin' to send me up the river."

"I assure you I'll do everything the law permits to obtain an acquittal."

Moroconi scrutinized Travis intently. "A cop doin' me favors. Go figure."

"Mr. Moroconi, our time together is limited. Can we discuss your case?"

Moroconi folded his arms across his chest. "Shoot."

"Did you know the victim, Miss Mary Ann McKenzie?"

"Oh, yeah. I knew the bitch."

Travis bit down on his lower lip. "And . . . how did you know her?"

"I was at the bar where it all started that night. You know, O'Reilly's. She comes struttin' in, tryin' to get some action, swingin' her cute little ass around. Personally, I think she got what she deserved, the stupid cunt."

Travis felt his heart beating faster. Cool off, he told himself. You're the man's zealous advocate. "Did you see what happened?"

"At the bar, yeah. After she'd flung her fishy smell all over the place, she sashayed out the front door. A gang of studs sittin' in the corner decided they wanted a piece of that and followed her. Didn't surprise me what happened. I knew it was comin'."

"Did you attempt to warn Miss McKenzie?"

"Why? Hell, I don't care what the little twat says. She wanted it." He laughed. "Maybe not exactly what she got, but she wanted it."

"And what did you do when you saw these men follow her out of the bar?"

Moroconi shrugged. "I had another Scotch and soda."

Travis redirected his eyes to the file. "Miss McKenzie says you were one of the men who attacked her."

"She's fucked in the head."

"She picked you out of the lineup."

"She remembers me from the bar. So what?"

"She says you urinated on her and forced a Coke bottle—"

"Well, she's wrong, goddamn it! Don't you see?" Moroconi leaned across the table. "The stupid slut had been fucked blind! She couldn't tell me from Elvis!"

Travis coughed. "She also states that you suggested tying her to the bumper of her car—"

"Look, you shit-faced shyster, I'm innocent. Are you going to help me or not?"

"I'm—" Travis took a deep breath and closed his eyes. His stomach was churning like the ocean during a storm. "It's not necessary for you to plead your innocence to me. In fact, I wish you wouldn't. I'm simply trying to uncover facts that could assist your defense."

"Shee-it." Moroconi blew air through his teeth. Bits of spittle flew across the room. "All you're interested in is covering your ass. Just like everybody else."

"I assure you that isn't—"

"Just keep the goddamn trial going. Can you do that?"

"I'm not sure I understand—"

"Just keep the trial going, asshole! How long will the feds' case take?"

"Three or four days."

"Fine. Throw in a lot of objections and make sure it doesn't end any sooner. I'll take care of myself."

"I don't think that's a very good strategy—"

"Are you my mouthpiece or ain't you?"

Travis hesitated. "I'm your court-appointed attorney—"

"Then do what I say."

"I think I could help you—"

"You better just try to help yourself, jerkwad."

Travis's head twitched. "What do you mean by that?"

"I mean exactly what I say. People are trying to get me, in case you haven't figured it out, chump."

Oh great, Travis thought. A conspiracy theory from the paranoid defendant. I suppose the rape was committed on a grassy knoll. "Why do you assume—"

"Why do you figure I got hauled in by the police?"

"I understand there was an anonymous tip. . . ."

"What a lucky coincidence. Shit. They saw a chance to nail my butt to the wall and they took it. In spades."

"I really don't understand—"

"Are you blind? Jesus, why do you think you're here? Do you really think my last lawyer just disappeared? Decided to go to Tahiti or somethin'? There are people who want me *gone*, asshole.

That's why they framed me for this rap, and that's why they're gonna make sure I do serious time for it."

Travis frowned. "And who are these alleged people?"

"They're people who'd cut your fuckin' heart out just to see what it looks like, that's who!"

Travis heard the guards returning. Time was up already. Sad thing about it was he was relieved—although the trial would start shortly and he hadn't gleaned any information he could use in court. "I don't feel I can adequately represent you without more cooperation on your part, Mr. Moroconi. The judge won't like it, but perhaps I should withdraw. He'll deny the motion, but if I just don't show up—"

Moroconi sprang out of his chair and lunged at Travis. Travis jumped, falling backward in his chair. Moroconi tried to dive after him, but the handcuffs restrained him.

Guards ran down the corridor and shoved the key into the cell door. Moroconi twisted and strained on the tabletop, spitting and cursing, looking as if he might burst free at any moment. Thank God for those handcuffs, Travis thought. The handcuffs I wanted removed.

Moroconi fought the guards as they hauled him to his feet. "Just make goddamn sure you're there today, shyster. I don't care what you do, I don't care what you say. Just keep the trial going. Understand?"

Travis nodded slowly.

"Good." Moroconi smiled, baring his yellow teeth, as the guards dragged him out of the cell. "See you in court."

# 9

8:45 a.m.

Travis bumped into Cavanaugh as he hurried through the courthouse. He surveyed her stuffed attaché case and determined expression and drew the obvious conclusion.

"Not you again?"

"I'm afraid so, counsel. Double jeopardy doesn't apply to prosecutors." She placed her briefcase on the conveyor belt of the X-ray machine. "Blaisdell asked me to handle the Moroconi case weeks ago. You have a problem with that?"

"No. It just seems a little unfair. You can't be in full fettle so soon after yesterday's crushing defeat at my hands."

They passed through the metal detector and started down the corridor to Courtroom Three. "Spare me the egomania, Byrne. Today's case is a whole new ball game."

"In what way?"

"Have you met your client yet?"

"Uh, yeah."

She smirked. "Then you know. Face it, you're going down in flames this time. Even if the evidence wasn't all against you, which it is, your client is such a disgusting little creep the jury will send him to the slammer anyway. It's hopeless."

Travis tended to agree, but he wasn't about to let her know that. "We may have a few surprises for you."

"Don't try to buffalo me, Byrne. You haven't had sufficient prep time. It's going to be a case of the blind leading the repugnant."

"We'll see."

"And if you're hoping to make a deal, forget it. We already tried. Your client refused all plea bargains. You're stuck with him till the bitter end."

Travis veered off toward the men's room. "I'll just have to make the best of it. See you in five minutes."

"I'll be waiting. With bated breath."

Travis pushed open the door and entered the bathroom. It was a tiny room—one sink, one urinal, one stall. The walls were composed of a grungy green tile streaked with mildew. Given the seemingly permanent odor, Travis preferred short visits during which he could conceivably hold his breath for the duration.

The urinal bore an out-of-order sign, so he used the stall. After he finished, he pushed open the door and stepped out.

There were two men in dark suits standing outside the stall. Staring at him.

"Excuse me," Travis said. He tried to push past them to get to the sink. The man on his left, an older man who was chewing a cigarette, leaned away from his much younger companion, blocking Travis's way.

"Hey, what do you think—"

Before Travis could finish his complaint, the cigarette man slammed him back against the wall. Travis's head thudded against the tile; bursts of light flashed before his eyes.

"Look," Travis said weakly. His brain felt scrambled. He realized he was slurring his words. "There are . . . s-security guards outside and—"

The cigarette man drew back his fist and punched Travis in the soft part of his stomach. Travis cried out in pain and fell forward onto his knees. The man blasted his face with the back of his fist. Travis's head smashed against the stall door. Blood trickled from his nose.

The younger man reached for Travis's throat. Fighting to clear his blurred vision, Travis grabbed his assailant's hand and squeezed down on a pressure point. The man cried out. Travis tried to wrench the man's arm behind his back, but before he could finish, the cigarette man chopped the side of his neck with his flattened hand. Travis fell back against the wall, releasing his grip on the young man's hand.

The cigarette man grabbed Travis again, this time by the collar of his jacket, and hauled him up to eye level. Travis's stomach burned; every movement was excruciating.

"Lose, asshole."

Travis tried to form words, but his lips were numb and unresponsive. "I don't . . . understand. . . ."

"You unnerstand enough." The man reached down and clamped his hand onto Travis's groin. "Feel that? I want you to remember what that feels like. Your balls are in my hands." He grinned malevolently. "In a minute, we'll disappear. But don't be fooled, asshole. Your balls will still be in my hands. You're gonna lose."

The man squeezed tightly. Travis screamed in pain. His knees weakened; he tumbled back down to the floor. The cigarette man shoved him away and started to leave, then whirled around suddenly and kicked Travis in the gut, in the same aching spot he had hit before.

Tears clouded Travis's eyes. "What . . . do you *want?*"

The man sneered. "You know what we want. Now you need to figure out what you're gonna do about it. If you decide not to cooperate, it'll be the last decision you make. We've taken care of punks like you before and we'll do it again."

Travis wanted to shout for help, but found he had no breath, no voice. He clutched his stomach helplessly.

"Just remember. We'll be watching, asshole." The two men left the bathroom.

Travis lay in a crumpled heap on the floor beneath the sink. He was gasping for air like a drowning man. His groin and stomach were on fire. He wanted to crawl up to the mirror and see if there was any permanent damage, but he couldn't manage it. He hurt too much.

He felt the warm blood flowing out of his nostrils, forming a sticky puddle around his mouth. He hoped his nose wasn't broken.

After all, he was due in court in less than five minutes.

# 10

## 3:00 P.M.

Cavanaugh was still voir-diring the jury.

She was taking no chances. Travis had been on the opposite side of a trial from her at least half a dozen times in the past year, and she had never taken nearly so long to select a jury. Usually it was the defense that wanted to know every minute detail about the jurors' lives.

Maybe she was still stinging from her defeat the day before, Travis mused. Whatever the cause, it had gone on too long, and if it took much longer, his head was going to explode. Judge Hagedorn had been relatively understanding when Travis stumbled into the courtroom fifteen minutes late with a bandage on his nose. Hagedorn probably didn't buy Travis's story about falling down the stairs, but he let it pass, and he recessed the proceedings every hour or so to allow Travis to soak his head and vomit. Who could ask for anything more?

For some reason he didn't quite understand himself, Travis didn't want to explain what had really happened. He didn't understand the situation well enough; it might have a negative impact on Moroconi's case. Or maybe it was just pride—the big burly ex-cop didn't want to admit he'd been trashed by two goons in the little boys' room.

Travis heard a noise in the back of the courtroom. He jumped, jerked his head around. No, it wasn't them; it was some spectator in a blue-and-white seersucker suit. Never seen him before. Looked harmless.

It had been this way all day—every time Travis heard a noise, he sprang out of his seat and his pulse shot off the scale. He wasn't sure what he feared most—that the two men from the bathroom would return, or that they wouldn't. He dearly wanted another go at them, but the way he felt right now, the result would probably be much the same. Or worse.

Travis silently cursed himself. The fact of the matter was they got the drop on him. It was humiliating. He was only thirty-six, for God's sake. He'd been trained to protect himself and to subdue assailants. But in the bathroom, he'd been a human punching bag. Sure, they caught him off guard, but there was more to it than that. Somewhere in the course of quitting the force, going to law school, and burying himself in the books—he'd gone soft. He'd forgotten how to fight with anything other than his mouth.

Speaking of which . . .

"Mr. Byrne, I repeat—do you have any questions for the jury?"

He looked up at the bench. Hagedorn was staring at him impatiently. Cavanaugh must've finished while he was grumbling to himself. Hope she didn't say anything too objectionable.

"Yes, your honor." Travis rose to his feet. "I have several questions."

"Please limit yourself to thirty minutes," Hagedorn said crisply.

"Thirty minutes!" Travis approached the bench. Cavanaugh followed close behind. "Your honor, counsel for the prosecution has questioned the jury panel for over five hours!"

"That's just the point," Hagedorn said. "She's surely explored every area of potential prejudice by now. I don't think it's necessary for you to rehash the same material."

"Judge, I can assure you I won't be repetitious—"

"I can assure myself of that, counsel. Your thirty minutes begin now."

"Your honor, this is grossly prejudicial. The court can't—" He froze, immediately realizing his mistake. Never tell a judge what he *can't* do. Never.

Hagedorn's face grew stern. "This court has the inherent power to set guidelines for the conduct of trials, as you well know."

"But, Judge, if the prosecution talks for five hours, and I only talk for half an hour, the impression left with the jury will be that the prosecution has the better case."

"This is not an evidentiary stage of the trial, counsel. This is merely voir dire."

"Sure, that's what the textbooks say. But as a practical matter—"

"Twenty-nine minutes, counsel. And counting."

Travis pushed away from the bench. What was going on here? Since when did the Honorable Charles E. Hagedorn engage in this kind of blatant favoritism? He glanced at Cavanaugh, but she looked away. No appeal to that quarter. She might not agree with the ruling, but she was smart enough to take a break when she got it.

Travis calmly approached the jury, trying to act as if nothing unfavorable had occurred. The jury couldn't hear what went on at the bench, but they could usually figure out who the judge liked and who he didn't. Travis couldn't let that happen here; he had too many strikes against him as it was.

He smiled pleasantly. "Ladies and gentlemen, how many of you are familiar with the phrase *presumed innocent?*"

A fter Travis finished questioning the jury (just under the thirty-minute deadline), Hagedorn took the lawyers into chambers and they eliminated jurors that either side thought could harm their case. Unfortunately, Travis suspected that any juror with common sense and good taste was detrimental to his case, but that was hardly a basis for dismissal.

Afterward Hagedorn called a recess for the day. Thank God. Travis's head was throbbing and his nausea had never subsided. He made a beeline for the back of the courtroom.

Dan Holyfield stopped him at the door.

"Dan!" Travis said, surprised. "What brings you to the courtroom? Couldn't resist my offer to second-chair?"

Dan didn't smile. "I came over because—" He stopped and stared at Travis's face. "My God, what happened?"

Travis touched his bandaged nose—still sore as hell. "A little accident in the bathroom."

"You're getting dark circles under both eyes. Your nose may be broken."

"Damn. I hope not. I'll stop at the emergency room on the way home."

"See that you do."

"Surely you didn't come down here just to do your Marcus Welby impression."

"True." Dan looked around, then pulled Travis to one side. His voice dropped to a whisper. "I'm afraid I have some bad news."

The blood drained from Travis's face. "Not about Staci?"

"No, no. Staci's fine. At least, as far as I know. This is about Seacrest."

"Tom Seacrest? The attorney who had this dog case before he disappeared?"

"Right. Except he didn't just disappear." Dan gripped Travis by the shoulders. "He's dead, Travis. He's been murdered."

A cold chill shot down Travis's spine. *We've taken care of punks like you before and we'll do it again.* "Who—who did it?"

"The police haven't the slightest idea. His body was found on the shore of Lake Palestine—but he didn't drown. He was killed—in the most god awful way you can imagine. Someone poured lighter fluid on his face and genitals, then set him on fire with a blowtorch. Then stabbed him with an ice pick about twenty times. Seacrest died slow and horribly."

Travis's mouth went dry. "When did this happen?"

"They're not sure. The body's been rotting for a couple of days at least. My friend at the police station tells me the corpse is all green and bloated, chewed by animals, picked at by birds."

Travis's eyes closed. Someone truly evil was involved in this. Someone—what was the phrase?—*someone who'd cut your fuckin' heart out just to see what it looks like.*

"I want you to drop this case, Travis."

"Tempting, I have to admit . . . but I can't do that."

"I think you should."

"Why? We don't know that there's any connection between Seacrest's death and the Moroconi case. Seacrest just happened to be working on it when he was killed. He was probably working on ten other cases, for that matter."

"Given the character of your client—"

"My client has been behind bars for weeks. He couldn't have had anything to do with it."

"Still, I'd feel more comfortable—"

"I can't drop the case, Dan. I've been appointed by a federal judge."

"Let me speak to Charles. I've known him since law school. I'm sure I can make him see reason—"

"No way, Dan."

"Just let me talk to him."

"Dan—no. I can handle this myself."

Dan squared his shoulders. "Travis, I don't like to pull rank, but last time I looked at the letterhead, my name was above yours. I'm your boss, and I'm telling you I want you out."

"Or what? Get real, Dan—I know you're not going to fire me. I have more respect for you than anyone else in the world. But I can't drop a client in the middle of a trial."

"Travis—I don't mean to interfere. I'm just concerned about you."

Travis did his utmost to sound reassuring. "Don't worry about me. I'll be fine."

"This from the man who looks like he lost a fight with a refrigerator. I don't suppose you'd care to tell me what really happened?"

Travis looked away. "Well . . ."

"As I suspected." Dan stepped toward the doorway. "Take care of yourself, Travis. You have an extremely promising future. Don't get in over your head."

"I'll do my best."

"Mr. Byrne?" Travis heard a voice from the other end of the courtroom. "May we talk to you for a moment?"

"Excuse me, Dan. Duty calls." Travis approached a couple, a young woman in a blue print dress and the man in the seersucker suit he had noticed earlier. "Yes?"

"My name is Curran." He was a skinny man with no chin. "This is my sister, Sarah."

"What can I do for you?"

"Mary Ann McKenzie is our sister."

Oh God, not now. Anything but grieving relatives.

"I've spoken to some people around town about you," Curran said. "You get high marks, especially for someone who's only been out of law school for a year. I hear you're especially clever at finding legal technicalities to get your clients off."

"I know the law and I'm willing to apply it, if that's what you mean," Travis replied.

Curran reached into a manila envelope and withdrew two eight-by-ten-inch photographs. "Have you seen these?"

The top photograph showed a smiling, red-haired teenage girl in a ruffled blue dress standing beside a straggly-looking geek in a blue tuxedo. "I take it that's your sister," Travis said.

"It was taken two years ago, on prom night." Curran shuffled the photos. "Now look at this."

Travis examined the second photograph and gasped. It was a close-up of Mary Ann taken at the crime scene, but this one hadn't been in the file. She was lying beside a dirt road, her body broken and twisted unnaturally, skin flayed from her face and arms. It was nightmarish.

"Where did you get this?" Travis said, suddenly short of breath. He turned the photo facedown.

"I don't think that's important," Curran said. He turned the photo faceup and held it in front of Travis's eyes. "I'd hate to see the man who did this get off on a legal technicality, wouldn't you?"

Travis looked away. Wordlessly, Curran returned the photos to the envelope. He put his arm around his sister and left the courtroom.

# 11

## 10:25 P.M.

Travis sat in his office, the contents of his trial notebook spread all over his desk. The office was dark except for the lamp burning on his desk. Mary Ann McKenzie would take the stand soon, and Travis knew he would either win or lose the case depending on how he handled her. He nibbled at a stale Caesar salad and reviewed his cross-examination notes for the tenth time.

Or tried, anyway. He took another bite, then pushed the take-out container away with disgust. He was really learning to hate salads. And Caesar salads were the worst—cold, soggy, and slimy. Even when they claimed the anchovies were gone, Travis knew they were still there. What kind of weenie could survive on this hamster chow?

He knew the answer to that question well enough. The kind of weenie who gets pummeled in the men's room by two ham-fisted thugs. He tried to concentrate on the case, but his mind kept drifting back to the day's bizarre series of events. His interview with his client—the most revolting man he had ever met, much less represented. The pressure tactics from the victim's family. Hagedorn's version of a kangaroo court. Learning that Seacrest bought the farm. And the incident in the bathroom.

*Damn!* He slammed his fist down on the desktop. That shouldn't have happened. Which was beside the point, or as the older lawyers said, "immaterial, inconclusive, and irrelevant." It happened, whether he liked it or not. He should have told Dan what happened—he knew that—but somehow, he just couldn't admit he'd been caught with his fly open by those two creeps.

What were they after? Surely there was more involved than a trial fix. All indications at this point were that Moroconi was well on his way to the big house. Assistance from outside forces seemed grossly unnecessary. Why take the risk? Unless they had a different objective in mind.

Travis's head suddenly rose to attention. Behind him, in the lobby outside his office, he heard a shuffling noise.

He bolted from his chair and pressed himself against the wall. Was he imagining things again or . . .

No. He heard the shuffling again. Louder now. Footsteps— several of them. And they were drawing closer.

This time, by God, they weren't going to get the drop on him. He grabbed the letter opener on his desk and whirled through the open office door.

"Freeze, punks! I've called the cops." Travis spun through the lobby, trying to look in every direction at once. He stopped, pivoted, then whirled around the other direction. Unfortunately, his foot struck the coffee table. He stumbled, waved his arms madly trying to regain his balance, then fell flat on his back.

He lay on the floor for a second, dazed. When he finally opened his eyes, he saw two men in long overcoats staring down at him.

Instinctively, he covered his stomach. *Please God, not again.* "Who . . . are you?" he whispered.

One of the men reached into his coat and withdrew a badge.

"I'm Agent Janicek. This is Mr. Holt. We're with the FBI. The Joint Organized Crime Task Force, to be specific."

"You're . . . *feebees*—" Travis propped himself up on one arm. "Then you're not going to . . ."

Janicek offered a hand and pulled Travis to his feet. "We'd like to have a word with you."

"You'd like . . ." Slowly, Travis was getting a grip. "How did you get in here?"

"Does it really matter? We're here, obviously. Let's talk."

Travis brushed off his suit. "I suppose this is about the McKenzie case."

"Not exactly. We want to discuss your client."

"Moroconi? What about him?"

Janicek was in his midforties, judging from the pronounced wrinkles around his eyes and the gray patches in his brown hair. "How much do you know about Mr. Moroconi?"

"Not much. I just met him this morning."

"And you've made no attempt to investigate his . . . background?"

"I haven't had much time, and the court-appointed-attorney retainer won't pay for private investigations. Even if it did, I'd investigate the crime, or perhaps the victim. Not my own client."

"Then you know little about Mr. Moroconi's past."

"Next to nothing."

Holt, a dark man with a bug-eyed expression, looked harshly at Janicek. "I told you this wouldn't work. He's a lawyer; he's not going to divulge anything voluntarily. We should've brought him in. Tried a few procedures."

Travis had thought Holt looked like a class-A moron the first moment he saw him. It was nice to have his judgment confirmed so soon. "A few procedures? Is that a threat?"

Janicek shook his head. "I'm sure that won't be necessary. Mr. Byrne will be happy to help us. Won't you?"

"That depends on what you want."

"Of course it does. Let me tell you about Alberto Moroconi. A few years ago he was a bagman for the Outfit."

"The Outfit?"

"You know. The boys. The mob. La Cosa Nostra."

"Moroconi was with the mob?"

"Right. The Gattuso mob, to be exact."

"Gattuso?" Travis's forehead creased. He might not be on the force anymore, but he still followed cases of that magnitude. "I thought you whiteshirts shut down the Gattusos a few years back."

"We did," Janicek said proudly, as if he took personal satisfaction in the Bureau's success. "For the most part, anyway. It was one of the great success stories of the Joint Task Force, a demonstration of what could be achieved when the feds and the locals work together and centralize our databases. Instead of trying to get criminal convictions, we used the asset-forfeiture provisions in the RICO Act. Civil verdicts are much easier to get than criminal convictions; after a prima facie RICO case is made, the burden of proof shifts to the crooks. We seized all property that might have been used or obtained in connection with a crime. Which with these guys was virtually everything they had. When we took away the toys, we cut the heart out of the mob. Pretty soon we had all the informants we needed to shut them down permanently. There were just a few loose threads, a few fish that slipped through the net. Al Moroconi was one of them."

Travis still couldn't believe it. "Moroconi used to be with the mob? The real-life, honest-to-God *mob*?"

"There's no such thing as *used to be* with the mob," Holt said. "Once you're in, you're in for life."

"Agent Holt would know," Janicek said. "He's our resident guru on mob activities. He's one of those obnoxious pricks who acts like he knows everything—except that Holt actually does."

"I have an eidetic memory," Holt said, displaying a touch of pride himself. "I never forget anything. I could tell you about dozens of illegal deals in which Moroconi is believed to have been involved. He was a *made man*—a member of one of the highest levels of the organization."

"Then you're not interested in the pending trial at all," Travis said, finally catching the drift.

"Correct. It's Moroconi we want. We've been specially sent on this errand by the head of our department. We've been looking for Moroconi for years, ever since an informant clued us in to his importance. But he disappeared when the Gattusos went down, and he's kept a low profile ever since. Until he was stupid enough to get arrested on this rape charge."

Stupid enough? Travis wondered. Or, as Moroconi suggested, *framed.* "So you want to talk with my client in connection with this Gattuso case."

"The Gattuso case is closed," Janicek said. "History. But we still need to interview him. Just to clear up a few details. A stolen slush fund, a witness who disappeared. That's all."

*Sure it is. What aren't you telling me, Janicek?* "Are you offering immunity?"

"Well, let's just say that if—*if*—he spills something we like, a deal might develop."

Travis shook his head. "No dice. If you want to negotiate, we do it up front. Otherwise I'm advising my client to remain silent."

Holt pursed his lips. "We could agree that nothing Moroconi tells us can be used against him in the current trial."

Hardly a sacrifice, Travis thought, since the current trial looked like a sure conviction already. "Sorry, boys, but I can't advise my client to relinquish something that might be of value to you unless you reciprocate."

Janicek glanced at his associate. An unspoken message seemed to pass between them. "I'm afraid we're not prepared to offer immunity at this time."

Travis shrugged. "Then I guess we have nothing to discuss."

He saw Holt grit his teeth and ball up his fists. Janicek reached inside his coat and withdrew a card. "This is my boss's card, Mr. Byrne. If you change your mind, just dial that number and ask for

Special Agent Henderson. See the password at the bottom of the card? That'll get you through. Call anytime, night or day. We monitor the phone constantly."

Travis took the card. "I don't think I'll be calling."

"Keep the card anyway. You never know." He opened the front door, then paused. "There are any number of reasons why a guy like you might need the FBI."

# 12

## 11:30 P.M.

The man in the trench coat lit another cigarette. How long did it take to drag out a prisoner, anyway? Christ—as much money as he'd paid to get in here, you'd think he'd be entitled to better service.

He sucked deeply, then exhaled the smoke in perfectly formed little rings. At last one of the guards shuffled up to the conference cell, Moroconi in tow. The guard unlocked the door and shoved Moroconi into the chair on the opposite side of the table.

"Remember," the man in the trench coat said to the guard, "you didn't see me, you didn't hear me, and you don't know who I am."

"Right, right," the guard replied. "Forgot all about it." He rubbed his hands together. "I bet you could prevent any sudden spurts of recollection, too."

The man in the trench coat blew a stream of smoke toward the guard. "You've already been paid."

"Paid for arranging the meeting. I ain't had nothin' for keepin' quiet."

"Don't get greedy, my friend."

"Hey, a guy like me's got to look out for himself. They don't pay us peanuts here and—*awrk!*—"

The guard emitted a short gurgling noise as the man in the trench coat grabbed him by the throat. "Don't play games with me, you pissant. If anyone found out about this meeting, you'd be in as much trouble as me. Probably more. I could talk my way out of it. A dumb shit like you would just sit there and take the punches. You'd be fired—you might even face criminal charges. Then you could spend some quality time with these inmates you've been so kind to over the years. Wouldn't that be fun?"

A look of undisguised terror crossed the guard's face. It was more than just the realization that the man could do everything he threatened. It was the realization that he would.

The man in the trench coat took another drag from his cigarette. "I haven't even mentioned what I personally would do to you if you talked. So keep your mouth shut, okay?"

"Yes, sir. I will. I promise." The guard backed away the instant he was released. "Hell, I was just playin' with you. You know, shootin' the bull. I wouldn't tell anyone. You know I wouldn't."

The man didn't look at him.

"Swear to God. I really really—"

The man tapped his cigarette ashes onto the floor. "Leave."

"Yes, sir. Right away, sir." The guard stumbled backward through the cell door. "You two will have complete privacy. Absolutely." He locked the door and faded down the dark corridor.

The man's lip curled around his cigarette. "Schmuck."

"You're tellin' me," Moroconi said. "You ain't been livin' with him."

"You have my sympathies."

"You can keep your sympathies. Just gimme what I want. Have you got it on you?"

"No. But I can get it. Have you got the money?"

Moroconi smiled thinly. "No. But I can get it."

"I see. We have a stalemate then. Who's going to make the first move?"

"I'm not goin' anywhere soon."

"Good point. How are you going to get the money?"

"I'm not. I'm gonna tell you where it is. When our deal is done."

The other man leaned back in his chair. "I'm afraid I detect a distinct lack of trust."

"Detect away, Sherlock. When you spring me and get me what I want, you'll get paid."

"You're demanding an inordinate amount of goodwill on my part."

"Wouldn't you? If you sell me short, I'm headed up the river. You're my last chance."

"Have you no faith in the judicial system? Or your attorney?"

"He's an ex-cop. No favors from him. Once an asshole, always an asshole. I tried to set him straight this mornin'. He acted like he couldn't stand to be in the same room with a lowlife like me. Self-righteous pig. What do you know about him?"

"At the moment, not much. But that will change soon."

"When you learn somethin', let me know. I wouldn't mind having the chance to stick that pig where it hurts."

"If the opportunity presents itself, I'll be happy to oblige." The man blew cigarette smoke through his teeth. "I guess you've heard what happened to his predecessor."

Moroconi's face became noticeably less animated. "No. What?"

"Fish food. Washed up on the shore of Lake Palestine. They're not sure how long he's been there."

"What happened to him?"

"The word isn't out yet officially, but . . ." He paused dramatically. "It involves fire."

"No shit! Then—"

The man nodded.

"Look, I can't screw around anymore. As long as I'm stuck in here, I'm a sitting duck."

"That fact has occurred to me."

"You son of a bitch." Moroconi's face and neck muscles tensed. "All right, goddamn you. I'll go first. I'll tell you where you can get the money. Half of it, anyway. After I'm out, and you've delivered the goods, I'll see that you get the other half."

"That's acceptable. Under the circumstances." He inhaled deeply. "Six to the right, two to the north, three to the left. Commit that to memory."

Moroconi made sure he had it, then asked, "How are you gonna get me what I want?"

"Not to worry."

"I don't think you should come here like this again. It's too risky."

"Agreed. Next time I'll visit during the day."

"Are you crazy? I'll be in the courtroom all day long. They've got five sergeants breathing down my neck from start to finish."

"I'll arrange something. Tonight I wanted us to have the opportunity to talk face-to-face. Privately. That shouldn't be necessary again. I'll get you what you want."

"I don't see how."

"You don't have to. I'll take care of it."

"Listen to me, chump. I'm tellin' you, they won't let you near me!"

"Of course they will." He ground his cigarette out on the table. "I can do anything I want, Al. I'm with the FBI."

# WEDNESDAY

*April 17*

**1 3**

8:50 A.M.

"C'mon, Charlie, you gotta help me out here."

"Sorry, Travis. Courtrooms give me the shivers."

"It'll only be for a little while."

"Ten seconds would be ten seconds too long. Get someone else."

Travis was inside the courthouse coffee shop pleading with Charlie Slovic, the proprietor. "There's no one else here who fits, Charlie. You're a perfect match."

"Besides, who would watch the shop while I'm gone?"

"I'll take care of that," Travis assured him. "I promise. You won't get into any trouble. Think of it as your civic obligation. Kind of like jury duty."

"I've never done jury duty."

"Well then. You owe us."

"Sheesh." Charlie turned down the coffee burners. "I really don't want to do this, Travis."

"But you will. That's what makes you a great American. Am I right?"

Charlie sighed. "Yeah. Right."

Opening statements passed without any major surprises. On behalf of the prosecution, Cavanaugh gave new meaning to the word *melodramatic*. Travis thought she overdid it—this situation was already so supercharged with emotion that it reeked of overkill. But the jury didn't appear to mind. Their attention was riveted to her, except for occasional diversions, when Cavanaugh would describe a particularly horrific act and the jury would glance at Moroconi with disgust.

Travis's opening statement was much shorter and hinged upon a single point. He didn't contest the fact that Mary Ann McKenzie had been raped—the medical evidence established that beyond any question. He didn't try to dissuade the jury from sympathizing with her; as he assured them, he felt for her, too. The only question was whether Al Moroconi was a member of the gang that assaulted her. In order to convict, Travis told them, they would have to find that Mary Ann's identification of Moroconi was trustworthy. Beyond a reasonable doubt.

Hagedorn instructed the prosecution to call its first witness. To Travis's surprise, Cavanaugh led with Mary Ann McKenzie. He had expected her to testify, but not right off the bat. The usual prosecution strategy was to build up to the victim—establish the crime through medical and forensic testimony, then bring on the victim for a devastating wrap-up. But for some reason, Cavanaugh had decided to lead with her ace.

Mary Ann McKenzie took the stand. She was sworn in, her voice choking on the phrase *I do*. Not a good sign, Travis thought. If she can't get through the oath without a choke, cross-examination might prove impossible.

She looked terrible. Her face was partially wrapped in bandages and still covered with large blue-black bruises. Travis knew she was undergoing reconstructive plastic surgery to restore some semblance of her former face. He also knew it wouldn't work; this was permanent damage, far beyond the curative powers of the surgeon's scalpel. Her neck and right arm were in a body cast—probably due to injuries sustained as she was dragged behind the car. She appeared weak, pale, and emaciated.

Cavanaugh began the direct examination. Travis noted that she was using her nice-nice voice; some questions were barely louder than a whisper. After passing through the preliminaries, Cavanaugh brought Mary Ann to the night of the incident.

"Would you please tell the jury what you were doing that night?"

Mary Ann's lips parted, and her voice emerged in a hoarse whisper. "I went to O'Reilly's. It's on Mockingbird. Near campus."

"Is this a place you frequented?" Cavanaugh asked.

"I'd never been there before in my life."

"Why were you there that evening?"

"I was looking for Dierdre, my roommate. A sorority sister told me she might be there. She was supposed to loan me her psych notes so I could study for an exam we had the next day."

"Did you find Dierdre?"

"No."

"What happened?"

"I searched all through the bar. She wasn't there, so I left. As I crossed the parking lot these men jumped out of nowhere and grabbed me."

"How many were there?"

"Six. Three black men, three white. I think. Everything happened so quickly."

Cavanaugh advanced toward the witness stand. "Can you tell us what happened next?"

"They threw me down on the asphalt and . . . hit me. In the face. Several times." She pointed to a still-vivid abrasion just beneath her left eye. "That's when I got this. They hit me so hard—I was afraid I'd lose my eye. Then they took my keys out

of my purse, threw me in the trunk of my car, and closed the lid."
She turned toward the jury, eyes wide. "It was so . . . *terrifying*. I
was trapped in the trunk—I couldn't see, I couldn't hear. I didn't
know what they were going to do to me. I was so scared."

Cavanaugh stood beside Mary Ann, careful not to block the jurors' view, and addressed her in a quiet voice. "When did you see
them next?"

"After they stopped the car. They opened the trunk and pulled
me out by my hair. We were somewhere near White Rock
Lake—I'm not sure exactly where." Her hands began to tremble.
"Two of them pinned me down to the ground. It was wet and
muddy. I tried to get away, but there were so many of them—and
they held me so tight. I was helpless."

"What happened next?"

Mary Ann looked down at her lap. "One of them ripped off my
slacks and . . . and—" She turned away and covered her face with
her hands.

"Did he rape you?" Cavanaugh asked.

Technically, Travis knew Cavanaugh was leading the witness.
He also knew that if he objected, the jury would crucify him.

Mary Ann nodded her head. Tears began to appear in the corners of her eyes.

"I'm sorry," Cavanaugh said. "You have to answer verbally for
the benefit of the court reporter."

After several false starts, Mary Ann managed to say, "Y-Yes. Yes.
They all did."

"How many of them?"

She shook her head. Tears were streaming down her face. "All
six of them. Some of them more than once. The third one"—she
clenched her eyes shut—"he peed on me."

"The man urinated on your body?"

She nodded. "In my mouth. On my breasts. All over me. Then
he flipped me over on my stomach, pressed my face into the mud,
and said—that thing."

"I'm sorry, Mary Ann, but you need to tell the jury what he said."

Mary Ann looked as if she would rather die, but she eventually answered the question. "He said, 'I bet she likes it doggie-style, stupid cunt.' And then he—he—oh *God*!" Her voice dissolved into uncontrolled sobbing. "I begged them to stop! It hurt so much! I begged them! But they just kept on and on. I was crying, pleading. And they laughed at me!"

Travis checked the jury. Her outburst had electrified them. If they had any questions about her veracity before—which Travis seriously doubted—the questions had evaporated.

Cavanaugh paused to allow Mary Ann to collect herself. "Did you recognize any of the men?"

Mary Ann raised a trembling hand and pointed at Moroconi. "He was there."

"Was he the one who urinated on you?"

"No. He came after that. Fourth." Her eyes seemed to be turning inward, as if she were experiencing the whole nightmare over again. "He was so mean. He hurt me. On purpose. He pounded on my breasts. He tore me. Inside. I was bleeding and crying, and he didn't care. The doctors say I'll never be able to—to—" Again her words were drowned in tears.

"Have children?" Cavanaugh completed.

Mary Ann nodded. "Y-Yes."

"And you subsequently were forced to undergo an emergency double mastectomy. Correct?"

Mary Ann covered her chest. "Yes."

"Do you recall anything else Mr. Moroconi did or said?"

"Yes. He was the one who suggested they tie me to the back of my car and drag me."

"Why would he want to do that?"

"He said, 'Just to teach the dumb bitch a lesson.' "

"Subsequent testimony will show you were dragged for over a mile," Cavanaugh said quietly. Counsel was testifying, but Travis wasn't about to protest. "What happened after that?"

"They tossed me back in the trunk, drove around for several hours, then threw me out on the side of a dirt road. Like I was . . . just a piece of garbage." Her voice was beyond tears; it took on an empty, despairing tone. "I hurt so bad. I felt so . . . ruined. I just wanted to die. That was the only thing I kept thinking. I just wanted to die."

# 14

10:45 A.M.

When Mary Ann finished, the courtroom was deadly silent. Several of the jurors were crying.

Travis knew he would have to break this spell. He would have to play the villain and ask Mary Ann the tough questions. He also knew that even if the jurors ultimately agreed with him, they would hate him. Who wouldn't?

"Psst."

It was Moroconi, hissing into Travis's ear.

"Yeah?"

"Ask how often she gets laid."

*"What?"*

"Ask her about her sex life. I bet she's had a good fuck or two in her time."

"Brilliant suggestion," Travis said. "You're a real sweetheart."

"Listen to me, Mr. Big-Shot Attorney. I've seen this routine played before. The jury might be a little pissed off at first, but once they hear about all the other times she's had sex, all the different positions she's tried, and all the different guys she's screwed, they'll change their minds. They'll wonder if she wasn't looking for some action in that bar that night, if she didn't maybe ask for what she got."

"Get a grip, Moroconi," Travis said emphatically. "No way."

"What do you mean? You got to do this."

"I don't got to do anything. Especially not for—" He stopped himself just in time.

"For what? For a guy too dirty for you to touch with your lily-white hands? I tell you, this is a sure winner!" Moroconi's face tightened. "Who's the client here?"

"You are. And I'm the attorney. An officer of the court. And I'm not doing it."

"You self-righteous son of a bitch. What the hell *are* you plannin'?"

"Just wait and see."

"You prick. You'll be sorry you screwed with me."

Hagedorn pounded his gavel on the bench. "Mr. Byrne! I hate to interrupt what is undoubtedly a fascinating conversation, but may I inquire if you would like to cross-examine this witness?"

Travis rose to his feet. "Yes, your honor. I would. But may I request a brief recess before we begin?"

Hagedorn glanced at his watch. "Well, we could probably all use a break. Court will resume in five minutes."

T ravis didn't have a nice-nice voice, but he was going to have to fake it as best he could. If the jury thought he was being mean to Mary Ann McKenzie—prematurely—they'd never listen to another word he uttered.

"Miss McKenzie, my name is Travis Byrne, and as you probably know, I represent the defendant. I'd like to ask you a few questions, if that's all right."

"Certainly," she said, barely audibly.

"I know this is very hard for you, ma'am. If you need to stop at any time, just tell me."

"All right."

"Do you feel able to proceed?"

She nodded.

"Thank you. I appreciate your cooperation." Surely that was a sufficient show of sympathy. Now to get on with it. "Ma'am, when you were first questioned by the police, you didn't identify Mr. Moroconi by name, did you?"

"Of course not. I didn't know his name. I'd never seen him before that night."

"You gave the police a physical description, though, didn't you?"

"I . . . told them what I remembered."

"You told them"—Travis glanced down at his file and read from the police report—"that you were assaulted by three white men and three black men. You described one of the white men as having black hair, an average build, and medium height."

"Right. That's Mr. Moroconi."

"Would you tell the jury where you actually identified Mr. Moroconi?"

"At the lineup. The next day."

"And how did the police select the men who would stand in the lineup?"

"Objection," Cavanaugh said, rising to her feet. "Beyond the personal knowledge of this witness."

Hagedorn shrugged. "If she doesn't know, she can say so. The witness will answer the question."

Now that you've told her what to say, Travis mused. Thanks a bunch, Judge.

"I'm afraid I don't know," Mary Ann said, to no one's surprise. "You'd have to ask the police officers in charge."

"Believe me," Travis said, "I will. Tell me what happened at the lineup."

"Five men came out and stood on the other side of a one-way

mirror from me. The officer in charge asked them all to say . . . something."

Travis didn't remember that being mentioned in the police report. "What did he have them say?"

"He had them repeat the statement"—her voice trembled—"about liking it doggie—"

"That's all right, ma'am," Travis said, cutting her off. Stupid mistake. If you don't know the answer, don't ask the question. "And did you identify Mr. Moroconi?"

"Oh yes. Almost immediately."

"By his voice or his appearance?"

She thought for a moment. "By his appearance."

Thank goodness. Travis picked up his file. "I'm looking at the police photograph of the other men in that lineup, ma'am. One of them is significantly taller than Mr. Moroconi. One of them is probably in his sixties and one of them looks barely old enough to drive. Isn't that correct?"

"I don't remember what the others looked like."

"Your honor, I request permission to publish this photo to the witness and the jury. It has been premarked as Defense Exhibit Number One and its authenticity has been stipulated to by the prosecution."

"Any objections?" Hagedorn asked.

Cavanaugh shook her head no.

Travis handed copies of the photo to Mary Ann and the bailiff, who delivered it to the nearest juror. "Mr. Moroconi was the only man in the lineup who fit the general description you gave the police, wasn't he?"

"I never thought about it," Mary Ann said. "He's the one who did it. I know that."

"And that's why Mr. Moroconi is in court today, isn't it?" Travis continued. "Because you identified him in that lineup?"

"I suppose."

Travis pushed away from the podium. It was a visual cue to the jury that something important was about to happen. "The only thing I haven't been able to figure out, ma'am, is how you could possibly have recognized him."

"Wh-what do you mean?"

"Ma'am, this incident occurred between eleven P.M. and two o'clock in the morning, isn't that correct?"

"I believe so."

"There was no moon that night, was there?"

"I have no idea."

"Believe me, there wasn't." He glanced at Cavanaugh. "And if counsel isn't content to take my word for it, we can have the judge look in the almanac and take judicial notice of the fact." He returned his attention to Mary Ann. "There's no artificial lighting out at White Rock Lake, is there, ma'am?"

"No, I don't think so."

"No lights, no moon. Middle of the night. In other words, it was dark."

"It was dark. That's true."

"You didn't see Mr. Moroconi in the parking lot, did you?"

"Well . . . no."

"Mr. Moroconi isn't the man who threw you into the trunk, is he?"

"No."

"You spent the entire drive to White Rock Lake alone in the trunk of the car, right?"

"Yes."

"You were then assaulted by six men, one after the other, correct?"

Cavanaugh jumped to her feet. "Objection, your honor. Asked and answered. I see no reason to drag the witness through these horrible events a second time."

Hagedorn pursed his lips unpleasantly. "I assume Mr. Byrne is building toward something new."

"That's correct, your honor."

"Then you'd better get there quickly. But the objection is overruled."

Travis continued. "Mary Ann, you were assaulted by two black men first, correct?"

"That's right."

"And the third man beat you, then rolled you over facedown, right?"

Her head slowly lifted. "Yes. But—"

"And you remained facedown for the remainder of the assaults, right?"

"Yes, but—"

"And after the last man finished, you were tied to the back of the car. Still facedown, right?"

"Y-Yes."

"And you remained in that position when you were placed in the trunk again, barely conscious, then deposited on the roadside hours later, where you remained until you were discovered by the police the next morning, correct?"

"That's . . . correct."

"Did Mr. Moroconi put you in the trunk?"

"N-No."

"Did he take you out and leave you on the side of the road?"

"No, that was someone else. The first one."

The jury was watching him now—Travis could see it out of the corner of his eye. They were beginning to follow his line of reasoning. "Miss McKenzie, you said you didn't see Al Moroconi in the parking lot. You obviously didn't see him when you were locked in the trunk. When you arrived, it was a dark, moonless night, and you were immediately accosted by your assailants. The third man, to use your own words, pressed your face into the mud. You remained facedown in the mud until you were put back in the trunk—by another man—and subsequently tossed out on the roadside—by another man."

A few of the jurors were nodding. Nonetheless, Travis decided to ram the point home. "Ma'am, you didn't see Al Moroconi in the parking lot, you didn't see him in the car, and you didn't see him at the crime scene. When *did* you see him?"

Tears were once more streaming down her cheeks. "I—I don't know exactly." She released a heart-wrenching cry. "But it was him. I know it was."

"Isn't that because you *want* it to be him? Because you *want* someone to be punished for the horrible crime visited on you?"

"Objection!" Cavanaugh shouted.

"Sustained."

Travis proceeded undeterred. "Miss McKenzie, can you tell me with absolute certainty that the man sitting at defendant's table is the man who assaulted you?"

She raised her chin defiantly. "Yes. Absolutely."

"Take a good look, ma'am. I want you to be certain."

"I'm certain. He's the one. I'll never forget that face as long as I live."

"I see." Travis approached defendant's table. "Sir, would you please produce your driver's license?"

He did so.

"Permission to publish this to the jury?"

Hagedorn nodded.

Travis handed the license to the bailiff and waited as it was slowly passed down the two rows of jurors. "As you can see, ladies and gentleman, the man now sitting at defendant's table is Charlie Slovic, a nice gentleman who runs the courthouse coffee shop. He switched places with the defendant during the break. Mr. Moroconi is waiting out in the hall." He turned toward the back of the room. "Sergeant."

The sergeant at arms stepped outside and returned with Moroconi. Together they walked to the front of the courtroom.

"As you can see, there is a resemblance between Charlie and my client. Both have dark hair, a medium build, medium height. But they are far from identical twins. Any clear-thinking person should be able to tell them apart." He turned toward the witness. "Mary Ann, isn't it true that you identified Al Moroconi simply because he was the only man in the lineup who came close to fitting your general description?"

She didn't answer.

"Isn't it equally true that you would've identified any medium-sized, dark-haired male in that lineup? Just as you identified Charlie Slovic in the courtroom today?"

"No," she said weakly. "I—I—*saw* him—"

"That's all right, ma'am. We'll let the jury answer that question. Nothing more, your honor."

**15**

11:45 A.M.

At the lunch break, after the jury was excused, Travis left his client in the trusting custody of his five guards. He needed to stretch his legs. Unfortunately, traffic out of the gallery was slow. This case was drawing standing-room-only crowds and five minutes passed before the courtroom emptied. He pushed his way toward the door, only to find himself face-to-face with Curran McKenzie.

"What did you bring me today?" Travis asked. "Her baby pictures?"

Curran stared at Travis, his face fixed like granite.

Obnoxious wimp. Travis tried to push past him. "If you'll excuse me . . ."

"Sarah and I saw what you did to our sister up there," Curran said as his kid sister appeared beside him.

"Every defendant is entitled to cross-examine his accusers. I was just exercising my client's constitutional rights."

"This is all a game to you, isn't it?" Curran said with undisguised contempt. "An entertainment. An easy way to make a buck."

"You don't know what you're talking about, kid."

"The hell I don't. You're a whore, Mr. Byrne. A filthy, two-bit whore."

Sarah McKenzie took her brother's arm. "Curran, let's leave. We don't want any trouble."

Still glaring, Curran followed his sister out of the courtroom.

"Self-righteous prig," Travis muttered to himself.

Cavanaugh strolled up beside him. "A meeting with the president of your fan club?"

"Not exactly. That's Mary Ann McKenzie's brother."

"I know. I've had some heated conversations with him myself. He's more interested in results than the legal process."

"So he's furious with you, too."

"I never said he was furious. We've just had heated conversations. Lest you forget, Travis, I'm one of the good guys."

"And what does that make me? I'm just doing my job."

"That's what they said at Nuremberg." And on that note, Cavanaugh left the courtroom.

Travis started after her, but a figure passing just outside the courtroom doors caught his eye. Was that . . . ? My God, *it was*! It was the man from the bathroom, the son of a bitch with the cigarette.

A tremor of cold fear shot through Travis's body. He'd spent the past twenty-four hours fantasizing about what he would do if he ever saw that man again, and now that he had, he was paralyzed.

He forced himself forward, consciously moving one foot at a time. He was not going to let this man get away. Finally getting in gear, he rushed out of the courtroom and plunged down the corridor.

Just as Travis rounded the corner a reporter stepped in front of him, almost tripping him. "Excuse me, Mr. Byrne. I'm from the *Morning News*. Could you please answer a few questions?"

"Get out of my way!" Travis growled.

Another reporter, a woman with a minicam operator hovering behind her, blocked his path. The red light on the minicam flickered. "Surely you can answer just a few—"

"Not now!" Travis shouted. He shoved her aside. The woman fell back against the minicam operator and both tumbled to the floor. An elderly guard shouted at Travis as he plunged down the corridor. He burst out the front doors of the courthouse.

He looked up and down Commerce Street, but saw no sign of the man from the bathroom. *If* that's who he had seen. At any rate, the man was gone now.

The sun went behind a cloud, and it started to rain. A flurry of umbrellas covered the courthouse steps as the guard tottered out the door. "I'm sorry, Mr. Byrne, but rules are rules. We can't have you—"

"I'm sorry, Harry. Thought I saw someone I knew. Guess I was wrong. I'll come back and apologize."

"Well . . . I reckon that'd be all right."

Travis returned to the courthouse, glancing back over his shoulder. Had that been the same man? He was almost certain it was.

And if so, what did he want? Or *who* did he want?

# 16

**6 : 22 P.M.**

The federal marshals transferred Moroconi from the courthouse to the midway detention room, where he waited for county sheriff's men to escort him back to his cell. The feds didn't have their own holding cells in Dallas County; they had a contractual agreement with the state to use their space as necessary.

The marshals pushed Moroconi into the detention room and began looking around impatiently. "I don't know where the hell those state cops are," one of them grumbled. "Lazy slobs. They think their whole life is one big trip to the doughnut shop. Never want to do a damn thing they don't absolutely have to."

He removed Moroconi's handcuffs and shoved him down in a chair. "They think they have it so tough. They ought to take a walk on the federal side, just for a day or two. Spend an hour at Leavenworth. Find out what tough really is." He sneered at Moroconi. "Couple days with scumbags like you, they'll be begging for a nice job at Burger King."

"The feeling's mutual," Moroconi mumbled.

The other marshal's eyes flared. "Wiseass. Let me bust him in the chops, Frank. We'll say he was trying to escape. Just once, that's all. I'll make it count."

Marshal Frank grinned. "I'm sure you would, Jim, but forget it. This sleaze is on trial, remember? If he shows up in court tomorrow all beaten up, the prosecution's case goes into the dumper. And our ass is grass." He leered eye to eye with Moroconi. "We'll just wait. After he's convicted, he'll be sent to the pen. And the cons there just love rapists."

"Oh yeah," Marshal Jim replied. "Those that give, so shall they receive."

The two men laughed uproariously and walked to the door. "Now we'll be right outside, Moroconi. Don't even think about trying to leave."

"Shucks, Frank, don't spoil the fun. I'd like to see him make a break for it." Marshal Jim patted his pistol. "I'd enjoy having the opportunity to apprehend a fleeing felon."

Still laughing, the two men strolled out the door and locked it behind them.

Moroconi sat in his chair, inhaling deeply, trying to suppress his temper. Miserable bastards. I'd like to meet them just once when they didn't have a goddamn holster strapped around their bloated bellies. He made two more entries on his mental list of people he wanted to take care of, along with Travis Byrne and his old pals Jack and Mario.

Once he was certain they were not returning, Moroconi walked to the far left corner of the room. He examined the paneling on the ceiling. Standard sound-resistant panels held in place by thin metallic strips. He'd tried them the first night he was left in here—they wouldn't budge. But tonight just might be different.

He counted panels, starting with the one directly above his head. Six to the right, two to the north, three to the left. That's what the man said. He drew his chair beneath the panel, stood on the chair, and pressed up.

It moved. Standing on his tiptoes, he pushed up and tossed the panel back. *Yes!* Mr. FB-fucking-I actually came through.

Moroconi grabbed one of the now exposed cross beams and pulled himself up into the opening. Not an easy task, but he hadn't been doing those chin-ups on the bunk bed in his cell every night for nothing. As quietly as possible, he replaced the ceiling panel. Careful to put his weight on the cross beams, he slithered through the small enclosed space between the ceiling and the roof.

Eventually, Moroconi reached a small ventilation window on the far wall of the building. Pushing with all his strength, he moved the rusty window slowly upward. At last the opening was wide enough for him to slip through, feetfirst. He lowered himself out, then dropped onto the porch just outside the front doors of the building.

The lights inside the lobby were on. Moroconi could see his two federal friends silhouetted inside. He thumbed his nose silently, then turned away. Unfortunately, he didn't see the steps until he had already stumbled over them. Losing his balance, he tumbled down the steps and crashed headfirst onto the concrete sidewalk.

*"What the hell?"*

Moroconi rolled over and saw Marshal Frank running to the door, pistol raised. Damn those goddamn steps!

Moroconi jumped to his feet, sprang up the steps, and slammed the edge of the door on Frank's hand. Frank screamed and dropped his gun.

Marshal Jim rushed through the other door. Moroconi tackled him, knocking him back into his buddy. In the half second that bought him, Moroconi picked up Frank's gun.

"Son of a bitch," Frank said breathlessly. "That's my gun."

"Then I'll give it to you," Moroconi replied. He fired. Blood spurted from Frank's neck. The wounded man's face went ashen, then he crumpled to the floor.

Panicked, Marshal Jim turned and ran. Moroconi shot him in the back.

Moroconi shoved the gun in his pants and sprinted toward the street. He knew he had to hurry. Cops and sheriffs and marshals and every other cocksucker wearing a badge would descend in a matter of moments. He bolted toward downtown Dallas, where he knew he could lose himself in no time at all.

# 17

6:45 P.M.

Here they were again—Mario, Kramer, and Donny—
gathered together in Mario's downtown office. These little status reports had become a regular unpleasantness in Mario's
life since the latest crisis developed. Occasionally they accom-
plished something; more often they did not. Either way, another
meeting meant more time with Kramer. And that made Mario's
blood run cold.

Not that Donny was much better. He'd come in earlier to beg
his uncle Mario to make him a lieutenant. Right. In the first
place, Mario explained, you can't be a lieutenant unless you're a
*made man*, and Donny wasn't. What's more, Mario thought but
did not say, you can't be a *made man* until you've successfully
completed a hit, Donny, and you couldn't successfully complete a
hit on a butterfly. Donny was fortunate Mario had agreed to accept him at all. There'd been a lot of bitching among the boys.
Understandably so.

"You never told me, Donny," Mario said. "How did your intro-
duction to Mr. Byrne go?"

"Smooth as shit," Kramer answered for him, " 'cept that Donny almost got himself turned into a hostage."

"I did not!" Donny said. He leaped off the sofa. "Byrne got one good shot in, that's all. When I wasn't looking. I got out of it right away."

Kramer laughed. "You got out of it when my man Mr. Hardcastle smashed Byrne's head against the wall. Otherwise you'd be doing time in the federal slammer right now."

"That's not true! Uncle Mario, make him shut up!"

Mario raised his hand. "Boys, boys, boys. Let's not behave like children. I take it Mr. Byrne received our message?"

"He received it all right," Kramer said. "Like a swift kick in the balls. Problem is, he's too dumb to take it to heart."

"Are you certain of this?"

"Positive. Hardcastle was in the courtroom today. I got a full report."

"What? He went in person!"

"Relax, he was careful. Byrne never saw him."

"For your sake, I hope you're right." Mario fell back and made a steeple with his fingers. At least Kramer hadn't gone himself. Kramer probably couldn't get near any law enforcement officer in the entire state of Texas without being identified. "What was your man's evaluation of Byrne's courtroom performance?"

"He's good," Kramer said. "What's worse, he's shrewd. He's not actin' like Moroconi is a great guy—or even that he likes him. He's not sayin' that the rapes didn't happen and he was a real sweetie pie to the victim. He made one point—that she didn't get a good enough look to identify Al. It ain't much, but if he makes the jury believe it, he'll win."

Mario brooded for a moment. "I thought you told me this case was a guaranteed conviction. With a long sentence attached."

"That's what my contacts at the police station were sayin'. I guess that was before Byrne made the scene."

"I don't know why you're acting like this Byrne prick is so great," Donny said, pouting. "He's just a stupid, fat policeman."

"Who almost broke your hand," Kramer added.

"That's not true!" Donny ran up to Mario's desk and hovered. "Uncle Mario, tell him to stop saying that!"

"Please, Donny. We're not on a playground and this is not recess."

"But he's picking on me!"

Mario buried his face in his hands. It was hopeless. Absolutely hopeless. Perhaps he could tell Monica her son had been killed in a train wreck.

"I don't mean to be an alarmist," Kramer said. "The feds still have a strong case. Odds are Al is going to do some major-league time. But I make no guarantees."

"Recommendations?"

"Nothin' drastic. Not yet. I'll keep an eye on Al. And Byrne. You said before we'd take more . . . extreme measures if necessary. I hope you meant it."

Mario folded his hands. "I meant it."

"Good. Then I'll continue to monitor the situation carefully."

Mario raised his chin. "They've found Seacrest."

"I know. I made sure they did."

"Perhaps you should make sure Mr. Byrne knows, too."

Kramer grinned. "Not a bad idea."

"Do you need more associates?"

"Nah. I've already got eight men on Byrne, diggin' into his background, watchin' him everywhere he goes. Listenin', too."

"Good."

The phone rang. Mario answered it, then passed it to Kramer. "It's for you."

Kramer took the phone. After a moment, he covered the receiver and whispered, "It's one of my contacts at the jailhouse." He listened for several more seconds. "What? *Gone?*"

"What is it?" Mario asked. "What happened?"

Kramer ignored him. After a few more minutes, he tossed the receiver back into its cradle.

"Talk to me," Mario demanded. "What happened?"

"A hell of a lot, apparently," Kramer said. "Two guards shot, one of them dead."

"What the fuck are you talking about?"

Kramer reached into his pocket and withdrew his lighter. "The holding cells," he said quietly. "Our friend Al busted out."

"You can't be serious!"

"I'm afraid so." He held the lighter between them and gazed at the orange flame. "You'd better lock your doors tonight, Mario. Al may show up on your doorstep. And he won't be deliverin' a candygram, either."

# 18

### 7 : 1 0 P.M.

Travis leaned against the headboard of his bed. He was wearing his favorite woolly pajamas; he had the covers tucked under his arms and headphones clamped over his ears. He'd finally given up trying to prepare for the next day of trial, only to find he couldn't sleep. Sure, it was early, but he'd barely slept at all the last two nights. He should've crashed the instant his head hit the pillow. Maybe he'd gotten his second wind; he just didn't feel tired. He was probably too keyed up about everything that had happened the past few days.

He decided to sample the stress-reduction tapes Gail had given him a few days ago. If stress reduction was supposed to be synonymous with mind numbing, the tapes were a smash success. As tedious as they were, he thought he'd surely drop off to sleep. But he didn't. His mind kept wandering back to the case, those cruel assaults, those gruesome pictures. Mary Ann McKenzie. With her lovely red hair.

He yanked the earphones off and stopped the tape. He resisted the temptation to throw the recorder across the room; it was

Staci's Walkman, after all, just on loan. He punched his pillow and stretched out across the bed, hoping the reclining position would induce sleep.

It didn't. What was wrong with him? He supposed he could check his blood pressure. Gail had insisted that he buy a blood-pressure monitor. And when he didn't, she bought it for him. Her idea was that he could wear it all day long and check himself every fifteen seconds or so. If your blood pressure is up, she said, just stop whatever you're doing and relax until it goes down. Travis delicately tried to explain that he wasn't wearing that stupid monitor all day long and that he couldn't stop a trial just because his blood pressure was up. And when she looked on the brink of tears, he strapped the contraption around his upper arm and started pumping.

For that matter, he mused, why stop with blood pressure? Maybe he should purchase a home EKG monitor. And while he was at it, a home heart defibrillator, just in case he needed a cardiac massage some chilly evening. What could they cost—ten, fifteen thousand dollars? A small price to pay to avoid the specter of the heart attack that hadn't happened. Yet.

A bell rang. It took Travis a few seconds to identify it as his doorbell. He wrapped himself in a robe and plodded to the front door. He really needed a peephole, he reminded himself for the millionth time.

He turned on the porch light and opened the door. "Yes?"

The young woman standing outside was sixteen, maybe seventeen tops. She was dressed in a tight-fitting green tube top that clung to her flat breasts and revealed an ample expanse of flesh above the miniskirt hugging her hips. "You must be Travis Byrne," she cooed with outstretched arms. "Tonight's your lucky night."

Travis blinked. He hadn't fallen asleep, had he? Then how could he be dreaming? "Do I know you?"

She stepped through the door and curled her arms around his neck. "The question is—would you like to get to know me?" She planted a kiss on his lips.

Travis twisted away. "Wait a second. What's going on here?"

She smiled. "Anything you want, darlin'. Absolutely anything."

"I don't understand. How do you know my name? Did someone put you up to this?"

"I came when called."

"Called? Who called?"

"I assume you."

"You assume wrong."

"Then I must be a gift. Who cares? It's all arranged. Take advantage, baby." Her thin lips curled up to form a wicked smile. She snuggled closer, pulled open his robe, and began planting kisses on his chest.

"Look," Travis said, trying unsuccessfully to push her away, "I don't know what your game is, but I don't want any part of it."

She frowned. "What's wrong? Is someone else here?"

"No."

"You're gay."

"I am not!"

"Jaded? Getting too much?"

"Well . . . look, lady, I don't mean to be rude, but I want you to leave."

She uncurled herself from his neck. "It's because of my tits, isn't it?"

Travis tried not to look. "I beg your pardon?"

"My tits! I told Tony I'd do better if he'd pay for some implants. He says they're not safe. I think he's just cheap."

"Look, miss, I don't care what size your, er . . ."

"Sure, you say that now, but if I was a D-cup, you'd be slobbering all over me."

"Not true. I'm just not . . . interested."

"Oh?" She pressed herself up and down his thigh. "I guess that's a roll of quarters in your pants then?"

Travis whisked her around and steered her through the open door. "Either you've got the wrong address, or this is a perverse prank being played by someone with an extremely weird sense of humor. In any case, I have a big day ahead of me, I need my sleep, and I don't need any more stress. So good night!"

Her shoulders drooped. "But I can't go back without finishing the job. You have no idea what kind of trouble I'll be in."

"I'm afraid I can't help you."

"I don't mind dressing up."

"Good night, miss."

"I'm fluent in all twenty-six positions."

"Twenty—?" He pressed his hand against his forehead. "I said, good night!"

"I brought my own gear!" She started to itemize, but it was too late. The door was firmly shut.

# 19

7:53 P.M.

Al Moroconi couldn't believe it—he was free! After weeks of stale air, staler food, and constant hassling by shit-for-brains guards, he was finally free.

He'd never really thought it would work. Stupid FBI dickhead—what did he know? Moroconi was willing to give it a whirl—what did he have to lose? But it had worked!

He raced down Commerce, trying to stay out of the light. Word must already be out; soon every cop in Dallas would be circling the area looking for him. He needed a car and he needed it fast.

He veered into the parking lot of Orpha's Lounge, a sleazy-looking bar with no windows, just a large neon sign that flashed BEER every other second. Lots of cars at Orpha's, he noted happily.

He looked around for a coat hanger, a heavy object, a sharp stick—anything. He searched for several minutes without success. It was too dark; even if something had been there, he wouldn't have found it.

He heard a shuffling noise coming from the bar. A tired, half-dead drunk was stumbling out of Orpha's all by his lonesome.

Moroconi grinned. Excellent—the answer to his prayers. Like taking candy from a baby.

Moroconi circled around the parked cars and came up behind the drunk. Moroconi waited until the man walked to his car—a big black pickup truck with oversize tires. While the man groped clumsily for his keys Moroconi wrapped his arm around his throat and pulled him down hard. The drunk fell face first into the gravel and lay there dazed.

Moroconi reached into the man's pocket, took his keys, and started the truck. The tires squealed as he whipped the truck around the parking lot and headed toward Commerce.

He briefly considered running over the drunk, just for the hell of it. What was it the kids said? *Ten points for the old man!* But he didn't have time for that, fun as it might be, and besides, blood-spattered tires might catch a cop's attention. It would be a long while before that drunk was able to file a police report, and Moroconi would have another car by then.

He pulled onto Commerce and zoomed down the road. He had to get out of downtown before the cops got their act in gear. In fact, he needed to get out of Dallas altogether.

And then, once he was safe, he was going to make a few phone calls to some old friends. . . .

# 20

### 8 : 58 P.M.

"Hello?"

"How's my friendly neighborhood FBI traitor?"

"Christ! Al!" The agent covered the receiver with his hand. Thank God he wasn't using the speakerphone.

He quickly scanned the office. No one was around, except, of course, Mooney, who was walking toward him with a notepad. Efficient little twerp. He'd seen the light flash on his monitor board. Might've known Al would call when that squid was on duty.

"Should I take the call, sir?" Agent Mooney asked.

"No, thanks. I'll handle it. It's one of my informants."

"I see. I'll monitor on the extension."

"No! I mean, I'm perfectly capable of taking my own notes. Continue with what you were doing, Mooney."

Mooney eyed him oddly, but returned to his desk in the next room. Mooney had just been assigned to this special team; he was the typical asskissing backstabber. Just waiting for you to make a mistake he could ram down your throat. He didn't care much for the look Mooney gave him as he left. If someone even suspected what he was doing . . . Well, he'd have to watch Agent Mooney very carefully.

He uncovered the receiver. "Al?" he whispered.

"In the flesh. Free as a bird. Can you believe it? Your plan actually worked, you dumbass son of a bitch!"

"Of course it worked. I told you it would. Why are you calling me here?"

"We got some business to conduct."

"I told you we would—"

"Screw that plan, *compadre.* It takes too long, and I don't have time to jack around."

"What do you mean?"

He heard Moroconi plug another quarter into the pay phone. "Haven't you heard?"

"Heard *what?*"

"There were some complications. People got hurt."

"Hurt! How bad?"

"I didn't have time to take their pulse. I think one of them's dead, though—I shot him in the fuckin' neck. The other one might pull through."

The agent was stunned silent. That stupid, vicious—

"Don't bother askin' if I'm okay," Moroconi said. "I know you're real concerned. I'm fine."

"Oh, my God. This is awful. Do you have any idea what you've done? You've ruined everything. And—my God! You shouldn't have called me here."

"Why? 'Fraid someone might be listenin'?"

"Who the hell knows? This changes everything. Hang up the damn phone."

"What about our rendezvous?"

"Fuck the rendezvous! It's too risky. You could be caught any second."

"We made a deal, you chickenshit. I want the list."

"Look, as soon as things calm down, I'll get back in touch with you."

"No way, asshole. We do it tonight."

"I can't possibly—"

"Do you want to do this deal or not? I can always take my business somewhere else. There must be others like you."

There was an extended pause. "Fine. Have it your way. Where do we meet?"

"I'm not going to tell you over your might-be-bugged line, chump. Call me from a pay phone."

"What's the number?"

"Ready to play a little baseball?"

"Oh, Christ." He rustled through his desk drawers, groping for a pad of paper and pencil. "All right. Ready."

"It's the top of the fifth and Tucker's three-and-two with two outs. The man on third had seven hits on the eighth day of the ninth month and two strikeouts with all three bases loaded. Are you gettin' this?"

He grunted as he scribbled down the proper numbers in the proper order.

"There's a change-up. Jones pulls a slider and two men slip by. That's six since the relief pitcher left at four o'clock. At the top of the seventh, it's three up, three down, eight points behind. He decides to reverse it. Plan B. Got it?"

He reversed the numbers, added carefully, and examined the resulting phone number. "Got it."

"Guess you learned somethin' in crime school after all. I'll be waitin' for you. Don't dawdle. Send the little woman my best."

Before the agent could spit back his reply, the line went dead.

# THURSDAY

*April 18*

# 21

## 1 2 : 5 2 A.M.

Travis was having a wonderfully weird Daliesque dream. He fantasized that he was in court, but it wasn't Dallas County Court, and it wasn't federal court—it wasn't even the Supreme Court. It was the Court of Celestial Appeals. Travis was arguing with great passion and persuasion, pleading with the jury not to spare someone's life, but to *return* a life—to grant Angela a second chance. He was really on a roll; he had the jury in the palm of his hand. He was winning, and in just a few seconds it would all be over and Angela would be back. . . .

And then the phone rang.

Travis fumbled in the dark and knocked the phone onto the floor, mercifully silencing the bell. He fell out of bed and crawled around till he found the receiver. "Geez," he mumbled, "do you know what time—"

"Ain't you lawyers on call for your clients whenever we need you?"

"Moroconi?" Travis stared at the phone, disbelieving. "How can you—where are you?"

"I'm out, Byrne."

"You're *out*? How the hell can you be out?"

"How do you think?"

"I assume the President didn't grant you a pardon while I slept."

"You got that right."

"Did you bust out?"

"In a manner of speaking."

Travis turned on the lamp on his nightstand. The harsh light made him squint, but it was just as well—he had to clear the cobwebs out of his brain somehow. "Listen to me. You'll never get away with this. You need to turn yourself in."

Moroconi snorted into the phone. "You must be kiddin'."

"Think about it. What are you going to do, run for the rest of your life? Sooner or later you'll be caught. Probably sooner. It would be smarter to let the judicial process run its course. We were making real headway in court today—"

"Aw, cut the bullshit, shyster. You know damn well the fix is in. The police can put a schmuck like me behind bars anytime they want to. And they want to. Someone got to them. Hell, most of those jurors assumed I was guilty the minute I walked into court."

"That isn't always true—"

"Besides, I can't turn myself in. If I go anywhere near a police station, they'll blow my head off and ask questions later."

Travis pondered for a moment. There was some truth in that. Especially if anyone had been hurt during the breakout. "All right, how about if I pick you up? We'll go in together."

"What's to say they won't kill you, too?"

"They won't," Travis assured him. "They'll listen to me."

"What if they want me to do extra time for the attempted escape?"

"You've already brought that on yourself, Al. The best I can do now is see that you don't aggravate matters."

There was a long silence on the other end of the line. Travis could tell he was thinking—but *what* was he thinking? "All right," Al said at last. "If you come meet me, I'll go in with you. If you promise you won't tip off the cops first."

"I promise. This is the wisest course of action, believe me."

"Meet me at the West End. In front of the Butcher Shop."

Travis nodded. "I know the place. It's near my office. I'll be there in half an hour. See you then."

Travis hung up the phone and began dressing. He didn't relish the prospect of being alone in the dark with Al Moroconi, but he didn't see any workable alternative. He tried to imagine what the bar association would advise, but the Rules of Professional Conduct didn't cover bizarre situations like this one.

He considered calling the police—but no. He had made a promise. A promise given in the course of legal counseling, no less. That was sacred. He'd do exactly what he had promised—he'd pick up Al and drive him to the station.

Besides, what did he have to fear from Al Moroconi? After all, the man was his client.


The brown-haired technician wearing the headphones smirked. "Did you get all that?"

His boss nodded. "West End. The Butcher Shop. Half an hour."

"Maybe sooner. It won't take Byrne half an hour to get there."

"Depends on how long it takes him to get his head together. Did you get a trace on Moroconi?"

"No. But he was calling from a pay phone. He'd be gone before we could get there. Doesn't matter. We know where he'll be in half an hour."

"True." He walked to the back of the truck. "Better keep monitoring. Just in case."

"Your wish is my command." The technician changed the tape on the reel-to-reel recorder and reactivated the machine.

The other man buttoned his overcoat and stepped into the bracing night air. "By the way, if I haven't mentioned it lately, you do damn fine work."

The technician smiled. "That's why you pay me the big money, Mr. Kramer."

## 22

### 1 : 2 0 A . M .

Travis exited Stemmons Freeway and headed for the West End Historic District, just north of Commerce and west of Lamar. He pulled into the empty parking lot on the opposite side of the railroad tracks. It was the closest open parking; he hoofed it from there.

The streets were quiet; all the restaurants and boutiques were closed. The West End had been refurbished several years before and converted into a trendy upscale shopping and dining haunt. A less panoramic version of San Antonio's Riverwalk. The yuppies were all in bed tonight, though, as any sensible person would be at this time of the morning.

Travis jogged over to the main cul-de-sac, the last of several smaller sequential culs-de-sac, just outside a glass-walled shopping mall. He tried to pretend the run didn't bother him. It was barely a fourth of a mile. A sprint like that couldn't tire a he-man like him, could it? He laughed bitterly. Of course it could. He was old and out of shape. A punching bag for bathroom bullies.

After weaving past several closed buildings, he arrived at the Butcher Shop. It was his favorite restaurant in the West End. Most of the other joints served prissy sculpted food in minuscule portions, usually topped with sun-dried tomatoes or asparagus tips. California food, he called it. The Butcher Shop was about the only place in the entire area you could get a decent steak, something you could sink your teeth into.

Steak—my God, he remembered that. Vaguely, anyway. A delicacy from his presalad days. He jogged back and forth outside the restaurant, swinging around an iron lamppost, trying to shake off the chill. It was a brisk night for April; downright cold, actually. He hoped Moroconi wouldn't be late. He began to realize how nebulous his instructions had been. What exactly was their plan? If Moroconi was going to turn himself in, why didn't they just meet near the police station? And where exactly were they going to meet? Should he be looking in the alley behind the building, in the trash bins, or what?

Fortunately, Travis didn't have to anguish over these questions for long. He heard tires squealing in the distance; probably not all that loud, but jarring in the silence. Soon he could see the source of the commotion—a large black pickup truck. But these were pedestrian-only streets. How . . . ?

He immediately saw the answer to his question. The truck exploded through a ground-level barricade without even slowing down. Splintered wood flew skyward, but the truck kept coming. From one of the smaller culs-de-sac, the truck roared up the curb and advanced along the main sidewalk. It burst through a sidewalk café, crushing white wire chairs under its wheels and sending tables flying. The truck passed through another small cul-de-sac, jumped another curb, then dropped into the main cul-de-sac.

Travis froze in his tracks.

The truck executed a full three-hundred-and-sixty-degree turn, laid rubber with all four tires, and came to a squealing stop in front of the Butcher Shop.

Moroconi leaned out of the window. "Whaddya think? Am I ready for the Demolition Derby?"

Travis gripped the truck door. "What the hell are you doing?"

"I didn't want to be late. Since you're such a hot-shit lawyer and all."

"Where'd you get the truck, Moroconi?"

"It's a loaner from a buddy down at Orpha's Lounge."

"I'll just bet." Travis opened the truck door. "Get out of there, you moron. We'll take my car to the station. No reason to volunteer additional felony charges."

"Shee-it!" Moroconi shook his head. "You are some kind of stupid, aren't you? Did you really think I was going to let you haul me back to the cops?" He thunked Travis in the center of his chest. "That I busted out just so you could drag me back?"

Travis's forehead became one long furrow. "I don't understand. If you're not coming with me, then why—"

Travis never had a chance to finish his sentence. Suddenly, they were both engulfed by brilliant white light emanating from the other end of the cul-de-sac.

"Who is it?" Travis shouted, squinting into the light. "Who's there?"

No response.

Without saying a word, Moroconi pulled a crumpled piece of paper out of his pocket and shoved it into Travis's hand.

"What's this?" Travis asked. "I don't want this. Who's shining that light?"

Travis stared into the white sheen, his eyes watering. It had to be a supercharged searchlight, souped up to a couple thousand or so candlepower. He could make out the shadowy outline of the man holding the light, and at least one other man standing beside him. Each had his right hand extended. Travis assumed they were holding guns.

One of the men spoke. "If you hand over that piece of paper, Byrne, it's just possible you'll live to see the sunrise."

"What, *this*?" He held out the paper. "I don't want this. What the hell is it?" Travis stared into the blinding light. "Who are you?"

There was no answer.

"Moroconi," Travis spat, "what's going on?"

Travis saw Moroconi ease back into the truck.

"Stay right where you are," a second voice shouted. After a moment's hesitation, the voice added: "Police."

*Police?* Travis could understand why they might come after Moroconi. But this was hardly standard police procedure, unless a lot had changed since he left the force.

Moroconi gunned his engine. Travis whirled around. My God, what was he doing?

The first voice returned. "One more move and we start shooting!"

Moroconi leaned out the driver's-side window. Travis's heart sank when he saw Moroconi leveling a gun. Moroconi fired, and a nanosecond later, the bright light went out. Travis heard glass smash and clatter onto the sidewalk.

Moroconi threw the truck into first gear. Gunfire erupted almost immediately. Travis shoved the paper into his pocket and dove away from the truck. The hell with attorney–client loyalty; he was getting out of the line of fire.

Travis rolled back onto his feet and surveyed the action. Whatever else he might say about Moroconi, he couldn't accuse him of being gutless. Instead of trying to escape, he was careening straight toward the shadow men on the sidewalk, who continued to fire off shot after shot. One of them hit the windshield, shattering it into a million pieces. Moroconi kept on coming.

At the last possible moment the men leaped away. The man on the right got clear of the truck; the other one didn't. He screamed, his terror-stricken face transfixed in the headlights. The truck crushed the man against the red brick wall of the Butcher Shop. The impact was loud and sickening, a horrifying crunch of metal and flesh. Travis wondered if Moroconi had killed himself as well.

He didn't have to wonder long. The truck jerked into reverse. It separated noisily from the brick wall and did an about-face in the cul-de-sac.

Travis rose to his feet and saw the remaining shadow man do the same. He was groping around on the pavement—must have lost his gun.

Suddenly Moroconi swerved around and aimed the truck at the gunman. The man plunged into the darkness, making a beeline for a narrow alley between buildings. Moroconi couldn't possibly follow him. He reversed the truck and headed back toward the sidewalk café he had trashed on his way in.

Just as Travis thought the worst might be over, he heard the unmistakable sound of a bullet whistling by not more than a foot from his head. Guess the man located his gun, Travis thought; he must be firing from within the alley. And Travis was a sitting duck.

In the split second during which Moroconi's truck approached, Travis realized it was his last chance to elude the gunman. He could hardly outrun him, and recent events had indicated he wasn't likely to overpower him in hand-to-hand combat either. He watched the truck carefully, concentrating on its speed, its direction. As the truck swerved around him Travis jumped onto the back bumper and clutched the tailgate for dear life.

Moroconi blasted through the café again. Naturally, he was too stupid to follow the path he'd cleared before. He had to annihilate more tables and chairs, making the ride good and rocky. Travis glanced back and saw the gunman run to the center of the cul-de-sac. The gunshots sounded like distant claps of thunder. They weren't even close. It was too dark, and the truck was moving too quickly.

Moroconi took a sharp curve, flinging Travis sideways against the tailgate. He held on desperately, gripping the back of the truck with all his might. Moroconi hit another curb, and Travis felt the full impact shoot through his arms and shoulders. He knew he couldn't hold on much longer. But he also knew he had to get farther away. If that goon with the gun had a car nearby, he could easily drill Travis before he got back to his own car.

The wind blasted through Travis's hair and stung his eyes. His arms were beginning to ache. Travis saw Moroconi glance into his side-view mirror, then grin from ear to ear. He knew Travis was hitching a ride.

Moroconi began to swerve back and forth for no reason, sending the truck lurching over the road. Travis gritted his teeth and held on tight. His hands were sweating profusely, making it even more difficult to maintain a solid grip.

Moroconi hit the railroad tracks flying. The impact knocked Travis into the air. His hands slid crossways, then his chin struck the tailgate. He was practically horizontal across the back bumper, hanging on by his fingertips. Moroconi took another sadistic swerve, and it was over. Travis flew off the bumper and smacked down onto the gravel.

He lay motionless for a long moment, taking a physical inventory. He knew it was only a few feet from the tailgate to the ground, but he felt as if he had fallen off the top of the Statue of Liberty. He hurt like hell, but all his extremities were still attached. He opened his eyes in time to see Moroconi leaning out the truck window, laughing hysterically as he drove off into the distance.

Travis forced himself to his feet. His chest ached. The pain was so sharp he could barely catch his breath, but he made himself jog the rest of the way to the parking lot. He had to reach his car before the man with the gun did. From there he could try to determine what was going on.

And what the hell he was going to do next.

# 23

## 2 : 00 A.M.

Travis wheeled his car onto Walnut Hill Lane, passed his apartment building, and parked his car on the far side of the block. Maybe he was being overcautious, but he wanted to play it safe. After all, he might be slow, but he wasn't stupid. Those goons had known him by name, and they hadn't shown up at the West End just then by coincidence. They might have followed Moroconi—God knows he was making enough noise—but if so, how did they get into position with that searchlight so quickly? It just wasn't possible. And that left two scenarios. Either they had followed Travis, or they had eavesdropped on his phone conversation with Moroconi.

Travis didn't have to be an ex-cop to know how painfully simple it was to bug a telephone line. Any fool with the right equipment and a vo-tech course in electronics could accomplish it. And based on recent experiences, Travis didn't think he was dealing with fools.

Travis spent the drive to his apartment considering his choices. He could go to the police—but then, the goons behind the searchlight had claimed to be police. They sure as hell didn't act like the police, but someone must've helped Moroconi break out of jail. He couldn't have done it without inside help. If the police department was tainted, going to them would be risky—possibly suicidal. No, he had a better, safer plan, at least for starters. But to exercise it, he needed to get inside his apartment.

He eased out of his car slowly, checking both sides of the street. He started jogging down the block, wincing at the sharp stabbing sensations in his chest, then he decelerated to a brisk walk. He just hoped all this stress didn't trigger his ulcer. That was the last complication he needed now.

Travis cautiously rounded the corner and peered down the street outside his apartment. A green four-door sedan was parked about ten feet north of the entrance. Exactly where he would be, Travis reflected, if he were staking out the building. Travis spotted two heads slumped low in the front seat.

He turned back the way he'd come, careful not to attract any attention. He couldn't risk being spotted while he was so far away from his car.

His head ached. What was he going to do now? He couldn't possibly go through the front door without being seen. And the back entrance was boarded up.

He had to get in there, though. Otherwise he didn't stand a chance.

# 24

## 7:45 A.M.

Travis waited for Staci at the corner where he knew she met the bus every weekday morning. As soon as she appeared, he stepped out from behind a cluster of elm trees and whistled.

"Travis!" Staci ran to him. "Omigosh! What happened to you?"

Travis hadn't even considered his appearance. After his beating in the men's room, his pummeling on the back of Moroconi's pickup, and being up all night, he realized he must look awful. "Nothing serious, honey."

"Travis, your clothes are torn, your face—"

"It's nothing. Really." A yellow school bus pulled up to the corner. "Look, I need your help."

"Oh boy! Are we going to work on your big case?"

"Well, in a way. I was wondering . . . do you know where your two friends from the basketball court are?"

"Doc and Jameel? They're on the bus."

Travis scanned the windows. He recognized them—they were sitting together in the back row. "Staci, I don't have time to mince words, so I'm just going to ask this directly. Do they have much experience at . . . well, housebreaking?"

"Travis, they're my *friends*—"

"You told me they'd been picked up on B and E's. I don't want to arrest them. On the contrary, I want to hire them."

"Hire them?"

"Yeah. I need someone with . . . expertise in this field."

"Way cool. I'll talk to them. If they can't do it, I'm sure they know someone who can. But only if I get to come along."

"That's out of the question."

"Why? I can be quiet. I can be real sneaky."

"Trust me, Staci. I feel bad enough about this as it is. I'll probably get hauled up on child-endangerment charges. I'm not going to compound matters by getting you involved. Besides, you could be recognized and traced back to me. I need people I don't know."

Staci's lower lip protruded. "You never let me do anything fun anymore."

"We'll do something fun when this is all over. I promise. Now get your friends before the bus takes off, okay? I shouldn't be standing out in the open like this."

Staci sulked but nonetheless climbed into the bus. A few moments later she descended with her two tall friends.

"It's okay," she said to the bus driver, who was eyeing Travis suspiciously. "He'll take us to school. He's one of the family." The driver tipped his hat and drove away. "Practically," she added, after the bus was gone.

Travis extended his hand to the two boys. Smirking, they took his hand and shook.

"Staci says you got a job for us," Jameel said.

"That's right," Travis replied. "I want you to break into an apartment."

"Hoo-*ee*!" Doc exclaimed. "Boy, when you cops turn, you turn *bad*."

"It's nothing like that," Travis said. "This job isn't even illegal."

The boys' faces fell, crestfallen.

"It is, however, dangerous," Travis added.

They perked up. "What we looking for? TVs, VCRs?"

"You can take whatever you want for yourself," Travis said. "I need some clothes, and a wallet—with the cash intact—and a briefcase."

Doc and Jameel poked one another in the ribs. "No problemo," Doc said. "Whose place we gonna hit?"

Travis scrawled an address on a scrap of paper. "Mine."

**25**

8:30 A.M.

Doc and Jameel strutted down Walnut Hill Lane, bouncing a basketball, chanting a Hammer rap lyric. They pointedly took no notice of the dull green Chevrolet or the men seated inside. The men in the Chevy, however, noticed them. The driver emerged from the car, crossed the street, and met Doc and Jameel at the foot of the front steps to Travis's apartment building.

"You boys live here?" The man from the Chevy was younger than they expected, pasty-faced and obviously nervous.

"Maybe," Doc bluffed. "Who wants to know?"

"I'm lookin' for a man named Byrne. Travis Byrne. Short, thick, on the heavy side. You know him?"

Jameel's eyes twinkled. "What if we do? What's in it for us?"

Grudgingly, the Chevy man shoved his hand into his pocket and extracted two twenties. After reading the boys' expressions, he dipped back into the pocket and extracted four more. "That's all I got."

Jameel snatched the money from him. "Then it'll have to do."

"So how about it? You know Byrne?"

"Not me," Doc said, grinning. "How 'bout you, Jameel?"

"Never heard of him," he said. "Sorry, chump."

"Now look here—"

"Was a dude like that here a while back," Jameel added. "Ain't seen him for some time, though. Like weeks maybe."

"Damn. I figured we had the wrong address."

"Anything else we can do for you?" Doc inquired.

"I guess not." The Chevy man headed back toward his car, and Doc and Jameel walked up the front steps of the apartment building. In the reflection in a window, Doc saw the man return to his car, wake his companion, and talk agitatedly into a cellular phone. A few seconds later, he started the car and drove away.

Grinning, Doc and Jameel scrambled up the stairs.


The housebreakers returned to the bus stop about an hour later with two garbage bags draped over their shoulders.

"What happened?" Travis asked. "Did you get in?"

"No problemo." They tossed the garbage bags to Travis.

"You seem disappointed."

"Easy pickins," Jameel explained. "Breakin' into a guy's apartment with his permission. Ain't no challenge."

Travis grinned. "I'm sorry there wasn't more excitement."

Doc chimed in. "It got a little hairy when that nervous dude in the Chevy stopped us."

"What? What did you tell him?"

"Told him you moved away, bro. What else?"

"Was he someone who might be . . . well, a professional criminal?"

"If he be in the mob, he must've been drafted." Doc laughed. "He was some kind of pansy."

Travis wondered if he was the same man who was in the courthouse men's room. It would help if he knew. "Maybe I should've gone myself."

"No way, bro. Even a pansy can be deadly if he's packin'. And this one was. 'Sides, there was another dude slumped down in the front seat and they were both barkin' at someone else on a car phone. Sendin' us was the smartest thing you ever did."

"I really appreciate this, guys. How can I thank you?"

Jameel looked out the corner of his eyes. "Well . . . you could help dee-fray our expenses."

"Right, right." Travis took his wallet out of the garbage bag and handed them six twenties. "Will that do?"

"Superfine," Jameel said, snatching the bills. "Been a good long time since we've seen that much cash. Right, Doc?"

# 26

## 9:40 A.M.

After changing clothes in his car, Travis followed a serpentine route downtown. He wanted to ensure that if someone stumbled across him, he couldn't be traced back to Staci. After he had taken enough random turns to lose even himself, he pulled over to a pay phone. He opened his briefcase and withdrew the object he'd wanted out of his apartment most of all: the business card for Special Agent William Henderson.

Before entering the phone booth, he plugged thirty-five cents into a street-side newspaper stand. Both page-one stories in the *Dallas Morning News* attracted his immediate attention. The paper announced that Alberto Moroconi, criminal defendant on trial for the rape-beating of Mary Ann McKenzie, had escaped from the detention room of the federal courthouse last night. One guard had been wounded during the escape, another was killed. Police were unsure how he eluded the marshals, but said that he must've had help from someone on the inside.

Another story reported that the West End was hit by a spree of vandalism, destruction, and murder. Again, police were uncertain what exactly had occurred, but the paper cryptically indicated that they had reason to believe escapee Moroconi was involved. For undisclosed reasons, the police were withholding all information regarding the murdered man.

A boxed item at the bottom of the second page disclosed that the police were searching for Moroconi's attorney, Travis Byrne, in connection with both incidents. A photo of Travis, probably clipped from the Dallas County Bar Directory, accompanied the notice. According to the article, an ongoing police investigation indicated that Travis was intimately involved in both crimes, and maybe several more besides.

Travis crumpled the paper in his fist. Someone had gotten to the police. And the press. How did they learn about the West End shoot-out in time to make the morning edition? Travis knew from a previous libel case he had handled that the morning edition was put to bed around three A.M.—only shortly after last night's incident occurred. There was only one explanation: someone at the newspaper was in close contact with Moroconi—or the men behind the searchlight.

Travis plunked a quarter into the pay phone and dialed the number on Henderson's card. It rang twice before it was answered.

"Hello. American Exports."

Travis blinked. "I'm—I'm calling for Agent Henderson."

"One moment."

Travis heard several clicks on the other end of the line, then a computerized beep that indicated his call had been transferred. "Hello?"

"Agent Henderson?"

"Henderson is unavailable at the moment. Who's calling, please?"

Blast! Where's the Special Agent when you need him? "This is Travis Byrne. I want to talk to Henderson. This is important."

"As I said, Henderson is unavailable, but I'm familiar with your situation. Please tell me what happened."

Travis was perplexed. Where the hell was Henderson, and who was this chump on the other end of the line? Holt? Janicek? Travis couldn't tell. The voice sounded weird; he was probably using one of those mechanical gizmos to distort his voice. Travis knew only one thing for certain—he needed help, and he needed it quick.

"Okay," Travis said, "get out your pencil. This ordeal began sometime after midnight, when I got a phone call from a client who's supposed to be behind bars. . . ." He told the story as briefly as possible—including the shoot-out at the West End and the stakeout of his apartment.

"Mr. Byrne," the man on the other end of the phone said, "listen to me carefully. You said Moroconi shoved a piece of paper into your hands. Have you looked at that paper?"

"No, I haven't had time to think about it. Should I?"

"Absolutely not. Under no circumstances should you look at that list. This is a matter of grave importance."

List? How did he know it was a list?

"Mr. Byrne, we need to bring you in."

"Bring me in? What does that mean?"

"It's obvious that you've become involved with the Outfit."

He recalled his conversation with Agent Janicek. "Gangsters?"

"Quaint, but accurate. They'll be trying to obtain what you now have, and if they believe you've read what's on that paper, they'll try to kill you as well. You need to be placed in protective custody."

"Excellent suggestion. Where do I meet you?"

A pause. "My computer indicates that you're currently at a pay phone near the intersection of Abrams and Mockingbird."

Travis felt the hairs on the back of his neck stand up. He didn't think he'd talked nearly long enough for a trace to be completed.

"Why don't we pick you up in the alley behind the grocery store on Abrams?" the man continued. "So as not to attract attention."

So as not to attract attention? Something about that phrase

bothered him. "Nothing personal, but I'd rather meet somewhere in the open. I haven't had much luck with clandestine meetings lately."

"That would raise the possibility of detection by the persons who are looking for you, Mr. Byrne."

"I'll take that risk. How about the Northpark Mall? Just off Central Expressway. Say, in the package-pickup alley behind Sears."

Travis heard the scratching of a pen on the other end of the line. "Got it. The recovery team will be there at eleven hundred hours. Stay out of sight until then."

Travis checked his watch. More than enough time. "Okay. I'll be there. Will Henderson be coming?"

"Unlikely. He probably will not have terminated his current engagement."

"How will I know you?"

"Do you recall the password on Agent Henderson's business card?" Travis said that he did. "Be prepared to use it." The line disconnected.

Travis hung up the phone and shoved his hand into his pocket. He knew he shouldn't look, but he couldn't resist the temptation. The FBI agent had definitely pricked his curiosity. Besides, if he was going to remain alive, he needed to have as much information as possible.

*List?* Travis examined the paper top to bottom, back and front. He held it up to the sun and watched the light seep through.

List, huh? He felt his confidence in the friendly neighborhood FBI seeping away.

The paper was blank.

# 27

9:50 P.M.

The FBI agent pressed his fingers against his throbbing temples. Thank God Henderson wasn't in. That would have screwed everything up. Although that was about the only complication that hadn't occurred yet. First, Moroconi botched his flawless escape plan, then he intentionally dragged Byrne into this mess just for spite. He didn't have much doubt about who was having Byrne's apartment watched, either. Everything that could possibly go wrong was going wrong.

And of course there was the goddamn list. Did Moroconi really give it to Byrne? After all his trouble to get the damn thing, would he give it away just to sign Byrne's death warrant?

He realized he made a major-league mistake when he got into bed with Alberto Moroconi. If he just hadn't needed the money . . .

There was only one solution. He would handle this rendezvous himself. He'd take Simpson along. Simpson was a new, fresh-faced recruit—eager to please, unquestioning. He'd do what he was told. And if Simpson needed any help keeping his mouth shut afterward, he'd haul out those pictures he had of Simpson with his male roommate. Most feds wanted to follow in the footsteps of J. Edgar Hoover, but Simpson took it a bit too far.

"Excuse me, sir. Are we going to log that call?"

He snapped out of his reverie. It was Mooney again, no surprise. The same sniveling idiot who got in his way every time he turned around.

"I was listening on the extension, sir," Mooney added.

The FBI agent maintained a calm, even demeanor while silently calling Mooney every swear word he knew. This definitely complicated matters.

"I believe standard procedure is to log the call and fill out a report," Mooney continued. "Then I would recommend a staff meeting to consider our options and assemble a field team to deal with this situation."

"Would you indeed?" And if I don't, you'll file a report accusing me of incompetence. Or dishonesty. Or both. You need to be taken care of, Mr. Mooney. "I'm afraid we don't have time for a meeting."

"This is very unorthodox, sir."

"You can't always play by the book, Mooney. A good agent knows that."

"We should at least wait for Henderson to return. He's due back shortly."

"Sorry, that's impossible."

Mooney looked at him strangely. Did he suspect? "If you won't wait for Henderson, sir, then I feel I should accompany you. As an independent observer."

"You? Why—" He bit down on his tongue. On second thought, *yes*, that was a splendid idea. That would work out perfectly. "Fine, Mooney. Get your gear. We leave in five minutes."

Mooney departed for the locker room. Excellent. With any luck, the whole affair would be resolved before Henderson even knew about the phone call.

He had to recover that damn list before it was traced back to him. He had to pin the rap for everything on Byrne. And with Mooney along, he could accomplish both goals at once.

Agent Janicek took his gun out of the desk drawer and slid it into his shoulder holster. He would get that list back. No matter what he had to do.

## 28

### 1 0 : 5 5 A.M.

Travis walked cautiously down the package pickup driveway of the Northpark Sears and positioned himself behind a trash dumper. He wasn't sure why, but this rendezvous made him nervous. Something about the situation didn't click. At the moment, however, he didn't seem to have any other options.

After a few minutes, a long black sedan with leaded-glass windows pulled sideways across the driveway. Sideways, Travis observed—preventing any other cars from coming in or going out.

Another minute passed. What on earth could they be doing in there? Travis felt himself tensing up. Why don't they get this show on the road?

At last three men in tan overcoats, much too heavy for the season, stepped out of the car. They looked like FBI agents; all they lacked were gray fedoras. Unfortunately, they were too far away for Travis to identify them.

They did not approach. They stood outside the car, conferring.

Travis wiped the sweat from his brow. My God, what were they waiting for?

Finally one of the men took a step forward. "Travis Byrne?" the man said, not too loud, not too soft.

Thank God. "Present," Travis said, stepping out from behind the trash bin. "Over here."

The man's gun was out from under his overcoat before Travis even realized he had moved. Travis ducked instinctively, and the bullet whistled over his right shoulder and ricocheted off the back wall. He flattened himself on the gravel just before the second bullet flew over his head. Crawling like a baby, Travis scrambled back behind the dumper. What the hell was going on here?

"Come on out, Byrne. You're just wasting our time."

No thanks, Travis thought. At least I'm wasting it in a reasonably safe place.

"I don't understand," Travis heard the third man say—the one with the curly blond hair. "Why did we open fire? We were supposed—"

Travis heard another shot, then a cry of pain. He peeked over the top of the dumper. The man with the gun had shot his companion. *He shot one of his own men!*

"Ten seconds, Byrne. Then we come after you."

Travis heard him count to ten, then heard the snap-crackle-pop of gravel that told him the two remaining men were approaching. In the six inches between the gravel and the bottom of the dumper, Travis could see Hush-Puppied feet shuffling down the driveway. He tried to think—what had his police training taught him to do in a situation like this? All those drills must have been worth something. Only one answer came to him. If you're totally helpless: bluff.

"Don't come any closer," Travis shouted. "I'm armed."

The footsteps stopped. Travis could see the Hush Puppies shifting weight, deliberating. He knew the questions that would be going through their minds: was he lying, and if not, what was he packing?

"We don't want to hurt you, Travis," said the man with the gun.

"You have a funny way of showing it," Travis muttered.

"Throw down your weapon and come with us peacefully."

To the morgue? No thanks. One of the two pairs of feet skittered away. Of course—he was going to do an end run, try to come up on Travis from behind. If Travis was going to make a break for it, the time was now.

Travis turned and bolted toward the Sears service entrance. As soon as he emerged from cover, he heard the first man yell, "He's moving!" A second after that, Travis heard him fire another shot.

Too quickly. He was reacting, not aiming. Travis's practiced ears could tell the bullet was more than a yard away from him. He kept barreling forward, zigzagging back and forth—an erratic target was a lot harder to hit. He grabbed an iron railing and vaulted over just as he heard another bullet zing by. Closer this time, but not close enough. He reached the service entrance and yanked at the door.

It was locked.

Travis glanced back over his shoulder. Both men were running toward him, trying to get close enough to get a decent shot off. Travis pounded desperately on the door.

A dark, unshaven man in a gray service uniform opened the door just a crack. "I'm sorry, sir. You need to deposit your invoice at the front register, then—"

Travis yanked the door open and shoved the man out of the way. He raced through the warehouse, careening down corridors lined with refrigerators and washing machines and power tools. Seconds later he heard the two alleged FBI men hit the door and race through.

Travis had no idea where he was going, but he knew if he stopped he was a dead man. The endless rows of merchandise were like a maze. And he was a stupid rat trying to find the cheese.

He plowed through a group of uniformed workers huddled around a clipboard.

"Hey, what's the—"

Travis didn't stop. He kept on running, sending the clipboard flying into the air. No time to inquire about exit doors. Judging by the sound of his pursuers' footsteps, they were closing in on him.

Finally Travis came to a wide set of double doors. He smashed through and found himself on the main retail floor. Before he could stop himself, he careened into a display of wedding crystal. A punch bowl and some stemware shattered on the tile floor. A man behind a cash register whirled around. "Just a minute—"

Unfortunately, Travis didn't have a minute. The two men in the unseasonable overcoats burst through the double doors and spotted him almost immediately. Travis plunged further into the store, hoping against hope they wouldn't fire in front of witnesses. It was just possible that he could lose them in the shopping mall.

After a crash-and-smash detour through the perfume and hosiery departments, Travis found himself in the main thoroughfare of the mall. He was panting and gasping for air. He probably hadn't run like this in years. His overweight body was complaining mightily.

He blended into the main stream of traffic, then glanced back over his shoulder. His trackers were still there, but following at a discreet distance. Apparently, his hope was fulfilled—they didn't want to be seen gunning him down before hundreds of witnesses. He passed the Hickory Farms outlet, the Suncoast Video store, and the food court. He was hungry and he wanted to pick up some food—some *real* food, with meat in it—but he didn't think that advisable at the moment. His immediate objective was to get back to his car and get the hell out of here.

He circled the food court and retraced his steps. A quick glance confirmed that his pursuers had done the same. They were walking faster now, closing the gap. They knew what he was trying to do, and they were determined to prevent it.

Travis reentered Sears and spotted a small group of people talking, apparently on their way back to their cars. The group was composed of three couples, all well-dressed yuppies. Travis plunged into their midst.

"Excuse me," he said to one of the men. "Do you have any jumper cables?"

"Sure," the man replied, stroking his salt-and-pepper beard. "In the back of my Land Rover. Car trouble?"

"Yeah. Wouldn't you know? I try to do some shopping for the little woman's birthday, and my car won't start."

"That stinks," said one of the other men. "We were just gonna pop into the wine shop. If you don't mind waiting, we'll be happy to help you out."

Travis tried to maintain his facade of calm. "The trouble is—I'm supposed to meet the little woman at eleven-thirty. And it's her birthday."

"Ye gods," the first man said, checking his watch. "We'd better move fast. We'll come back for the wine later."

"Thanks," Travis said. "I really appreciate it."

Travis fell into step with them, careful to keep his newfound friends between himself and the two men in the overcoats. He didn't have to look over his shoulder; he knew they were still back there.

After providing a lame story about his gimp leg, Travis convinced the group to go to their car first, then drive him to his own car. All seven of them squeezed into the Land Rover; Travis kept himself in the middle. He instructed the driver to park his car in the aisle between two parking rows, blocking oncoming traffic. Travis then crawled into his car and put it into neutral, resisting suggestions that he give it another try first. Travis steered while the others pushed his car in front of the Rover. As he stepped out of his car he saw the long black sedan with leaded windows pull into the same lane, just behind the Rover. It was waiting.

The first man, whom Travis had now learned went by "Buzz," attached the jumper cables to the two cars' batteries. After a believable period of time Travis tried his engine and—what a surprise!—it started right up.

After letting the car charge briefly, Buzz removed the jumper cables and closed the hood of Travis's car. "Well, that should take care of—"

Travis never heard the rest of the sentence. He floored the accelerator and peeled out of the parking lot. In his rearview mirror, he saw the sedan press forward, but they couldn't get around the Land Rover. The sedan honked, then someone leaned out the window and began shouting. Buzz closed his hood, got into the Rover, and tried to get out of the way. He eased forward, the sedan riding his rear bumper.

Travis was already at the Park Lane intersection and the light was green. He turned right and shot down Park Lane, leaving the sedan and its occupants well behind. He took the first exit, turned right into a residential section, and wandered aimlessly for fifteen minutes.

When he was certain he had lost them, Travis pulled over to the side of the street and rested his forehead against the steering wheel.

Somehow he'd managed to give them the slip. But where could he go now? He couldn't go anywhere he would normally be expected. Driving was itself dangerous; they could easily identify his car. Whoever *they* were. He slapped the dash with the flat of his hand. Why would the FBI try to kill him?

He didn't know what was and wasn't safe, who could and couldn't be trusted. All he had were guesses. And if he guessed wrong, it might prove fatal.

# 29

## 12:22 P.M.

**H**enderson was enraged. "You did *what?*"

"I organized a recovery team to bring Byrne in," Janicek said, folding his hands calmly in his lap.

"Without my authorization?"

"You weren't around," Janicek said, with barely a hint of derision.

"You knew I'd be back."

"We couldn't wait. The man was desperate. Claimed his life was in danger. We had to hurry."

"Goddamn it, your haste got an agent killed!"

Janicek examined his fingernails. "We had no reason to believe Byrne was armed or dangerous."

"Well, you should've, Janicek. You should've planned for every contingency."

"I'm sorry, sir. I tried to act according to regulation. But the first thing I knew, Byrne was shooting at us and poor Mooney was dead."

Henderson threw his coat bitterly on the floor. He was a big barrel-chested man with rugged features, now contorted by his anger and frustration. "Did he say whether he'd looked at the list?"

"He claimed he hadn't."

"Which doesn't tell us a damn thing." Henderson pounded his fists together. "I can't believe that list got out in the first place. Have you tracked down the leak yet, Holt?"

Holt stepped forward. "I have compiled and committed to memory the names of all the people who had access, sir."

"And what is your conclusion?"

"That would be premature. Any number of agents could have obtained clearance. Any of us could have."

"Thank you very goddamn much, Mr. Holt. Tell me something I don't know!"

"Sir," Holt said, "I'm formally requesting authorization to interview every agent on our special team. Separately. See what they have to say for themselves. See if they have any knowledge they shouldn't."

"We can't do that," Henderson said. "Among other reasons, we don't have time. We have to recover that list before it's sold or made public."

"With all due respect, sir, that won't be easy," Janicek said. "Byrne is a cold-blooded killer."

"Are you sure? It just doesn't make any goddamn sense."

"I told you what happened," Janicek said. "What other explanation can there be? Simpson, Mooney, and I arrived at the appointed place. When I demanded the list, Byrne opened fire and shot Mooney. He would've killed us all if he'd had the chance."

"But *why?*"

"Apparently he plans to keep the list," Janicek replied. "Maybe Moroconi was acting for Byrne when he acquired it. Maybe they're in it together. We've checked Byrne out. He's not a wealthy man."

Henderson pressed his knuckles together. It still didn't add up. He'd already checked with Simpson, though, and he had confirmed Janicek's story in every detail.

"Well, what the hell are we going to do?" Henderson asked, his teeth clenched.

"I don't see that we have a great deal of choice," Janicek said. "Damage control is our first priority. If it's possible to preserve the integrity of the list, we have to do it. And that means we have to get Byrne. Immediately. Before he's found by someone else. We're not the only group in town chasing him, you know."

Henderson's eyebrows shot up. "What are you talking about?"

"I'm talking about Moroconi's old business acquaintances."

"They're after Byrne, too?"

"There's no other explanation for what happened at the West End. The initial target was Moroconi. But Byrne's got the hot potato now, so they'll want him. And frankly, if they find him first, there won't be enough left for us to scrape up with a pizza knife."

"And they'll have every name on the list," Henderson said solemnly.

Janicek nodded in quiet agreement. "Names and addresses."

There was a long silence during which all three of them thought the same thought. It was Holt who said it first. "We have to find Byrne before they do, sir. And if we have to kill him, then we have to kill him. In all likelihood, we will."

**30**

2 : 0 0 P.M.

Another office, in another high-rise, on the opposite side of town. Shadows masking the grim faces of the participants.

Mario pressed a hand wearily to his forehead. "Can someone please explain what is going on? How did this simple plan for the elimination of one penny-ante pissant turn into a major disaster?"

Kramer's face became taut, distending his long, gruesome facial scar. He spoke in measured tones that in no way prevented Mario from realizing Kramer would like to set his face on fire. "That ain't fair. Most of this operation has been flawless."

"One of your own men was killed!" Mario shouted. From the safety of the sofa, Donny smirked. "What the hell is so flawless about that?"

"That was a mistake," Kramer admitted. "Hardcastle fucked up and he paid the price. Still, most of our goals have been achieved. Such as watchin' the phone lines and locations connected to Byrne. That's how we got our first lead to Moroconi. That's how we learned he had the list. That's how we interrupted their little rendezvous at the West End."

Yes, Mario thought, that was Kramer—quick to bulldoze over this gaping hole in his heretofore unblemished record of stylized sadism. Why had the family endured him for so long? Sure, he was proficient, but he was unpredictable. And expensive. At least fifty thousand dollars a hit. Hell, the Outfit was teeming with poor slobs desperate to finish a hit so they could become *made men*. And Mario never paid them more than ten thousand a shot. Sure, there were risks, but anytime a murder was actually *planned*—wasn't executed in the heat of the moment by an enraged spouse or jealous boyfriend—the chances of the police ever figuring out who did it decreased dramatically. All in all, Kramer was convenient, but unnecessary. So why the hell were they still using him?

"Yes, you discovered the rendezvous at the West End, but once you arrived, what did you do?" Mario demanded. "You screwed up!"

"There was . . . some confusion. I dunno why Hardcastle identified himself as a cop."

"The police line was a great idea," Donny said. "In fact, I suggested it."

"That figures," Kramer said with disgust.

"I thought that if Byrne took us for police, he'd surrender quietly."

"Brilliant." Kramer pulled out his lighter. "Unfortunately, Moroconi, who had busted out of jail a few hours before, had a slightly different reaction."

"I couldn't predict that!" Donny screamed. "He always blames me, Uncle Mario. It's not my fault."

"Of course it's your fault, you little shit!" Kramer shouted back. "Your stupidity got one of my men killed!"

"Uncle Mario, make him stop!"

Mario covered his face with his hands. "Please, gentlemen.

Must we always have this squabbling? No wonder we can't accomplish anything. We're our own worst enemy."

"Our worst enemy is our blood relations," Kramer muttered.

"Have there been any traces of Byrne since the West End incident?"

"Yes," Kramer answered. "My agents have confirmed that he didn't go to his apartment or his office, or the courthouse, or any of his other usual haunts. He's on the run, probably feeling like a cat in a Doberman cage. He finally turned up at a shopping mall."

Mario looked incredulous. "A shopping mall?"

"Yes. Northpark Mall. One of my contacts reported the incident."

It was Donny's turn to snicker. "Yeah, an hour after Byrne left."

Kramer fired up his lighter and held it about an inch from Donny's nose. The message was unmistakable.

"Look," Kramer said, "I planted all the right info with my boys at the police station, and they fed it to those unquestioning vultures at the press. Byrne is a wanted man. He's got nowhere to go, nowhere to hide, and he can't run forever. Just gimme some more time. I'll give you his fat ass on a silver platter."

"Any thoughts on what this wanted man was doing at a public mall?" Mario asked.

"My source tells me he was running, like he was being chased. He thought there mighta been some gunplay."

"The police?"

"So soon? Fat chance."

"Then we must assume that the people who lost the list are now attempting to reclaim it."

"I'd say that's a fair conclusion."

Mario spread his hands across his desk. "Mr. Kramer, I want that list. Bring it to me."

"A tall order," Kramer said.

"But one I feel confident you can fill."

"It won't be enough to just find Byrne, then. We have to find him before anyone else does."

Mario nodded. "I concur. Do it."

"And when I find him? What then?"

"You may do whatever you like with *him*, Mr. Kramer. Indulge yourself. Just bring me the list."

"And what if he's with Al when I find him?"

Mario smiled. "All the better. Shoot to kill."

# 31

### 4:45 P.M.

Travis slipped into the phone booth and closed the glass
door behind him. As he dialed he scanned in all direc-
tions, watching for suspiciously slow cars or anyone taking an un-
healthy interest in his license plate number.

Gail picked up the phone. "Holyfield and Associates."

"Put me through to Dan."

"Omigosh! Travis! Is this you?"

"Shhh!" Travis hissed into the receiver. "Don't say my name.
Someone could be listening. Just act as if this is nothing out of the
ordinary and put me through to Dan."

"But, Travis, everyone is so worried—"

"Gail—"

"I don't care what anyone says. I know you didn't have anything
to do with those murders."

"Gail, transfer my call to Dan."

"I just wanted you to know—"

"Gail, *do* it!"

"Right, right . . ." Travis heard a series of electronic beeps as his call was transferred.

"Hello?"

Travis recognized the voice at once. "Dan, are you alone?"

"Travis! Where are you?"

"Dan, please don't say my name. We don't know who might be listening."

"What are you talking about? I'm alone."

"Dan, just let me talk. I can't stay on the line for long. They might trace the call."

"They? Who on earth—"

"Dan, I'm not going to be able to finish the trial. Send Abigail or someone else over to make an appearance—"

"The trial has been suspended, Travis."

He swore silently. "Because I didn't appear in court."

"Plus the fact that your client broke out of jail last night."

Of course. How stupid of him. Normally, the voluntary disappearance of the defendant wouldn't halt a trial (if it did, they'd all disappear), but when both the defendant and his attorney vanished, it could definitely gum up the works.

"Was Hagedorn angry?"

"What do you think? He held you in contempt and issued a bench warrant for your arrest. Which is convenient, because I understand the police are looking for you anyway. Charles didn't have much choice under the circumstances. You haven't been disbarred, Travis, but of course, the day isn't over yet."

"I had to stay away, Dan. Someone's looking for me. Someone who wants to kill me."

"What could be safer than a courthouse?"

"Dan, I got the hell beaten out of me in the courthouse a few days ago."

"Come into the office, then. I'll see that you get every possible protection."

"Sorry, Dan. I've already driven by the office. Someone's parked across the street from the front door, and there's a thug pacing up and down the steps. I'm certain they're watching for me."

"I'll personally escort you upstairs."

"I'm not putting you in danger."

"Travis. The police think you were involved in a shooting at the West End."

"It isn't true, Dan. I mean, I was involved, but only as a target. You've got to believe me. People are trying to *kill* me."

"Travis . . ." Dan inhaled slowly, choosing his words with care. "I know you've been under a lot of stress lately. We've all been trying to get you to slow down. You've been working much too hard."

"I haven't gone bonkers, Dan."

"No, of course not. You're just a little . . . stressed. Paranoia sets in. . . ."

"You wouldn't think I was paranoid if you'd lived my last twenty-four hours. People *are* trying to kill me, Dan. And it appears to involve both the police and the FBI, so don't suggest that I turn myself in to either one."

"Where did you get the idea that—"

"I don't have time to go into it. Just relay a message to Judge Hagedorn. Tell him I apologize, that I regret the inconvenience to the court, and that I would've appeared if it had been at all possible."

"I will, Travis, but I don't see what good it's going to do."

"Thanks. Bye." He disconnected the line.

There was one more call Travis wanted to make. He looked the number up in the directory dangling beneath the pay phone. Sure enough, it was not the number on Henderson's business card. He dialed.

"Good afternoon. Federal Bureau of Investigation."

"Yes." Travis tried to muffle his voice with his hand. "Could I speak to Special Agent William Henderson?"

"Extension, please."

"Uh . . . I'm sorry, I don't know it. Can you look it up?"

He heard an annoyed *hmmph* on the other end of the line. After a few moments the voice returned. "I show two Hendersons—a George and a Phoebe. No William."

"Perhaps he's located in an office outside Dallas."

"Sir, I'm looking at the directory for the entire FBI. All offices."

"Perhaps I have his title wrong."

"I show no William Henderson with any title."

"Are you certain?"

A long exasperated sigh. "Yes, sir, I'm certain. Will there be anything else?"

"How about an agent named Janicek?"

She checked. "I'm sorry. No Janicek."

Travis felt a sinking sensation in the pit of his stomach. "What about Holt? Check for Holt."

"I show a Clara Holt in Seattle."

"No, this was a man."

"Strike three," the woman said. "Does this mean you're out?"

"Yeah," Travis murmured. "As a matter of fact, it does." He hung up the phone.

Travis stood in the booth, utterly clueless about his next move. If they weren't FBI, who the hell were those people? How could he fight them when he didn't even know who they were?

He jumped back into his car and floored it. He had no idea what to do. The only thing he knew with clarity was what he couldn't do. He couldn't go to the police, or the alleged FBI agents, or his friends—at least not without taking a serious risk of getting killed, and maybe getting others killed as well.

What was left?

## 32

**5:30 P.M.**

Special Agent Henderson sat at one end of a long conference table with Janicek, Holt, and three other agents.

"Status report," Henderson said gruffly. "Why haven't we located Byrne yet?"

"I think I can answer that, sir," Holt said. "We haven't located him because he's smart, and because he knows he's being hunted. Also, Dallas is a very large city, and we're not entirely certain he's still in Dallas."

"Surely our combined forces can bring in one renegade lawyer."

"Easy to say, sir. Tough to accomplish. We know he hasn't gone to any of his usual places. If he's smart, stays out of sight, and doesn't drive his car much, it could be days before we track him down. Even weeks."

"That's unacceptable."

"That's reality. We're focusing on the car. Logic suggests he's going to stay close to it, at least until he has a chance to swap it for something else. We've got men combing every parking lot, every used-car lot, every public garage, and every other place a car might be left in the greater Dallas/Fort Worth area. But that takes time."

"We haven't got time. For all we know, he could be selling the names on that list one by one."

"May I say something?" Janicek leaned across the table. "I think it's essential that we instruct our agents to be careful and to take a defensive, shoot-on-sight posture."

Henderson raised an eyebrow. "Oh?"

"The reality is," Janicek continued, "he's already suckered us once. I don't want to lose any more men."

Holt shook his head. "It's hard to believe the man we saw stumbling around his office a few nights ago is in league with the mob. It's contrary to everything I know about organized crime."

"It's possible Byrne's now working on their behalf at this time," Janicek suggested. "He may have used his connections to gain access to the list but is now acting for his own profit."

"Then it would follow logically that Byrne engineered Moroconi's escape. That's equally difficult for me to believe."

"Look," Janicek said angrily, "Simpson will confirm that we barely got away from him alive. Byrne is a murderer."

"I've already spoken to Simpson," Henderson said evenly. "He did confirm your report. Where is he tonight?"

"I've got him . . . monitoring calls in the Austin office," Janicek said quickly. "They, uh, had an absence on the switchboard."

"I see."

"Sir, I'm requesting Code Eleven alert status and top defensive posture. We can't afford another screwup. We have to bring that list home." Janicek paused decisively. "Byrne is expendable."

Henderson nodded. "From what I hear, we'll be saving the government a long protracted trial on a variety of complicated legal issues if we take Byrne out. But what if he doesn't have the list on his person?"

Janicek shifted his weight uneasily. "That strikes me as unlikely."

"Probably right," Henderson murmured, eyeing Janicek carefully. "Very well, then. I'll advance this to Code Eleven. Defensive posture, kill authorization. I'd rather it didn't come to that, but . . ."

"We must recover the list," Janicek repeated. "Lives are at stake. People are counting on us to protect them."

Henderson nodded his head grimly. "You're right, of course. Gentlemen, bring back our list. And if you have to kill Byrne in the process—do it."

After the meeting ended, Janicek walked down the rear stairs, crossed through the basement, unlocked a door, and entered a private room equipped with state-of-the-art eavesdropping equipment.

Janicek patted Simpson on the shoulder. "You did a good job covering me with Henderson." Simpson squirmed but did not twist away. "Hear anything of interest?"

"Not really. Byrne called his boss, but he didn't say anything we didn't already know." Simpson tapped his right earphone, then pushed a few buttons on his computer console. "And the line disconnected before I could get a lock."

"Damn! What happened?"

"Byrne hung up. And at the last possible moment, I might add. This guy knows what he's doing. What is he, a fed? Spook?"

"Neither," Janicek said. "Ex-cop."

"I can get you a general region."

"Don't bother. He's already left it. How's the tape?"

"Crystal clear. For whatever it's worth."

Janicek exited the room, carefully closing and locking the door behind him. Soon their entire team would be gunning for Byrne, but he couldn't count on them to take care of his problem. He had to find Byrne and Moroconi before Henderson did. Otherwise there could be some very damaging revelations about Janicek's role in Moroconi's escape. And the leaking of the list. And Mooney's murder.

No doubt about it—he had to be the first one to talk to Byrne. And the last.

# 33

8 : 1 0 p.m.

Travis crept up the wooden stairs to apartment 13X, concealing a roll of industrial-strength duct tape under his windbreaker. Thank goodness these apartments were separate units, well off Forest Lane, amply spaced. They could make a lot of noise and still not be heard by any of her neighbors.

He pressed his ear against the door. He heard a steady drone inside. Television, probably, or maybe a radio. As gently as possible, he tried the doorknob. To his astonishment, it turned. Where did she think she lived, Smallville, U.S.A.? Imagine having an apartment in Plano, just a few miles from Dallas Metro, and not locking your front door. She was asking for trouble.

Yeah, he repeated to himself, she was asking for trouble—as if that might somehow assuage his guilt about what he was about to do.

As quietly as possible, Travis pushed the door open and poked his head through. He was right the first time; it was the television. John Tesh and Leeza Gibbons were rhapsodizing about the latest celebrity bio. "Unrestrained and relentlessly honest," they said. "One of the great books of our time."

Travis heard clattering noises from the kitchen. He shut the front door and tiptoed through the living room. She was facing the stove, her back to him, stirring something in a copper pot with a wooden spoon. As gently as possible, he placed his hands on her shoulders and whispered, "Don't be scared."

Cavanaugh screamed. Frantically, Travis covered her mouth, just as they'd instructed him at the academy. It barely reduced the volume. He grabbed a dishrag and shoved it in her mouth. This did a considerably better job of muffling her, but in the meantime, she began fighting back.

She stabbed him in the side with her spoon. Travis winced, and as his grip loosened she whirled around and opened a drawer. She grabbed a two-tined barbecue fork and thrust it toward his abdomen. Travis grabbed her wrist and tried to force it down to her side. He was probably a hundred and twenty pounds heavier than she was but, by God, she fought like a champion. She grabbed his hair with her free hand, jerking his head back.

He knocked her hand away and stomped on her right foot. While she was still reacting to that blow, he grabbed her right hand and forced it down hard against the kitchen counter. She dropped the barbecue fork.

Straining with all her might, Cavanaugh reached across the counter for her battery-charged mixer. Travis tightened his grip on both her arms and slowly brought them down to her side.

He twisted her head around and forced her to face him. "What's wrong with you?" he spat out. "You know who I am. I'm not going to hurt you."

Her response sounded something like *Mmmmhmphfrulumm-mmphmm.*

Despite the restraint on enunciation created by the dishrag, he gathered the general tenor of her reply. "If I remove the rag, do you promise not to scream again?"

Her eyes burned straight into his, but she made no sound.

"Look," he added, "I brought plenty of duct tape. I could wrap you up and leave you gagged all night, but I'd prefer not to. Will you promise not to scream?"

She continued glaring for a long time, then twisted her left wrist free, raised a finger, and tapped her wristwatch. *One minute.*

"Fine," Travis said. "That's all I need." He removed the dishrag.

"What the hell do you think you're doing?" Cavanaugh shouted. "Let me tell you, mister, I'm a charter member of Women Take Back the Night, I've had serious martial-arts training—"

"I'm not going to hurt you."

"You're damn right about that. My boyfriend should be back any minute. And I've got a Doberman in the other room."

"Oh? He's awfully well behaved."

"He's trained to keep his distance. But the second you try to get rough with me, *pow!* He'll be all over you like a bad dream."

"Uh-huh. Look, Cavanaugh, I need someplace to spend the night."

"You've come to the wrong place, you pervert."

"I just want to hide out. With someone I can trust."

"Then why the hell are you here? We barely know each other."

"That's more or less the point. Everyone I know well is being watched. Every place I would normally go is being watched. Or bugged. Or both."

"Oh, please."

"It's true. Didn't you wonder why I didn't show up for trial to-day?"

"I assumed you were on the lam with your deviant client. That's what the papers said."

"Well, the papers were wrong. Why would I help Moroconi? You know what he is."

"That hasn't stopped you from representing him."

"A judicial appointment. You were there at the time—you know I didn't want the case."

"I recall you didn't object too strenuously."

"It doesn't make any sense for me to go on the lam with Moroconi."

"It makes sense if you helped him escape. Which is what I heard."

"Who's starting these rumors? I didn't even know about the breakout until it was already a fait accompli."

"I heard he had inside assistance—"

"Does that mean I was the accomplice?"

"Coupled with your disappearance immediately thereafter . . ."

Travis clenched his jaw. "Look, all I need is a place to stay the night. I can't go anywhere and I can't sleep in my car—that's what everyone will be looking for."

"Who is this *everyone*?"

Travis hesitated. "I'm not entirely sure. Maybe the mob, maybe the police. Maybe both. And the FBI."

"*And* the FBI? Wait, don't leave out the CIA. And the military-industrial complex. What about Elvis? Or Lee Harvey Oswald? Maybe he was in on this, too."

"You don't have to believe me. Just give me a place to crash."

"Open my door to a raving maniac who's in contempt of court and wanted by the police, federal marshals, and possibly a federal agency or two. Yeah, what could be simpler?"

"C'mon. For old times' sake."

"What old times? You mean our face-offs in countless trials during the past year? In most of which, I might add, you've trounced me. Let me tell you, Byrne, those old times haven't exactly endeared you to me."

"Just for the night."

"No way. I'm an officer of the court. A federal prosecutor, no less. I can't harbor fugitives."

"I'm desperate here." He glanced at the roll of tape inside his jacket. "Don't make me—"

"Don't even think about it." She struggled to pull away from him. "And don't try any more rough stuff. I wasn't kidding about my martial-arts training."

"Cavanaugh, I'm at the end of my rope—"

"I'll scream. Man, you can't believe how I'll scream. What you heard before was just a warm-up."

"I can't let you do that." He reached into his coat pocket, pointed a finger, and pushed it forward. "If you scream, I'll shoot."

"Give me a break. I used to be a skip tracer, remember? I handled guys tougher than you on a regular basis. And I know the difference between a finger and a gun."

"Are you positive?"

"As a matter of fact, yes." And to prove it, she screamed. True to her word, this scream was twice as loud as the previous one.

Travis clamped his hand over her mouth. Cavanaugh bit down on his palm.

*"Owww!"*

Cavanaugh ducked under his arm and ran out of the kitchen. Travis whirled around and raced after her, catching her about halfway across the living room. He tackled her around the legs and brought her crashing down to the floor, knocking over an end table and a lamp in the process.

"Goddamn you, Byrne, I'm calling the police—"

Travis shoved the dishrag back in her mouth. He pulled himself directly on top of her and pinned her shoulders to the carpet. Cavanaugh thrashed her head and twisted back and forth, but he maintained his grip.

With one terrific burst of energy, she bent forward at the waist and butted her head against his. Travis pulled back but not in time to avoid the blow. He clutched the carpet and tried to maintain his bearings. Next thing he knew, she was pulling her legs out from under him. He stiffened his muscles, but not in time to prevent her knee from connecting with his groin. He shouted and his eyes watered, but did not loosen his grip. He grabbed her arms and stretched them out flat on the carpet.

"Goddamn you, Cavanaugh." He felt her chest heaving, her breasts pressing against him. He was suddenly keenly aware of her musky perfume. "If you keep this up, you're going to spend the night taped to the radiator."

She continued to struggle, if anything even more strenuously than before.

"Fine, you stubborn—" Pressing her arms down with his knees, he grabbed the duct tape and began wrapping it around her hands.

# 34

9:00 P.M.

The dark-haired man carefully slid the nightscope onto his gun. It was more complicated than it looked; a number of minute notches had to be correctly aligned. It was designed to be difficult. With equipment on this level of sophistication, amateurs were not welcome.

He checked his night goggles—perfect operating condition. He strapped them onto his belt. Ditto for the Fujinon binoculars—lightweight, waterproof, and almost infinitely powerful. He strapped on a tiny Tessina minichip camera, just in case he wanted to memorialize a license-plate number.

He searched through his closet. What else? Better safe than sorry. He added a small but powerful Xenon flashlight. An electronic stethoscope. Tiny microportable transceivers.

It had been years since he last used equipment like this. He had almost forgotten the pleasure of being able to see in the dark, being able to hear what others could not, being able to sneak up on someone unawares. He checked all the devices and made sure he remembered how each worked. He supposed it was like riding a bicycle—you never forgot.

He tugged a Kevlar vest tightly around his chest, aligned his shoulder holster, put his shirt back on, then strapped the loaded Sam Browne belt around his waist. He checked the equipment still snapped in their compartments from the last time he had worn the belt—spare handgun, Puukko knife, Bianchi handcuffs, tear gas, Mace, brass knuckles, ammunition. A travel kit for commandos. And the whole thing, fully equipped, weighed less than ten pounds. It wouldn't slow him down a beat.

Finally he examined the new SSI tracer bug; once it was activated, he could follow someone from as much as twenty miles away. It had cost him a pretty penny; in fact, it had cost him almost everything he had. But if he tracked down his quarry, it would be worth it. He had to assume he would need everything; after all, this time he was on his own.

No one was going to help him. Who could? No one else had managed to locate his prey so far. His buddy at the police station said the man was being tracked by the FBI—or someone calling themselves the FBI—as well as the police and some heavy-duty criminal types. But so far, no one had found him. Not that that meant anything. He had a few tricks up his sleeve that the others did not.

He had spent years at this kind of work; it was what he did best. Finding someone others couldn't—someone who didn't want to be found. Some jobs took longer than others, but he never failed.

He didn't really need all this high-tech paraphernalia, but he was accustomed to it, and there was a certain comfort in it. As he had been told by his superiors so many times in the past: your best weapons are your eyes, your ears, your hands. Two skilled hands can kill more quickly, more efficiently, and with less chance of detection than all the electronic gizmos in the world.

He slid noiselessly out the door. Time to begin, before the trail became even colder. He had no actual clues to his target's location;

but he had contacts. Not much, but it would have to be enough. He had to find the man before the others did. If he got there last, or even second, it would be too late.

He slid behind the steering wheel of his Jeep and turned the ignition. He felt exhilarated to be back in action, doing something important. Perhaps more important than anything he had ever done before. He *would* complete this mission. Successfully.

And when he did, Travis Byrne would get exactly what he deserved.

# 35

9 : 45 P.M.

Travis smiled at Cavanaugh, who was securely taped to a kitchen chair. He dipped her wooden spoon into the pot he had taken from the stove and tasted the contents.

"Mmm," he murmured appreciatively. "What do you call this?"

Cavanaugh's reply was something like *blmflkmbtk*. It was the most the dishrag duct-taped in her mouth would allow.

"Bell-pepper soup? Whatever it is, it's good."

Cavanaugh bowed her head in acknowledgment.

"Who would've guessed that the tough lady prosecutor would be a great cook?" His eyebrows bounced up and down. "I wonder what other talents you've been hiding?"

Her reply was muffled but nonetheless forceful. Upon reflection, Travis was grateful that he couldn't understand what she was saying.

"Oh, I found your dog in the back room, hiding in the closet. Don't worry, I fed him. He's cute. Not exactly a Doberman, but cute."

Cavanaugh's eyes narrowed.

"I don't hate toy poodles the way some guys do. You know, some people would rather have a pet rat than one of those yippy yappers. Not me. I like them just fine."

He grinned, hoping she might return some indication of amiability. He was sorely disappointed.

"Maybe you're bored. Is that it? Look." He withdrew two large blue marbles from his coat pocket, placed them in his right palm, and held out his hands, knuckles up. He swirled his hands back and forth, over and under, up and down. "Okay, which hand are the marbles in?"

Cavanaugh's expression did not change.

"Look, I'm sorry about taping you up. You left me no choice."

Cavanaugh did not appear sympathetic.

"I'm not kidding. I didn't want to bother you. Really. I just wanted your help. If anyone can figure a way out of this mess, I thought, Cavanaugh can. Got any suggestions?"

Her only response was communicated through angry, glaring eyes.

Travis sighed. He dipped the spoon back in the pot and slurped more soup. "I feel guilty eating in front of you. Can I get you some milk or something? I promise not to poison it."

Cavanaugh kicked with both feet, then twisted from side to side, straining against her bonds. It was no use. She was securely fixed in place.

"If you agree not to scream, or call the police, or try to get away, I'll untie you. You wouldn't have to be civil to me. What d'ya say?"

No reaction.

"Oh well." He finished the soup, then sat on the floor, his arms folded across his lap. "I'm going to tell you everything that's happened to me since Moroconi busted out of jail. Maybe you can come up with some ideas. Okay?"

Cavanaugh glared at him with stony eyes.

"Okay. Good. Well, it began when I got this phone call in the middle of the night. . . ."

This time Kramer met Donny in the corridor outside Mario's office. He snuck up behind him, grabbed a suspender, then let it pop.

"*Owww!*" Donny cried.

Kramer grabbed Donny by the throat. "Whatcha been up to, Donny-boy?"

"Nothing. Nothing at all." His eyes looked as if they were about to pop out of his head. "You're hurting me."

"I know," Kramer replied. "That's why I got this shit-eatin' grin." He reached into his pocket with his free hand and removed a fistful of handwritten notes. "Look what I found."

"Hey! Those are mine! What were you doing in my desk?"

"Looking for backstabbing crap like this!" He threw the notes on the floor. "You've pushed your ass into my affairs once too often, Donny-boy."

Donny struggled futilely against Kramer's grip. "You can't hurt me. I'm family."

"So?"

"So you're nothing. You're just a sick bastard Uncle Mario uses to clean up shit too dirty for any normal—"

He never finished the sentence. Kramer's fist brought it to a premature conclusion. Donny fell to his knees, his hand pressed against his face, tears in his eyes.

"What is the meaning of this?"

It was Mario, standing just behind them.

"Just handlin' a little discipline problem," Kramer replied. "Nothin' important."

"He hurt me!" Donny cried, rubbing his jaw. "He's just mad because—"

"Silence!" Mario bellowed. "I've had all the petty bickering I can bear. Mr. Kramer, if I ever decide to hire you to enforce discipline within the family, I will let you know."

Kramer muttered something under his breath.

Mario bent down and retrieved the notes, glanced at them, then dropped them in a trash can. "Donny, surely you didn't think I needed you to set me straight?"

"I just wanted to keep a record. So you'd know why Kramer keeps screwing up."

Kramer's eyes widened, enraged. "You candy-assed son of a—"

Mario cut Kramer off with a wave of his hand. "If you ever hope to become a lieutenant, Donny, you must learn to follow instructions and observe the chain of command." He turned to face Kramer. "I must admit, however, that to a large extent I share Donny's concerns. Mr. Kramer, you have a reputation for efficiency that knows no bounds. As a result, you have been trusted with matters of great delicacy." His voice swelled in volume. "So why the hell can't you take care of *one* third-rate crook and *one* fucking lawyer?"

Kramer stuttered uncertainly. Mario interrupted before he could complete a word. "I don't care to hear your excuses." He placed his hand roughly against Kramer's chest, shoving him back. "One more chance, Mr. Kramer. That is all that remains to you. One more failure, and you will no longer have any association with this family. You will be invisible to us. Transparent. A ghost. Do you understand?"

Kramer didn't answer. His teeth were clenched tightly together.

"I said, *do you understand?*"

Kramer nodded his head slowly. "I understand."

"Perfect." Mario extended his hand to help Donny up, who was still lying on the floor.

"Thanks, Uncle Mario. I told you what a screwup he was—"

"Donny, shut up. You've been no more successful than Mr. Kramer. Indeed, I have to wonder whether your forced association with Mr. Kramer is the reason for his atypical incompetence."

"Uncle Mario!"

"I'm shipping you back to your mother, Donny. It pains me, but I must tell Monica you have no place in this family. Not as a lieutenant, not even as the lowliest foot soldier. Perhaps we can reconsider when you have matured, say, in thirty or forty years. But for now, I want no part of you. Goodbye."

*"But, Uncle Mario!"*

It was no use. Mario was already down the hall and out of sight.

Donny stared at Kramer, who was standing stiff as a board, obviously seething. He'd never seen anyone talk to Kramer like Mario just did. Served the bastard right.

He decided to run back to his room before Kramer snapped out of it and started slugging again. He wasn't going to pack, though. He couldn't believe Mario would really ship him back home. This was a warning, that's all. Shape up or ship out.

So he would shape up. He would prove to Uncle Mario that he could be a valuable asset to the organization. By accomplishing what Kramer could not.

He would kill Travis Byrne stone-cold dead. And not make a mess of it.

# FRIDAY

*April 19*

**37**

1 : 0 0 A . M .

Travis had recounted everything that had happened since Al Moroconi called him the night before. Cavanaugh listened quietly and patiently to the entire story—not that she really had any choice.

"So you see where I am," Travis concluded. "There's nowhere I can go. There's no one I can trust. Visiting friends would be fatal, both for them and me. So I came here."

Cavanaugh leaned forward, the dishrag still wedged in her mouth. "Mmmwhtantfmmmeeee?"

"I'm sorry," Travis said. "I missed the last part."

Cavanaugh kicked up her heels, sending the chair within inches of capsizing.

"For the millionth time, I'll take the rag out of your mouth if you won't scream. You don't have to help me. Just promise you won't try to attract any attention."

He waited a long time. Eventually, her head moved slowly up and down.

Travis crawled over beside her. "This is going to sting a little. Should I do it all at once, or slowly?"

She rolled her eyes.

In a quick jerk, he ripped the duct tape off her face. Cavanaugh made a noise, but it was muffled by the dishrag. He yanked it out of her mouth. "Does this mean you believe what I told you?"

"No," she replied curtly. "It means I'm tired of having a dirty dishrag in my mouth. *Blech!*" She rubbed the tip of her tongue against the roof of her mouth. "You could at least have used something clean."

"You didn't allow me much time to look around."

"That was the same towel I used to mop up the spilt soup!"

"So? I thought the soup was delicious."

"It's better on a spoon than a dishrag. I think you're totally delusional, Byrne. But even if what you say is true, what do you want from me?"

"I told you. I just need a place to crash for the night."

Cavanaugh glanced at the clock on the wall. "You've half-accomplished that goal already."

"Of course," he added, "any recommendations you could make would be greatly appreciated."

"I recommend counseling, Byrne. Intensive, psychiatric counseling. Shock therapy, perhaps."

Travis ignored her. "Didn't you say you used to be a skip tracer? You must know all kinds of dodges for finding people who have disappeared."

"That was a long time ago, Byrne."

"So? I've seen you in the courtroom. You have a great memory."

"For some things, yes. For others, no. That's a part of my life I try to block out."

"But this is an emergency—"

"Don't you hear what I'm saying, Byrne? This is not a part of my life I wish to remember. Do you have any idea what that might be like?"

Travis looked down suddenly. "I have . . . some idea, yes."

"Good. Then leave me alone. And get me the hell out of this chair."

"Do you promise not to try to get away?"

"Get away? I *live* here Byrne, remember?"

"I can't untie you unless you promise not to leave."

"Why not? Christ!" She struggled against the tape strapping her to the chair. "What's the matter? Are you afraid this hundred-and-five-pound woman will overpower you?"

"Frankly, yes. You damn near got away the last time we struggled. I'm not taking any chances." He smiled slightly. "After all, you are a martial-arts expert."

"This is probably how you get your cheap thrills. Bondage. S-and-M fantasies."

"Oh, please—"

"I bet that's it. I'm surprised you haven't been sitting over there jerking off."

"Such language. Next time I'll put a bar of soap in your mouth."

"Sicko."

This was the drawback to overpowering people and taping them to the kitchen furniture: they tended to be somewhat hostile afterward. "Look, I understand how you feel. Some guy you only know from the other side of the courtroom breaks into your apartment, and for all you know he may be a . . . a . . ."

"Psychosexual sadist who likes to tie women up?"

"Those weren't exactly the words I had in mind, but . . ." He cleared his throat. "The point is, I understand how you must feel, but I can't let you leave."

There was a long silence. Travis could feel her eyes scrutinizing him. It didn't matter. It was too late and he'd been at it too long. He was beyond caring.

"Okay," she said suddenly.

He looked up. "Okay what?"

"I promise not to turn you in. I promise I won't try to leave. Mother, may I please be untied?"

His eyes brightened. "Then you do believe me."

"Wrong. I'm just dead tired. In case you haven't noticed, it's after one in the morning, somewhat later than my usual bedtime. I'm weary to the bone, and I'm not likely to get any sleep duct-taped to a kitchen chair."

"Okay." Travis took a knife from the kitchen and cut the tape.

Cavanaugh rose slowly from her chair. Her knees creaked. "Oh God." She ripped the cut tape from her clothing. "Well, you can stay up all night if you want, Travis, but I'm going to bed. I have to work on another case tomorrow." She walked wearily toward the bedroom, then stopped. "You can sleep on the sofa if you like. It folds out."

"Thanks."

"I'll see you in the morning. Don't wake me. I plan to sleep in."

"I'll be as quiet as a mouse."

"And don't get the wrong idea, pal. This is for one night and one night only. As soon as the sun rises, you're out of here."

"Agreed." He hesitated. "And thanks. I really appreciate this."

"Don't get sentimental. I might change my mind yet." She closed her bedroom door.

He threw himself down on the sofa and tried to relax. It was no use. Whether he liked it or not, he had a thousand stray images racing through his head, a thousand loose ends, a thousand unanswered questions.

He took a legal pad from Cavanaugh's briefcase and started sketching a diagram of what had happened so far. He drew the FBI on the left, Moroconi on the right. But where did he put those men at the shopping mall? Were they with the FBI, or the police, or the mob? And who were the men at the West End? Where did they fit into his diagram?

He was dog tired, but he was never one who could rest first; he had to get the work done before he could even think about relaxing. Like in the poem, the woods were pretty damn dark and deep and he had miles to go before he could sleep.

He had to figure out what to do. Where to go. How to get himself out of this mess.

Before it was too late.

**38**

2 : 3 5 A . M .

Kramer cruised into the apartment-complex parking lot just off Forest Lane, lights dimmed. Sure enough, there it was—Travis Byrne's car. The license plate and description were both perfect matches.

His broad smile made the scar on the side of his face crinkle. This would show Mario. He had been certain his men would find the car eventually, but in truth he had thought it would take longer than this. Sometimes you just get lucky, he supposed. Of course, some of the luck could be attributed to the time-tested technique of putting the fear of death into a group of men who were basically spineless bootlickers. Part of the luck was also attributable to Byrne's own stupidity—why was he still in the Dallas metro area? If Kramer had been on the run, he'd be in Chicago by now. Maybe Paris.

Byrne's car was empty. Kramer slid a thin, long sheet of metal between the window glass and the car frame, pushed it down about a foot and a half, then jerked it to the right. He heard a popping noise that told him the lock had been sprung.

He crawled into the car and began rooting around. Nothing particularly suspicious—a change of clothes, an overcoat, a briefcase. Kramer popped open the briefcase and examined the contents. A lot of boring documents written on long legal paper. Some pens, pencils, yellow Post-Its. And a business card.

Now, that was interesting—Kramer had heard of Special Agent Henderson and knew what the man really did. Who had contacted Byrne, he wondered, and why? He slipped the card into his pocket.

Nothing else in the car seemed particularly noteworthy. Nothing indicated in which of the apartments Byrne was hiding.

Kramer considered his options. He could set the car on fire. That would be fun. That would give him great pleasure. And that might bring Byrne out of hiding.

On the other hand, he considered, it might just tip Byrne off and send him scurrying out the back window. No, he should figure out which of these apartments Byrne was in. Once he knew that, he could use a more direct approach. And if that didn't work, he thought, grinning, he could still blow the car to hell and back—with Byrne in it. That would be Plan B.

Yeah, that's the ticket. He strolled across the parking lot, crisscrossing toward the main office building. He casually passed the front door, glancing at the lock. Piece of cake. And the office would undoubtedly have files identifying every tenant. And from that list, he could likely deduce which apartment Byrne was in. He would just look for someone Byrne would be likely to know—a coworker, or a relative, or another lawyer. He'd start with the apartments nearest Byrne's car.

Kramer returned to his car. He checked the trunk and found all his favorite tools—cans of gasoline, lighter fluid, an incendiary blowtorch, cord. He examined a small brown box, barely three by four inches. Everything was there—a tiny triggering mechanism, a smidgen of plastic explosive, and four hundred nails. Ready to go. He crawled under Byrne's car and locked the box into place.

He'd get Byrne in the apartment, or later when he ran to his car. Either way Kramer would get him, and have a little fun in the process. And then he'd be in a position to make that fat fucker Mario regret talking to him like he did.

There were going to be a few surprises for Mr. Travis Byrne in the morning.

**39**

9:30 A.M.

Travis rolled over, groaning, and untangled his body from the living-room furniture.

"Pffst—wha—?" He had carpet hair in his mouth. He was lying on the floor in a twisted knot between the coffee table and the sofa. He stretched his legs and tried to remember when he had finally conked out. His neck and back were stiff; pins and needles shot through his legs. He might be awake, but his legs weren't.

He tiptoed into the kitchen, careful not to wake Cavanaugh. The cabinets were still littered with utensils and ingredients for the bell-pepper soup.

He wondered if Cavanaugh had anything for breakfast. He opened the refrigerator and found it well stocked: milk, orange juice, eggs, bacon. Much more than he could have found in his own kitchen. He congratulated himself for holing up with someone who cooked.

He decided to start with coffee. He couldn't find a coffeemaker, but he did locate a jar of instant. He pulled a brass teakettle out of the cupboard, filled it with water, and turned the heat up high.

The doorbell rang. He frowned. Who would be here at this time of—

He checked his watch. It was already nine-thirty. How could he have slept so late?

He rushed to the door, hoping he could get rid of whoever it was before Cavanaugh awoke. If she was aroused too early, she was certain to be grumpy. Come to think of it, she was certain to be grumpy in any case, but the less provocation the better.

He peered through the peephole. The face was unfamiliar—which was good. A tall, medium-sized white male in a spiffy-looking blue suit and tie.

"Package," the man said.

Why would someone be delivering a package? Then it dawned on him—Cavanaugh had said she was going to work on a new case. She probably had the files couriered to her apartment to save herself the trouble of lugging them.

He shook his head; he really was getting paranoid. No one could possibly know he was here.

He opened the door. "Hello."

The man smiled politely. "Good morning. I'm delivering some documents for"—he glanced at the label—"Laverne Cavanaugh."

Travis grinned. No wonder everyone called her by her last name. "I'll take it."

"I'm afraid I need a signature."

"But she's still asleep."

"That's all right. You can sign for her." He handed Travis a pen.

Travis took the pen and started to sign Cavanaugh's name. "Uh-oh." He turned the pen upside down and shook it, but nothing happened. "Out of ink."

"Hell," the courier said. "I'll have to go back to my car and get another one."

"That's all right. There must be another pen somewhere around here. Let me look."

"Hey, thanks," the man said.

"No problem." Travis returned to the living room. The courier stepped inside and closed the door.

Travis tried to find the pen he had been drawing diagrams with last night, without success. Probably lost somewhere in the depths of Cavanaugh's shag carpet, he mused. He went into the kitchen and began opening drawers—everyone had a few thousand pens in a slovenly kitchen drawer, didn't they?

Travis returned to the living room. "I found—" The courier was gone. Come to think of it, why did the man come inside? And why did he shut the door? Unless—

Travis whirled around, much too late. He took a sucker punch in the soft part of his stomach, exactly where he had been hit a few days before in the men's room.

Travis fell to his knees, struggling to maintain consciousness. The courier's knee rose sharply and struck him under the chin. Travis fell backward, striking his head on the floor. He peered up blurry-eyed at his attacker. The man reached inside his attaché and withdrew a medium-sized gun with a silencer.

Travis commanded his fog-filled head to clear. By God, he wasn't going to let another two-bit bully get the drop on him. He caught the man's foot just before it struck his rib cage. He pulled, sharp and hard; his assailant lost his balance and fell back into the kitchen. The man clutched the counter to keep from falling. Travis crawled after him and punched him in the side.

Travis grabbed the hand holding the gun and pressed his thumbs down on the pressure points. The courier screamed and dropped the gun. Travis kicked it into the living room.

The man jerked open a drawer, searching for anything he could use as a weapon. He found a battery-operated carving knife. Damn Cavanaugh and her upscale kitchen appliances! In an instant the man had flicked the power switch. The knife roared to life.

Travis moved away as quickly as possible. An ordinary knife would be frightening enough—anything that made a noise like that he definitely did not want to come into contact with. The courier was waving the knife wildly back and forth, advancing like

D'Artagnan, pressing Travis against the stove. Travis realized that he had run out of room to maneuver. The man with the knife was barely a foot away from his face.

Travis grabbed the teakettle he had put on to boil. Ignoring the heat radiating from the brass handle, he threw the boiling water at his assailant. The man ducked, but not quite fast enough. He cried out as the water scalded his face.

"Son of a bitch!" the man shouted. He clutched his face. "You'll pay for that." The man advanced again with the knife; Travis held out the kettle as a shield. He searched for a potential weapon, but there was nothing within reach more dangerous than a plastic place mat.

The courier forced Travis into the living room. Travis dodged the sofa but slipped on the papers he'd left lying out the night before. He plummeted onto the coffee table, shattering the glass top. The man grinned malevolently and lowered the knife. . . .

Suddenly, out of the corner of his eye, Travis saw Cavanaugh swing her briefcase directly into the back of the man's head. The carving knife took flight; Travis ducked as it soared over his head. The man fell to his knees, eyelids fluttering. Cavanaugh hit him again, then once more for good measure. He fell in a crumpled heap on the floor.

It took Travis several seconds to gain some semblance of his normal voice. "Good morning," he said finally.

" 'Morning," Cavanaugh replied. She was wearing a shimmering blue nightie. "Sleep well?"

"Not bad. It was the wake-up call that was rough."

"So I see."

"I thought you were asleep."

"I was, till you two started clattering around in the kitchen."

"My apologies."

"Well, under the circumstances, you're forgiven."

Just as Cavanaugh finished her absolution the courier jumped up and tackled her from behind, knocking her onto Travis. The man raced out the front door.

Travis felt Cavanaugh's warm skin through the nightie as she lay on top of him. She was surprisingly soft for such a likely bulemia candidate. "I'm going after him."

Cavanaugh grabbed his arm, pulling his back. "Don't be a fool. If one goon found you, there could be others. And they might all be waiting outside."

"If they know where I am, I've got to leave."

"Granted. But let's get organized before we make a break for it. If we run out half-cocked, we'll get creamed."

"We?" His eyebrows rose. "Does this mean—"

She rummaged through her closet and pulled out a duffel bag. "It means you've successfully dragged me into whatever the hell trouble you're in."

"I can't let you come with me. It's too dangerous."

"What am I going to do, stay here and wait for the next hit man?"

Travis frowned. He didn't like the conclusion, but her logic was incontrovertible. "All right," he said. "Get dressed. The sooner we're out of here, the better."

# 40

9:45 A.M.

Donny strolled into the apartment parking lot, eyes twitching every which way at once. He didn't see Kramer, but with a psychopath like him, it was best to exercise caution.

This was Donny's big chance to prove himself to Mario. Kramer was on his way out; Donny would step forward as his replacement. A *made man*. A lieutenant. After he heard one of Kramer's men had found Travis's car, he never let Kramer out of his sight. He trailed him from a respectful distance; he was certain Kramer hadn't spotted him.

He'd followed Kramer to the parking lot, then waited in his car for almost four hours until Kramer left. Fool. Kramer was probably planning some elaborate execution; Donny would nail Byrne before Kramer returned. It was simple, really. All he had to do was watch Byrne's car, and when he returned to it, Donny would blow his face off. He patted the stolen gun in his coat pocket. Simple.

Donny tried the car door. To his surprise, it was unlocked. He crawled into the front seat and looked around. Nothing particularly unusual, except that it was a mess. Fast-food bags all over the floor, moldy french fries in the crevices of the seats. A briefcase, but nothing inside but the usual shyster paraphernalia. He looked for a car key but didn't find one. Even Byrne was smart enough not to leave that lying around.

He crawled out of the car. As he emerged a yellow Dodge Omni whipped past him.

*Whaaat?* He crossed through the parked cars to catch another glimpse of the Omni as it passed down the other side. This time he saw him clearly. Travis Byrne was sitting in the passenger seat.

Damn! Some goddamn bimbo was driving; he must've hijacked a ride. Donny wanted to slap himself; he should've seen that coming. But there was no time for self-recrimination now. To salvage anything out of this mess, to prevent Mario from shipping him home to his mother, he was going to have to follow that car.

He had parked his own car a good distance away so it wouldn't be seen. If he ran to it, he had no chance of catching Byrne. Instead he leaped back into Byrne's car and started groping around under the steering wheel. Most of the technical aspects of criminal life eluded Donny, but the one thing he was able to do was hotwire a car. He'd been doing it since he was twelve. Most of his teenage income had derived from this lucrative pursuit.

He found the critical wires under the steering column, jerked the red wire free, and touched it to the green. The engine turned over like a dream.

Donny smiled. He hadn't lost the old touch. He'd catch Byrne and the bitch before they passed through the entrance gate.

Still smiling, Donny thrust the automatic transmission into reverse, heard an odd clicking noise, and watched as the world turned into a haze of molten white. He never heard the explosion, and was spared the realization that he would never become a lieutenant.

**41**

9:55 A.M.

The shock waves threw Travis against the dash of Cavanaugh's car. Cavanaugh slammed on the brakes.

"What the hell was that?"

Travis clutched the passenger seat, trying to regain his bearings. "I dunno," he said dully. He turned around and saw a cloud of smoke billowing from the parking lot, the same section in which he had parked. "But I'm suddenly very glad we're in your car and not mine."

Travis pulled his jacket close around him. He was feeling a distinct chill. How many more close shaves could he possibly hope to escape? He'd like to think he was surviving on his wits, bringing to bear years of police training, experience, and acquired wisdom. But he had a nagging suspicion that he had just been lucky. And this kind of luck wouldn't hold out forever.

"We need to go someplace safe," he said quietly.

"Such as? As far as I can tell, no place is safe as long as I'm with you. You need to figure out who the hell is trying to kill you."

"Thanks, Einstein."

"The way I see it, your link is Moroconi. He's the one known factor. We know what he is, we know what he looks like."

"True. But we don't know where he is."

"And that, my friend, is why you need a skip tracer."

"What are you saying?"

"You've gotten me messed up in this but good. It's only a matter of time before they figure out I'm with you and start looking for me. And my car. If they could find you at my place, somewhere you've never been before in your entire life, in less than twelve hours—well, it won't take them long to find me."

Travis looked at himself reproachfully in the mirror. He hated to admit it, but she was right. He had involved her. He'd put her life in danger just as surely as his own.

"We need some answers, Byrne. And quick. And for that, we need Moroconi. Do you know his phone number?"

"Sure," Travis said. "Just dial *M* for Murderer."

"I take it that's a *no*. Fortunately, I have an inkling how we might find him."

Travis felt a swelling in his chest. For the first time since the dawn of this nightmare, he had some small hope that he might survive it. "How do we start?"

"By checking the phone records on that call Moroconi made to you night before last."

"How? By strolling casually into Southwestern Bell?"

"Just let me take care of that, Byrne." She pressed down on the accelerator and merged onto the LBJ Freeway. She pulled into the fast lane, hit her best cruising speed, and opened the console between the seats.

"What are you looking for?"

"The phone," she muttered. She yanked out an old floppy fishing hat, complete with lures hooked around the brim.

"You like to fish?" Travis asked.

"I *live* to fish," Cavanaugh replied.

"Really?"

"Is that so incredible?"

184 ■ WILLIAM BERNHARDT

"Well ... you always seemed more the white-wine-and-croissant type to me."

Cavanaugh rolled her eyes. "I may surprise you."

"You already have."

She withdrew a small handheld tape recorder. "I use this to take notes sometimes," she explained.

"I've seen you talking into it in court. I always assumed you were calling me names."

"You may have been right." She slipped the tape recorder inside her purse, then reached back into the console and withdrew a small portable phone. She clipped it onto her dash and plugged it into the lighter. Then she pressed a series of fifteen numbers.

"Who are you calling?" Travis inquired.

"An old friend. He owes me a big favor. And he works for the phone company." After a momentary clicking, Travis heard the line ringing.

"Hello? Crescatelli here."

"John? It's your old pal Cavanaugh."

"Cavanaugh? Hey, it's been a while. I heard you went legit."

"Yeah, yeah. Listen, John, I don't have time to play 'Auld Lang Syne.' I need help. I'm in trouble, see. Very dangerous players are looking for me, including perhaps certain law enforcement agencies, and you'd be in big trouble if anyone found out you were talking to me."

There was a brief pause, a few clicks, then: "What's that? I'm sorry, there must be some static on the line. Who is this again?"

Cavanaugh smiled. "Bless you."

It sounded like Crescatelli was blowing into the receiver. "Damn these car phones. The reception is horrible. Who's calling, please?"

"John, I need access to a central switchboard computer terminal with the records for the last forty-eight hours for all lines in the greater Dallas/Fort Worth area. Like, for example, the one you're probably sitting in front of. And I need to make calls without being traced."

Crescatelli pounded the phone against something solid. "I can't believe this crappy reception. It's these new fiber-optic cables, you know. They don't work worth beans. Look, whoever this is, I expect to be at my terminal until six o'clock tonight, but between twelve-thirty and one-thirty everyone else in the office goes to lunch, so I'll be here all by my lonesome. If you can't get a better connection, you might consider coming by in person."

Cavanaugh nodded. "Maybe I will. Talk to you later, John." She pushed the red button, disconnecting the line.

"Travis," she asked, "how would you like to pay a visit to the inner bowels of Ma Bell?"

# 42

12:40 P.M.

Travis stood in the midst of row after row of electronic switching equipment and tried to act more comfortable than he really was. He didn't think anyone would recognize him; he was certain he'd never been here before. Somehow, though, that didn't make him feel a bit safer. He'd never been to Cavanaugh's apartment before, either, but that didn't prevent them from finding him.

He was hiding behind dark sunglasses and beneath the brim of Cavanaugh's fairly ridiculous fishing hat. Sure, it shaded his face, but he wondered if it didn't attract more attention than it deflected. And it clashed with his necktie.

John Crescatelli was a jumbo-sized man whose fingers skidded across his computer keyboard at a speed faster than the eye could follow. The terminal was connected by shiny metal cables to a series of metal boxes, each equipped with flashing lights, buttons, and LED displays. To Travis, the place looked like a set from *Star Trek*, but Cavanaugh assured him it was all standard-issue telecommunications equipment.

"As I mentioned on the phone," Cavanaugh said, "I need to be able to make phone calls that cannot be traced."

Crescatelli nodded, apparently nonplussed. "May I ask why?"

"No. And let me remind you that I am not here, I never was here, you've never talked to me, you don't know who I am, and you wouldn't help me if you did."

"Roger." He gazed at the ceiling. "Someday I must seek a cure for this dreadful habit of talking to myself. I guess it stems from the fact that I'm fundamentally a lonely person."

Cavanaugh smirked. "We'll stand behind this row of beeping gizmos, just in case someone wanders in early from lunch."

Crescatelli continued to stare at the ceiling. "What was that sound? The wind? Man, they really need to do something about the drafts in here." He shuffled the papers on his desk. "Maybe this would be a good time to start outlining my doctoral dissertation—just in case I ever decide to go to college. In order to make an untraceable call, you need to understand about tandems."

Cavanaugh scribbled into her notepad. "Tandems. That rings a bell."

"The tandem is the key to the whole Bell telephone switching system. Each tandem is a carrier line with relays capable of switching other tandems in any toll-switching office in North America, either one-to-one or by programming a roundabout route through other tandems. If you call from Dallas to Tulsa and the traffic is heavy on all the direct trunks between the two cities, the tandem automatically reroutes you through the next best route, say for instance, through a tandem down in Shreveport or Houston, then up to Denver, then Wichita, then back to Tulsa."

"Thanks for the fascinating background info," Cavanaugh muttered. "So how do you make the untraceable call?"

"When a tandem is not in use, it whistles."

Travis blinked. "Whistles? Like Yankee Doodle Dandy?"

"Mental note," Crescatelli said. "Remove all frivolous asides from dissertation before publication. Anyway, when a caller dials a long-distance number, he is immediately connected to a tandem. The tandem stops whistling and converts the number into multi-frequency beep tones, then transmits the tones to the tandem in the area code the caller wishes to reach."

"Yeah, yeah, yeah," Cavanaugh said. "I've got the general idea. Get on to the good stuff."

"You would think this system is utterly immune to interference—who could talk to a tandem? No one could—until someone invented the first blue box." Crescatelli reached into his bottom desk drawer and withdrew a small blue metal shell case. "You see, Ma Bell got careless. She allowed some egghead on the East Coast to publish an article in a technical journal which, in passing, revealed the actual frequencies Bell uses to create those multifrequency tones. Who'd have thought anyone would notice? Well, one squid at MIT read that issue. And half a day later he'd created the first blue box."

Crescatelli flipped open a panel on the box to reveal a numeric keypad similar to that found on a telephone receiver. "Of course, Bell subsequently had all issues of that journal yanked from every library in the country. But it was too late. The entire AT&T switching system operates on twelve electronically generated combinations of six master tones—those are the tones you hear sometimes after you dial a long-distance number. The tone for each number is a combination of two fixed tones played simultaneously to create a certain beat frequency. Once those frequencies became public knowledge, all a guy had to do was get a Casio keyboard and a tape deck and record the tones. Play back the recording into a phone receiver and presto!—you've made a long-distance phone call without touching the dial."

Cavanaugh was writing frenetically. "So your tape recorder can now make a long-distance call, something I could've done with my fingers. So what?"

Crescatelli shook his head. "I suppose for certain doubting Thomases it will be necessary to explain every little step. Remember the tandem networks? The blue box is programmed with tones that emulate the inactive whistling of a tandem. When the blue-box operator wants to call from Dallas to Tulsa, he might start by calling a toll-free number in Ypsilanti. The tandem in Ypsilanti is seized and starts listening to the beep tones that tell it which number to ring. Meanwhile, a mark is made on the Dallas office accounting tape noting that a call from your number to the Ypsilanti toll-free number has been initiated. The blue-box operator then sends a tone that emulates the inactive whistling of the tandem. The tandem assumes the caller has hung up and stops ringing the toll-free number. As soon as the blue-box operator stops sending the signal, the Ypsilanti tandem assumes the trunk is again being used and listens for a new series of tones to tell it where to call. The blue-box operator beeps out another number, say to Poughkeepsie."

"Why would anyone call Poughkeepsie?" Travis whispered. Cavanaugh swatted him.

"The tandem relays the call. The blue-box operator can go on like this indefinitely, whistling his way from one tandem to the next, till he decides to connect with his ultimate destination. When he does, he can talk as long as he wants—'cause it's all going to be charged to the owner of that first toll-free number. More importantly, for the purpose of those on the lam, the call cannot be traced by normal methods, and even abnormal high-tech methods will require much longer than usual."

"Why is that?"

"Say someone has a trace on the receiving phone; his trace won't run back to the caller's phone—he'll go back to the last tandem in the chain—and then the one before that, and the one before that, and so on and so on. Slowly. Eventually he'll get back to the caller's phone, but I'd like to think most people would have the sense not to talk that long."

Travis whispered to Cavanaugh, "Did you get all that? Or any of that?"

"Enough," she said, nodding.

"As any fool can see," Crescatelli continued, "this information could easily be put to nefarious purposes, especially by cheapskates who don't want to give the phone company its due. Come to think of it, it would probably be irresponsible to write this dissertation. I think I'll scrap the whole idea." He sighed. "What the heck. I'll probably never go to college anyway."

Cavanaugh stepped out from behind the machinery and quietly slipped the blue box into her purse. "You're a gem and a half, John, but you've only taken me halfway home. How can I trace a phone call made in the past—one that's already been disconnected? And don't tell me it can't be done. I work for the federal prosecutor's office. I know it can."

"Then again," Crescatelli reflected, still staring at the ceiling, "there might be some legitimate uses for the article I envision. After all, once you understand about tandems, there isn't much you can't do with the phone system. Every major city has a central accounting computer that maintains their phone records. Of course, this is done for billing purposes, not out of any desire to aid law enforcement officials, but it does come in handy when the police want to know everyone who's called a particular line within a given time period."

"How do we access the central computer?"

Crescatelli batted a finger against his lips. "How does one access the central computer? Well, if you have a modem, you do it just like you call anyone else. All you have to know is the number."

"Then we need the number of the central accounting computer for Dallas," Travis said.

"Fortunately," Crescatelli said, "the number of the Dallas computer, now displayed on this terminal screen, is totally top secret. I shudder to think what might happen if an unscrupulous person got hold of it."

Cavanaugh jotted down the number.

Crescatelli punched a few more numbers on his terminal. "While I've been sitting here musing I've managed to take the phone line connected by modem to this computer through eighteen tandems crisscrossing the United States. Not absolutely necessary, but it would be best if this inquiry were not easily traced back here, just in case someone should become suspicious. Of course, I'm just doing it to remind myself how it's done. Anybody could call on this line now and it couldn't be traced back for twenty years."

Crescatelli stood, stretched, and yawned. "All this brain work is tiring. I'm going to get a Coke. Maybe a doughnut, too." He pushed his chair back and sauntered toward the kitchen.

"A prince among men," Cavanaugh whispered as she slid into his chair.

"No kidding," Travis said. "You must've saved that guy's life."

She began punching keys on the terminal keyboard. "As a matter of fact, I did."

"How?"

"Oh . . . it's a long story."

"So shorten it."

"Before John went legit, which was before John was John, he was a phone phreak. That's with a *ph*."

"What's a phone phreak?"

"A telephone hacker. Used blue boxes and other devices to help friends make freebie long-distance phone calls. Not exactly admirable, but hardly a crime against humanity. Despite the fact that he was married, had one baby and another on the way, the phone company decided to make an example of him. John went underground. I was assigned to find him. I didn't."

"You mean, you did, but you didn't turn him in."

"Whatever. John is basically a good man, and I didn't think an entire family should be destroyed just because Daddy made a dumb mistake he'll never repeat. I've always had a soft spot for underdogs." She looked at Travis awkwardly, then returned her attention to the terminal. "Did you follow all that rigmarole about switching tandems?"

"Not by a long shot."

"Then watch." She keyed up the modem and punched in the number on the computer screen. After a few moments they heard a typically shrill recorded operator voice say: "You have reached the central accounting records for area code 214. If you wish to make an inquiry, press one. If you wish—"

Cavanaugh pressed one.

"Please dial the number you wish records displayed for at the sound of the tone." After a short pause they heard a beeping noise. "What's your phone number, Byrne?"

He told her. "Why?"

"Just wait and see."

Almost immediately, the screen filled with a long list of dates and times, each numbered sequentially. Beside the time and date stamp was a numeric indication of the length of the call.

"Good Lord!" Travis exclaimed. "That's every phone call I've received in the past week!"

"Right you are."

"What an enormous invasion of privacy."

"You're wrong, if only because your *privacy* was an illusion. Big Brother has been watching all along. You just didn't realize it. Anyway, did you answer any calls after Moroconi phoned you?"

"No. I haven't been there."

"Good. Then we just need to take down the number of the last completed call to your phone." She punched the number up. Travis noted that the date and time corresponded to Moroconi's call. Cavanaugh highlighted the entry, then pressed the return key.

"Please hold," the computer said.

Cavanaugh withdrew the tape recorder from her purse and pushed the record button. A few seconds later they heard the seven beeps of a phone number, as if dialed on a Touch-Tone phone.

"Thank you," the recorded voice said.

"Bingo!" Cavanaugh exclaimed. She disconnected the phone line. "We got it."

"We got what?" Travis asked, mystified. "A bunch of beeps?"

"Boy, you're not following this at all, are you? How did anyone so slow-witted ever beat me so many times in court?" She rewound the tape, lifted the receiver on the desktop phone console, and played the beeps back into the receiver. After a few clicking noises, they heard the line ring.

Cavanaugh grinned proudly. "Can I cook, or can I cook?"

Someone lifted the phone on the other end of the line. "Million Dollar Motel." The voice had a foreign accent. "Can I help you?"

Cavanaugh's eyebrows bounced up and down. "What room is Al Moroconi in?"

"Moroconi." They heard some shuffling of papers on the other end of the line. "There is no Moroconi here."

Travis took the phone. "He's a medium-sized, dark-haired guy, with greasy skin and an unpleasant expression."

"Oh, yes. I know the gentleman. He did not register under that name."

"Big surprise."

"If you can hold on, I will connect you to his room."

"No, no, no," Travis said quickly. "I want to surprise him. Just give me his room number."

"Oh, no, sir. So sorry, but I am not permitted to disclose that information."

Travis's voice deepened. "Look, this is Sergeant Abel T. Stoneheart of the Dallas Police Force, badge number 714, and if you don't give me that room number in five seconds flat, I'll send a platoon of squad cars out to search every room in your place. Including your office."

There was an audible drawing of breath on the other end of the line.

"They'll be there in less than five minutes," Travis added. "Think you can clean up that quickly?"

The desk clerk cleared his throat. "I believe the man you are looking for is in Room 14."

"Fine. We're on our way. And you'd damn well better not tip him off before we arrive, or I might bring you in for questioning in his place. That could take days. And I've heard the strip search is particularly unpleasant this time of year."

The man's voice became a dry, raspy whisper. "I understand, Sergeant, sir. My lips are sealed."

"Keep it that way." Travis slammed down the receiver. "See? I learned something in my former life, too."

"Right. Deception and intimidation."

As if on cue, Crescatelli wandered back into the room. Travis and Cavanaugh skittered away from his terminal.

"Oh, my goodness," Crescatelli said. "I left my terminal up. With all those tandems connected. I'd better clear those out right away." He punched a few keys. The screen went blank.

"Well, that takes care of that," Crescatelli said. "Whatever I was connected to, there's no trace of it now."

Cavanaugh put her hands on his shoulders, leaned forward, and kissed him on the cheek. "Thanks a million, John. We're even now."

He shook his head. "Not by a long shot. But we're closer."

She smiled and kissed him again.

"What was that?" Crescatelli asked. "I felt a sudden breeze against my cheek. I'm going to *have* to talk to the guys in Climate Control. It's always too hot or too cold, and the thermostats are no help. Nothing around here ever works."

# 43

2 : 4 5 P.M.

C avanaugh exited Belt Line Road and eased her Omni into the parking lot of the Million Dollar Motel, careful not to attract undue attention. After all, they probably weren't the only people in town looking for Alberto Moroconi.

The Million Dollar Motel appeared to have been financed with approximately one one-millionth of the funds specified in its name. A wire fence restricted access to the rooms in theory, but the fence was broken by so many vandal-cut holes as to make it ridiculously ineffective. The swimming pool was coated with green fungi; it looked as if it hadn't held more than puddles of rainwater in years. The ugly pink paint was peeling; leaden flecks curled away from the walls. Travis wondered if the place didn't fulfill the legal description of a toxic-waste dump. He was not surprised to find that, as its flickering neon sign announced, there were VAC NCI S.

"So," Cavanaugh said, after she parked her car near Room 14, "you think your client would hole up at this ersatz Bates Motel?"

"I think it reeks of Moroconi's personal style. Emphasis on
*reeks*."

"Okay. What's our plan?"

"Our plan?" Travis shrugged. "I suppose we're going to bust the
door open and grab Moroconi by the short hairs before he has a
chance to slither away."

"Once a cop, always a cop. And people wonder why prosecutors
lose so many cases on technicalities."

"I'm not trying to build a federal case. I'm trying to extract information from a walking waste pile who's standing trial for a sex-
ual felony and is wanted for murder. This guy has very little to
lose. If you stop to read him his Miranda rights, you might as well
kiss your pretty little butt goodbye."

She gave him a withering look. "I suppose that's a compliment,
of sorts. But I plan to ignore it. Okay, Dick Tracy, you do the
busting, I'll bring up your rear."

They scanned the outer perimeter of the motel, saw no one,
and stepped out of the car. Travis held back the fence while
Cavanaugh stepped through a conveniently placed hole. He
glanced at the desk clerk, visible through the large bay window in
the front office. He appeared to be reading a magazine and didn't
notice them.

Travis and Cavanaugh silently approached Room 14. Travis
aimed his foot at the door.

"Don't you think we should knock first?" Cavanaugh whispered.

"No." Travis kicked the door just below the doorknob. The
thin, warped plywood splintered and cracked down the middle.
Travis kicked again, this time opening a hole wide enough for his
arm. He reached through, turned the knob, and unlocked the
door.

He burst into the room just in time to see someone crawling
beneath the bedcovers. Travis dove onto the bed, throwing his
arms around the cloaked figure.

"Don't bother trying to get away, Moroconi. I've got you." His captive squirmed and kicked, trying to get free of the bedspread and Travis. Cavanaugh tried to help, to little effect. Despite their best efforts, one foot got free of the covers and kicked Travis between the legs. Fortunately, the aim wasn't exact.

"Damn it, Moroconi, hold still!" Travis shouted. He ripped the bedspread away—to find a dark-haired teenage girl wearing a black lace teddy and too much makeup. What's worse, her face was familiar.

"This is Moroconi?" Cavanaugh asked. "He's changed a lot since he got out of the slammer."

"Not hardly," Travis said, staring at the girl. "Where is he?"

"Al? I dunno." The girl looked puzzled; then, suddenly, a smile of recognition appeared. "Hey, you're the sex weirdo."

Cavanaugh raised an eyebrow. "I take it you two have met?"

Travis took the girl roughly by the arm, and scrutinized her face. *Yes*—it was the same scantily clad young woman who had waltzed into his apartment two nights before. "What are you doing here?"

She lifted her chin defiantly. "This is my room. What are *you* doing here?"

Travis pressed her back against the headboard. "We don't have time to play around. Where the hell is Moroconi?"

"You're hurting me."

"I could do a lot worse. Where is he?"

"I'm not sure," she said, squirming. "He left sometime last night."

Travis pushed her away and crawled off the bed. "Is he coming back?"

She rubbed her arm. "I don't think so. He took all his stuff."

Travis paced back and forth beside the bed. "And what's your story? Who are you, his long-lost sister?"

Cavanaugh looked pointedly at Travis. "Somehow I don't think that's the answer," she said, popping a lace garter beneath the girl's teddy.

Travis's face flushed red. "How long have you known Al?"

"Since night before last."

"Night before last? The same night you were in my apartment? The night he broke out of jail?"

"Al broke out of jail?" She covered her mouth with her hands. "Omigod. Are you a cop?"

Travis intentionally failed to answer. "How did you meet him?"

"I was on my usual corner downtown late that night, after I left your place. Al drove up in a pickup and asked if I wanted a date."

"I thought so," Travis said. "You're a—"

"I'm a private entrepreneur," she interrupted.

"Right."

Cavanaugh sat down on the bed beside the girl. "Relax, kid, we're not cops. We won't bother you, we won't report you. We just need to know as much about your trick as possible."

The girl seemed considerably relieved. "Well, he's about five foot seven with black hair—"

"We know what he looks like," Travis barked. "What else can you tell us?"

"Well, he's heavily into bondage, and his favorite snack is edible panties—"

Travis turned away, thoroughly disgusted. He spotted a pair of handcuffs dangling from the headboard of the bed. "We don't want to hear about his kinky ..." Travis searched for the right word, but it wasn't in his vocabulary. "We want to know about his other activities. Do you have any idea where he's gone, or what he's been doing?"

"He was gone for several hours yesterday. That's all I know."

"He must've said something when the two of you were together."

"Mostly it was just grunting noises."

Travis pressed his fingers against his temples. "If Moroconi isn't coming back, why are you still here?"

The girl shrugged. "Checkout time's not until three o'clock, and the room's paid for. It's a decent place. Lot nicer than where I usually stay."

To say the least. Travis silently swore. Sometimes, Travis Byrne, you are an insensitive son of a bitch. She was obviously just a pawn in this scenario. And how could he help but feel sorry for anyone who thought the Million Dollar Motel was a pleasant change of scenery?

"Look," he said more quietly, "are you sure you can't think of anything that might help us find . . . Al?"

She shook her head.

"One more question. Who sent you to me the other night?"

"I dunno. Someone had the money delivered, then called on a pay phone and gave me your address. I assumed you were calling the shots, till you started acting so strange."

"So you just go to any address someone phones in, without checking first?"

She drew her shoulders back. "Most people are delighted to see me. Most normal people."

"You don't ask your employers many questions."

"My employers prefer it that way."

"Okay, okay. Why don't you collect your belongings and leave."

"Do I have to?"

"Yeah. We're not the only ones looking for your buddy Al. But we're the only ones who don't carry big guns."

"Oh. Okay. I'll go." She jumped off the bed, then hesitated. "I don't suppose you'd be interested in a quick date?"

Travis stammered incoherently.

"If you'd like," Cavanaugh said dryly, "I could step outside."

"We could do whatever you like," the girl added.

Travis shook his head. "No, really . . ."

"I could call a friend. You know, two at once."

"Uhh, no . . ."

"We could use this." She reached under the bed and withdrew a foot-long wooden handle with long gossamer-looking angel hair dangling beneath.

A profound line creased Travis's brow. "What on earth is that?"

"It's the Cosmic Spider." She leaned forward and whispered the rest into his ear.

"Good Lord! That's . . . that's . . ."

She giggled. "It's kinda fun, actually."

"Look, miss, you really need to get out of here."

"You like guys, don't you? I should have known. The only time I get turned down is when the trick likes boys better."

"I do not like boys better. I mean, I don't like them at all. I mean—"

Cavanaugh stepped between them. "I hate to break up this beautiful moment, but why don't we let the teenager report back to her boss? You and I can search for any clues Al might've left behind."

"Right, right." Travis reached for his wallet. "Look, here's sixty bucks. I'm sorry it's not more, but I'm tight on cash right now and I may need—"

"Oh, no," the girl said. "I never accept handouts. I'm a working girl."

"It's not a handout. It's compensation for your illuminating information. And an apology for the rough stuff on the bed."

"That's all right," she said, snatching the cash from his hand. "I'm used to it."

# 44

### 3:00 P.M.

The man in the black stocking cap slowly approached the yellow Dodge Omni, shielding himself from the view of the desk clerk in the front office. If his contacts back at Orpha's Lounge were right, and Moroconi had stayed here, he was gone now. Using his binoculars, he scanned the parking lot. No black pickup.

There did appear to be someone in Moroconi's room—someone who wanted to be there badly enough to break down the door. A barely dressed teenage girl had just left the room. He didn't recognize her—hotel whore, probably. But who was inside?

He crept closer and listened to the voices in the room. It sounded as if they were searching; probably trying to determine where Moroconi had gone. He didn't recognize the female voice, but he was certain the man was Travis Byrne.

He touched the shoulder holster attached to his Kevlar vest. He slowly removed the gun, keeping it out of sight inside his jacket. He could slip inside the room, take care of Byrne, and slip out again. No one would be the wiser. Perhaps this mission would be easier than he had anticipated.

He started toward the door, then hurriedly retreated to the shadows. Someone was leaving the front office and walking briskly toward Room 14. He shouldn't have procrastinated; he should've just gone in there and—

Well, it was too late now. The desk clerk was probably investigating the gaping hole in the door. He'd call the cops soon, if he hadn't already. It wasn't safe to be here any longer.

He eased his gun back into the holster, then opened one of the compartments on his Sam Browne belt and removed the tiny SSI tracer. He quickly crept into the backseat of the Omni. It would be better to hide the tracer among their personal belongings; they might be tempted to switch cars later. He opened a black leather briefcase and slipped the device inside.

The tracer had a range of twenty miles. Now he'd be able to follow them from a distance, with no risk of being spotted. Never mind this temporary setback—his time would come.

And when it did, Travis Byrne's time would come to an end.

## 45

### 3 : 1 5 P.M.

After the girl left, Travis and Cavanaugh searched every cranny of Moroconi's motel room. They tried to be as thorough as possible while still remembering that their entrance had been less than subtle and was bound to attract attention, possibly from the police.

Travis ransacked the bathroom while Cavanaugh rummaged through the closets. "So," she said, "last night when you gave me the story of your recent life, you somehow omitted your encounter with that cute little tartlet."

Travis made an indistinct coughing noise.

"Care to explain how you ran into the juvenile jailbait?"

"A criminal attorney comes into contact with people from all walks of life. . . ."

"Don't tell me she's a client, Byrne. Dan Holyfield wouldn't let her through the office door. I somehow got the feeling you and she had a more prolonged, intimate acquaintance."

"Well, you were wrong. It was a very brief, bizarre acquaintance." He reflected for a moment. "Although, in light of what's happened since, it's beginning to make more sense."

Cavanaugh wriggled under the bed and grabbed something soft and rubbery. "Perhaps Moroconi hasn't gone too far," she said. "He left his tennis shoes." The well-worn tennies were filthy and riddled with holes; she held them at arm's length by the tips of her fingers.

Travis emerged from the bathroom. "He left a half-empty shampoo bottle, too, but I hardly think we can expect him to return for it. Especially after he sees what I did to the front door."

"Here you go, Byrne." Cavanaugh tossed the tennies to him. "They look like they might be your size."

Travis caught them, then grimaced. "These are disgusting. I'm dumping them." He dropped the shoes into the trash can. They plopped in with a clang.

In addition to the clang, Travis heard a crinkling noise. He bent down on his knees and began rummaging through the trash can. "There's something in here."

"I know," Cavanaugh said. "Mostly Big Mac wrappers and used condoms. I for one feel better about this whole situation now that I know Moroconi practices safe sex."

Travis continued digging through the disgusting contents of the trash can. He found a strip of cotton, apparently torn from an undershirt. It was stained with blood. He had found traces of blood around the shower drain, too. Was Moroconi hurt? Perhaps by that crash into the wall at the West End?

A moment later Travis withdrew a torn and crinkled envelope.

"I didn't see that," Cavanaugh said, walking toward him.

"It was wrapped up in one of the McDonald's bags." He shot her a pointed glance. "Police officers are trained to be thorough."

He flattened the envelope on the dresser. There were no markings on it, except for a corporate logo in the upper left corner that identified the letter as being sent by the Elcon Corporation. There was no return address.

"Mean anything to you?" Cavanaugh asked.

"Not offhand, but if we—"

Travis stopped when he heard footsteps outside the room. He sprang back and positioned himself beside the door, waiting to club whoever stepped through.

"Heavens to Betsy," the man outside the door said. His hands were pressed against his face. "Who has done this terrible terrible thing? My boss, he will kill me."

Travis slowly emerged from behind the door. The speaker was a diminutive gentleman of Indian descent, or perhaps Pakistani. The badge on his lapel said that he was the front desk clerk and that his name was Bob.

"Uh, we don't know how this happened," Travis said. He hated to lie, but the circumstances left him little alternative. "We just thought we'd come inside and see if anyone was hurt."

"What in the holy moley has happened?" the desk clerk cried. "Was there an explosion of a small nuclear device?"

"Like I said, we just showed up." Travis grabbed Cavanaugh's hand and tugged her toward the door.

"Are you the gentleman who called about Room 14?"

Travis stared at the carpet. "Nah. I was just in the neighborhood. . . ."

"Oh, my. This time I shall be fired for certain. It is the cracks."

Travis blinked. "I'm sorry?"

"The cracks. They all have it up their noses. They take one whiff and they think they are invincible. They say, I can handle it and then *powie!* They go through a door."

Travis decided to play along. "Yeah, this probably is the work of some drug-crazed fiends." He tugged Cavanaugh more emphatically. "We'd better get out of here."

"Wait," the clerk said. "You must fill out forms, report to the police."

"Sorry," Travis said. "No time."

"Stop!" The clerk followed close behind them. "You must stay. I am not kidding with you."

They piled into the Omni and Cavanaugh backed away, ignoring Bob's protests.

"Back out without turning around," Travis muttered. "So he can't get your license-plate number."

Cavanaugh followed instructions. The desk clerk followed them all the way out of the parking lot, never quite catching up.

Once there was sufficient distance between them, Cavanaugh turned the car around and accelerated out of sight. She never noticed the Jeep waiting for them on the side of the highway, much less the blinking red light inside her briefcase.

# 46

4 : 3 0 P.M.

Travis hung his head low as a patrol car whizzed by them on Belt Line Road.

"Ten to one that cop is headed to the Million Dollar Motel to investigate a reported break-in," Cavanaugh said.

"That shouldn't attract too much interest."

"Not until the clerk describes the suspects who sped from the scene of the crime. Then every available officer on the force will descend on the place."

"And the press can add breaking and entering to their list of my alleged crimes," Travis mused. "Oh well. At least I really committed this one."

Cavanaugh checked traffic on all sides for more police cars. "Incidentally, Byrne, where am I driving?"

"You're asking me?"

"Yes. I'm tired of running this third-rate Bonnie and Clyde outfit. I got us to Moroconi—his room, anyway. Now you tell me what we do next."

"Well, we need to figure out what the Elcon Corporation is,

and what its connection is to one Alberto Moroconi. Unless I'm missing something, it's the only clue we have."

"Sound reasoning." She barreled into the fast lane and switched over to I-365. "But that doesn't tell me where to drive."

"Don't feel bad. It doesn't tell me anything either."

She punched Travis in the shoulder. "Snap out of it, Byrne. Show some of that resourcefulness you've been using to undeservedly win all those trials."

"This is different."

"I don't see why. Pretend you're a client with a problem. Where does the superstar lawyer go to unearth information about the mystery corporation?"

"I'd probably check the records in the secretary of state's office."

"In Austin? Nothing personal, Byrne, but I don't think we'd make it alive. Got anything closer to home?"

"You don't have to go to Austin. The secretary of state's records can be accessed by computer."

"Excellent. How do you do that?"

"I haven't the foggiest idea."

"Well, what would you normally do when you need corporate records?"

"I'd ask my secretary to get them."

"The pampered life of the private practitioner. You do half as much work and make twice as much money." She fumbled with the console between the seats and withdrew Crescatelli's blue box. "Looks like we get to try this gizmo out early, Byrne. You're going to call your secretary."

"I'd rather not get Gail involved."

"The call can't be traced."

"Nonetheless, I don't want to run the risk."

"Then what do you suggest?"

"Let's use one of the legal on-line services. Lexis, or maybe Information America."

"This is all gibberish to me, Byrne. We lowly prosecutors have to use the books in the library."

"My condolences. Dan has all the state-of-the-art research toys."

"So you want to go to your office?"

"Are you kidding? We'd be killed, as would probably everyone else there."

Cavanaugh exited from the highway, turned left, and pulled into the parking lot of a 7-Eleven. "Well, I refuse to continue driving around aimlessly. Until you give me a destination, I'm not budging."

Travis eyed the suspicious and sleazy characters waiting to use the pay phone. A beefy man with multiple tattoos was arguing with a man in a motorcycle gang jacket. "I'm not sure this is an ideal hangout. . . ."

Cavanaugh's arms were folded firmly across her chest. "Then suggest something better."

Travis watched the argument escalate. Switchblades would be flying any minute. "What about SMU? At the law library. They have all the on-line computer services, and they usually get free access. It should be relatively quiet if we go tonight."

Cavanaugh considered. "I don't think we should go anyplace quite that public. Too many chances of being seen by the wrong persons."

"I agree it's risky, but as you said, we have to do something. SMU sounds like the best option."

"All right. SMU it is." She started to turn the ignition.

Travis laid his hand on hers. "Wait a minute." He opened the car door.

"Good God, you're not going to try to break up that fight, are you?"

"No." He left the car, carefully avoiding the fracas, and approached a row of coin-operated newspaper stands. Something had caught his eye—something disturbingly familiar. He plugged thirty-five cents in and removed the afternoon paper.

After scanning it quickly, he returned to the car. "Take a look at this." He tossed the paper to her.

Cavanaugh examined the photograph plastered on the bottom half of page one. "Travis . . ." she said eventually, "that's *you*."

"No kidding. Nice profile, huh?"

"And you're with that girl. The one we found in Moroconi's room."

Travis snatched the paper back. The two of them were standing just inside his apartment; her scantily clad arms and legs were wrapped all around him. The article discussed new evidence discovered about "lawyer on the lam" Travis Byrne, his associations with organized crime, his repeated use of courtroom trickery to return career criminals to the streets and, of course, his known fraternization with prostitutes.

"How did that get into the paper so quickly?" Cavanaugh asked.

"This was taken two nights ago," Travis explained. "Plenty of time."

"But—why?"

"Someone's trying to smear me," Travis said bitterly. "Not content to put my life in danger, now they're going after my reputation as well."

"Any idea who might be behind it?"

"The article indicates that the press is getting its info from the police. Probably the same informant that fed them the last batch of false information about me."

Travis turned to the continuation of the story on page two, read for a while, then gasped. "Oh my God."

"What? What is it?"

Travis passed the paper back to Cavanaugh. "The remains of my car, that's what it is. The explanation for the explosion and the cloud of smoke we saw as we left your apartment."

The picture showed the wreckage of a green compact car that looked as if it had been ripped apart from the inside out. The roof was blown off and flung to one side. The frame was punctured by hundreds of tiny nail holes. Shattered glass lay in a ring all around the wreck. The car was destroyed, its remains blackened by fire.

And the caption identified the wreckage as an automobile registered to Travis Byrne.

"Thank God you weren't in it," Cavanaugh said quietly.

"Yeah." Travis pointed to the relevant paragraph of the article.
"I wasn't. But someone else was."

# 47

7:00 P.M.

Travis and Cavanaugh sat before a computer terminal in the back of SMU's Underwood Law Library. He had chosen this terminal deliberately—it was tucked away behind the stacks and shielded by a private carrel. Just the thing for a lawyer on the lam with a yen for research.

On-line legal services often made their databases available to colleges for free; they hoped lawyers in training would learn how to use them, become dependent upon them, and pay big bucks for them when they were out in the real world. Travis and Cavanaugh were able to get a terminal without any problem.

Travis pushed buttons on the keyboard and watched the screen glow blue. "I've accessed the secretary of state's files. Now let me see what I can pull up." He typed *Elcon Corporation* and hit Enter.

"Now this is interesting," Travis said. "I'm not the first attorney to probe into the Elcon Corporation recently."

"Really? Who else?"

Travis moved the cursor to the indicated line. "Thomas J. Seacrest. Moroconi's first attorney. He did the exact same thing."

Travis checked the date. "And later that same day, he disappeared. Until he turned up murdered."

"I can't imagine that any great secrets are going to be revealed in documents filed with a government agency."

"Corporations are required by law to submit certain information," Travis replied. "For instance, the corporate charter, the articles of incorporation, and the name of the registered service agent. See? I'm pulling up the corporate charter now."

"I'm tingling with excitement."

Travis scanned the paragraphs of legalese that composed the charter. "Seems to be your basic garden-variety Texas corporation. No unusual clauses or provisions. Formed about thirty-five years ago. Merged with another Texas corporate entity a few years ago."

He depressed the Page Down button, scanning as the pages passed. "Here's the name of the corporate president. Apparently there's a managing board of directors, although I can't find the name of the CEO. Ever heard of this president?"

Cavanaugh read the name on the screen. "Mario Catuara. Doesn't ring any bells with me."

"Me neither. Here, take down his office address. I think we should check him out."

Cavanaugh didn't respond.

Travis glanced up at her. "Did you get the address?"

Cavanaugh placed a finger across her lips. She was looking over the top of the carrel toward the other side of the library.

"What is it?" Travis whispered. "What do you see?" He sat up and craned his neck.

Cavanaugh pushed his head down. "Stay out of sight."

"What are you looking at?"

"A man who came in about five minutes after we did. He's been sitting in the same chair ever since. A chair equidistant between our carrel and the front door."

"So?"

"Maybe nothing. But that's where I'd sit if I wanted to keep an unobtrusive eye on us and ensure that we couldn't leave without his knowing about it."

Travis dropped a pencil and, under the pretense of recovering it, took a look under the carrel. He saw the man right away; there weren't that many people in the library, and the man appeared to be reading a *Southwestern Reporter* page by page. It was a dead giveaway. No one read case reports; someone might look up a case, but no one sat around reading them like they were Agatha Christies. He might as well be holding the book upside down; it was just a prop.

"You're right," Travis whispered. "He's waiting for something."

"Probably for us to leave so he can drill us. He's got a very suspicious bulge inside his windbreaker." She laid her notepad on the carrel. "I'm going to talk to him."

"Wait." Travis grabbed her wrist. "I'll go. I'm the one he's looking for."

"All the more reason you should stay here. While I distract him you can get the car."

"No way."

Cavanaugh pushed him back down. "Relax. He won't try anything here. And he may not recognize me. Let me see what I can find out. Who knows? We might actually learn something if you don't kick his teeth out first. Just make sure you have the car waiting outside if I have to make a break for it."

"Too risky."

"I'm willing to take the risk."

"For me?" He raised an eyebrow. "You're starting to sound like you might give a damn what happens to me."

"Perish the thought."

C avanaugh walked the long way around the room, past the law reviews and through the regional reporters. She came up behind the man, hoping to catch him by surprise.

"Excuse me," she said. "Are you a law student?"

The man turned around slowly. His eyes were masked with dark sunglasses, his hair was covered by a baseball cap.

"Uh . . . yeah," he answered. "I am."

"Great. Maybe you can help me. I'm looking for the *Pacific Reporters*. Can you tell me where they are?"

"Uh, right. I always forget where those are shelved." His voice was muffled and indistinct. He scanned the identifier tabs on the end of each row of books. "Yeah, here they are. I thought so."

"Thanks a million," Cavanaugh said. "And could you help me find this cite?" She scribbled a citation on her legal pad—*512 P.2d 1204.* "I'm a secretary, see, and this complex legal gibberish baffles me."

The man shifted awkwardly from foot to foot. "You know, I'm just a first-year student, and I haven't figured those codes out either. Sorry."

"Oh, that's all right. I'm sorry to bother you. Oops!" Cavanaugh dropped her legal pad so that it fell almost between his legs. After a moment's hesitation the man picked it up. While he was bent over, his windbreaker rose and Cavanaugh spotted the equipment belt strapped around his waist.

"I'm sorry," she said, bopping herself on the side of the head. "I'm such a klutz sometimes. I shouldn't have bothered you."

"No problem."

"I feel awful about interrupting your studies. You've probably got finals this week."

He nodded. "Yeah, finals. They're a bear."

"Right. Finals in mid-April."

The man moved toward her, arms extended.

Cavanaugh started to move away, but the man seized her wrist. He tightened his grip and twisted, sending flashes of pain through her arm. He pushed her backward into the relative seclusion of the stacks. She tried to pull away, but he grabbed her other arm and held fast. She tried to toss him over her shoulder, but he was too heavy and too strong.

"You've already blown it," Cavanaugh said, her teeth clenched. "No one has finals in April. Just as no one could get through a semester in law school without learning how to look up a case citation. If you don't let go of me in two seconds, I'll scream."

"If you scream, you die," the man replied matter-of-factly. He pressed his thumb against a spot behind and below her ear. "Feel that? Hurts, doesn't it?"

Cavanaugh tried to answer, but couldn't. The sudden pain shot through her head like a lightning bolt. Her eyes watered. This man knew what he was doing.

"The right amount of pressure applied to the right point can kill someone in the blink of an eye," he said. He pressed even harder. "And I know exactly where to apply the pressure."

Tears streamed out of Cavanaugh's eyes. What had happened? This man had placed her entirely under his control in a matter of seconds.

"I saw your boyfriend leave." His lips brushed against her ear. "Take me to him." He twisted her arm behind her back.

Cavanaugh could barely think, the pain had become so intense; it was as if he had driven an iron spike through her skull. She couldn't take him to Travis, but she knew she couldn't take much more of this, either. She felt as if her head might snap off at any moment. She began to pray for unconsciousness.

"Three seconds," the man whispered. "Then I'll finish you off. Where *is* he?" He pressed his other thumb on the same point behind her other ear, doubling the pain. Cavanaugh's lips parted, but the sound she made was merely a whimper. It was all she could do.

"Let go of her."

Cavanaugh heard a deep voice behind her. *Travis?* But he had gone to the car. . . .

She felt a jerking, then a loosening of the man's grip. She opened her eyes, tried to focus. It *was* Travis. He had come behind them and wrapped his necktie around the man's throat.

"Let go of her!" Travis barked, twisting the ends of the tie. The man slowly removed his fingers. She felt a great rush as blood streamed back into her head. The pressure points still ached, but it was an aching of relieved tension, not of impending death.

"Don't even think about going for any of those fancy weapons you're carrying," Travis ordered. "Who are you?"

The man didn't answer.

"What is it you want?"

The only reply was a defiant glare.

Travis twisted the tie as firmly as possible around the man's windpipe. Still no response.

Travis heard a stirring noise from the front of the library. Apparently they'd caught the attention of the front desk librarian. Using the necktie like a leash, Travis swung the man around and sent him reeling into a nearby reading room. He slammed the door shut and pushed a carrel in front of the doorway.

"That'll slow him down for thirty seconds or so," Travis said, grabbing Cavanaugh's hand. "The car's outside. Let's go."

**48**

7 : 2 5 P . M .

Cavanaugh dove into the passenger seat and slammed the
door behind her. "Drive like hell, Byrne."

"Got it." He threw the stick into first and zoomed out of the
parking lot.

Cavanaugh didn't speak for several minutes. Then, finally: "You
saw the belt he was wearing?"

Travis nodded.

"I can't be sure," Cavanaugh said, "but I think that's what some
of my military clients call a Sam Browne belt."

"What the hell is that?"

"It's specially designed for people going into combat situations.
Soldiers, spies, terrorists. It holds a lot of ammo and assault gizmos."

"I saw a bulge under his jacket, too," he said. "A holster with
a gun in it?"

"I think that's a safe assumption."

"Did you recognize any of the gadgets on his belt?"

"I only got a quick look, but I've seen some of it before, usually in narcotics cases. He had an infrared nightscope, for instance. High-powered, compact binoculars. What the pros call a Puukko knife—specially designed for quick, clean kills."

"Who would carry lethal crap like that?"

"Anyone who wants to. It's available. Pawnshops, soldier-of-fortune mail-order houses, wherever." She paused. "But you know who really loves this stuff?"

"Who?"

"Spooks. CIA agents."

"*CIA?*" Travis felt a sudden catching in his throat. In addition to the mob? On top of the police and the FBI? Who *wasn't* involved in this? Who *didn't* want a piece of Travis Byrne?

"Why the CIA?"

"Beats me. But of course I don't really understand why anyone is involved, or what it is they're involved in."

"Good point."

"Maybe the guy just has connections to the CIA. Or the military. Access to their equipment."

"An unpleasant possibility."

"Yeah." Cavanaugh looked down at her lap and fidgeted with her fingers. "I wanted to thank you, Byrne. For . . . you know. Bailing me out of that."

"Don't mention it."

"No, I want to mention it. The truth is, I've been kind of . . . well, I've been kind of crappy to you. Maybe it's because you play hardball in the courtroom and you've screwed up my win–loss record. Maybe it's . . . something else." She gazed out the window. "You could've just driven away. But you didn't. So—thanks."

"My pleasure," he said quietly.

She pounded her fist against her hand. "I can't believe I was so . . . helpless."

"That spook was obviously well trained. He would've clobbered me if he'd had half a chance."

"I hate being so . . . vulnerable."

"We're way outmatched. You shouldn't have gone by yourself."

"I didn't think he would try anything in the middle of the library. How did I know he was some trained super-killer?"

"From now on, assume the worst about everything and everyone." Travis wasn't sure, but he thought he saw Cavanaugh shudder. "Did you recognize him?"

"No. You?"

"I never got a good look at his face."

"Ditto. For a moment I thought there was something familiar about him, but I couldn't pinpoint it."

"Well, give it some thought." Travis reentered the highway, merged into the fast lane, and zoomed into the darkness.

"Do you think he's following us?"

"If he isn't, he will be soon."

"How?"

"I don't know. How did he find us at the library? How do these people keep finding us wherever we go?"

"I'm not tipping anyone off, Travis."

"I didn't mean to suggest that you were. It's just mysterious, that's all. Christ!" His muscles tightened in frustration. "Get that blue box out. I'm going to make some phone calls."


The librarian found the man pounding on the door of the reading room. First she insisted on asking idiotic questions, then she took forever to move the stupid carrel out of the doorway. As soon as the path was clear, he pushed her aside and raced out of the library.

He started his Jeep and activated the monitor, trying to pick up the signal of the tracing device he had placed in the briefcase. Nothing. Absolutely nothing.

He bashed his head against the steering column. What was wrong with him? First he let Byrne sneak up on him, then he let him get beyond the tracer's radius. A simple mission, and he had blown it.

He bit down on his lower lip till it bled. It was starting all over again. The screwups. The headstrong craziness. The failure to observe procedures. This is what had gotten him kicked out, and now, when it really mattered, he was doing it all over again.

He would never get Byrne at this rate. He'd be lucky now if he even found him again. All he could do was drive around the city, all night long if necessary, hoping to stumble within twenty miles of wherever Byrne was now. Barely better than a needle in a haystack, but it was all he had.

He removed a city map from the glove compartment. He would cover the city systematically, one section at a time, picking the roads that would eventually bring him within twenty miles of almost everything. With luck, they would stop somewhere for the night and he'd have a chance to zero in on them. And if he didn't get them the first time, he'd start all over again. And again, and again, and again. He would drive forever if necessary. He would ignore the fatigue, the despair, the pain. He would regain what he had lost.

And by God, the next time Travis Byrne would not get away from him.

## 49

8:00 P.M.

When Kramer entered Mario's office, it was almost entirely dark. The gooseneck lamp was off. Only the subtlest hint of a silhouette informed him that Mario was in his usual place behind his desk. All he could see were two incandescent eyes burning across the room.

Mario spoke first. "It was Donny?"

Kramer ran his finger up and down the scar on his face. "Uh . . . yeah. It was."

A very long pause. "What am I to tell his mother? He was her only son. My only nephew."

"I—I don't know. Sir." Kramer shoved his hands inside his pockets. "I didn't know Donny was followin' me. Hell! Donny was stupid as shit, but I still wouldn't have—"

"Don't speak ill of the dead."

"Sorry." The hypocrisy of the moment was beginning to overwhelm him. As if Mario really gave a damn. "Look, we all knew what Donny was. He had no future with us—"

"Does that mean he deserved to die? To be burned alive? Ventilated by hundreds of nails?" Mario's voice boomed out of the darkness. "Should we dispose of all our castoffs by sealing them in a car with one of your demented death traps?"

"It was a good idea. A smart backup plan. Just in case the first line of assault didn't work."

"Which it didn't."

"That's . . . true. Like the bumper stickers say, shit happens. You can't blame me for that."

"You sent a hireling to perform a job you should have done yourself. You weren't even there."

"I couldn't have passed as an office courier. My . . . appearance would've aroused his suspicions."

"This is simply another attempt to excuse your failure. A ghastly failure that has now cost us two men. Including my nephew."

"Give it a rest. You never liked Donny any better than I did. Just stay cool a little longer and I'll serve Byrne's head to you on a silver platter. Moroconi's, too."

"Your time is up, Mr. Kramer." Mario rose to his feet and slowly emerged from the shadows. "For many years I have believed you were not a desirable member of our organization. In the old days, perhaps, you had a place. But now you are a relic. In this latest matter, you have proven your obsolescence. Although I have given you every possible chance, you have failed to deliver Moroconi. You haven't even been able to find a stupid lawyer. And in the course of this catastrophic failure, you have cost men their lives and threatened the integrity of our entire organization."

Kramer withdrew his lighter from his pocket and flicked it. The flame cast a dim glow through the darkened room. "Fine. You wanted to chew me out, you've chewed me out. I suppose I gave you an openin'. Now can I get on with my job?"

"You don't have a job, Mr. Kramer."

"*What?*"

"I am relieving you of your duties in this matter. In fact, I am relieving you of all responsibilities for my organization."

"You can't do that!"

"Can't? I already have. You are no longer connected with us, Mr. Kramer. Whatever tenuous connection you once may have claimed is now and forever severed."

"I was workin' for this family before you were—"

"None of that matters, Mr. Kramer. I'm in charge now. And I have given you your walking papers. So walk."

"You're serious!"

"Very." He stepped closer to Kramer. "If I see you around here again, I'll have you killed."

Kramer stalked toward the door, his teeth clenched, his fists balled up in rage. That explained why the room was so goddamn dark, he realized. Mario must have bodyguards in here. Otherwise he would never dare speak like that.

Kramer slammed the door behind him. Fucking pissant. The Outfit had shot straight downhill since Mario took over. Now they all wore business suits and pretended they were Wall Street tycoons. They didn't know who they were anymore. They didn't think they needed him.

Mario was just trying to scare him, Kramer told himself. He just wanted Moroconi and Byrne brought in. And this was his way of ensuring that Kramer worked night and day to make that happen. Bastard.

Fine. He'd bring in Byrne. He had hoped to do it with a minimum of fuss, but since Mario was in such a goddamn hurry, he'd expedite matters. He'd continue with his main plan—tracking Byrne—but he'd put his contingency plan into action as well. One or the other was bound to produce results.

After all, Byrne might be able to hide himself. But he couldn't hide all his friends, too.

**50**

8 : 1 5 P.M.

T ravis asked Cavanaugh to pull over to a relatively unpop-
ulated QuikTrip.

"Sure you understood what Crescatelli told you about the blue
box?" he asked.

"Well enough. But make it quick, okay?"

"I'll do my best." They got out of the car and walked to the
phone booth. Cavanaugh closed the glass door and opened the
blue box.

"This will take a few minutes," she said, "while I line up eight
or ten trunks. You stand guard."

"I can do that." Travis watched as she dialed an 800 number
randomly chosen from the phone book. She did seem to know
what she was doing, and for that he was grateful. He hadn't absorbed enough of Crescatelli's lecture even to feign competence.
He was so absorbed in watching Cavanaugh work that he didn't
notice the woman with the poodle until she was directly under his
nose.

" 'Scuse me," she said. "Can I get to the phone, please?"

Travis could barely make out her face—it was buried beneath layer upon layer of makeup. She was chewing gum and her hair was in curlers. Now that Travis noticed, the poodle was in curlers, too.

"I need to use the phone," she said.

"It's occupied."

"There's a three-minute limit," she said, cracking her gum for emphasis. She pointed to a sign on the phone-booth door.

"I'm sorry," Travis said. "This is very important."

"So is my call! If I don't call Maurice, he'll cancel our appointment. Then poor Sugar Pie and I will have to wear our curlers all week."

"Maybe there's a phone inside you can use."

"There isn't. I already asked."

"Well, I'm afraid this one is tied up."

"This is an outrage! I shop here regularly. I'm probably their best customer."

Travis assumed that meant she bought her cosmetics here. "Ma'am, if you'll please go away, I'll give you five bucks for your trouble."

She slapped the money away. "What do I look like, a streetwalker?"

Travis decided not to comment.

"I don't want your money. I want the phone. I have a constitutional right to use the phone. And by God, I intend to!" She pivoted on one foot, dog in tow, and stomped back into the store.

Travis saw her stop at the cash register and complain bitterly to the clerk. Just Travis's luck—he had to run into the only woman in Dallas who thought she had a constitutional right to talk on the phone.

Cavanaugh was punching in numbers, and the red light on the blue box was still glowing. Apparently she hadn't gotten to a line she considered sufficiently safe yet. And if they disconnected the line now, she would have to start all over again.

The woman with the poodle reemerged from the store with an

extremely reluctant clerk. Thank goodness I'm wearing the sun-glasses and hat, Travis thought. By now, he had probably made the tabloids, and this woman undoubtedly read them every day.

"Uh, pardon me," the clerk said, shuffling his feet. "There's a three-minute limit on the phone."

"There are two of us," Travis said, gesturing toward Cavanaugh. "So we get six minutes combined."

"You've been on the phone for more than six minutes," the clerk observed. "But actually, you get no time, because you aren't customers, because you haven't bought anything."

So the clerk was a literalist. Swell. Travis searched his brain for a new tack; the situation was becoming desperate. Ridiculous, but desperate.

"Ma'am, how long has your dog had poodle herpacocci?"

The woman looked at Travis blank-faced. "Had what?"

"Poodle herpacocci. Well, the full medical name would be"—he took a deep breath—"streptocardioencephalodoggy herpacocci, but I don't see any reason to get bogged down in a lot of Latin, do you?"

The woman appeared stricken. "You think my Sugar Pie has a disease?"

"Surely you've noticed." Travis bent down beside the dog. "The bloodred eyes, the discolored toes, the waxy quality of the coat. Oh yes, it's a clear-cut case."

"Are you a—"

"Yes, of course. Am I to understand that this dog is not under-going treatment?"

"Why, no—"

"My God, woman!" He glared at her accusingly. "Some people shouldn't be allowed to have pets."

The woman made a choking sound, her hand clasped against her throat. "Sugar Pie . . . if I had only known . . ." She cradled the dog in her arms.

"You need to get that dog to a veterinary hospital immediately, ma'am." Travis made a snorting noise. "You'll probably want to wait until after you make your phone call."

"Don't be ridiculous. I'll go right now." She started toward her car, then stopped. "Wait a minute. Can't you treat him?"

"Of course not," Travis said. "I'm using the phone."

He stepped into the glass booth with Cavanaugh and closed the door. Confused and concerned, the woman carried her dog to her car and sped away.

A large smile playing on his lips, the clerk returned to his cash register.

"Holyfield and Associates."

"Hello, Gail?"

"Travis! Is that you?"

"Yes. Thank goodness you're still at the office. Now, stay calm—"

"Oh my God, oh my God, oh my God! Travis, what's happened to you?"

Thanks for staying calm. "I'm in a lot of trouble, Gail."

"I know! I keep reading the awful details in the newspaper."

Great. All my sins revealed. "You really shouldn't believe—"

"And those pictures of you and that . . . little girl. I had no idea you were so *lonely*, Travis. You know, if you had just told me . . ."

Travis felt his face flushing. "Gail, those pictures were trumped up. I didn't really . . . you know."

"You didn't?" She sounded almost disappointed.

"Gail, I called to give you a message—go on vacation."

"Vacation? I don't think I can—"

"Gail, you haven't taken a vacation for years. Cancún is a paradise this time of year. Go."

"Well, I'll have to check my bank account. . . ."

"Good news. Dan is paying for this one."

"He is?"

"Yeah." He doesn't know it yet, but he is. Even if it has to come out of my salary. "Think of this as an assignment, Gail. Be out of town before sunrise."

"But *why?*"

"I don't want to go into it on the phone, but it's best for all concerned. Trust me."

She paused. "All right. I'll go."

Thank you. He was glad to be spared the explanations. "Now connect me with Dan."

"I don't know if he's free—"

"Tell him his favorite fugitive is on the line. I think he'll take the call."

"All right, hold on."

A few seconds later he heard: "Travis? Where the hell are you?"

"It's best we don't go into that. . . ."

"What do you think you're doing, running all over the city, leaving a trail of dead bodies?"

"I'm sorry if I've created any inconvenience—"

"*Inconvenience?* I've spent the last two days fielding phone calls about you! My God, I've never dealt with a disaster of this proportion. My firm has never been linked with organized crime or . . . prostitution! And they say you've killed some men, Travis."

"Well, I haven't."

"You need help, Travis. You can't handle this on your own."

"I'm not . . . entirely on my own—"

"Does that mean Cavanaugh is with you?"

That caught him off guard. "What makes you think—"

"That's Charles Hagedorn's idea. Cavanaugh disappeared about twenty-four hours after you did. Didn't show up for some meetings today with Washington bigwigs. Put the U.S. Attorney's Office into a frenzy."

"So why would the judge connect that to me?"

"Well, it's quite a coincidence, wouldn't you say? The attorneys on both sides of a high-profile case disappearing? Just after the defendant does. Hagedorn's notion is that you kidnapped her to prevent the Moroconi case from being tried in absentia."

"That's the lamest idea I've ever heard."

"I agree, but that hasn't stopped the judge from spreading it around town. Your reputation is going into the dumper in a hurry, Travis. I've managed to keep the judge from filing a bar grievance until we can sort this out, but your failure to appear is not helping anything. Did I tell you the judge issued a contempt citation against you?"

"Yup."

"And *still* you won't appear? My God, you're in deliberate contempt of court. You might as well take your law license and tear it into tiny little pieces!"

Travis closed his eyes. This was not helping. "Dan, I want you and Gail to leave town."

"I beg your pardon!"

"You heard me. I already told Gail to take a vacation. At your expense. Take it out of my salary-deferral fund. I'll sign the papers when I can. And I want you to leave, too."

"And who would run this office?"

"I don't care. Shut it down if you have to. Just get out of there."

"Why?"

"Isn't it obvious? I'm afraid these killers will try to get at me through you."

The silence on the other end of the line was heavy and protracted. Travis could almost hear him deliberating. "All right. If you want us to make ourselves scarce, we will. But let's all go together. Let me meet you somewhere safe."

"No can do," Travis said. "It's too risky."

"We'll go directly to the airport."

"No. If I leave Dallas, I'll never get to the bottom of this. Besides, I'm trying to get you out of danger, and traveling with me would have the opposite effect."

"Travis—"

"That's my final word, Dan. Things are bad already, and I think they're about to get worse. I want you and Gail out."

Dan sighed, resigned. "Fine. We'll go."

"Thank you. Oh, and can you do me another favor?"

"I live to please," he said wearily.

"Check on Staci. If she can't leave town by herself, I'm going to ask her to meet you. You'll take care of her, won't you?"

"Of course. If you'll promise to come see me as soon as you can."

"Thanks, Dan. I owed you before, but now, even more so. I won't forget this."

He disconnected the line.

"You're pushing your luck," Cavanaugh said, tapping her watch. "Don't talk so long next time."

Travis mumbled an incomprehensible answer and dialed another number.

**5 1**

**8 : 2 5 P . M .**

Fortunately, she answered the phone herself.

"Hello, Staci?"

"Oh my gosh. Travis? Is that really you?"

"Yes. Now listen—"

"Travis, where are you?"

"I can't tell you that."

"Travis, you've been in all the papers."

"I know, honey. Listen—"

"Travis . . . those things they're saying . . . They aren't true, are they?"

"Of course not, honey—"

"Aunt Marnie says they are. She says she was always suspicious of you. She says it isn't natural for a guy your age to be so interested in a teenage girl."

That never prevented Aunt Marnie from accepting the money I gave her, Travis thought. He wondered if any of it got spent on Staci. "Sweetheart, listen to me. This is very important."

"I knew something was wrong when you asked Doc and Jameel

to break into your own apartment. Someone's trying to hurt you, right?"

"Staci, just listen—"

"Tell me where you are, Travis. I'm coming."

"*No!* Absolutely not! Now listen to me." He heard her steady, expectant breathing as she quieted. "You're right, people are trying to hurt me, and I'm afraid they might try to get at me through my friends and"—he swallowed—"loved ones. So I want you to leave Dallas."

"Leave Dallas? Where would I go?"

"What about your uncle Jacko? In Oregon."

"Uncle Jacko? He's not even a real uncle."

"Can you think of anyone else?"

Silence on the other end of the line.

"Jacko it is, then. Dan will make your travel arrangements." He gave her the phone number. "If you need any money, use that credit card I gave you last year for emergencies."

"What if Aunt Marnie won't let me go?"

Travis swore silently. This was advice he hated to give. "Go anyway," he said softly.

"Okay. Wow."

"Are you writing all this down?"

"I can remember."

He only hoped that was true. But at times her attention disorder was extremely pronounced—her powers of concentration were low and she couldn't be expected to retain anything. "This is very important, honey. Don't mess around. And don't tell anyone where you're going."

"I don't like this, Travis," she said. "It's not right—running off when you're in trouble."

"It is right, honey. It's the most right thing you can possibly do." He exhaled, much relieved. "I can't stay on this line any longer. I'm going to hang up."

"Travis?"

"Yes?"

She stalled, apparently unable to say what she wanted to say. "Be careful."

"I will."

"If you don't come see me soon, I'll punch your lights out!"

"Understood." He hung up the phone and climbed back in the car with Cavanaugh. "Now. We need to talk to that Elcon corporate president, but I suppose we'll have to wait until morning. In the meantime, let's find a safe place to catch some shut-eye. I wouldn't object to getting something to eat, either."

"Any suggestions?"

"No. I don't know what's safe." He gripped the steering wheel tightly. "I don't understand how these people keep finding me wherever I go."

"Well, we have to stay somewhere, so pick a place."

Travis shrugged. "Cheap motel."

"Fine. Just don't make it the Million Dollar."

"Deal." Travis glanced uneasily into the rearview mirror.

Cavanaugh leaned closer to him. "You think someone's following us?"

Travis thought a long time before answering. "I don't know," he said finally. "I just don't know."


"**D**id you get it?"

The technician pressed the headphones closer to his ears. "I think so. . . ."

Kramer slapped him brutally across the side of his face, knocking him out of his chair. "Don't tell me what you *think*, goddamn it! I need results!"

The technician lay sprawled on the floor of the truck, stunned. "I'm—I'm sorry. I got it. Every word."

"When is she leaving? Where is she going?"

Crawling back to his feet, the technician related everything he had heard.

"Then there's still time."

"Do you want me to arrange for some of the boys to meet her?"

"No," Kramer replied. "I've depended on assistants far too much already. I'm going to take care of her myself."

The technician tossed the headphones down beside the recorder. He felt nauseated—not from the blow, but from the thought of Kramer "taking care of" a teenage girl. "I don't understand, sir. How will this help you find Byrne?"

"It won't." A wide, leering grin spread across his pocked face. "Byrne will come to me."

## 52

### 10:40 P.M.

Travis and Cavanaugh sat side by side on the ratty double bed in their fleabag motel room. They purposely chose low-end accommodations, both to stay out of sight, and because they knew their cash on hand couldn't last forever and using credit cards and automated tellers would be suicide. Without discussion, they had agreed to share a room—safety in numbers. They'd stopped at a gas station, and while Cavanaugh gassed up, Travis grabbed an assortment of unnutritious snacks—beef jerky, potato chips, pork rinds, and every other high-fat fried food he hadn't eaten in months.

"Kind of sliding off the cholesterol-free diet, aren't you?" Cavanaugh observed.

"Right now I need stress reduction. And I don't care if I gain a few pounds getting it."

"Certainly that's always been my approach to dieting." She opened a jumbo bag of Chee•tos. "Topic one. First thing tomorrow, we need to get a new car."

"Fine. I've got forty-five bucks left."

"I'm serious, Byrne. Whoever crashed my apartment knows my name, and if they know my name, all it takes is a phone call to get a description of my car and the license-plate number. Plus that goon at the library may have seen the car. We need new wheels."

"But if we buy a new car, we'll have to register it."

"True. That's why, much as it pains me, I conclude that we should acquire a new vehicle by less than legal means."

"Am I hearing these words spoken by Little Miss I'm an Officer of the Court?"

Cavanaugh snatched his pork rinds. "Our lives are on the line here. Legal ethics are a swell concept, but I'm not prepared to die for them."

"And how are we going to acquire this automobile by, uh, less than legal means?"

"Leave it to me."

"You're the expert." He paused, then added, "Laverne."

She slugged him on the arm. "Byrne, if you start calling me Laverne in the courtroom, so help me—"

"Relax, relax. I wouldn't do that. Besides, surely you realize we're both going to be disbarred."

"That makes me feel much better."

"It's not such a bad name. Laverne, I mean. Has kind of a warm . . . grandmotherly feel."

"Just what I was hoping for." Cavanaugh sighed. "I always wanted a friendly name. The kind of name people have that other people . . . well, *like*."

"Such as what?"

"Oh, I don't know. Daisy, maybe."

"Daisy? Like Blondie and Dagwood's dog?"

She cast her eyes toward the ceiling. "One year when I was in college, during spring break, I decided to drive from Dallas to San Francisco to visit an old high-school friend. A brief adventure. I drove it nonstop—just me, the radio, and lots of No Doz. Anyway, along the way, somewhere in Arizona, I think, I picked up this hitchhiker."

Travis's eyes widened. "You? A hitchhiker?"

"I was younger then. I didn't know any better. He was what my parents would've called a hippie, even then. Long stringy unwashed hair, a guitar, fringed jacket. He was a folksinger, or wanted to be. He played a few tunes for me in the car. He wasn't bad." She turned away suddenly. "I'm sorry. I'm boring you."

"No, please continue. I'm fascinated. This is so unlike the Madame Prosecutor I've come to know and . . . know."

"Yeah, well . . ." She waved her hand aimlessly. "The hitchhiker asked me what my name was. I went by my initials then—L.C.—but he wouldn't settle for that. He wanted to know what the letters stood for, and I eventually told him."

"And then what? He left in outrage?"

"No. He grew very quiet, then said, 'Well, I'm going to call you Daisy.' "

A smile played upon her lips. "And he did, for the whole drive to California. Called me Daisy. I loved that name. It was so . . . soft. And romantic. It was everything I had never been but always secretly wanted to be."

"What happened?"

Cavanaugh shrugged. "He got out in Monterey. I never saw him again. And no one has called me Daisy ever since."

"Did you ever tell your parents you wanted a name change?"

"My parents are dead. Sailboat accident off the Gulf Coast. When I was fifteen."

"Sorry. I didn't know."

She nodded slightly. "Doesn't matter."

"Must've been rough on a fifteen-year-old."

"I always wanted to go to law school, but after my parents died, I lived with an aunt who didn't want me and couldn't afford me. Paying for a college education was out of the question. After about six months of just bumming around, one of my low-life high-school friends got me into the skip-tracing business. Hell, at the time, I thought he was a big shot. Wore expensive shoes, jewelry. At least he could pay his bills, which was more than I could manage. He showed me the ropes. Eventually took me in as a partner."

"You mean . . . in the business sense?"

Cavanaugh looked into his eyes, as if evaluating how much she could trust to tell. "I mean in every sense."

"I see."

"It was fine for the first two years. Then, almost all at once, it fell apart. He started saying we should take separate vacations, see other people, crap like that. He thought that was the kind approach, the sensitive guy's way out. I think he was a coward. It would've hurt less if he'd just disappeared one day."

"That's when you left the skip-tracing racket?"

"Yup. I had made some money; he was reasonable about letting me keep most of what I earned. I finished undergrad in three years, took the LSAT, applied to South Texas, and got in. After law school, I worked for the Attorney General's Office, then the DA, and now the U.S. Attorney's Office. And that pretty much brings us up to date. I thought I had a promising career. Everyone seemed to like me, I got good reviews—and then one day this crazed lawyer with a roll of duct tape broke into my apartment and taped me to a chair. Now half of Dallas is gunning for me."

"Sorry about that."

"What about you, Byrne? You probably hail from some small farm town and have a cute little gray-haired ma who bakes you apple pies on your birthday."

"No. My parents are gone, too. Mom when I was young. Dad when I was at the police academy."

"Oh."

"Yeah."

She paused. "At least your father got to see you on the way to becoming something. He must've been very proud."

Travis laughed bitterly. "Not hardly. He thought I was throwing my life away. To use his own words, 'chasing a childish dream of playing cops and robbers.' "

"What did Dad want you to be?"

"Same as him. A trial lawyer."

Cavanaugh placed her fingers against her lips. "So he never got to see you become one of the best courtroom attorneys in the state. That's a pity." She was quiet for a moment. "How did he die?"

"Heart attack. Stress-induced. And yes, to answer your next questions, he was overweight, he ate too much of the wrong foods, and we'd had a big argument about my future the night before."

Cavanaugh waited a long time before breaking the silence. "Will you tell me why you quit the police force?"

Travis's face became stony. "Why? That was a long time ago. Before Moroconi. Before the world turned upside down."

"I heard . . . I heard something horrible happened."

"You heard right. I don't think you want to know."

She placed her hand carefully over his. "I do," she said quietly. "I really do."

I t was the middle of April, over four years before, on a beautiful, sunshine-filled Dallas day. Travis was off duty, and he and Angela were enjoying a leisurely afternoon on the town, heading nowhere in particular, reveling in the luxury of one another's company.

"I feel guilty, Angel," Travis said, clasping her hand tightly. "In a few minutes we'll be at Adamson Park. They have a great merry-go-round. We should have brought Staci."

Angela tossed back her luxurious, waist-length red hair. "Staci will be fine." She touched the ring on the fourth finger of her left hand. "Besides, after June, she'll be seeing you every day."

He squeezed her hand. "I guess that's right. Any clues yet how she feels about me?"

"She adores you, Travis. Isn't that obvious? You two are buddies."

"Yeah, she adores me as a buddy. But what's she going to think of me as a daddy?"

Angela poked him in the ribs. "You'll do fine, you insecure twerp. You couldn't be any worse than the creep who fathered her."

"Staci may feel differently."

"She won't. She barely knows Alan. Neither of us have heard from him in years. You've been much more of a father to her than he ever was."

Travis thought about that for a while. "Think Alan will come back?"

"No chance. Well, not unless I come into a large inheritance or win the Publishers Clearing House sweepstakes." She threw her arm around his shoulders. "We both love you madly. So just relax, okay?"

He grinned. "Okay. You're the boss."

They rounded the corner and saw a crowd of people huddled in the middle of the street. Travis slowed, holding Angela back with one hand. What was the big attraction?

As they came closer he realized it was some kind of disturbance. A man in his late thirties or early forties with a gray-flecked beard was standing in the street, shouting obscenities, grabbing at people as they passed. He was big, broad-shouldered, frightening. His tone was hostile; he seemed to be on the verge of exploding.

Angela tugged on Travis's arm. "Let's go back the way we came."

Before she could steer him away, the owner of the corner pawnshop approached Travis. They recognized each other; Travis regularly patrolled this neighborhood.

"Travis!" he shouted. "Can you help?"

"What's going on?"

"It's that crazy bastard in the middle of the street. I don't know if he's drunk or high or what, but he's driving all our customers away."

"Probably just a vagrant who wandered over from the park," Travis said. "He'll likely move on in a few minutes."

"Are you kidding? He's been here for almost half an hour. And he gets more violent every minute. We need some help here. This part of town is dangerous enough without this kind of crap scaring everyone away."

"Why don't you call Morrison? He's supposed to be cruising this beat today."

"I called. Nobody came."

Travis groaned. That was Morrison. He probably found a jaywalker to occupy his time so he could ignore his radio for an hour or so. "I'm really not prepared—"

"You are now." The pawnshop owner slapped a .38 into Travis's hand. "I took it off the top shelf. It's loaded."

"Great. Well, let me see what I can do."

Angela held tight to his arm. "Travis—this is your day off."

"I know, honey. It'll just take a minute."

"You promised we would spend the day together. Just you and me."

"I know, Angel. And we will." He removed her hand and plunged into the thick of the crowd.

The gray-bearded man was becoming increasingly abusive. "Goddamn satanistic sons of bitches!" he cried at the top of his lungs, his face upturned toward heaven. "It's a plague. A plague on us and our children." He pointed into the crowd. "There's a fornicating whore. I can tell by the way she stands! And there's another!" He rushed into the crowd, sending a teenage girl running. "Repent, sinner! Jee-sus God Almighty!"

Travis reluctantly approached the man. "Okay, padre. Show's over. Why don't you come with me?"

The man's eyes opened wider than Travis would've thought possible. He flung himself at a young woman, ignoring Travis completely. "God is coming for you, whore of Babylon! He's coming for all of you!"

Travis steeled himself. Of all the loonies he came into contact with on a regular basis, he hated the religious loonies worst of all. "It's time for you to go to confessional, your holiness. At the county drunk tank, most likely. Come along."

Suddenly the man reared up, raising his hands clawlike above his head, like some kind of wild beast. He glared at Travis, literally snarling. "Get thee behind me, Satan!"

Travis blanched. The man's distorted visage was horrifying. "Look, don't try to get rough—"

The man growled at him. *"Get away from me!"*

Travis drew his gun. Technically, this was a violation of regulations—his life wasn't in immediate danger. But it wasn't his gun anyway and he wasn't taking any chances with this nut. He leveled the gun, chest-high.

The man's eyes blazed; his teeth bared. He looked as if he were suddenly possessed with a demonic fury. "Would you threaten me, pimp of Satan?" He crouched low and rushed toward Travis.

Travis fired into the air, but it had no effect. The man slammed into him like a bull hitting a matador, sending Travis careening across the street. Several people screamed; most of the crowd scrambled to get out of the way.

Travis tried to grab the madman by the neck. He was strong, almost inhumanly so. Travis could feel his breath on his shoulder. The man was trying to bite him! His teeth were extended like fangs; drool dripped from his mouth. Either this man was insane, or he was doing a hell of an imitation.

Bringing his right hand around, Travis clubbed the man on the top of the head with the butt of his gun. The man grunted, wavered. Travis hit him again. He fell to his knees.

The man's entire body relaxed, as if the demon had been exorcised. His eyes receded; his expression became flat, placid. Travis grabbed his arms and twisted them behind his back. The man from the pawnshop brought him a pair of handcuffs. Travis snapped the cuffs over the lunatic's wrists.

The man shrieked at the restraints. "You're hurting me!"

"You should've thought of that before you decided to sample this week's designer drug, asshole."

"I mean it. You're killing me! I got a pin."

Travis frowned. "A pin?"

"Yeah, a pin. A big one. In my arm. Got it in Vietnam. I can't stand to have my arm twisted back like that. Feels like it's gonna snap."

Travis grabbed his wrists and pulled the man to his feet. "Sorry, jerkface. Protocol."

"Cuff me in the front, man. I ain't goin' anywhere."

That was contrary to standard procedure. But the man did appear to be in extreme agony.

"All right, you whiny little perp." Travis brought the man's arms around and snapped the cuffs in the front. He grabbed the chain between the cuffs and began to lead him away.

They had barely traveled ten feet when Travis heard a tremendous clanging noise, followed by what sounded like a round of gunfire. It seemed to be coming from the warehouse across the street, the building the crowd had been blocking for the last half hour. Before he had a chance to investigate the shots, he heard a scream from behind.

*"Travis!"*

It was Angela. She was at the front of the crowd, waving her arms desperately. *"Look out!"*

Travis turned too late. Before he could stop him, the man had reached under Travis's jacket with his cuffed hands and snatched his gun.

"Sinful sons of bitches!" the man bellowed, waving the gun wildly in the air. "Hellspawn of Satan!" The crowd scattered.

"Put that down!" Travis commanded.

"Yes, Jesus! I will slay thy enemies!" His voice rose in pitch to a crazed squeal.

"*Give* me the *gun!*" Travis shouted.

"I'll fucking give it to you." The man brought the gun back down and aimed it at Travis's head.

Travis grabbed the man's wrist. The gun fired; the bullet went over Travis's shoulder. He tackled the man and brought him down hard. The man's head thudded on the concrete. His eyes fluttered, then he seemed to drift into unconsciousness.

This time Travis took no chances. He rolled the man over and pinned his head down with his knee.

"Someone call the police," Travis shouted. "Someone call—"

He stopped short. Few if any of the crowd were watching him. They were huddled about ten feet behind him. Travis could see two feet protruding from the circle, two feet in red lace sandals.

He felt a dry catching in his throat. Steadying himself, he advanced toward the new center of attention. The crowd, now deathly silent, parted and let him pass. Don't let it be. *Don't let it . . . !*

It was Angela. She was lying on the sidewalk, her eyes dark, blood streaming from the opening in her chest where the bullet had struck. The red blood matted her red hair.

Travis grabbed her hand and called her name, but she didn't respond. He called louder and louder, screaming, but it was no use. He felt for a pulse, but there was nothing there.

He pushed himself away, horrified. He knew that he should do something— get a doctor, or call an ambulance—but it was too late. Much too late.

For both of them.

C avanaugh didn't speak for a long time. Travis couldn't. He was exhausted, in every way a man could be. It was too painful—the recollection of that hideous day.

Cavanaugh's hand never left his.

"What was it?" she asked finally. "Crack?"

Travis's voice was hollow. "I never heard. Turned out there was a robbery going on in the warehouse across the street, which explained the loud noises and the gunfire. The man was a diversion—a way of luring employees out of the building and keeping them occupied. And keeping other people out."

"So that horrible man—it was all an act?"

"Oh, I don't think so. He was high as a kite. Probably thought it would give him strength, help him do his miserable little job." His head shook. "He cut a deal with the prosecutor. I never saw him again. I heard he got twenty years for felony murder."

"Then—"

"She was dead," Travis said flatly. "Long before the paramedics arrived."

"Oh . . . God, Travis. I—I'm—"

"Staci was taken in by Angela's sister, Marnie. She didn't really want Staci, as Staci well knows, but she had little choice. I still see Staci whenever I can, but it isn't the same. We were almost a family. Now . . ." His voice trailed off.

"I—I don't know—" Cavanaugh took a deep breath, tried again. "I don't know how you—" She couldn't seem to make herself talk coherently, so she stopped trying. Instead she leaned over and pressed her lips against his.

Travis was startled. He flinched instinctively, then gradually relaxed. It was a slow, tentative kiss, but it soon became something more, as caution gave way to arousal.

The first kiss was followed by another, then another. His hand slipped behind her neck; his fingers stroked her hair. Neither of them said a word; it was as if speaking would break the spell—make them acknowledge what they were doing.

After a moment they broke apart, gasping, and then, just as suddenly, he was on top of her, horizontal on the bed. Her hands roamed through his hair, around his neck, under his shirt. His mouth nibbled her earlobe.

He suddenly realized her fingers were moving down his shirt, releasing each button in turn. Just as smoothly, she removed her own blouse. Travis pulled away, but she drew him closer and held him there, refusing to let him withdraw.

His hand gently explored her body. When he paused, she clasped his hand and urged it back to her. Both of them were breathing like long-distance runners, but neither one took notice. His lips brushed against her breasts; he felt goose bumps rise on her soft skin. He pressed his face down hard against her; his stubbled chin tickled her nipples.

They were both moving at once now, twisting, turning, pressing, fumbling with snaps and zippers, trying to forget, trying to remember. They were everywhere at once, but somehow it seemed to work. Travis forgot everything—forgot the world that was hunting him, and the memories that were haunting him.

The last layers of clothing peeled away, and Travis knew there was no turning back. They were committed now—oblivious to the consequences, oblivious to the risk, oblivious to the squealing of the cheap motel bedsprings. For a brief moment the world was rightside up once more.

**53**

11:05 P.M.

"And where do you think you're going, young lady?"

Staci froze in her tracks. Aunt Marnie had spotted her before she made it halfway through the kitchen. Staci had tried to be as quiet as possible, but somehow Aunt Marnie had still managed to catch her. She was like a giant squid; her tentacles were everywhere.

Staci briefly considered possible answers. Slumber party? Late-night basketball game? Prom night? Forget it. She was carrying a stuffed backpack and a pillow. She obviously didn't plan to be back anytime soon.

"I . . . told you Travis called me," Staci began.

"Yes." Marnie placed her hands on her hips. "So?"

"He says I shouldn't stay here tonight."

"Is that right? So you were planning to just take off without even telling me?"

"Well . . . if I told you, I didn't think you'd let me go."

"You were right about that. And just what was it your criminal friend has in mind for this illicit rendezvous?"

"It isn't anything nasty. You don't know what you're talking—"

Marnie slapped her across the face. The sudden blow startled Staci, instantly provoking tears.

"Watch your lip, young lady. I deserve a little more respect than that. I didn't have to take you in, you know."

"I know," Staci whispered.

"I've been suspicious of your precious Travis Byrne for a long time. Paying so much attention to a young girl. Buying her presents, taking her on trips. It isn't natural."

"Travis is the most decent guy on earth," Staci insisted.

"That's not what I read in the papers," Marnie pronounced. She pointed to the front-page article on the kitchen table. "I always suspected he was a pervert, and now my suspicions have been confirmed."

Staci surreptitiously eyed the kitchen door. Only about ten feet away. If she moved quickly, she might get out before Marnie could stop her. "That story in the paper was totally wrong. Travis told me."

"Oh, he told you, did he? Well then, that settles it. Use some sense, girl! He's not going to admit he's a pervert. Especially when he's trying to get you to . . . come to him."

"You're wrong. He doesn't want me to come to him. He won't let me come to him. He wants me to meet Dan and—"

"Dan?" Marnie interrupted. "Who is he? Some other old pervert?"

"He's Travis's boss. He's a lawyer."

"A lawyer who likes little girls?"

Staci threw down her hands in frustration. "I've never even met him before!"

"And Travis expects you to run off in the middle of the night and meet this sicko you've never met before? I don't think so."

"Then can we go to a hotel?" Staci pleaded. "Anywhere other than here."

"My Lord, but you have a lot to learn. Angela just spoiled you, that's all. She lived in a fantasy world."

Staci's face darkened. "Don't say mean things about my mother."

Marnie jerked Staci violently by the shoulders. "Don't you tell me what I may and may not say. You live in a dreamworld, just like she did. You have no idea what things cost. As if I could afford to put you in some expensive hotel. You already cost me far more than I can afford."

"What about the money Travis gives you?"

That remark slowed Marnie down, if only momentarily. "Money? What did he tell you?"

"He didn't tell me anything. But his secretary, Gail, told me he sends you two hundred dollars a month to help take care of me. So where's my two hundred dollars, Aunt Marnie?"

"You brat." She slapped Staci again, even harder than before. "I'll beat you till you beg for forgiveness."

Staci made her break for it. She twisted away and raced toward the kitchen door. Unfortunately, the sliding bolt was engaged; by the time she unlocked it, Marnie had her by the throat.

Marnie whirled her around and brought the flat of her hand sharply against Staci's face. That was the third slap on the same side; it stung. Staci tried to push her away, but she wasn't strong enough.

Marnie raised her arm, this time with her fist clenched. The blow caught Staci just below her right eye and sent her head thudding back against the door.

*No more.* Staci grabbed Marnie's arm and twisted it—she gave her what the kids at school called an *Indian burn.* Marnie screeched, obviously startled to see Staci fight back. Staci used the moment of surprise to good advantage. She raised her right sneaker and kicked Marnie in the shin. Marnie fell back against the kitchen counter. Without wasting a second, Staci flung the door open and raced outside.

She was free—she'd made it! She couldn't help but smile, but she didn't slow down. She wasn't going to give Marnie a second chance. She kept running full out, without looking back.

The tall thin man appeared out of nowhere. Before Staci realized what was happening, he had clamped a hand over her mouth and wrapped his arm around her neck. Another man appeared out of the darkness and grabbed her by the waist. The cloth the first man held over her mouth smelled like Pine Sol. She felt herself growing dizzy and faint.

"Is she the one?" the second man asked.

The tall man nodded. Staci couldn't see his face clearly, but there was something wrong with it, something . . . deformed. He grabbed her Disney bracelet and with a sudden jerk ripped it off her arm. "She's the one."

Staci tried to struggle, but it was becoming increasingly difficult. Her whole body seemed heavy and tired.

"Relax," the second man said. "No one's going to hurt you."

"Right," the tall man echoed. "Well, not for twenty-four hours, anyway." He began to laugh.

It was the last sound Staci heard before she drifted into unconsciousness.

# SATURDAY

*April 20*

# 54

6:30 A.M.

As soon as he saw the number on his LED screen, Agent Janicek jerked the phone out of the cradle.

"Moroconi? Is that you?"

The voice on the other end of the line whispered, "I don't know. Is it safe?"

Janicek punched two buttons on his control console. "It's safe. You're on a secured line."

"Mooney isn't listenin' in?"

"Mooney—" The corners of his mouth turned up slightly. "Mooney won't be bothering me anymore."

"What happened?"

"He had an unfortunate accident. Died in the line of duty."

"Duty? Workin' with you? What'd you do, send him into a cross fire for a can of beer?"

"As a matter of fact, he was killed by your former attorney Mr. Travis Byrne."

"Byrne!" Moroconi sputtered into the phone. "You must be

kiddin'. That wimp wouldn't pull the wings off a butterfly. You set him up."

"I don't see any reason to discuss my business with you, Moroconi. Why did you call?"

"I got the word you were lookin' for me."

"You heard right. I need the list back."

"So why are you tellin' me?"

"Because I think you've still got it. You might fool the mob, but I know damn well you'd never give that list to Byrne. I want it back."

"No way."

"This is serious, Moroconi. I have to have it. Have you made any copies?"

"Not yet."

"Then don't. Bring me the original."

"You little turd. Have you forgotten we had a deal? You sure as hell took my money fast enough."

"I'll return it. It's too risky now. I think Henderson is suspicious."

"Well, isn't that too bad for you?"

Janicek clenched the phone tightly. "It'll be too bad for you, too, you bastard, if I decide to tell everything I know."

There was an extended silence, interrupted only by Moroconi's raspy breathing into the receiver.

"Goddamn list isn't complete as it is."

"What do you mean?"

"I mean it isn't right!" Moroconi shouted. "I wanted Jack. Before I did anyone else, I was going to do Jack. But he isn't there. The address on the list is wrong."

"That can't be. The list is checked and updated constantly."

"Well, it's goddamn true, you chickenshit."

"If the list is incorrect, then you shouldn't mind giving it back."

"Wrong. That list is my insurance policy."

"What do you need it for now? Just stay out of sight. They'll never find you."

"They already have, asshole. I got mail while I was holed up at the motel. Hand-delivered."

"From . . . them?"

"You got it. Elcon, that's what they call themselves. Pissants. Trying to scare me off, like I was some second-grader."

"Don't be a fool, Moroconi. You can't beat them. The smartest thing you can do is keep a low profile and get the hell out of town."

Moroconi seemed to consider. "Maybe you're right. But I got some business to take care of first."

"Revenge is for losers, Moroconi."

"Not the way I do it."

"You're playing with fire. If you know what I mean."

He laughed. "But I won't be the one who gets burned."

"Why don't we meet somewhere and try to come up with a concerted plan of action? Two heads are better than one."

Moroconi released a slow whistle. "You son of a bitch. You're tryin' to set me up, aren't you? You're gonna kill me!"

"Moroconi, you're becoming paranoid—"

"Like hell. You're tryin' to lure me somewhere so you can off me just like you did that dick Mooney. Just to save your own sweet ass."

"That's ridiculous—"

"Don't lie to me, you cheap motherfucker!"

*"I'm desperate!"* Janicek shouted, then checked himself. He looked outside his office door. No one appeared to have heard, thank God. "Henderson suspects. Do you know what will happen to me if he figures it out?"

"You should've thought of that before you got greedy. You knew the risks you were takin'."

"I didn't know you were going to shoot two guards! I didn't know you were going to kill some hood at the West End!"

"Your escape plan was fucked. I had no choice."

"My plan was flawless. The only thing that was fucked was *you.*"

There was another long pause. Janicek could hear Moroconi muttering under his breath, but he was fortunately unable to hear what he was saying.

"I won't be callin' anymore," Moroconi said, finally. "Don't come lookin' for me." He paused, then added: "If I see you, I'll kill you."

**55**

7:02 A.M.

Kramer rubbed his hands together with expectation. The recent turn of events had been extremely promising. A successful capture last night, and now a positive ID on that damned yellow Omni. Who could ask for anything more?

Mario, probably, but that was beside the point. Mario would get everything he wanted—the end of Travis Byrne, the end of Alberto Moroconi, and his own personal copy of the list. And then, once the job was completed, Kramer had some settling up to do with Mario. This time he wouldn't be satisfied with an invitation to the family picnic. No one treated him the way Mario had. No one.

In fairness, he supposed he had to give Mario his due. His carefully choreographed displays of temper had produced the desired result. Kramer had stepped up his efforts—doubled them, to be exact. And Donny had been inspired right into oblivion. Kramer had sent every available thug in Dallas after that yellow Dodge Omni. This had increased his expenses a thousandfold; he probably would be hard-pressed to make a profit off this deal now.

Bottom line, though: he wanted Byrne—and Byrne's new bitch lawyer assistant. And now he had them.

He was on a high grassy ridge overlooking the Black Angus Inn with the five best sharpshooters he knew. Five rifles were trained on the yellow Omni in the parking lot.

And just in time. Even from this distance, Kramer could see two heads, one above the driver's seat, one above the passenger's. Soon they would back out and try to become invisible on the LBJ Expressway. Kramer didn't intend to give them the chance.

Kramer brought his hand down and his men opened fire. An uninterrupted cascade of bullets rained down on the Omni. The windows shattered; glass flew everywhere. The car lurched and shuddered as its small frame was riddled with lead. The heads above the seats fell over.

One of his men tapped Kramer on the shoulder. "The gas tank?"

Kramer resisted the temptation. That would be beautiful. But premature. "Not yet. Let me confirm the kills and take a few photos for Uncle Mario. Then you can blow the thing sky high."

Kramer scanned both sides of the ridge. So far the shooting didn't appear to have attracted any attention. He climbed down and crossed the parking lot. Smoke was still rising from the shattered hull of the Omni. Its tires had gone flat; it drooped over the asphalt like vehicular roadkill. Pleased, Kramer strolled up to the car and peered into the front seat.

Pillows. They were pillows. Well-dressed pillows, but pillows, nonetheless. Pillows wrapped in shirts and coats, propped up so that a head-shaped circlet of fluff appeared just above the seat cushions.

They were way ahead of him. They had ditched the car and left nothing but the pillows behind. They had fooled him.

Kramer pounded his fist on the hood of the car. *Goddamn them!* They had played him for a fool.

Kramer glanced up the ridge. Already his men were headed this way. Soon they would know he had been tricked, and then, within hours, everyone else would know. Travis Byrne had already tarnished his reputation. Now he had caused irreparable damage.

Kramer strode resolutely out of the parking lot. His men called to him, but he ignored them. He didn't need them, he didn't need Mario—he didn't need anyone. This wasn't an assignment anymore. This was personal.

This was a score to settle, a score between Vincent Kramer and Travis Byrne. No more fake couriers, no more firebombs, no more plugged pillows. Next time it would be just him and Byrne.

Byrne was going to die. Slowly. And Kramer was going to enjoy doing it, too.

So what if Byrne and that bitch had gotten away again? It didn't matter. After all, he still had the girl.

**56**

7:30 A.M.

Travis fumbled with the shift stick in their newly acquired Hyundai. He rarely drove a standard and barely remembered how.

Cavanaugh was staring out the passenger-side window. Something was on her mind. He'd have given a million dollars to know what she was thinking, what she thought about him. About them. But so far, no clues.

They had scarcely spoken all morning. And neither had made any reference to the night before.

"I think this was a good idea," Travis said tentatively. "Stealing a car, I mean."

Cavanaugh continued staring out the window. "Does that mean you won't be turning me in?"

"Definitely. How long do you think this car will be safe?"

"Hard to say. I assume the owner will report it stolen as soon as he notices. Certainly we shouldn't drive it longer than twenty-four hours."

"And then?"

"Assuming you still haven't straightened out this mess, or that we haven't been killed? I suppose we'll steal another one."

"Isn't that risky?"

"Oh, in a remote sort of way. You know, there are teenagers who steal eight or ten cars every weekend and never get caught. Of course, they know what they're doing."

Something about Cavanaugh's manner bothered him. She was definitely acting different this morning. Perhaps that was only natural—things had changed. Still, he had hoped she wouldn't be too awkward or . . . regretful.

"Cavanaugh," he said quietly.

"Yes?"

"There's . . . something I want to tell you. Especially after last night." He took a deep breath. "I have a confession to make."

Her head slowly turned. "You're married."

"What? Oh, no—"

"You're living with someone."

"No, I—"

"Oh God! You have some kind of disease."

"No, no!" Travis wiped his brow. "It's nothing like that. It's just that . . . well, it's about why I broke into your apartment. I know I said I chose you because I trusted you. And that was true. But I also knew that you used to be a skip tracer, and it seemed to me that since I needed to locate someone who had disappeared . . ."

There was a painful silence in the car. "You used me."

"It wasn't like that. . . ."

"You've been soft-soaping me the whole time," she said. "You came to me so I would find Moroconi for you!"

"Please, Cavanaugh—I know it sounds awful, but it really wasn't like that—"

"You used me to trace Moroconi's call, and you used me again last night in bed!"

Travis was horrified. "Cavanaugh—*no!*"

Cavanaugh suddenly burst out laughing. She pressed her hand against her mouth, trying to quiet herself, but the laughter continued. Several moments later she gained sufficient control to speak. "Travis," she said, gasping for air, "I figured that out about ten minutes after you showed up."

"You did?"

"Of course I did. What do you take me for?"

"Then you're not angry?"

"I was just toying with you. You are kind of a stuffed shirt sometimes."

A wave of relief passed over him. "I was afraid you hated me."

"Well, I wasn't too keen on being taped to a chair. But the circumstances were rather extreme, so I've decided to forgive you."

"And . . . last night?"

"That, Travis, was entirely mutual. And extremely pleasurable."

Travis wrapped his hand around hers and squeezed.

"Let's pull over and buy the morning paper," he suggested.

"Why? You'll only become more depressed."

"What else can possibly be said about me? That I wear panty hose under my business suits? That I sleep with chickens?"

"They'll think of something."

"Someone is working double time to slander me, and I want to stay on top of the latest developments."

He pulled into a nearby convenience store, then jumped out of the car and bought a paper.

When he returned to the car, less than a minute later, his face was ghostly white.

"See?" Cavanaugh said. "I told you not to read that crap. What did they—" She stopped in midsentence. She could see that there was something else involved, something more than character assassination.

She took the paper from his limp hands. At the top of page one, she saw the expected story on the Moroconi-Byrne manhunt. Scanning quickly, she learned that the police had received an anonymous note from someone who claimed to have been at the West End the night of the shoot-out. The note contained a message—for Travis Byrne. Although it was believed to be a threat of some sort, police were uncertain of its precise meaning.

The message on the front side of the note was only four words long: *We have the girl.*

On the flip side, in small, scribbled letters, someone had written: *Moroconi's motel room by midnight. Or she dies.*

And in the same box with the note, the police found a charm bracelet bearing tiny gold figurines of various Disney characters. Inquiries were proceeding.

Cavanaugh laid down the newspaper. "It's Staci, isn't it?"

"Newspapers frequently receive threats like that," Travis said evenly, "but they almost never print them."

"Maybe they thought it would persuade you to turn yourself in."

Travis shook his head. "Someone with the police or the paper is involved in this. Or is controlled by someone who is."

"What are you going to do?"

"I don't have any choice."

"Travis, you can't turn yourself in to these fiends. They'll kill you!"

"If I don't, they'll kill Staci."

"Maybe not. Maybe they're just bluffing."

"Given all the people who have been killed so far, I think that's unlikely."

She grabbed him by the shoulders. "Travis, I won't let you do this. It's suicide."

He turned away. "What else can I do?"

Cavanaugh reread the note as reported in the paper. "You've got until midnight. That gives us about sixteen hours."

"To do what?"

"To locate Moroconi. To find out who's behind this. And stop it!"

"That's an impossible deadline."

"We have to try!"

"I suppose." Travis's face was tight and grim. "But if we haven't found them by—no. If we haven't found *Staci* by midnight, I will turn myself in to them."

"They'll kill you, Travis."

Travis nodded. "I know."

# 57

8 : 5 0 A . M .

Travis parked the Hyundai in the parking garage for Reunion Tower, the high-rise home of the Elcon Corporation. He backed into the space so the car's license-plate number
wouldn't be easily visible. If they were going to find him again, by
God, they were going to have to work for it.

He and Cavanaugh entered the office building together, Travis
still disguised with sunglasses and fishing hat. They checked the
office directory and rode the elevator to the twenty-fourth floor.

The Elcon offices were small and low-key; they didn't look as
if many visitors were expected. As Travis peered through the glass
in the front door, he saw a small reception area with a slender bru-
nette secretary presiding. She wasn't swamped with work; in fact,
she was concentrating on a crossword puzzle. Oh, well, Travis
mused. It's Saturday. In the back, he saw a large door that led to
an inner office. Travis had to assume that was the lair of Mario
Catuara.

"Think she'll let us see him?" Cavanaugh asked.

"Hard to say. He may not be in."

"Maybe we should concoct some kind of plan."

"You complicate things too much, Cavanaugh. The direct approach is usually best. Let me take a stab at her."

"So you can turn on your animal magnetism?"

"I just think I might have more success with her than you." Before Cavanaugh could reply, Travis pushed the door open and strolled inside.

The secretary was humming something. Travis thought it was *"Qué Sera Sera,"* but it was hard to be certain when she had the eraser end of a pencil in her mouth. He approached, smiled, and sat down on the edge of her desk. She was in her late thirties at least and, he noted, she wasn't wearing a wedding ring.

"Hi there," Travis said cheerily. "My name's Sam Jones. I'd like to see Mr. Catuara. I'm an old family friend."

"Do you have an appointment?"

"I'm afraid not. But he'll want to see me."

"Is he expecting you?"

"In a way."

"That's odd," she said, "since he isn't even here."

"Well . . . do you expect him in later?"

"No." She batted a pencil against her desk.

"Well . . . do you know where he is?"

"Of course I do," she replied.

"Well . . . would you like to tell me where he is?"

She seemed to be considering at great length. "I suppose it wouldn't hurt. Since you're an old family friend. He's at his home."

"Oh. And where is that?"

"You're an old family friend, and you don't know where he lives?" Her voice carried more than a hint of suspicion. "I'm not authorized to release that information."

"Maybe you could give me his phone number." With which Crescatelli could obtain his address, Travis thought.

"No."

"Aw, what could it hurt?"

"I don't know," she said. "And I don't plan to find out."

"Mr. Catuara will be mighty disappointed if he finds out I was in town and he didn't get to see me."

"I'll take that risk."

"Look, it's vital that I talk with him today. As soon as possible. Can I at least make an appointment?"

"I'm not authorized to make appointments for Mr. Catuara. He does that for himself. I can take a number, though, and ask him to call you."

"No, that won't work." Travis searched his brain for a different approach. He leaned across her desk, hovering precariously over the out box, and stroked her chin. "Are you sure you can't help me out here?"

"I'm afraid not," she replied frostily.

"I bet you have his home address right there in your Rolodex," Travis continued. "You could just sort of . . . look away for a moment. I'd be very appreciative." He ran his fingers across her cheek and down her neck.

The secretary removed his hand from her face. "I'm afraid I'm going to have to ask you to leave, Mr. Jones. Or whatever your name is."

"There must be some way you can help me."

"I can help you out the door. That's it."

"But surely—"

She picked up her phone. "I'm calling Security. They take a dim view of office mashers."

"But I didn't—"

"Five more seconds, then I cry rape."

"I'm going, I'm going." Travis slid off the desk. "I'm gone."

Cavanaugh was waiting for him in the hallway outside. "Good work, Casanova."

"You were watching?"

"From a respectful distance. You should've let me go. Your act isn't exactly subtle."

"How was I supposed to know she would be—"

"What? Offended by your heavy-handed pseudosexual advances? You were supposed to get into her Rolodex, not her pants."

"Pseudosexual? What's that supposed to mean? I can't tell if you're mad or just jealous."

"*Jealous?* Why, you insufferable—" She swung her fist around and socked him on the shoulder.

He rubbed his arm vigorously. "All right, since I'm such a loser, let's hear your brilliant plan for getting Catuara's address."

"Well, the easiest methods are all gone now because she's going to be suspicious of anyone who comes near that Rolodex. We need a diversion."

"And so you're going to . . . what? Do a striptease in the lobby?"

"Just stay out of the way and watch, pig."

She marched back toward the elevators and directed Travis's attention to the fire alarm.

"You're not going to set that off, are you?"

"Why not?" Cavanaugh responded. "It'll ring for maybe ten minutes until Security discovers there's no fire. But the secretary will have to leave her office."

Travis shrugged. Maybe it wasn't such a bad idea, even if it was hers.

Cavanaugh pulled the handle. There was a delay; it was probably a silent alarm that triggered something on the security people's control panel. After about ten seconds, a very audible alarm sounded. The shrill wail filled the twenty-fourth floor. Travis and Cavanaugh ran back to the Elcon offices and positioned themselves around the corner where they could keep an eye on the office door.

Workers strolled out the few other offices that were open on Saturday morning, mumbling variations of "Is this another drill?" and "I don't have time for this." The floor emptied, except for the Elcon office.

Finally the front door opened. Travis watched as the secretary stepped out of the office . . . and locked the door behind her. She continued down the hallway to the stairwell.

"She locked the door," Travis said.

"Thanks for the color commentary," Cavanaugh replied. "I noticed."

"Well, Ms. Former Skip Tracer, do you know how to pick locks?"

"With lock picks. But I don't have any."

"Know anyplace we could get some?"

"Yeah. But not before she gets back from the fire drill."

Travis shoved his hands into his pockets. Looked like this was strike two.

**58**

1 0 : 0 5 A.M.

"This is a monumentally ridiculous idea," Cavanaugh observed.

"Cut me some slack. We tried your idea. It bombed."

"This from the guy who tried to seduce the secretary on top of her desk."

"Would you forget about that? As far as I'm concerned, we've each got one out. But this ploy will drive the ball over the fence."

"I like the macho sports analogies, but I'm reserving judgment on your conclusion." She put on his windbreaker and tucked away the Rolodex and the pencils they bought in the office-supply store downstairs. "Maybe I should take your sunglasses. Tell her I'm from the Council for the Blind."

"And you said I was insensitive." He took her by the shoulders and steered her toward the door. "Don't overact, Cavanaugh. The simpler the performance, the better. Go."

Cavanaugh marched into the Elcon office before the secretary had a chance to instruct her otherwise. "Good morning. My name is Marilyn Smith and I'm raising funds for the Mars Initiative."

The secretary peered up from her crossword. "You're—what? From Mars?"

"Yes, Mars. We believe the American space program has been moribund for too long. We want to see some action—not just talk, but actual missions. American citizens exploring the final frontier, reaching for the infinity of the stars. Will you assist us?"

"I don't exactly know what I . . ."

"Patriotism begins at home."

"But I really wouldn't know what to do."

"It's very simple." Cavanaugh reached into her jacket and withdrew the pencils. "Just a few dollars from you can help guarantee the immortality of the species. All you have to do is buy these special commemorative space pencils."

The secretary took one from the box. "They look like ordinary number-two pencils to me."

"You don't want us to spend all our funds producing cheap souvenirs, do you? Of course you don't. Now, if you'll simply donate enough to buy all of these"—she fanned the pencils across the desk—"you'll become an associate member of the Society for the Mars Init—oops!"

She feigned stumbling and spilled the pencil box. The entire assortment dropped onto the floor behind the secretary's desk. The secretary jumped back as if they were ballistic missiles.

"Oh, my goodness. I'm such a klutz," Cavanaugh said. She started to walk around the desk. "Here, allow me to help."

"Just stay where you are," the secretary said, motioning her back. "I'll get them."

The secretary bent over and began collecting the pencils. As soon as her head was below the desktop, Cavanaugh silently removed the dummy Rolodex—identical to the secretary's except that all the cards were blank—and switched them. She tucked the real Rolodex inside her jacket.

A second later the secretary rose with the pencils. "Here. Now please leave."

Cavanaugh sniffed. "Well, fine. I guess some people just don't care about the immortality of the species." She grabbed the pencils and slid out the door, grumbling about coffee-break patriots.

After the office door closed, Cavanaugh shoved the real Rolodex into Travis's hands. "Get the address."

Travis removed the card for Mario Catuara, then set the Rolodex on the floor just outside the office. Together, they scrambled for the elevators.

"How long till she notices her Rolodex is blank?" Cavanaugh asked.

"Until her first phone call. Let's hope that when she finds the real one outside the door, she'll stop worrying about it."

"And what are we going to do?"

Travis smiled thinly as the elevator doors closed. "We're going to pay Mr. Catuara a visit."

# 59

### 4:00 P.M.

Agent Simpson slid the memo onto Janicek's desk while he talked on the phone. As soon as Janicek read the first sentence, he put down the receiver, cutting off the speaker in midsentence.

Success.

He knew they could do it. They were the goddamn FBI, after all. Sort of. If they wanted somebody found, they were found.

The information in the files about Jack's current location was not up-to-date. That was because no one cared. If he didn't want FBI protection anymore, that was fine with them. They'd save a ton of money; he could look after himself. On the other hand, if the FBI wanted to find him, they could, Janicek had reasoned. And this memo proved he was right.

Jack had changed his name again, but he made the stupid mistake of using one of the credit cards the FBI had supplied to him. The charge was made at a casino; the idiot was probably desperate, probably a second away from getting his head bashed in. Anyway, that was the lead they needed. From there, tracking him down was a simple exercise in detective work. He hadn't gone far. Janicek could be there in about an hour.

And that was exactly what he planned to do, as soon as he got out of this office. Jack was his most reliable lead to Moroconi. Moroconi had said that he was planning to *do* Jack first. Which was okay with him. But when Moroconi finished with Jack, Janicek would be waiting for him.

M ario removed a huge imported cigar from his desktop humidor, bit off the end, and lit it. He propped his feet up on the elegant desk in the den of his home on the outskirts of Fort Worth and let the pungent smoke course through his lungs. With each puff, he felt his tension evaporating.

Mario had been through tough times, both before and after he became president of the corporation, but these past few days had been a real son of a bitch. He'd been so tense his chest felt like granite. He imagined he could feel his arteries hardening. That bastard Byrne, and that worse bastard Kramer, had put him through the wringer. Finally, for the first time in a week, he had a chance to be alone, to relax, and to contemplate the future.

He smiled when he thought about his recent displays of rage. What performances; he should be up for an Oscar. He had actually bullied Kramer, the meanest, sickest sadist on God's green earth. The whole time Mario had felt as if his knees might give out, as if his thin facade of authority might crack and reveal the terror-stricken coward within. But it never did. He had brought it off without a hitch, and managed to inspire not only Kramer but his worthless moron nephew as well.

A thin smile curled around the huge cigar. Yes, he'd inspired Donny—right into his grave. He must be a great actor if he made Kramer believe he had the remotest iota of grief about Donny's demise. More like relief; an annoying fly had been swatted— by someone else. He supposed he would eventually have to call

Monica and give her the news. He wondered if she might not be as relieved as he was.

Mario had Kramer by the short hairs. He didn't know why people treated hit men like they were demigods. They were just sociopaths—serial killers who found a way to make a living doing what they enjoyed most. Kramer's flawless record that he was so goddamn proud of was ruined. Mario hated Moroconi and Byrne and wanted them both rubbed out, but it was almost worth the delay just to see Kramer squirm. Just to have an excuse to get that sick sack of shit out of his organization for good.

Mario chuckled just thinking about the mighty Kramer shooting holes in a bunch of pillows. Thank God he'd had some of his own men on Kramer's tail, or he would surely have never heard about it. Travis Byrne had shaken Kramer but good. Kramer was a desperate man, losing his grip by inches. Eventually he would make the big mistake, and the world would be a better place as a result.

Mario was enjoying himself for the first time in days when the green phone on his desk rang. He frowned. The ringing was jarring—an intrusion on the little moment of pleasure he had carved out for himself. He considered ignoring it, but realized that would only postpone the inevitable.

"Yes?" he snapped, snatching the phone.

"Sir, it's Madeline. From the office."

Right. Madeline. Lucky she identified herself. Madeline—nice legs, big butt. He'd screwed her a few times after he hired her, then forgot about her. Why hadn't she been fired yet? Just another administrative detail he was going to have to deal with himself. If you want something done right . . .

"Why are you calling me at home, Madeline?"

"I just wanted to ask you—"

"Forget it, Madeline. It's over between us. And I told you never to use this number unless it's an emergency."

"No, you don't understand." There was a protracted pause on

the other end of the line. Mario could imagine her dense wheels spinning in their grooves, throwing sparks into a vast void. "Something very . . . strange happened in the office today."

"Strange?" Mario put his feet down on the floor. "What do you mean, strange?"

"My Rolodex went blank."

Another imbecile. Even stupider than Donny. "Look, you know the procedure for ordering office supplies—"

"And then I found the real one outside my door."

"Madeline, I don't know what you're talking about. Start at the beginning and tell me what happened!"

"First, this guy I've never seen before enters the office and starts coming on to me like a ton of bricks. I told him to take a hike. I'm not cheap, Mario, you know that. He wanted to get close to me in a bad way. In the office! Can you believe that?"

The only thing Mario couldn't believe was that the man was unsuccessful. "Is this some stupid ploy to make me jealous, Madeline?"

"Of course not. The thing is, he acted like he was interested in me, but the whole time he kept looking at my desk. Then he started pumping me for your home address. And then, later on, I notice my Rolodex has been replaced by a brand-new blank one, and about ten minutes after that, when I'm on my way to the ladies' room, I find my Rolodex in the hallway outside the door."

Mario was finally getting the drift. "Does this Rolodex contain my address?"

After a pregnant pause, Madeline confessed. "It did. The card is missing."

Mario's hands tightened into little fists. "And what about our esteemed CEO? Is his address in there?"

"Oh no," Madeline said hurriedly. "I don't have his address written down anywhere."

"Thank God for that." Mario felt a sudden throbbing between his temples. "Are you sure you don't know who this stranger was?"

"Sorry. I've never seen him before."

"Have you been reading the newspapers lately? For instance, the articles about Travis Byrne and Alberto Moroconi?"

"Oh no, I don't read the papers. Don't watch the TV news either. It's too depressing."

Not as depressing as you, you worthless cunt. "Was the man medium-size, dark-haired, rat-faced?"

"Oh, no. That wasn't him at all."

So it wasn't Moroconi. Unfortunately, Mario didn't know what Byrne looked like well enough to describe him. "All right, Madeline. You did right by calling me. If anything else unusual happens, or if you see that man again, phone me immediately. Understand?"

"Sure. If you like, I could come by the house—"

"That won't be necessary." Mario hung up the phone before she had a chance to say another word.

He ground his cigar out on the desk blotter. The holiday was over.

He paced back and forth across his den. Who the hell could it have been? Byrne? The FBI? Even if it hadn't been Moroconi in the office, he could have sent an accomplice. Come to think of it, if Moroconi asked enough of the old boys, he could probably find Mario's house. . . .

This is intolerable, Mario thought. He would not be threatened, especially not in his own home. He hated to give Kramer an entry back into the organization, but . . . he needed someone he could count on. Someone ruthless. He could always ditch him again later.

Kramer wasn't in, but Mario left a message with his point man and told him to send Kramer over immediately. As soon as he hung up the phone, he wondered if that was enough. Kramer had been slipping lately. Maybe he should call Tony and tell him to come out with a full security contingent.

Yeah. They could lay a trap and, when his visitor arrived, blow him to kingdom come. Mario would take this minor annoyance and turn it to his own advantage. That's what his father would've done. Damn straight.

He felt his confidence reasserting itself, just as he heard a click that told him the door to the den had been opened.

Mario whirled around and saw Al Moroconi standing not five feet away, a grin smeared across his face, and a snub-nosed revolver clutched in both hands.

"Surprise," he said.

**60**

**4:30 P.M.**

Travis and Cavanaugh were in the Big-D Pawn Shop, a barred-window emporium in one of the seediest parts of downtown Dallas.

Cavanaugh returned from a back office, her arms loaded with weapons of all shapes and sizes. "I've brought a vast assortment so you can have your pick of the lot."

"Aren't there registration requirements for handguns? Permits? Waiting periods?"

"Not here. Not for us, anyway. It pays to have friends in low places."

Travis glanced at the wiry man in the sky-blue leisure suit standing behind the counter. "I'm surprised a prosecution type such as yourself knows about a place like this," Travis remarked.

"I'm surprised you don't," she replied. "You're the one who represents the scum of the earth on a regular basis. Where do you think your clients get their guns? Kmart?"

"I never ask questions. It's better that way."

"I met Floyd back when I was a skip tracer," she explained.

" 'Bout the same time I met Crescatelli. I did him a favor, too—found a hood who'd stuck him with a lot of fake jewelry. Nothing crooks hate worse than crooks. He couldn't afford to pay me, so I let it slide. He owed me."

"You seem to have a lot of outstanding debts."

"Yeah. Lucky for you, huh?" She spread the array of weaponry across a counter. "Take your pick, Byrne."

Travis felt a hollow pounding in his heart. "Are you sure we should carry guns?"

"You want to bust in on this probable mobster unarmed? It's an incredibly stupid, life-threatening idea *with* guns. Without them, it's suicide."

"I don't . . . like guns."

"You don't— You used to be a cop, for Pete's sake!"

"That was before—" Travis leaned against the glass counter. It was all surging back. Everything he had worked so hard to suppress.

Cavanaugh placed her hand on his shoulder. "Travis, it wasn't your fault."

"If I hadn't had a gun . . . it wouldn't have happened."

"You're not thinking straight. If there hadn't been a crazy man who attacked you, it wouldn't have happened. If there hadn't been a crowd, it wouldn't have happened. If you didn't care about other people, it wouldn't have happened. It was a tragic juxtaposition of circumstances. But it wasn't your fault."

The aching in Travis's chest was almost more than he could bear. "I'm sorry, Cavanaugh. I don't think I could fire a gun. Ever again."

Cavanaugh sighed. "Okay. Could you at least *carry* a gun? That might keep someone from pulling one on you. For at least a second or two."

Travis reached for the nearest pistol and felt a tidal rush of nausea sweep over him. In a flash, the entire scene played out before his eyes—the frantic struggle, the report of the gun, Angela's face on the pavement, eyes dark. He shook his head and turned away.

"Okay," Cavanaugh said. "How about this multistrike weapon? It looks more like a toy than a gun. And it shoots red paint pellets."

Travis glanced at the weapon. It had two barrels, one mounted over the other, both oversized. She was right, it didn't look real—more like a Nerf gun.

He pointed to the second barrel. "More paint pellets?"

"Well . . . no. That one spews bullets."

"Paint pellets *and* bullets?"

"That's why it's a multistrike weapon. You have your choice."

Slowly, Travis reached out and picked up the weapon. His stomach was still churning, but not nearly so badly as before. It seemed so harmless. Maybe he could pull it off.

"Okay. I'll try," he said quietly.

"Great." She set aside a .44 Magnum and several rounds of ammunition. "I prefer something a bit stronger myself. Someone has to be ready for the bad guys."

She peered out the storefront windows and saw the orange sun beginning its descent. "It'll be dark in a few hours. Shall we wait till all the villains are snoring soundly in their beds?"

"No," Travis said. "Not while Staci's in danger. The longer we wait, the greater the chance that . . . something will happen to her. Let's go now."

H e had been driving the streets for over twenty-four hours, trolling like a psychotic serial killer in search of his prey. He had covered every district in metro Dallas, and then covered them all over again. It was boring, mind-numbing. But necessary.

It was his own fault. If he hadn't been such a stupid fool, if he hadn't allowed that amateur Byrne and his girlfriend to get away from him at the library, it would all be over now. But he had hesitated. He had been careless. And during that momentary lapse, they had managed to get away. He would not let that happen again.

He drove all morning, his eyes bouncing back and forth between the road and the tracing beacon scanner, until finally he saw what he was looking for. A red blip on the scanner. The homing tracer was on the same highway moving in the opposite direction.

He whirled his Jeep around and crossed over the white stone median. The bottom of his Jeep scraped, making a hideous noise and sending sparks flying. Not good for the vehicle, but he had no time to waste.

He pulled into the fast lane and floored the accelerator. The blip returned to his scanner, clear as a bell. His prey was maybe two miles ahead of him, moving fast. Excellent. Wherever the blip went, so would he.

He lightly fingered his pistol, his ammunition, his Puukko knife. Noting that the sun was setting, he checked his infrared glasses. Still operational. He was ready. All he had to do was tag along and wait for the right moment.

This time Travis Byrne would not get away from him.

**61**

5:05 P.M.

**M**ario awoke in a flash of panic. His body was suspended horizontally, but he couldn't tell where or how. He couldn't feel anything beneath him or above him. It was as if he was floating in midair. But that was impossible. If he was still alive.

He opened his eyes, but couldn't seem to get his bearings. Everything was black; he couldn't see anything, or touch anything, or hear anything. He was totally disoriented. He tried to move, but found his hands and feet were locked tightly in place. He was helpless, pinned down like a bug in the middle of . . . nothing.

What had happened to him? He remembered thinking he should call Tony to guard his home. But before he could lift the phone, his worst nightmare walked into the den—Al Moroconi, back from the dead. Moroconi had clubbed him over the head with his pistol, and Mario had awakened here. But where the hell was here?

Mario felt beads of sweat dripping down his face. If this was supposed to frighten him, it was working. He was terrified. And he was sweating profusely. It was extremely hot, especially beneath him.

He swung his body back and forth, as much as the restraints on his hands and feet would allow. He heard a rushing sound. Something trickled inside his shirt and down his shorts. Water? *What the hell?*

Suddenly the overhead lights burst on. Mario squinted, trying to shut out the offending light. His head began to throb. He heard a shuffling noise, then a soft, horrifying chuckle.

Mario slowly opened his eyes. He knew where he was. He should—it was his own basement rec room. He could see the pool table, the sauna, the high-tech exercise equipment. Of course—he was in the hot tub! Moroconi had tied him down in the goddamn hot tub!

"Get me out of here, you sick motherfucker!" Mario bellowed.

He saw Moroconi's leering face emerge over the edge of the Jacuzzi. "You ain't in a position to give orders."

"After my boys get here—and that won't be long—you won't be in a position to walk, you slimy bastard." That was it, Mario told himself, keep it rolling. His bluff had worked on Kramer; maybe he could cow Moroconi, too. "Get me the hell out of here!"

"Hot tubs are supposed to be relaxing, Mario. You don't seem relaxed at all. Here, lemme add some more water."

Moroconi disappeared momentarily from view. Mario heard the squeak of the faucet as Moroconi turned up the water flow. Twisting his head around as much as possible, Mario saw that he was stretched clean across the hot tub, floating atop the water, tied down to the jet hooks on the bottom. His head was already much higher than his hands. Soon the water would rise and stretch his arms to their full length.

The horrible truth struck him like a blow to the head. That was Moroconi's plan, of course. Once Mario couldn't rise any higher, the water would rush over his head—and he would drown. In his own hot tub.

"I called my boys just before you arrived, Moroconi. They

should be here in five minutes. Ten at the outside. If you're still here, you'll be dog meat."

"Izzat so?" Moroconi's grin was sickening; yellow teeth were visible between his lips. "Lemme tell you somethin', Mario. You've been out cold for over an hour. Your boys are runnin' late. If I didn't know better, I'd think you were lyin' to me."

Mario put on his nastiest sneer. "You're a dead man, Moroconi. Might as well go buy your coffin. When my boys are done, you'll be less than a smear on the carpet. We should've taken you out four years ago—"

"Yeah, you probably should have," Moroconi agreed. "You should have done *something* for me. But you didn't. You fucked me over and hung me out to dry. And now you're gonna pay for it."

Moroconi pursed his lips and spat, missing Mario's face by less than an inch. "How's the temperature in there?"

Mario swallowed. "It's . . . fine. Why?"

"Well, you still seem tense." Moroconi bent down and checked the thermostat on the side of the hot tub. "Only a hundred degrees? And they call this a hot tub?" He placed his fingers on the dial. "Here—let's crank it up to a hundred twenty, maybe one thirty. Oh, what the hell. Let's just go all the way." He turned the dial into the red zone.

"You crazy bastard! That's scalding!"

"No," Moroconi said. "One thirty would've been scalding. At this temperature, the flesh will peel off your bones." He folded his arms across his chest. "This kinda confuses matters, don't it? I'm not sure now whether you'll die from the heat or from drowning."

Mario felt his respiration increasing, his perspiration working overtime. Could it be that much hotter so soon? Or was he just losing his grip? He felt a drop slide down the side of his face and realized, to his utter humiliation, that it was not sweat. He was crying.

"Oh, poor little Mario," Moroconi said in a baby voice. "He's gettin' all upset. *Awwww.*"

Mario tried to speak, but choked. "What do you want, Moroconi?"

"I'm sure you know already."

"I don't have any idea!"

"I wanna square the record. I wanna piece of what everyone else got. And I wanna get even for what you and Jack did to me."

Mario could feel the water lapping at his cheeks. The temperature was definitely hotter. "If it's money you want, help yourself. I don't have much, but—"

"But Jack does? Goddamn right. He's living high off *my* fuckin' money!"

"Fine—get Jack! Let me out of here!"

Moroconi made a tsking sound with his teeth and tongue. He was savoring every minute of his sweet revenge. "That's my problem, Mario. I don't know where Jack is. But you do."

"You're wrong. I haven't seen him since he turned state's evidence. You've got the list. Or had it, at least. Can't you find him?"

"The list is wrong. I went to the address on the list, and he wasn't there. He's relocated himself."

"Maybe he has. What's that got to do with me?"

"I think you've been in contact with him, Mario. I think you must've helped him relocate."

"Me? Help that traitor? If I knew where he was, I'd cut his heart out." The water was trickling around his neck, burning his throat.

"It pains me to say this, Mario, but I think you're lyin' through your goddamn teeth."

"Al, if I knew where he was, I'd tell you. What do I care what happens to him?"

Moroconi leaned in close. "Don't fuck with me, Mario."

"I'm not! I wouldn't do that to you, Al."

"Liar." Moroconi reached down and pressed Mario's head beneath the water.

The steaming water flowed over Mario's face, his eyes, his lips. It was hot, much too hot. It burned. It felt as if the water etched into his flesh. He wanted to scream, but he had to keep his mouth shut tight.

Moroconi jerked Mario's head out by his thinning hair. "Enjoyin' yourself, Mario? Ready to talk?"

"I'm telling you"—he coughed, sputtered—"I don't know where—"

Moroconi lowered Mario's face back into the boiling caldron. Mario tried to keep his eyes clenched shut, to prevent the water from burning the skin off his eyeballs. All he could do was grit his teeth and wait.

He waited, but Moroconi didn't raise his head out of the water. Perverted bastard. This was just a scare tactic. He wouldn't—

Mario's lungs began to ache. He needed oxygen—now! He thrashed from side to side, trying to lift his head above the surface of the water. It was no use. Moroconi held his head down firmly. With his hands tied, there was nothing, absolutely nothing Mario could do. He felt himself growing faint.

Desperate for air, his lips parted, and the scalding water poured inside. Mario felt it burning his mouth, his tongue, coursing through his lungs. For the first shattering moment he realized he was going to die—

And then Moroconi lifted his head out of the water.

Mario came up coughing and throwing up water. Vomit spewed down his cheeks into the hot tub.

Moroconi laughed. "Gotcha worried that time, didn't I?"

"It's under the blotter. On my desk," Mario gasped, as soon as he was able to talk. "Jack's new address."

"Thank you, Mario. Most cooperative of you." He released Mario's head. It splashed back into the hot tub.

The hot water rose to the level of Mario's cheekbones. "Wait a minute. You said you'd let me go if I gave you Jack!"

Moroconi shook his head. "I said no such thing. You assumed I would let you go." He grinned. "You were wrong. Bye-bye, Mario. Hope you can hold your breath for a long time. Like forever."

He laughed again, even louder than before, and strolled upstairs.

**62**

5:15 P.M.

Travis and Cavanaugh approached the front door of the home of the Elcon president, Mario Catuara. It was an elegant house, obviously expensive, not far from Fort Worth, but very secluded. If they hadn't known exactly where they were going, they never would have found it.

Travis stopped when he got to the porch steps. The front door was open.

"Something's wrong," Cavanaugh said.

"I agree," Travis replied. "Someone got here before us."

"Moroconi? Or that creep from the library?"

Travis shrugged. "Who knows?"

"Why would Moroconi be looking for Catuara?"

"I don't know. But that envelope we found in his hotel room tells me they're connected somehow. Why don't you stay out here while I take a look inside?"

Cavanaugh grabbed Travis by the collar. "Spare me the chivalry. If Moroconi is in there, you're going to need someone who's capable of firing a gun."

Cavanaugh pushed the front door the rest of the way open and entered. Frowning, Travis followed close behind.

They made a quick sweep of the ground level of the house. Marvelously well furnished, but beyond that, they found nothing of interest. They did discover a staircase—nineteen steps going up, twenty steps going down.

"Let's cover both floors at once so he can't slip away," Cavanaugh whispered. "You take the basement. I'll take the upstairs."

Travis didn't argue. He tiptoed quietly down the carpeted steps and soon realized he had gotten the easier assignment. There was only one room downstairs.

The door was partly open and the light was on. Travis took a deep breath, then stepped through. He hit the deck, just in case someone fired at him. No one did. He crawled into the room on his hands and knees, then slowly rose to his feet.

It was a rec room—a high-class, state-of-the-art playhouse. Travis eyed the sophisticated exercise equipment, feeling a wave of envy he couldn't suppress. If he could afford to put gizmos like these in his apartment, maybe he could lose those extra pounds around his gut. Scanning the room, he saw a pool table, several pinball machines, and in the far corner—a hot tub.

There was something floating in the hot tub. Approaching, he saw it was a body—Catuara, unless Travis missed his guess. He was tied down in the tub, and his face was covered with water. He was not moving.

"Cavanaugh!" Travis yelled.

He reached into the water, then instinctively withdrew his hand. The water was blisteringly hot. He grabbed a towel from a nearby rack and wrapped it around his hand. Steeling himself, he reached into the hot tub and pulled the man's head above the water.

The man's eyes did not open, but Travis saw them move under the eyelids—a sign of life, however slight. He cut the ropes with a pocketknife he'd picked up at the pawnshop. After the man was free, he hauled him out of the steaming water.

It was at just that moment, when Travis's arms were wrapped

around the body and there was nothing he could do to defend himself, that he heard quiet footsteps immediately behind him. He felt a heavy blow on the top of his head, and before he passed out, he had a brief sensation of his face plunging into scalding hot water.

# 63

5:30 P.M.

The shorter, beefier of the two men checked his watch, then frowned. "I don't think he's coming."

"He'll come," Staci said defiantly. "I know he will."

"Just a few more hours till midnight."

"Plenty of time." Despite her outward show of strength, Staci was scared to death. Why was Travis taking so long? Why wasn't he here yet?

They were in a crummy hotel room somewhere in Dallas—Staci and the two men who grabbed her outside Aunt Marnie's house. There were two other men in an adjoining room who popped in from time to time. Staci didn't know anything about any of them, except that they all looked like crooks and they were all carrying big guns.

After she had regained consciousness, she had found herself tied to a stiff-backed, uncomfortable chair. They hadn't let her move since.

"Maybe he didn't get the message," Staci suggested.

"Unlikely. It was in the paper, right?"

The tall man with the long scar down the side of his face nodded. "My man at the newspaper never fails me."

"Maybe Travis doesn't have time to read the papers," Staci suggested. "He's been real busy."

"If I were gettin' the press coverage he's gettin', I'd read the paper," the shorter man said. "Wouldn't you, Kramer?"

The tall man's eyes widened. In one sudden, savage motion he clubbed the man on the side of his face.

Blood trickled from the corner of his mouth. "Jesus Christ! What was that for?"

"Names," Kramer whispered under his breath.

"Oh, shit. I didn't think." He looked down at Staci. " 'Course, that isn't his real name, you know. We all use aliases around here."

Kramer rolled his eyes. "Unlike you, she ain't a complete moron." He cast his eyes down at the girl. "You just signed her death certificate."

Staci only understood about a fourth of what the two men said, but she fully understood the import of that last remark. "What did he call you? I didn't even hear it. And I wouldn't remember it if I had. I've got a real short attention span. Really. It's certified and everything."

"It ain't gonna make much difference, in the end," Kramer said grimly. "Even if Byrne does show up—"

"He will. I know he will."

Kramer raised an eyebrow. "Then what's takin' so long?"

"I don't know, but I know there's a reason."

"I think Byrne has deserted you."

"He has not!"

"Maybe I screwed up. Maybe he never cared about you."

Staci's face flushed. "You *geekwad.*"

The short man raised his fists eagerly. "She can't talk to you like that, boss. Should I hit her?"

"Of course not. Idiot." Kramer stepped forward and, just as suddenly as before, swung his fist into Staci's face.

Afterward he rubbed his hand and smiled. "Rank has its privileges."

Staci began to cry. Her teeth and jaws ached; she had accidentally bitten her tongue.

"Stop bawlin'!" Kramer barked.

Staci tried, but she couldn't. It hurt too bad.

"Fine. Gag her." The short man stuffed a towel in Staci's mouth.

The door to the adjoining room opened, and a third man leaned in. "Simmons just called in," he said, looking at Kramer. "He's been talking to Mario."

Kramer's eyebrows rose. "What does Mario want?"

"He wants you to come to his home immediately. Didn't explain why. He left an address."

"Wow!" the short man exclaimed. "I ain't never been invited to his home. I didn't think anyone got to go. What do you suppose happened?"

"I dunno," Kramer murmured. "But it must be bad. He wouldn't call me unless the whole operation was in trouble." He grabbed his coat. "I'm leavin'."

"Fine," the short man said. "I'll watch the girl."

"No. Take her to the CEO."

"Really?"

Kramer nodded. "You know where he lives?"

"Sure, but—why?"

"If Mario is in danger, our CEO also may be threatened. You will deliver this invaluable insurance policy to him."

"Should I stay there with her?"

"No. She isn't going anywhere. You're needed here."

"What if Byrne shows up and there's no girl?"

Kramer made a steeple with his fingers. "What does it matter, really? We can kill him just as easily, whether she's here or not."

## 64

5 : 4 5 P.M.

When Travis awoke, he was lying faceup, staring at the ceiling. He wasn't sure where he was. The only things he could be certain of were that he wasn't in heaven and he wasn't in the overheated hot tub.

He touched his face; it felt tender and raw. Probably swollen and burned, too, but at least all the parts still seemed to function.

He rolled slightly to one side, sending shooting pains up and down his abdomen. Never mind, he thought to himself. I'm not drowning, and I'm not being burned alive. Maybe I'll just lie here for a moment.

He heard a soft rhythmic sound behind him—steady breathing. Twisting his head, he saw Cavanaugh hunched over the man he had dragged out of the hot tub. And—what the hell? She was kissing him!

He rolled his eyes to the back of his head. What an idiot he was sometimes. She wasn't kissing him—she was giving him mouth-to-mouth resuscitation. And it was working. Travis could see water spewing out of the man's mouth, and could see his arms and legs beginning to move.

An intense aching radiated through Travis's skull, reminding him that he'd been clubbed over the head. Cavanaugh must've hauled him out of the tub. Cavanaugh seemed to have everything under control. He'd just remain still and try to pull himself together. Who knew—maybe he could get some mouth-to-mouth for himself.

About half an hour later Mario sat on a beanbag chair in the rec room hunched over a half-filled brandy snifter. Travis pressed a fully filled ice pack to his forehead. Cavanaugh stood between them and listened.

"Moroconi hates me," Mario murmured. He spoke in short, breathy bursts, a few syllables at a time. "He left me to die. Must've clubbed you on his way out."

"What did he want?" Cavanaugh asked.

"He wanted an address. One he couldn't find on the list."

"There it is again," Travis said. "That damn list that everyone wants. What is it?"

"It's a list of squealers who were given new identities by the Federal Witness Relocation Program. Once the witnesses are relocated, there are supposed to be no traces of their former lives. No trail to be followed. But someone in Bureau 99 kept a list."

"Why?"

Mario inhaled the brandy fumes. "Don't ask me. Some overzealous bureaucrat, probably. Maybe it was necessary to forward payments, to make periodic checks. All I know is that the list exists. And Moroconi got it."

"Why did he want it?"

"He's looking for someone. Someone who turned state's evidence four years ago. Jack." He paused. "Moroconi wants revenge against Jack."

"Wasn't Jack on the list?"

"He was, but the information was incorrect." Mario swirled the brandy around his mouth and down his throat, savoring the artificial comfort. "The FBI are not the only ones who know how to relocate."

"Did Moroconi get the man's address from you?"

Mario's eyes lowered. "I had no choice."

"Then give it to me, too," Travis said. "I have to find him. It's my only hope."

"I can't do that."

"You gave it to Moroconi!"

"Because I had to. I don't want to do any more damage than has already been done."

"If you don't give me the address," Travis barked, "I won't catch Moroconi. He'll remain free." He paused, allowing the weight of his words to sink into Mario's brain. "And when he finds out you're still alive, he'll be back here for you."

This threat obviously caused Mario to reconsider, but he remained silent.

"Moreover, if you don't give me the address right now," Travis added, "I'm going to sink your fat butt back in the hot tub. And goose up the temperature. So *talk*!"

A shudder passed through Mario's body. "The address is beneath the blotter on my desk in the den upstairs. He lives about a hundred miles from here, not too far from Austin. But you'll never get in. He's got guards posted who stop everyone who comes in or goes out. He's got high-tech security equipment. And always a couple of bodyguards. At least."

"One problem at a time," Travis muttered. "Just give us—"

Travis was cut off by the ever-more-familiar sound of a bullet whistling overhead. He hadn't heard the gun fire; that made it all the more disturbing. He grabbed Mario by the neck and slammed him down on the carpet. Cavanaugh followed suit. He heard another bullet sail past.

"Where is he?" Cavanaugh mouthed.

Travis shook his head. "Outside the door, I think."

Travis pointed to their immediate right, and together they quickly crawled behind the pool table. Unfortunately, the table stood three feet off the ground. All the sniper had to do was crouch and—

Another whizzing sound. Travis heard a bullet smash into a leg of the pool table.

"This won't cut it," he whispered.

"What can we do?" Cavanaugh asked.

"Why are you asking me? I don't know."

"You're the ex-cop. What would a cop do?"

Travis grimaced. He heard the soft patter of footsteps on the carpet. Whoever was firing at them was moving closer. "Follow my lead." He rose up on his knees, pressed a shoulder against the pool table, and shoved. Good—the top separated from the legs, and the legs were screwed to the floor.

Cavanaugh lent her shoulder to the cause. Travis heaved and the tabletop fell forward off its base with a crash. Billiard balls and slate smashed onto the floor. The front legs propped the tabletop up at a forty-five-degree angle, creating a ten-foot-wide shield.

"How's that for cover?" Travis murmured.

"Better," Cavanaugh replied. "At least now he'll have to move away from the door."

"Unfortunately that doesn't change the fundamental fact that he's armed and I'm not. What happened to my gun?"

Cavanaugh shrugged. "I know I set mine down when I started mouth-to-mouth on Mario."

"Great."

Mario relaxed the expression of terror plastered across his face long enough to speak. "It's by the hot tub."

Travis stared at the hot tub—about twenty very exposed feet to his right. He didn't see his multistrike weapon. Must be on the other side. The side closest to the door, natch.

"I'm going to make a dive for the hot tub, Cavanaugh. Cover me."

"Cover you? With what?"

"Use your imagination."

Cavanaugh clenched her teeth and mumbled something he couldn't understand. He figured it was just as well. He crouched down near the end of the table and prepared to spring out.

He glanced back over his shoulder. "I'm ready."

He was startled to see Cavanaugh grit her teeth and grab a billiard ball. "Take this, you sorry son of a bitch!" she shouted. She reared over the tabletop and hurled the ball toward the door.

Travis heard the projectile clatter and ricochet around some exercise equipment, and heard their assailant drop to the floor. Good enough. He dove away from the table and scrambled toward the hot tub. He landed on his hands and executed a somersault that brought him right beside his gun. Not bad for a fat ex-cop. He grabbed his gun and scrambled back to the safer side of the hot tub, hugging the carpet.

Travis heard another bullet zoom over his head, this one much closer than before. Much too close for comfort. He flattened himself and tried to figure out what he was going to do next.

He heard a mechanical grinding sound coming from the door. No bullets followed. Something was wrong with their assailant's gun.

From his prone position, Travis saw Cavanaugh cautiously peer over the top of the pool table. "His gun is jammed!" she shouted. *"Go!"*

Travis took her at her word. He sprang to his feet, cocked the hammer back, aimed the barrel at the stocking-capped figure in the doorway, and . . .

And he could not pull the trigger.

"Goddamn it," Cavanaugh yelled. "Fire!"

He couldn't do it. His hands trembled, his fingers refused to move. He stared at the man in the doorway, fully aware that at any second he might clear the action and fire that gun. It didn't help. He still couldn't do it

"Travis—do something!"

The man in the stocking cap threw down his gun, pulled a long, curved knife out of his belt, and ran toward Travis. Travis hurled his weapon at the man's head. While the man ducked, Travis rushed him. Travis hit him around the waist and sent him careening backward. The man hit the wall, lurched away in the opposite direction, then tumbled backward into the boiling hot tub. He screamed.

The man beat his arms furiously, trying desperately to get out of the water. Travis knocked the knife out of his hand, then held him down by the shoulders. Cavanaugh ran out from behind the pool table, grabbed her gun, and trained it on the man in the tub. "Don't kill him," she said.

"I'm not letting him out just so he can come after us again," Travis grunted. "As long as he's fighting me, he stays in the water."

As if on cue, the man stopped struggling. Travis grabbed him behind the shoulders and placed a half Nelson lock around his neck. Once he was sure he had the man under control, he hauled him out of the water. Cavanaugh kept her gun trained on his skull the whole time.

The man's face was red and flushed and he looked as if he hurt. "Look at all this high-tech equipment he's packing," Cavanaugh said. She searched him, then systematically removed every gadget and weapon he carried, much of it now waterlogged and ruined. "This is the same man who attacked me at the library."

"Persistent son of a bitch," Travis muttered.

Cavanaugh ripped the man's stocking cap off his head. Travis's eyes widened.

It was Curran McKenzie. Mary Ann McKenzie's brother.

**65**

6 : 3 0 p.m.

Once Travis's eyes had retracted back into his head, he murmured, "This is the rape victim's brother."

"I know," Cavanaugh said, nodding. "I saw him in the courtroom, remember? Just after he talked to you. I believe you described him as an obnoxious wimp."

"Well, I got the obnoxious part right." He tightened his grip around Curran's neck. "Where'd you learn the commando tactics?"

"In the army," Curran spat out. "Green Beret, for your information."

"Where'd you get the spiffy CIA-issue equipment?"

Curran struggled futilely against Travis's grip. "I've maintained a few connections."

"Great. A man of mystery." He withdrew a canister from Curran's belt. "What's this? A time bomb disguised as a roll of film?"

"Just a roll of film. For the cameras."

Travis fingered the tiny binoculars. "And I guess this is how you spy on your neighbors."

Curran ignored him.

"So what's the story, super spook? Are you working for the Outfit or the FBI?"

A pained expression crossed Curran's face. "Neither one."

"Then what—"

"I'm on my own."

"On your own? Not a Green Beret anymore?"

"I had a disagreement with my commanding officer. Several, actually."

"But why are you following us? What do you want?"

Curran twisted his head around as much as Travis's grip permitted. "I want you dead."

"Me? Dead?" Travis stared back at him, dumbfounded. "What the hell did I ever do to you?"

Curran looked straight ahead and kept his mouth shut.

Cavanaugh pushed her gun into Curran's ribs. "Answer him."

"It's not what you did to me," Curran replied curtly. "It's what you did to my sister."

Travis released Curran's neck. "I didn't have anything to do with what happened to your sister."

"You had everything to do with humiliating her in court. You're doing everything you can to help Moroconi escape punishment for what he did to her."

"I was defending Moroconi, if that's what you mean. The prosecution's case against him is flimsy at best. Even scum are entitled to a fair trial. If you take that away, the whole system falls apart."

Cavanaugh stepped between them. "I don't think he's in the mood for a civics lesson, Travis. Look, Curran, I'm on the prosecution side of the courtroom. You can trust me. This desire to exact vengeance by projecting your anger onto the defendant's lawyer is very common, although most people don't do it with Puukko knives and laserscope rifles. But surely you can see you're misdirecting your anger. Your beef is against the men who attacked your sister."

"If I knew who those men were, I'd go after them," Curran said. "In the meantime, I'll settle for Byrne."

"Great." Travis slumped down beside the hot tub. "Just what I need. Someone else who wants to kill me."

"There are others?"

"Take a number, kid. I'm not sure you're even in the top five."

"Look, Curran," Cavanaugh said, "I'm sympathetic. I share your frustration. But I don't think you understand what's going on here. Why don't we all put away our big guns and just talk for a few minutes? Then you can decide if you still want to kill Travis."

Travis stared at her. "Put our guns away! And what if he decides he still wants to kill me?"

"One thing at a time, Travis. Can we talk, Curran?"

Curran frowned. "I suppose. As long as Byrne doesn't try to get away."

"He won't. I've got the car keys. *Mario!*"

Mario crawled out from behind the pool table. "Yes?" he whispered.

"Show us to the den, Mario, and unlock the liquor cabinet. We're going to have a nice, friendly chat."

While Mario retired to his master bedroom to pull himself together, Cavanaugh tried to convince Curran that Travis was as much a pawn as his sister had been. She explained that Travis had been appointed to represent Moroconi, that he had precious little choice in the matter, and that once appointed, he had an obligation to do his best to exonerate Moroconi. Most important, she tried to convince him that the last thing on earth Travis needed was another person trying to kill him.

"Who are these other people?" Curran asked, still suspicious. "Did you humiliate their relatives in public, too?"

Travis ignored the barb. "I thought one group was the FBI, but the FBI has never heard of them. I thought the other group was the mob, although the FBI assures me the mob has been cleaned out of Dallas. The paper trail leads to some corporation."

"I don't understand."

"Join the club."

Curran was silent for a moment. "Do you think these people who are after you could be the same people who attacked my sister?"

"I don't know," Travis said honestly. "Moroconi always claimed someone had framed him. At the least I think they know something about it."

"Then I'm in."

Travis blinked. "I beg your pardon?"

"You heard me. I'm in. I'll help."

"Forget it. I'm not letting you anywhere near a weapon."

"Wait a minute," Cavanaugh said. "What exactly are you saying, Curran?"

"I'm saying I want to help you."

"What do you think we're going to do?"

"Don't play dumb with me. I listened in on part of your conversation with Mario after you hauled him out of the hot tub. You're going after Moroconi."

"So?"

"So, I'm coming along. If these people know who attacked my sister, then I have as much right to go after them as you do."

"This isn't just a vigilante mission," Travis insisted. "They've kidnapped a little girl. I have to find her by midnight or they'll kill her."

"Then you'd better have me along."

"He has a point, you know," Cavanaugh said. "He's far better trained for this sort of mission than either of us." She eyed Curran carefully. "And you promise you won't hurt Travis till we're done?"

"I promise. Till we're done."

"Good. Travis, I think we should let him join the party."

Travis threw up his hands. "Cavanaugh, he tried to kill me!"

"But he promised not to try again. Till we're done."

"Oh, well then. If the man who's been stalking me for days *promises*, then fine. Here, Curran. Have a machete."

"I think he's okay," Cavanaugh said. "Just a little headstrong."

"Just a little—" Travis walked up to Curran and grabbed him by the lapel. "Look, Mr. Green Beret. How do I know you won't kill me in some gruesome super-secret way the first opportunity you get?"

"I gave you my word."

"I'd prefer a more tangible form of security."

"Like what?"

Travis pushed him away. "Forget it. Come on, Cavanaugh. We don't have time to mess around with him."

*"No!"*

The sudden rise in Curran's voice took them both by surprise. Curran's face was transfixed by some new, unrecognizable emotion. He seated himself in an armchair and stared into the fireplace.

"Mary Ann is more than just my sister," he said quietly. "She's my twin."

Of course. Travis had noticed the similarity in their features before.

"When we were growing up, we did everything together. We were the best of friends. She was always frail, timid. I was her protector. I was supposed to look out for her.

"I remember a time when we were in the fifth or sixth grade. I was supposed to walk her home, but I got sidetracked with some of my friends on the football team. Some bully hassled her on the way home. Actually, I think he had a crush on her but didn't know how to show it. Anyway, he pushed her down and scraped up her knee. She ran home crying. She scared so easily. When I saw her, I put my arms around her and said, 'I'm sorry, Mary Ann. I should have been with you. I'll never let anyone hurt you ever again.' "

Cavanaugh gently laid her hand on his shoulder. "Curran, you're not to blame for what happened to your sister."

"Oh?" His eyes burned into hers. "What do you know about it? I was visiting her when it happened. We had shared a pizza earlier that evening. I walked her back to her sorority house and heard her say she was going to that bar to find her roommate." He pressed his fingers against his temples. "I could have gone with her. She invited me. But it was late, and I was tired. So I left her alone. Just when she needed me most."

The three of them were quiet for several protracted moments. Only the crackling of wood in the fireplace disturbed their thoughts.

Travis walked out of the room and down the stairs. A few moments later he returned carrying Curran's gun.

"Here," he said, tossing it into Curran's hands. "You can come."

Curran's eyes slowly rose to meet Travis's. "You trust me with this?"

"You said you wouldn't try to kill me. At least not for a while. Right?"

Curran nodded. "Right."

Travis grabbed his own multistrike weapon and threw it over his shoulder. "Good enough for me."

A tiny smile appeared on Curran's face. "Maybe you're not so bad after all, Byrne. For a lawyer."

**66**

6 : 5 3 P.M.

Kramer had been suspicious from the start. After all, less than twenty-four hours ago, Mario had fired him and said he was to have no further association with the family. Now Mario wanted him to come to his home immediately. Was this some kind of setup? In fifteen years of working for Mario, Kramer had never been invited to his home. He hadn't even known where it was, and he suspected that his lack of knowledge was no accident. What the hell was going on?

To compound his suspicion, Kramer had seen a Jeep parked on the side of the private road leading to Mario's home, about five hundred feet from the front gates. Odd parking place, and not a car he would expect Mario to be driving. As if that wasn't enough, he found a green Hyundai parked not far from the Jeep. A quick call from his car phone told him the Hyundai was stolen.

Something unusual was happening at Mario's house.

As he approached the front door Kramer heard voices. Two voices, maybe three. None of them was Mario's. They were coming closer, approaching the front door.

Best to play it safe, Kramer decided. He'd fucked up too many times already; he wasn't taking any more risks. He ducked behind some tall hedges lining the driveway and waited to see who came out the door.

"I'm familiar with that area," Curran said as he, Travis, and Cavanaugh exited Mario's house. "I'll drive."

"Wait a second," Travis said. "I said you could come. I didn't say you could take over."

"I just thought it made sense, since I know my way around."

"I've lived in Texas all my life." Travis walked down the front steps and started across the large driveway fronting Mario's home. "I also know what some of the people on my tail look like. I'll drive."

"Suit yourself. I was just—"

Curran's voice suddenly faded away. Travis turned and saw that Curran had disappeared. One moment he was talking to Travis, and the next—

Cavanaugh pointed behind him. Travis whirled around just in time to see Curran dive over the hedge lining the driveway. What the hell did he think he was doing? Had he gone totally off the deep end?

A few seconds later Travis understood. Curran was rolling on the ground, wrestling with someone. Someone who must've been watching them.

Travis ran around the hedge. To his surprise, the man on the ground beneath Curran was not Moroconi. It was an older man, a tall man with a long, prominent scar on the side of his face. Travis had never seen him before.

Curran already had the upper hand. He was by far the stronger of the two, and he had pinned the man's shoulders down on the well-trimmed lawn.

The man reached inside his jacket for a gun. Curran knocked

it away with a quick, decisive slap of his hand. The man's other hand dipped inside his pants pocket and returned with a cigarette lighter. The man flicked the lighter, then pressed it up against Curran's face. Curran yelled, startled by the sudden burning sensation, but his hold did not diminish.

Travis ran forward and kicked the lighter out of the man's hand; it flew off into the hedge. Curran leaned forward and braced his arm just under the man's chin.

"I could kill you in three seconds," Curran said in a guttural voice. "And if you try anything like that again, I will."

The man relaxed. He stopped fighting.

"Who the hell are you?" Curran demanded. "Why were you watching us? And why are you carrying a gun?"

The man looked at Curran, then stared at Travis for a long moment. Then he glanced at Cavanaugh, who had just stepped behind the hedge. He didn't answer.

Curran brought his fists down on the man's chest. "I asked you a question! Who are you?"

The man gasped for air. He hesitated, then slowly formed the words. "I'm Inspector Henderson. With the FBI."

**67**

7 : 0 0 P.M.

"Henderson?" Travis said. "Why the hell are you sneaking around behind the hedges?"

The man shrugged, as best he was able with his shoulders pressed into the mud. "My goal is the same as yours. Finding Moroconi."

"And trying to recover your precious list, I'll bet," Travis said.

The man hesitated. Then: "That's right."

"How do we know you are who you say you are?" Cavanaugh asked. "Have you got any identification?"

"No, I'm undercover. I don't carry ID."

"So how can you prove you're Henderson?" Travis asked.

"Do you remember the password, Mr. Byrne? On the business card you received?"

Travis did. He didn't have the card anymore, but he definitely remembered the password.

"Good. Hickory dickory dock."

Travis answered. "The mouse ran up the clock."

"And the cow jumped over the moon." He grinned, crinkling his vivid scar. "Tricky, huh?"

"Yeah, you guys are regular geniuses."

"So he is who he says he is?" Cavanaugh asked.

"I guess so," Travis said. "I don't know how else he could've known the password. I called the FBI number in the directory, Henderson, and they said they'd never heard of you."

"We were trying to confuse you. Disorientation. After all, we were told you were a dangerous killer."

Curran did not relax his grip. "That still doesn't explain why you were watching us. In hiding."

"I didn't know who you were," he insisted. "I got a tip that something was going down at Mario Catuara's place, but I had no idea who the players were, or who came out on top. For all I knew, you could've all been mob enforcers. I was playing it safe till I knew who you were. I was about to identify myself when George of the Jungle here leaped on top of me."

Travis nodded. "Let him go, Curran."

With obvious reluctance, Curran did as Travis instructed. The man brushed himself off and rose to his feet.

"Look, Henderson," Travis said, "this whole affair is one gigantic mistake. I don't have your list and I haven't killed anyone. One of your own men killed that FBI agent."

"I know."

"You—" Travis stared back at him, stunned. "You *know?*"

"Of course." He recovered his lighter from where it had fallen. "I'll admit I was confused at first, but I figured it out eventually. One of our men went bad. Probably behind your alleged murder at the West End, too. Why would you want to kill those people? It doesn't make any sense."

Travis felt a wave of release rush through his body. "Then why are you after me?"

"After you? I'm here to help you."

Travis leaned against Cavanaugh for support; this was more good news than he could handle in a single sitting.

"I think we're both after the same quarry—Moroconi. Am I right?"

Travis agreed. Quickly, he told the man everything they had learned inside Mario's house, especially about where Moroconi was headed.

"We're on our way there now," Travis said. "Why don't you come with us?"

A slow smile spread across the man's face. For some strange, inexplicable reason, the smile made Travis shudder.

"I think that's an excellent idea," he replied.

"Good," Cavanaugh said. "Maybe you could call for some FBI backup."

"I'm afraid that's impossible. All my men are out on assignment. And by the time I got men reassigned from other departments—"

Travis completed his sentence. "Moroconi would've flown the coop."

The man tilted his head in assent.

"Well, at least you can join us." Travis glanced at Curran. "Any problems?"

Curran didn't say anything.

"Cavanaugh?"

"No. I like the idea of having a trained FBI agent along for the ride. As long as he doesn't shoot Moroconi before we can talk to him."

"I won't," the man replied. "I'd like to ask that gentleman a few questions myself."

"Good," Travis said. "Let's not waste any more time. Moroconi has almost an hour's lead on us as it is."

He agreed, still smiling. "Your car or mine?"

Kramer walked back to their cars with them. Not a bad recovery from a near-fatal blunder. He had been so intent on eavesdropping that he hadn't seen that idiot commando until he was flying over the hedge.

He had to think hard and fast if he was going to make this masquerade fly. At least he had managed to come up with the Henderson bluff, using the name and password he found in Travis's car. It was a calculated risk. He wasn't absolutely positive Byrne had never met Henderson, although it seemed unlikely. Henderson was a desk jockey—someone more likely to send flunkeys out to put the fear into a two-bit criminal attorney.

Apparently, Mario had blown it. Crumbled like a cracker. Gave away Jack's address. If Jack went down, he'd take the rest of the corporation with him. Byrne had to be stopped.

Of course, he'd been planning to take Byrne out anyway. Now he could be more than a paid assassin. He could be a hero. It wouldn't matter what Mario said about him, or what Mario tried to do to him. Mario would be the traitor, the weasel, the one who talked. Kramer would be the knight in shining armor, the mastermind who saved the family after Mario's blunder.

As they approached the Jeep Kramer noticed that the kid—Curran, they called him—remained a few steps behind him. Come to think of it, he was watching Kramer very carefully. Apparently the punk had some doubts about this alleged FBI man who dropped in out of the blue. Smart punk.

It was a perfect setup. He would stick to these people like glue, and let them lead him to Moroconi. Once that was done, he would simply wait for the right moment and blow Byrne's head off. On second thought, a bullet through the kneecap might be better—extremely painful and not immediately fatal. Then he would fire another bullet into an extremity every few minutes or so. Then set fire to his clothes. Slowly. It might take Byrne hours to die. Good. He wanted that shithead lawyer to suffer for what he had put him through. He wanted him to hurt.

He would just wait for the right moment, when this Curran punk was out of the way and not in a position to retaliate. Or he would kill Curran first. Whatever. He would probably have to kill them all, come to think of it, now that they had seen his face. Not that that particularly bothered him.

"We have to find Moroconi before midnight," Travis said. "Otherwise—" He didn't finish the sentence, but Kramer knew what he meant. He knew all about Staci's midnight deadline—since he'd created it himself and leaked it to his pigeon at the paper.

Byrne was holding the gun Curran had knocked out of Kramer's hand. He was obviously uncertain what to do with it.

"If it makes you more comfortable," Kramer bluffed, "you keep the gun."

"No," Travis said. "You're going to need it." He returned the pistol.

Kramer had to exert extreme control, but he managed to suppress his strong desire to laugh.

Thanks for the murder weapon, Byrne. Yours.

**68**

7 : 1 0 P.M.

In a small office on the penthouse floor of a high-rise in downtown Dallas, the real Special Agent Henderson stormed into
Agent Simpson's office. He was behind Simpson's desk before the
man had a chance to blink.

"Mr. Henderson!" Simpson cried, startled.

"Don't bother getting up," Henderson growled.

"Oh no," Simpson said, pushing himself out of his chair. "I
wouldn't dream—"

Henderson shoved him back down. "I want to know what's really going on, Simpson. And you're going to tell me."

"I don't know what you mean—"

"Bureau 99 is going to hell in a handbasket, that's what I mean.
I had a clean, perfectly functioning little team here, and suddenly
it's all gone to shit. I think we have a mole."

"A mole?" Simpson did his best to feign surprise. "Surely not."

"Spare me the crap. I'm onto you."

"Don't tell me you suspect that *I*—"

"No, I don't. You haven't the imagination." He hovered over

Simpson's chair; Simpson could feel his hot breath on his face. "But I think you know who it is."

"Why me?"

"You've always been a mindless little toady. Anything anyone wanted you to do, no matter how dirty, you were ready to do it."

Simpson tried to squirm out of his chair, but Henderson didn't give him an opening. "But, sir—"

"Mind you, I'm not complaining. There's a place for mindless toadies in every operation, as long as you know who they are and who they're working for. So that's my question, Simpson. Who are you working for?"

"You, sir!" Beads of sweat trickled down his brow. "I only take orders from you."

"Is that right? I just had some phone records pulled up from the central database in Quantico. Maybe you didn't know we had a double check on the phone monitor?"

Simpson's befuddled expression showed that Henderson had guessed correctly. "I didn't—"

"Funny thing. I found several unauthorized, unrecorded phone calls to Mr. Janicek's extension. And they all occurred while either you or the late Agent Mooney were supposed to be monitoring the phones."

Simpson desperately wanted to loosen his collar but feared it would be a dead giveaway. "You know, sometimes the switchboard gets so busy, it's possible I might miss a call—"

Henderson grabbed him by his shirt. "What really happened at that shopping mall, Simpson? I never believed for a minute that Travis Byrne killed Mooney."

"B-but—he did, sir. It was just like—"

"Bull. Makes no sense. And if he wasn't killed by Byrne, that means it was either you or Janicek."

He tightened his grip on Simpson's shirt, lifting him out of his chair. "One of you is going up the river, Simpson. Who's it going to be?"

**69**

8 : 1 2 P.M.

Travis and Cavanaugh hid in a grove of trees north of the large ranch-style home they had determined was the elusive Jack's current residence. It was a lovely, secluded area not far from Mountain Creek Lake. Curran had volunteered to make a preliminary sweep of the grounds. Although Travis had a hard time believing Henderson could be much help to him, for some reason, Curran had insisted on dragging the man along with him.

Travis tried to keep them in sight, using Curran's high-powered infrared glasses, but the slope of the hill obscured his view before they had traveled two hundred feet.

"How long have they been gone?" Cavanaugh whispered.

"Only about twenty minutes. Not long, really."

"Curran said he'd be back in ten."

"He was estimating."

"What if he's been caught?"

Travis tried to comfort her, even though her words only echoed his own thoughts. "Henderson is probably slowing him down."

"Henderson should know his way around the block if he's such a big FBI hotshot."

"Maybe he's been behind a desk too long."

"I suppose." She shuddered involuntarily. "Eerie-looking guy, though. Did you see that scar on his face? Gives me the creeps."

"Yeah. Well, you can't judge a book by its cover."

Travis was about to spin off a few more reassuring platitudes when he heard the barely discernible sound of approaching footsteps—a tiny crunching of leaves, an almost inaudible rush of air. It was coming from behind him, away from the house.

Travis's hand involuntarily went to his gun. He cursed himself bitterly. And just what did you think you might do with that gun, Byrne?

To his relief, he saw Curran trudging up the hill, Henderson a few steps in front of him. "How'd you get behind me?" Travis asked.

"Years of practice," Curran replied.

"So how's it look? Did you see any security?"

Curran and Henderson exchanged a meaningful look. "You could say that."

"A burglar alarm system?"

"True, they do have that. An electric touch-and-sound-sensitive system wired to every door and window in the house. Very sophisticated. Noise detectors, motion detectors. The works."

Travis swung his fist in the air. "Damn."

"Don't sweat it. The flaw with any system that big is that it requires a lot of power. I found the power source and cut it off. It's useless."

"So they're all in the house without power now?"

"What do you take me for? I didn't shut off all the power. I just cut the line feeding the security system. They'll never know the difference."

Travis's eyes brightened. "That's great. So we can just waltz on in."

"We can, assuming you can avoid the guardpost, the security cameras, the magnetic card gate, and the bodyguards."

Travis's chin fell. "Oh. Anything else?"

"Yeah. Moroconi's here. Henderson ID'd his silhouette in an upstairs window."

"Then I was right!" Travis thought for a moment. "If we can't get in, how did Moroconi?"

"My guess would be that he was admitted voluntarily. He seemed to be chatting with someone. And by the way, I never said we couldn't get in."

"Then you think we can?"

"I think it's possible."

"Okay," Cavanaugh asked, "how do we get past the security guards?"

"There are only two of them."

"I'm not that handy in a fistfight," Travis hedged.

"That's not the critical issue," Curran replied. "Frankly, I could take them both down myself. The issue is time."

"I don't understand."

"I could take them both out, but not before one of them triggered an alarm. Or called for help. That's why I need you."

"Wait a minute," Cavanaugh said. "If you can take out the burglar alarm, why can't you take out the phones?"

"I could, but the security guards might notice and they'd know something was up. I'll take the phones out once we've taken care of the guards."

"Why don't we just sneak past them?" Henderson asked. "You and I did it when we scouted the grounds. All those bozos are watching is the road in and out of the house."

"We probably could get past them," Curran answered. "But what if they notice a disturbance in the house after we break in? They'll get reinforcements, then come rushing in with big guns. And we'll be history. No, we need to take them out before we go inside."

"What if you do take these two?" Cavanaugh asked. "What about the bodyguards inside? What about the magnetic card gate? What about the security cameras?"

"One thing at a time," Curren replied.

T ravis and Curran approached the guardpost, one on each side, using the dense trees, brush, and darkness as natural camouflage. The post was basically a small shack with barely enough room for two men to sit. There were Dutch doors on both sides—top halves open, bottom halves closed. Presumably, one man covered incoming traffic while the other covered the outgoing. Both roads had a gate blocking the lane that could be raised by the guards.

Curran crept up to the Dutch door on his side, then sprang up to his full height. "Excuse me."

The guard nearest him jumped, startled to see a man suddenly appear in the doorway. "What the—" His hand moved toward the gun in his holster.

"Whoa! Calm down." Curran held out his hands reassuringly. "I don't want any trouble. My car broke down about a mile up the road and I can't get it started." He showed them the grease he had smeared all over his arms and face. "I thought maybe you'd have a phone."

The guard glanced at his partner, who shrugged. "I suppose that would be all right." He unlatched the bottom part of the Dutch door.

The instant the door was unlocked, Curran grabbed it and slammed it back into the guard. He doubled over the top of the door; Curran slammed it back again. The guard fell backward, knocking his partner against the control panel.

On the other side of the guardpost, Travis saw the other guard's hand groping for an alarm button. He leaped over the Dutch door and grabbed the man's hands. He heard Curran's fists connecting with some part of the other guard's anatomy, but he didn't stop to see what or where. His job was to make sure his man's hands didn't make contact with the control panel.

Suddenly Travis's guard bent forward and rammed his head into Travis's gut. Travis fell back with a shout. The guard dove for the control panel. In the midst of this sudden flurry, Travis saw Curran land another fist on his target. He was doing fine, but the guard was proving too resilient. Curran would be done soon, but not soon enough.

Travis grabbed his guard around the neck and jerked him away from the control panel just as the man's thumb was about to make contact with a large red button. He thrust the man's head downward; his chin struck the metal panel. He fell onto the floor, apparently unconscious.

Travis heard another punch and saw Curran's man fall to the ground in a similarly unconscious state.

"I can't believe it," Curran said. "You put your goon away before I did mine. How'd you do that?"

"Vitamins," Travis said, gasping for air. "Now take out the damn phones."

# 70

## 8 : 4 3 P.M.

Travis grabbed the guard by the back of his neck and shook him. He still didn't rouse.

"Nice job you did on him," Henderson commented. "He's out cold."

"That had more to do with the solidity of the control panel than the strength of my fists." He shook the man again. No reaction.

"Let me try," Curran said. He stood behind the guard, wrapped his arms under the man's shoulders and around his neck, then jerked him violently upward. Travis heard the guard's neck crack. His eyes shot open.

"Who the fuck—" The guard looked around furiously, then groaned. His head fell to one side.

Curran lifted the man's head and motioned for Travis to begin the inquisition. Travis searched back in the far recesses of his mind to his police days. Interrogation 101. Play on the suspect's insecurity. Make him uneasy, unsure. Don't let him know what you want. Let him wonder—

Oh, the hell with it. "Where's your security card? Punk," he added for dramatic effect.

The man stared at Travis, still semidazed. "My what?"

"Your entrance card. The little magnetic gizmo you stick in the box at the door so you can get into the house."

"Don't know what you're talking about."

"Yeah, right. Hold him tight, Curran."

Travis proceeded to search him. He followed standard police procedure; it was all coming back to him. He patted down the man's outer body, then came up on the inside of his legs and arms. In the man's shirt pocket, he found a piece of plastic about the size of a credit card with an electromagnetic strip on the back. "This it?"

Curran glanced at the card. "Probably. Let's sneak up to the house and give it a try."

The man sneered. "It won't work, you assholes."

"Did you hear that?" Travis said. "He says it won't work."

"What did you expect him to say? Be my guest?" Curran tightened his grip around the man's neck. "So why won't it work, chump?"

The man grimaced. "You ain't as smart as you think you are."

"I think he's referring to the voiceprint ID," Cavanaugh suggested. The man's immediate reaction told them she was right. "I've seen this equipment in operation before. You pop in the card and the machine asks you a few questions. Your voiceprint has to match the one the machine has on file."

"If he thinks that's going to stop us, he's in for a big surprise," Curran said. In the blink of an eye, he released his grip around the man's neck, whirled him around, and shoved him back against the guardpost. He held two fingers about an inch from each of the man's eyeballs.

"You see these fingers?" Curran asked. His voice was soft but dark; his expression was menacing. "Do you know how long it would take me to avulse your eyeballs? In case you don't know, that means to pop them out of their sockets."

The man shook his head slowly. He was staring at the two threatening fingers.

"About three seconds," Curran answered. "Believe me. I've done it before."

The guard's head was trembling. "You're a fuckin' lunatic."

"You know what? You're right." An evil leer crossed from one end of Curran's face to the other, transforming his boyish features into an eerie satanic mask. He rested his fingertips on the man's eyelids. "Two seconds left."

The guard's entire body shook, but he kept his mouth shut.

Curran pressed down on his eyelids. "One second left. And then—*pop!* go the eyeballs."

"Chrissake, *don't do it*!" The man's chest was heaving; he was on the verge of crying. "I'll do whatever you want."

"Good." Curran whipped him around again. "I'm going to tie you up now. Then we'll lead you to the front entrance to the house. We'll stick your card in the slot, and then you're going to say whatever it is you're supposed to say. You're not going to scream or yell for help. You might bring help, but not in less than three seconds. If you so much as peep, you may as well start shopping for a Seeing Eye dog. Understand?"

The man nodded nervously. Sweat dripped down both cheeks.

"By the way," Curran asked the guard, "has anyone else come calling today?"

"Yeah. Some other guy. I was told to let him in. 'Bout an hour ago."

"Who was he?"

"I don't know his name. Honest I don't."

"Medium-size, dark-haired guy? Ugly face?"

"That's him."

Curran glanced at Travis. "Your client's presence is confirmed." Curran wrapped a heavy cord around the man's wrists and shoved him toward the house. The others followed behind, careful to stay near the trees and in shadows.

Travis lagged behind. "Henderson," he whispered, "you're being awfully quiet."

"How long have you known this Curran fellow?"

"Oh, about half an hour longer than we've known you," Travis replied. "Why?"

"He seems . . . dangerous. Like a loose cannon. I wonder if we should be hanging so close to him."

Cavanaugh overheard. "What do you mean?"

"He's a lightning rod. Maybe we should let him stay well ahead of us. Deflect fire."

"I think we have to all stay together or we're history," Travis said.

The man nodded thoughtfully without comment.

The machine resembled an automated bank teller. Curran inserted the plastic card into the slot just beneath a small screen. The screen glowed blue; then the words *State Your Name* appeared in white.

Curran shoved the guard forward. "Elmer Thaddeus Brown," the man said.

Curran and Travis exchanged a look. *Elmer?*

The next screen asked for his job title. "Chief of security," the man replied.

The third and final screen read: *Password.*

The guard hesitated. Curran gently reached forward and placed a finger beneath each eyeball.

"Elcon," he spat out.

Elcon? Travis thought. Yet another connection between that corporation and the mob.

The blue screen disappeared, and a clicking noise told them the front door was open. Cautiously, they stepped inside. Once everyone was in, Curran closed the door behind them.

"Sorry about this," Curran told the guard, "but we need to reduce our risks." He reared back his fist.

Just before his hand connected with Elmer's face, Elmer ducked and rushed Curran. Curran was caught off guard; he fell backward against a sofa. Elmer's hands were still tied behind his back, but he managed to scramble toward the staircase. "Jack! Marty! *Trouble!*"

"Damn!" Travis raced forward and grabbed Elmer by his tied hands. Using the man's own momentum against him, he swung him around into a brick fireplace. Without the use of his hands, Elmer had no way to stop himself. He hit the bricks headfirst, then fell to the floor.

Barely a second later three men came rushing down the stairs. They were large, muscular types; there could be little doubt about their function in the household.

Before Cavanaugh could get out of the way, one of the men leaped over the banister, knocked her gun out of her hands, and shoved her down onto the carpet. Travis tried to intervene, but was stopped by another of the men, a tall, blond Nordic-looking behemoth. The blond took a swing at Travis's head. Travis ducked, but the man's fist still clipped him.

Out of the corner of his eye, Travis saw that Curran was having similar problems. The third bodyguard had him pinned against the wall, a large handgun wedged under his chin. Curran might know a hundred and five ways to kill a man, but he wasn't going to have a chance to implement any of them unless he got out of that chokehold.

He heard Cavanaugh scream, but couldn't see what was happening to her. A fist impacting upon his stomach reminded Travis that he had problems of his own. The blond knocked the breath out of him, and he hadn't the slightest idea where he had dropped his gun. The blond, however, had no such difficulty. He reached behind his back and withdrew a small revolver.

Travis grabbed the blond's arm and flung it up into the air. The gun was poised directly above their heads. Travis locked his arms and held on for dear life. Suddenly the blond shifted his weight and brought the butt of the gun down in a straight vertical line—on top of Travis's head.

He cried out. That hurt. He felt as if the blond had put an inch-deep gash in his skull. His eyes were watering, clouding over. He tried to tackle him, but the blond knocked him back with a swift boot to the chest. Travis fell to his knees.

Travis saw a shimmery outline of the blond leveling the gun at his face. He realized he was too dazed, too drained, and too far away to do a thing about it.

He heard a gunshot ring out. He was unsure what had happened at first; then he saw the blond fall face forward onto the carpet.

He heard another shot ring out. Behind him, Cavanaugh was lying on the floor while one of the assailants stood over her with a combat boot pinning her neck. The man's grip loosened, then he, too, crumpled to the floor. His wound leaked blood onto the white carpet.

Curran was still fighting. Travis ran to help, but saw that Curran had things under control. He had managed to reverse positions with his attacker and was slamming the upper half of his head repeatedly against the brick fireplace. Even Curran was startled, though, when the next gunshot rang out. The bullet caught the man in the neck; he was dead instantly.

"What the—" Curran whirled around, trying to figure out what had happened. "Henderson!"

He was standing by the front door, a smoking gun in his hand.

"You killed them!" Travis said.

"Yeah, before they killed you."

"Curran would've taken his man out soon."

"Maybe. We couldn't afford the risk. Or the delay."

"Couldn't you have . . . winged them or something?"

He ran the gun muzzle down the scar on his face. "The situation was getting out of control."

"But surely—"

"Don't give me a lot of crap, Byrne. Another second and you and the girl would've been dead meat."

Travis bit his tongue. The man probably had saved his life. And this would be a poor time to spread dissension in the ranks. "How are you, Cavanaugh?"

Cavanaugh rubbed her neck. The imprint of her attacker's boot was still visible, outlined in red. "Better than I was a few moments ago. Thanks, Henderson."

"At least someone approves," he grumbled.

"I didn't say that," Cavanaugh replied. "Don't they show you how to throw a punch at Quantico?"

"My evaluation of the situation was—"

"I'm surprised the FBI allows you to just summarily execute people."

"I'm authorized to take all necessary action in emergency situations."

"Still, that was just cold-blooded—"

"Cut him some slack!" Curran barked. "It was a tense situation. He did the best he could. He saved your butts."

"Yeah, although—"

"We don't have time for this. Jack and Moroconi could be crawling out the fire escape. Let's go upstairs."

Travis still didn't like it. Now a few more unnecessary deaths would be tallied under his name. But Curran was right—they had other tasks that took immediate precedence. Still, he didn't want this loose cannon near Moroconi. At least not until Travis had a chance to talk to him.

"Look, Henderson," Travis said, "we need someone to guard our rear. More thugs could show up at any moment. Reinforcements. Why don't you take a position behind the trees outside the front door? If anyone else shows up, you can come in behind them."

He frowned, obviously displeased.

"Not a bad idea," Curran echoed. "We don't all need to be upstairs with Moroconi. Do you mind?"

He took a long time before answering. "If that's what you want me to do, that's what I'll do."

"Good."

Grudgingly, he walked out the door to find a safe position among the trees.

Travis recovered his multistrike weapon from where he had dropped it on the carpet. "All right, team. Let's go meet the master of the house."

K ramer chuckled as he lit a cigarette and pressed it between his lips. Who would've thought that shit-for-brains Curran would be the one to come to his defense? He was the only one who had acted remotely suspicious of him before, and now he'd bailed him out of a tight spot.

It pained Kramer to be associated with such bleeding-heart amateurs, even if he was just waiting for a chance to rub them all out. What fucking idiots. Bursting into a room they knew would be guarded and then trying to slug it out with a bunch of professional bodyguards. If it had been up to him, he would've used firebombs, would've blown the entire house sky high. And he would've been safely tucked away in the forest, watching the beautiful billows of fire illuminate the hillside.

Christ—he had come with them hoping to kill Byrne and he had ended up saving the man's life! But it was too soon. He wanted Moroconi, and he couldn't blow away Byrne until he was certain he had him. Besides, he had the persistent feeling that Curran was watching him, even as he fought.

He wasn't thrilled about drawing guard duty, but if he had protested too much, they would've become suspicious. Actually, he reflected, this might work out for the best. Let those idiots find Moroconi, do all the risky stuff—and then deliver Moroconi into his hands. Yes, he realized, that was by far the most sensible plan of action.

After all, he could kill them anytime.

**71**

9:20 P.M.

Travis and Cavanaugh stood outside the closed door at the top of the stairs. Curran made a quick sweep of the other upstairs rooms and found nothing. Unless their targets had somehow escaped, they were behind that door.

Travis pointed toward the hallway corner, just below the ceiling. "Security camera."

Curran ignored it. "After a rollicking brawl and three gunshots, I have a hunch they know we're here." He gestured toward the door. "Shall we?"

Travis blanched. "What? Just open the door and stroll in?"

"What did you want to do? Sneak in through a ventilation shaft? You watch too much TV." Curran placed his hand on the doorknob. "Ready?"

Travis braced himself. He glanced at Cavanaugh, who was standing just to his side. She crossed her fingers and smiled. What a trooper. At least he had his police experience to fall back on. She was untrained but unafraid, steeling herself to plunge into almost certain danger. Hard not to feel strongly about someone like that.

The door swung open and they rushed inside. Travis had half expected to be greeted with gunfire. Instead he heard nothing.

The room was totally dark. Travis literally could not see his hand when he held it before his face.

He sensed movement beside him. Curran was pushing forward, exploring the darkness.

"Freeze," he heard a familiar voice say.

"Moroconi," Travis said. "Is that you?"

"Guilty as charged. For once. Nice to see you again, counselor."

See? Travis couldn't see a thing.

"That's right. I can see all three of you. You're outlined in the doorway, in the light from downstairs. But you can't see me, can you? What a goddamn pity." He laughed in his customary revolting manner. "I guess that gives me kind of an advantage."

"What's this all about, Moroconi? Why did you attack those people at the West End? Why did you set me up?"

"Because you're a self-righteous turd, Byrne. My mistake was leaving you eating gravel after I shook you off the back of my truck. I should've turned around and run over you five or six times."

Travis heard just the slightest shuffling noise on his immediate left. It didn't take a genius to figure out what Curran was doing. He was sliding his infrared glasses off his belt. Evening the score.

Travis tried to keep Moroconi distracted. "What about the list? Why did you have to drag me into that?"

Moroconi chuckled contemptuously. "You still haven't figured it out, have you, Byrne? What a fool."

"I was trying to help you, Moroconi. I still am. I haven't resigned from the case. Turn yourself in and we'll finish the trial. I promise I'll do the best job for you I can."

"Goddamn mouthpiece. You'll say anythin', won't you? What do you take me for?"

Travis took a tiny step forward. "I'm serious—"

"Don't move another step," Moroconi warned. "If you do, I'll blow your fuckin' head off."

Travis didn't doubt it. He had successfully managed to distract Moroconi, though. Even in the darkness, Travis could tell Curran was strapping the glasses over his eyes.

"Did you have anything to do with kidnapping Staci?"

"Staci? Who the hell is she? What am I bein' framed for now?"

"I'm just trying to figure out what the hell is going on."

"You and me both." Moroconi brushed up against something in the dark. A chair? "And I had a damn hard time gettin' my old chum Jack to talk to me."

So Jack was in the room. Funny that he hadn't said anything. Assuming he was still able to say anything.

Travis was sure Curran was getting ready to make his move. He fell silent and waited for a signal. He didn't have to wait long.

Curran's voice pierced the dark room. *"Get down!"*

Travis ducked, and he could hear Cavanaugh doing the same. A shot rang out from Moroconi's gun, but he had no idea where it went. Nowhere near him, anyway. He jumped to his feet, ran back to the door, and flipped on the lights.

The room was flooded by bright overhead bulbs. Moroconi stood behind a desk, squinting, waving his gun. Curran was already on top of the desk, and a moment later he knocked the gun out of Moroconi's hand. Curran brought his fist squarely into Moroconi's neck. Moroconi went reeling back against the windowsill.

"Are you all right?" Travis asked Cavanaugh. She nodded. Wherever Moroconi's wild bullet had gone, it hadn't been into her, thank God.

Travis ran to see if Curran needed help. He didn't. He had Moroconi pinned firmly facedown on the floor. Travis watched as Curran patted Moroconi down, then systematically pulled knives, condoms, and rolled-up wads of money out of his pockets. And a single sheet of paper.

Travis scanned the typewritten sheet. Names, aliases, addresses. This had to be the list. The real one.

Travis noticed red ink checkmarks beside four of the names on the list, the four geographically closest to Dallas.

"Blackmail," he murmured, more to himself than anyone else. "Not content to extract money from Jack, I'll bet Moroconi was planning to bleed bucks out of every ex-mobster on this list."

Speaking of Jack—where was he? The desk chair was facing the window. Travis swiveled it around . . . and found a man's body slumped in the chair, blood trickling down his face, a gag tied in his mouth. His face seemed familiar, but it was so contorted and smeared with blood it was difficult to see it clearly.

*"Jack?"* Travis said under his breath.

"That's him," Moroconi answered, twisting his neck around. Curran rammed his face back into the carpet.

Cavanaugh pushed Travis aside. She was holding two wet washcloths and a bottle of antiseptic. He had no idea where they had come from—probably the bathroom down the hall.

"You shouldn't have done this," Cavanaugh said, glaring at Moroconi as she dressed the wounds.

"The bastard deserved it."

"No one deserves to be tortured."

"What do you know about it, bitch?"

Cavanaugh turned away from him in disgust. "This isn't fatal," she told Travis and Curran as she wiped off the coagulated blood. "In fact, the cuts are minor. Moroconi was probably just scaring the man in his own sick way. I think he's in mild shock. It looks awful, but the blood is principally coming from just two superficial facial slashes."

"I had to!" Moroconi protested. "Fuckin' asswipe wouldn't talk."

Curran twisted Moroconi's arms painfully behind his back and tied them.

Jack was beginning to come around. Cavanaugh laid a cool washrag on his face and let it soak. The color gradually returned to his face. About five minutes later Travis decided he had waited long enough. He lifted the washrag off the man's face.

Yes. Now that the man had been cleaned up, there was no doubt in Travis's mind. He had seen him before.

He was the man who had created the disturbance in front of the warehouse four years ago. The man who had acted like a crazed religious lunatic. The man who had stolen his gun.

The man who had killed Angela.

# 72

9:41 P.M.

"It's you," Travis said breathlessly.

Jack turned away. "Shit. I was afraid you'd recognize me."

"Recognize you? How could I forget you?" Travis wiped his hand across his brow. "They told me you were doing time."

"They lied."

"What's going on?" Cavanaugh asked. "I don't understand."

"You and me both." Travis swung Jack around to face him eye to eye. "What are you doing on the outside? What's your connection to Moroconi?"

"Jesus T. Christ." Jack shook his head in disgust. "You still don't know?"

Travis grabbed him by his lapels. "What the hell are you talking about?"

Curran laid his hand on Travis's shoulder. "Stay calm, Travis. Let's just ask him some questions."

"I won't answer," Jack said.

Curran clutched the man's throat. "If you don't, I'll untie your

buddy Al and give him back his knife. I don't think he's quite finished cutting you."

Jack was visibly shaken. "Ask your stupid questions. What do I
care?"

"What's your real name?" Travis demanded.

"Who gives a flying fuck?"

Who did, actually? Travis realized he had only asked the question because that was standard police procedure. First line: Name.
Next he would probably ask for the man's Social Security number.

"What's your connection to Moroconi and Mario Catuara and
the rest of their gangland buddies?"

Jack sat in sullen silence. Curran grabbed him and shook him
hard.

"Don't you know what they do to squealers?" Jack shouted.
"The penalty for violating the *Omerta* is death!"

Curran gritted his teeth. "Don't you know what I'll do to you
if you *don't* talk?" When that didn't work, he slapped him several
times with the back of his hand. The contemptuous expression
melted into a *what the hell.*

"I was big in the Gattuso mob before the FBI shut it—" Jack
smiled. "Before the FBI *thought* they shut it down. I mean, I was
heavy-duty, locked in tight with the boys that mattered. The players. I got all the important jobs." He glanced at Travis. "Like the
one where I iced that bitch you were fuckin'."

Travis's fingernails dug into the palms of his hands. Stay in control. *Stay in control.* "I take it the mob wasn't altogether eradi-
cated?"

"Shit no." He picked something black out from between his
teeth. "See, we had us a contingency plan. Something to fall back
on."

"And what was the plan?"

"The FBI had the goods on most of the *made men*. But some
of us had been smart. We kept a low profile."

Lower than a rock, Travis suspected.

"We knew the feds were about to make their move. So we executed Escape Plan A. We merged."

"Merged?"

"Yeah. We'd bought a small corporation a few years before. Limited business, single shareholder. Small-potatoes stuff. And totally legitimate. The guy who ran the thing had no idea he'd married the mob. At first."

"He found out later?"

"He had to. Believe me, no one could write off the money that started pourin' through that corporation to increased market penetration. But the original owner just took the money and kept quiet. We wanted to keep him happy, see. We needed a place to stash the dough, someplace it would be safely waiting when we needed it. It was our golden parachute, right? Our private retirement fund. By the time this schmuck knew enough to be really concerned, he was in too deep. Besides, he was making money, real motherfuckin' money for the first time in his life. And he liked it."

"So when the FBI clamped down on all the known mob members, you and the other faceless ones phased into the corporation."

"Very smart." A tiny light began to shine in Jack's eyes. "It was a perfect setup. Instead of being criminals, we were suddenly legit businessmen. Everyone got titles—you know, president, vice-president—that kind of shit. It was a riot."

"That would be the Elcon Corporation."

"Right. The hell of it was, the stuff we did in the corporation wasn't any different from the stuff we did in the mob. Hell, some of it was worse, if you ask me. We still stole money and used whores and shit. Now all our new *made men* have MBAs and law degrees. And we get away with it!"

"Maybe *they* got away with it," Travis said, "but I notice Moroconi is still on the outside, and Mario said you turned state's evidence. What happened?"

"Al got greedy. He wanted a bigger cut—and threatened to screw the merger if he didn't get it. Basically, he was trying to steal money that wasn't his. The mob doesn't put up with that. Al al-ready had a huge private slush fund he'd squirreled away over the years. And now he wanted more. We had to do something. I wanted to turn him in to the feds, but Mario was afraid he'd squeal on us. We had to destroy his credibility—fix it so no one would believe anything he said."

"Why not just rub him out?" Travis asked.

"Believe me, it was considered. But we came up with something sweeter. We were concerned that the FBI was still snooping around for the kingpin. But they didn't know who he was. So I turned state's evidence."

"Why?"

"So I could tell the feebees—after a big show of not telling them—that the godfather was Alberto Moroconi."

Travis slapped his forehead. "No wonder the FBI wanted to talk to him."

Jack grinned. "It was perfect. The heat was off Mario, and Moroconi had to go deep undercover just to keep his butt out of jail. Killed two birds with one stone. I let the feds relocate me, and about a year after that, I let Mario—excuse me, *Elcon*—re-relocate me, so I'd be free of the feds and could cut myself back into the corporation."

"Which you did."

"True. A few months ago I got a tip from one of the boys about where Moroconi was hiding out. I spread some money around the police station and arranged for him to be hauled in on the first available major felony. Which turned out to be your rape case."

"Son of a bitch," Moroconi muttered.

"The mob shafted one of its own?" Travis said. "Whatever hap-pened to loyalty for life? Family ties?"

"Horseshit," Jack said. "Maybe you think the mob is about blood oaths and ring kissing, all that Hollywood shit. Let me tell you—in the real mob, the bottom line is always, 'Where's the money?' When Al wasn't profitable anymore, they cut him loose."

"So that's why Moroconi was out to get you," Travis said.

"Well . . . that and—"

"He stole my *fuckin'* money!" Moroconi shouted from the back of the room. Curran had tied him to a closet door.

Jack didn't deny it. "Before I went to the feds, I liberated Al's slush fund. Just to tide me over."

"I had six hundred thousand dollars," Moroconi yelled. "And he stole it!"

"It wasn't half enough," Jack said. "Pissant."

"If you were fixed for money," Travis said, "I'm surprised you didn't stay with the feds longer."

"Those assholes were totally incompetent. They couldn't protect their own dicks. This list crap is proof. Thank God they didn't have my address—I would've been dead days ago. I can take care of myself a hell of a lot better than they could."

Travis thought over everything Jack had told him. The jigsaw pieces were finally beginning to come together in his mind. And he didn't like the looks of the completed picture. "So when Moroconi broke out of prison, he came looking for you. Because you squealed on him."

Jack snorted. "Don't make him sound so noble. All he wanted was the money."

"And your butt," Moroconi added.

"In your dreams," Jack replied.

"Mario wrote to me a couple days ago," Moroconi said. "On his corporate stationery, no less. Threatening me, telling me to keep the hell away. I showed him."

Travis decided not to give him the bad news—that Mario was still alive.

"Anyway," Jack continued, "my men grabbed Moroconi when he burst in here, and I had some fun with him. When you fools burst in, I sent the boys downstairs. I heard the gunshots—I guess that explains how you got past them. Of course, this piece of shit Moroconi used that opportunity to take out his knife and rough me up a bit. Till he heard you three coming upstairs. That's when he hit the lights. He was scared shitless."

Travis noticed that Curran was peering out the corner of the window. "Has he just about brought this fascinating story up-to-date?" Curran asked.

"I think so," Travis replied. "Why?"

Curran removed his gun from its holster. "We're about to have company."

# 73

10:11 P.M.

Travis pressed close to Curran and tried to look over his shoulder. "Who is it?"

"I can't tell. But it's a man, and he's alone." They both heard the sound of the front door opening. "He's in the house."

Travis held his breath and listened to the soft footsteps crossing the living room downstairs. The intruder was undoubtedly surveying the scene, examining the dead men. Slowly, the footsteps moved toward the staircase.

Curran pressed himself flat against the wall beside the door. He raised his gun and held it suspended in the air.

"Is anyone up there?" The voice seemed harsh, authoritative.

"Who wants to know?" Curran fired back.

"I do. My name is Janicek. I'm with the FBI."

"Let him in," Travis advised Curran.

Curran frowned but obeyed. "All right," he shouted, "you can come up. But keep your hands in the air. If you go for a weapon, I'll shoot you dead."

Travis listened as the soft footsteps floated up the stairs. He pulled Cavanaugh closer to him. They both held their breath.

Travis recognized the man who stepped through the doorway, arms raised in the air. "I've met this man before," he said. "He visited my office and scared the hell out of me. He's FBI."

Curran slowly lowered his gun.

Janicek smiled. "I'm glad you remembered, Byrne. Your pal looks like he has an itchy trigger finger."

"Just cautious," Curran murmured.

"Why the hell did the FBI try to kill me at the shopping mall?" Travis demanded.

"We were acting on some . . . confused intelligence," Janicek said.

Travis noticed Moroconi, still tied to the closet door. He was being strangely silent. For the first time his obnoxious overconfidence seemed to have drained away. He almost looked scared.

"You've caught Moroconi. That's great," Janicek said.

"Yeah. And we recovered your goddamn list."

"That's wonderful. Can I see it?"

Travis hesitated. There was no reason not to hand the list back to the people who lost it, but something about this situation struck him as . . . odd. What was it?

Paranoia, he told himself. It's finally getting to me. He shrugged and handed over the list.

"Thank God it's safe again," Janicek said, shoving it into his pocket. "For all we know, Moroconi may have been planning to knock each witness off one by one."

"I suspect blackmail was more what he had in mind," Travis replied. "I have a lot of questions—"

"There'll be time for that later. I need to take this man into custody."

Janicek advanced toward Moroconi. Moroconi immediately moved away from him, as far as he could go while tied to the closet. "Don't let him near me," he said. "Please. Keep him offa me!"

Travis was puzzled. He hadn't expected Moroconi to go willingly, but he hadn't expected this reaction either. There was pure fear in Moroconi's eyes.

Janicek grabbed Moroconi roughly by the arm. "Don't give me any trouble."

"I'm serious!" Moroconi said. He was practically pleading. "This guy ain't what he seems."

That caught Travis's attention.

"Don't listen to him," Janicek said. "He's desperate. He's trying to confuse you."

"You mean he isn't with the FBI?" Travis asked Moroconi.

"No, he's with the FBI, but he's playing both ends against the middle. He's the one who *gave* me—"

Janicek's fist smashed into Moroconi's nose. Moroconi's head flew back and pounded against the closet. He tried once more to speak, and Janicek hit him again.

"What the hell was that for?" Travis demanded.

"He was getting out of hand," Janicek said gruffly.

"Out of hand? He's tied to the closet. What did you think he was going to do?"

Janicek proceeded to untie Moroconi. "Just stay out of my way, Byrne. Leave this to the professionals."

"You're not going anywhere until I get some answers."

"I don't have time to play twenty questions. Interfering with a federal officer in the execution of his duty is a felony offense!" He finished untying Moroconi and grabbed him by the arm. "I have to get this man into custody. I have to secure the list."

"Secure the list!" Moroconi said, blood dripping from his nose. "He's the one who gave me the list!"

*"What!"* Travis pushed Janicek away from Moroconi. "Is that true?"

Almost instantaneously, Janicek had his gun out of his shoulder holster. "Get out of my way, Byrne."

Travis stepped back cautiously.

Janicek jerked Moroconi toward the door, only to find Curran was blocking the way, gun raised. "You are obstructing an officer of the law!"

"Maybe so," Curran said. "But something about this smells."

"What do you care what happens to this piece of shit?"

"Not much, but I'm not going to let you execute him," Curran said.

"Stupid son of a—" Before Curran realized what was happening, Janicek swung Moroconi around between himself and Curran's gun. Curran almost fired, then stopped when he realized Moroconi had become the man's shield. Janicek shoved Moroconi into Curran, knocking him off balance, then clubbed Moroconi with his gun butt. Moroconi dropped to the ground like a rock. A second later Janicek pointed his gun at Curran's head and pulled back the hammer.

The sound of a gunshot electrified the room. Janicek screamed and fell to his knees. Clutching his chest, he tumbled to the floor.

Travis whirled around. "Henderson!"

He was standing in the doorway, gun drawn. "Thought you'd been inside too long," he said, entering the room. "Especially after I saw this clown go in. I got worried."

"Damn good timing," Travis said. "But did you have to use your gun again?"

"What did you want me to use? Harsh language?"

"Right." Travis picked up the phone on Jack's desk. "I'll call an ambulance."

Yet another voice echoed through the room. "Don't bother."

Travis looked up and saw an older man in the doorway, his hands in the pockets of a long overcoat.

"And who the hell are you?" Travis asked.

"I'm with the FBI," the man replied.

"Isn't everyone?" Travis said. "Or so it seems today."

"I'd be happy to show you my ID."

"Why don't you start by telling us your name?"

"As you wish," the man answered calmly. "My name is Special Agent William Henderson. You may have heard of me."

# 74

10:49 P.M.

The other man—the man they believed to be Henderson—whirled around to face the newcomer. Curran raised his gun and covered both Hendersons.

"Wait a minute," Travis said. "If you're Henderson, who the hell is he?"

"One of them is lying," Curran growled. "The question is which." Curran pointed at their first Henderson. "I've been suspicious of this one since he entered the picture. He doesn't look or act like any fed I've ever met."

"No, it's him!" shouted the first Henderson, pointing at the newcomer. "He's with the mob!"

"*He's* lying," the new Henderson said calmly. "Believe me, I've known who I am for years."

"How did you find us?"

"I followed Agent Janicek. When I arrived, I spotted this man hiding in the brush." He indicated the first Henderson. "When he made his move, I followed him in."

"You're with Janicek?" Travis said. "Janicek just tried to kill Moroconi."

"That can be explained."

"I called the FBI," Travis said. "They said they'd never heard of anyone named William Henderson. Either one of you."

"What did you expect them to do? Give you my phone number? My men and I work for a special subdivision called Bureau 99. It's kind of an FBI within the FBI. My work is extremely sensitive; I have one of the highest security clearances in the Southwest. After all, if the mob can get to me, they can get to any of the federal witnesses I've relocated."

"Our first Henderson knew the password," Cavanaugh reminded them.

"True," Travis said. He addressed the newcomer. "What's the password?"

"Which one? I know a dozen of them."

"See?" the first Henderson insisted. "He doesn't know it. That proves he's the imposter."

Curran grabbed the newcomer by the neck. "I don't trust anyone connected with this Janicek creep."

While they were talking no one noticed Moroconi pulling himself off the carpet and wiping a smear of blood from his face. He quickly surveyed the situation. *"Him!"* Moroconi shrieked, pointing.

The first Henderson glared at him.

"He's not the FBI! His name is Kramer. He's a fuckin' hit man!"

Kramer slammed into Henderson like a linebacker, square in the stomach, knocking him into Curran. Henderson doubled over and went reeling onto the floor; Curran fumbled for his gun. Kramer kicked Henderson's head against the desk. Henderson's eyelids fluttered, then closed.

*"Grab him!"* Travis shouted.

It was too late. Kramer was out the door. Moroconi started after him; Curran grabbed Moroconi around the waist. Moroconi swung his arms back and clubbed Curran on the shoulders. They both fell to the floor, struggling.

Travis didn't have time to help. Curran would eventually recapture Moroconi and Cavanaugh could look after Henderson. He wanted this killer Kramer.

Travis bounded downstairs and hit the first floor just in time to see Kramer fly out the front door. He leaped over the sofa, ran through the door, and hit the grass running. Kramer was making a beeline for the northern grove of trees, trying to disappear in the thick, dark brush. Travis couldn't see more than a few feet in front of him. If he let Kramer get too far ahead, he would lose him.

*Damn!* Travis ran as fast as he was able. Damn these stupid shoes, and damn me for getting so badly out of shape. He was doing the best he could, but Kramer was getting away from him. His lead had already doubled; soon Travis wouldn't be able to see him at all.

A sudden cry up ahead told Travis he had gotten a lucky break. Kramer must've tripped over a stump or something; Travis saw him fly into the air, then crash to the ground. It was just the chance he needed to catch up.

Kramer was lying prostrate in the mud when Travis reached him. Travis unstrapped his multistrike gun and aimed. "Don't move."

Kramer did not freeze. He lurched forward, grabbing at the gun. Travis managed to shove him back to the ground. This time he held the gun against Kramer's face. "Don't move or I'll shoot."

Kramer's face was covered with dirt and sweat, but that didn't prevent Travis from seeing the cold sneer that crossed his face. "I don't believe you."

Travis gritted his teeth and wrapped his finger around the trigger. Pull it, *damn it*! He knew he only had seconds at best before Kramer came at him again, but in the space of a single second every horrible memory raced through his head. Jack. Angela. Her face on the bloodstained pavement.

This was totally different, he told himself. This was a man who had tried to kill him. This was a life-and-death situation! He *had* to pull the damn trigger.

But he couldn't do it.

Kramer knocked the gun out of Travis's hands. Before Travis could move away, Kramer kicked up his feet and caught Travis in the abdomen. Travis sprawled onto the ground. He felt as if his chest were on fire. Before he could think what do to next, another kick landed in the same spot. He clutched his chest, writhing in agony.

Travis rolled onto his side, trying to squirm away, propping himself up with one arm. His ribs ached; he felt certain at least one was broken, maybe more.

Kramer reared back with his foot and kicked Travis once more in the gut. Travis screamed. His eyes were watering. The pain was so intense he couldn't think. Every time he tried to move, Kramer kicked him again.

Kramer shoved him over, then kicked him in the side. "Fuckin' piece of shit," he muttered. "Don't worry, I'm not gonna kill you. I'm gonna hurt you. Then I'm gonna burn you. Yeah—Byrne burns." He laughed. "Then I'll kill you."

Kramer removed his lighter from his pocket and lit it. He held it against Travis's face.

Travis cried out. Even after he moved his face away, he could feel the flame burning his flesh. Kramer moved the lighter to the other side of Travis's face. Travis screamed again. There was nothing else he could do. He couldn't run, could barely breathe.

Kramer lowered the lighter to the edge of Travis's jacket and watched as the windbreaker caught fire. "Welcome to hell, Byrne," he said. His eyes glowed with excitement.

Then, as he watched the flames catch on, he pulled out his gun, cocked the hammer, and aimed at Travis's kneecap.

Travis heard the shot. He winced involuntarily, bracing himself. It took him several moments to realize . . . he wasn't wounded. Before he could react, he felt about a hundred and fifty pounds slam down on his stomach.

After he regained his breath, Travis cleared the tears from his eyes and tried to figure out what had happened. He was still alive. His kneecaps were intact. And Kramer's body was sprawled across his lap.

And his jacket was on fire.

"Aren't you going to thank me?" Cavanaugh ran forward and beat the flames out with her coat. "Another second and you would've been about two feet shorter."

"Mucho gracious," Travis mumbled. It hurt to talk. "Where's Curran?"

"Taking care of Moroconi. How are you?"

"I've been better. Can you get this big lug off me?"

Cavanaugh bent down and rolled Kramer off Travis's stomach. Travis tried to help, but the strain was too much. He fell back to the ground, groaning.

"Oh God, Travis. You're really hurt, aren't you?" She put her hand behind his neck. "Are you going to be all right? Are you bleeding?"

"I don't think so. Except maybe internally. I think he cracked a rib."

"God. I'm sorry I didn't get here sooner."

Travis grunted, doing his best to speak coherently. "Not your fault."

She took his hands and held them against her cheek. "I don't want anything to happen to you, Travis."

He tried to smile. "Neither do I." After a moment he added, "I don't want anything to happen to you, either. Laverne."

She began kissing his face, then his neck, at first lightly, then less so. Despite the fire burning in his chest, he found it quite enjoyable.

# 75

11:55 P.M.

Henderson—the real one—finished wrapping a tight bandage around Travis's chest. Not an easy feat in the backseat of Henderson's sedan—while it was moving fast. Very fast.

"I think you should go to the hospital."

"Later," Travis said, wincing. "After I've found Staci."

"You should've ridden in the ambulance with Kramer and Janicek," Cavanaugh said, wringing her hands. "That would be a hell of a result—Kramer lives and you die."

"I'm not hurt that much," Travis said, hoping someone would believe him. He certainly didn't. "And it shouldn't take too long."

"At least let me go with you," Henderson insisted.

"No. He'll kill her if he sees you."

"Believe me, I know how to keep a low profile. I followed Janicek here, once I got Simpson to spill his guts. He never had the slightest idea I was following him."

"Thanks for the offer, but no. I won't risk Staci's life. I'll check in with you as soon as I'm done."

"Don't check in with me. Check in with the hospital. I'm not at all sure your ribs are going to survive this."

Travis ignored him. "I'll be okay. It won't take long."

"I still don't understand why you aren't going to Moroconi's old motel room," Cavanaugh asked.

"That's where the goons hired to kill me will be, but that's not where Staci is."

Cavanaugh nodded, then held out his gun. "Don't forget this. You might need it."

Travis took it from her wordlessly. Yeah, he thought, I might need it. But will I be able to use it?

A few seconds before midnight Travis stood on the front steps of an elegant Tudor-style home in the fashionable part of Plano. He rang the bell, but no one answered. Of course, he mused, given the size of the house, it might take ten minutes for someone to make it to the door.

But he couldn't wait. He felt exposed, standing out in the open like this. When no one came to the door, he tried the doorknob. It was unlocked.

He entered the foyer. The decor was impeccable. Heavy on the burgundies and mahoganies. Suits of armor, Victorian-era antiques. A man's house, decorated to a man's taste.

As Travis should know. He'd been here several times before. For dinner.

Travis heard footsteps approaching from the living room. He entered the room and waited. A few moments later a rear door opened and Dan Holyfield walked in.

"Travis! My God, it's you!" His face was the picture of concern. "What are you doing here? Are you still in danger? Why didn't you come to the office?"

"The office is being watched. Or was, anyway. Not to mention bugged."

Dan appeared horrified. "Are you certain?"

Travis nodded.

"At least you managed to get here safely. You can relax now, Travis. I'll take care of everything. I still think you should turn yourself in, but don't worry. I'll be behind you all the way, with every penny at my disposal. I won't rest until you're cleared of all charges."

Travis smiled thinly. "Don't bother, Dan. I have a new friend at the FBI who has already begun the process of clearing my name and getting the charges dropped. I imagine it'll be a lot easier for him than it would be for you."

Dan appeared relieved. "Well, that's great, Travis. Splendid. Come into the office Monday morning and we'll talk over this whole situation. We need to sit down and plan out your future. See where you go from here. Frankly, I think it's about time I made you a partner in the firm. Just come in Monday and we'll thrash out all the details."

Travis shook his head. "The office is too public for what I want to do."

"I don't understand. What is it you want to do?"

Travis seated himself in a comfortable upright armchair. "Give it up, Dan. I know almost everything. And I think I can deduce the rest."

"Deduce . . . ? I'm sorry, Travis, but you've absolutely lost me."

"What do you take me for?" A trace of anger tinged Travis's voice. "Did you think I would never figure it out? Hell, you just reminded me yourself the other day."

"Reminded you of what?"

"Of your small family corporation. The one to which you now devote the majority of your time. The corporation founded by your parents, Elsie and Conrad. Hence the name—Elcon."

The pleasant expression drained away from Dan's face. "What do you know about Elcon?"

"I know you were bought out by the mob. Excuse me, I guess

technically it was a merger. Forgive me if I don't get all the legal nuances just right. I'm not a corporate lawyer."

Dan's eyes lowered. "You have to understand what happened, Travis. I had no idea those men were connected to the Gattuso mob. They met me in business suits, ties—they looked just like the men you and I work with every day of the week. I had no reason to be suspicious."

"Did you check up on them? Complete a due diligence?"

Dan sighed. "Perhaps I jumped too quickly. The deal they offered me—it was everything I'd hoped for. I wanted to slow down, to get out of the grind of practicing law day in and day out. I'm almost sixty years old, and when a man reaches that age, he starts to think about retirement. And how he's going to pay the bills during his retirement."

"Pity you didn't stick with Social Security."

Dan made a snorting sound. "Don't be ridiculous. I didn't want to live in squalor and poverty." He gestured about the room. "Look at this place. Do you have any idea what it takes to maintain it? Do you have any idea what it takes to run it for a year? Social Security wouldn't pay for that chair you're sitting in."

"So you decided to sell out to a bunch of mobsters looking for a place to launder their loot."

Dan drew himself erect. "I told you, I had no idea they were connected with the Gattuso mob." His voice grew quieter. "At first. After a while . . . well, strange things began to happen. Inexplicably large amounts of money started pouring into the corporate coffers, money that wasn't tied to any of Elcon's business activities. And when I asked them about it, they told me to sit back and enjoy the ride. That's when I began to suspect that . . . they were something other than legitimate businessmen."

"Why didn't you go to the police?"

"I thought about it, Travis. I really did. But somehow . . . I don't know." He folded his hands in his lap. "Perhaps I'm just not as strong as I'd like to be. Somehow, I never made the call."

"They bought you off," Travis said. "And now they own you."

Dan didn't bother with a denial. "It would be difficult now . . . after all these years . . . to claim that I didn't know what was going on . . ."

Travis looked away. His eyes were beginning to sting. "Even if you let yourself be bought off, why the hell did you drag me into it?"

Dan's head tilted to one side. "Of course, the mob is the reason I gave you your job in the first place. I felt . . . responsible."

"Responsible?" Travis brushed the dampness from his eyes. "For what?"

Dan seemed genuinely surprised. "Haven't you guessed? That robbery you interrupted four years ago. The disturbance created by Jack Gable. That was a mob operation. They were robbing a building—I owned—for a reason. They had to create a cover story for the disappearance of some key corporate documents. To protect the integrity of the merger.

"You see, the IRS was after Elcon. They didn't know about the mob ties—but they knew there was something suspicious about the merger, and if they plowed around in the records long enough, they would've figured it out. We couldn't allow that to happen. So we created a robbery, to excuse our failure to produce the requested corporate documents. We told them they were all stolen. It worked."

Travis stared back at him, his head trembling. "Angela died . . . so your goddamn corporation could duck a tax audit!"

"Believe me, Travis, I had no idea you and Angela would be there that day. It was just a simple robbery. No one was supposed to get hurt. When it all went bad, I felt awful. Don't you see? That's why I put you through law school. That's why I gave you a job. I owed you."

Travis didn't know what to say. His heart felt as if it might pound its way out of his chest. "Did you know," he finally managed, "that your . . . *partners* were trying to kill me?"

"I found out. After you disappeared. From Mario Catuara, the acting head of the corporate entity. He was president, I was the CEO. That's how we set it up."

"You could have told me!" Travis shouted. "When I called you, you could have told me what was going on! You could have told me who was trying to kill me!"

"That would have been very difficult for me, Travis. Very difficult."

"No wonder you kept trying to get me to drop the Moroconi case. You knew all along."

Dan looked away.

Travis's teeth set on edge. "I'm turning you in, Dan."

"I . . . don't think you mean that, Travis."

"I do. I'm telling the FBI everything about you and Elcon."

"No." Dan rose suddenly from his chair. "No, you're not. Let me show you something." He walked to the rear door from which he had entered.

Travis saw a light click on. He pushed himself out of the chair and slowly walked to the other room. Before he entered, he removed his gun from his shoulder.

When he entered the library, his eyes were immediately focused on two persons just to the side of a large oak desk. The first was Staci. She was tied to an armchair; a gag was taped across her mouth. The second was Dan. He was pointing a small revolver at her head.

"You couldn't possibly fire before I put a bullet in this little girl's head," Dan said. "I want you to drop the gun, Travis. Now."

Travis hesitated. Police training told him never, under any circumstances, to relinquish his weapon.

"I'm serious, Travis!" Dan's hands were shaking. His finger was curled ominously around the trigger. "I want you to drop the gun!"

Travis bent down and placed the gun on the carpet.

"Thank you." He wiped the perspiration from his brow. "You can't imagine how sorry I am about this, Travis. I never wanted this poor girl to be taken. It was all that sadist Kramer's idea."

Travis took a careful step toward them. "Let her go, Dan. You don't need her now. You have me."

"I'm afraid I disagree. My life here in Dallas is shot. Just at the time when I was planing to settle down, I'm going to have to up-root myself. But I'm not going to be penniless. I—" His voice became high-pitched and strained. "I've worked too hard for that. I'm going to take all the money out of my personal bank accounts—and the Elcon corporate accounts—and disappear. But I can't do that until the banks open Monday morning. That means I have to prevent you from going to the police between now and then."

Travis bit down on his lower lip. "And how do you plan to do that?"

"This is so hard," Dan said. "So, so hard. You do see the dilemma I'm in, don't you, Travis? I don't want to hurt anyone. But I can't stand by and watch my life fall apart at the seams."

"You're going to kill me, aren't you, Dan?"

"I—don't see that I have much choice."

Travis nodded. The two men stared at one another from opposite sides of the room. There seemed to be very little left to say.

"At least let Staci talk to me for a minute before you kill me," Travis said finally.

"I—I'm sorry, no. I don't think that would be a very good idea."

"Then let me talk to her. Let me kiss her goodbye."

"I—I don't know—"

"I won't even remove her gag. All I'm asking for is one minute. Surely you owe me that."

Travis could see the confusion and despair in Dan's face. He was tearing himself apart, unable to decide what to do. "All right," he said finally. "One minute."

Travis approached Staci in calm, measured steps. "Hi, sweetheart," he said. He could see her eyes tearing, her hands shaking. She was scared to death.

"Sure I can't loosen her gag?" he asked Dan.

"I guess—I don't—" He swallowed. "No, I don't think I should let you do that."

"Suit yourself." Travis moved closer to Staci and crouched down to her level. "Don't worry about a thing," he said to her quietly. "Everything's going to be all right."

Staci rocked back and forth. Hard as she tried, she couldn't get free.

"When you get out of here, Staci, I want you to look up a friend of mine. Her name is—well, Cavanaugh. That's her last name. She knows who you are, and she'll make sure you're taken care of. I think you've been with Aunt Marnie long enough. Cavanaugh will help you make other arrangements. I don't think Marnie will protest much."

Tears spilled over the rims of Staci's eyes and trickled down onto her gag.

"You'll be fine. Don't worry about me. Really."

"Thirty seconds," Dan said.

"All right, all right." Travis winked at Staci. "How about one last trick, just for old times' sake?" He reached into his pocket. "Don't panic, Dan. These are just marbles." He slowly removed the marbles from his pocket, then opened his palm so that Dan could see that was all he had. "Two harmless oversize aggies. That's all."

He placed the marbles in his left hand, then held out his hands before Staci, knuckles up. "All right now. Watch closely." Travis's hands were a blur. They crossed, crisscrossed, turned upside down and right side up, one palm over the other, faster than the eye could follow.

"All right, Staci. Which hand are the marbles in?"

She shrugged. Travis knew her eyes were so blurred with tears she could barely see.

"What about you, Dan? Which hand do you think the marbles are in?"

"The left," he said, his voice squeaking. "They never moved."

"Well, let's just see." Travis extended his left hand to its farthest point and slowly unfurled his fingers, one by one.

The second he saw Dan's eyes divert to his left hand, he swung his right arm around and hurled the marbles at Dan's face. Dan instinctively raised his hands to block them. The gun fired; the shot went high. A second later Travis tackled him and knocked him onto the parquet floor.

Travis sat astride Dan trying to wrestle the gun from his hand. Dan did everything he could to aim the gun in Travis's direction. Neither was making any progress; it was a stalemate.

Suddenly Dan raised his knee into Travis's chest. The impact was not that hard, but it struck Travis exactly where he had been pounded by Kramer. The numbing pain returned, worse than ever. If his rib wasn't broken before, it certainly was now. Travis gasped, and in that moment Dan rolled away from him.

Travis grabbed at Dan's arm. He didn't stop him, but he did knock the revolver out of his hand. It skidded across the floor and under the desk. Dan ran for the front door.

Travis hauled himself to his feet. Every movement increased his pain a thousandfold. He forced himself to block it out, ignore it. Staci's life depended on him. Gritting his teeth, he lumbered across the room after Dan.

When he was almost through the room, Dan stumbled over the weapon Travis had left on the floor. He recovered quickly, but not quickly enough. Travis grabbed Dan by the collar and slung him forcefully down on the floor.

Travis grabbed his gun and pointed it at Dan's chest. "Don't move."

Perspiration dripped from Dan's face. He attempted a grotesque, unconvincing smile. "Travis, you—you wouldn't shoot me, would you?"

"Why not? You were going to kill me."

"Kill you? Oh, no—you misunderstood. I just wanted to delay you—"

"Save it, Dan. It's over."

"Over?" The smile faded from Dan's face and was replaced by something else, something far worse. "Over? My life over? Just because some stupid fat policeman is holding a gun on me?" He began to laugh, a thin, nasty laugh. "You're pathetic. This is Dan, remember? I know everything about you. And I know you don't have the balls to fire that gun."

Travis's eyes narrowed to tiny slits. He could feel the pounding of his heart, the aching of his chest. This was the man who had ruined his life, who had manipulated him from the start. The man who had lied to him, who had tried to kill him. The man who had terrified and threatened Staci.

This was the man who was truly responsible for Angela's death.

Travis's hands clenched the gun tightly. If ever he was going to recover his life, this was the time.

He wrapped his finger around the trigger and fired.

Henderson and Cavanaugh burst through the front door of Dan's house barely a second after Travis's gun sounded.

"What the hell . . . ?" Henderson scanned the foyer, then led the charge into the library. He saw the door standing open and entered, Cavanaugh close at his heels.

"*Travis!*" Cavanaugh ran to him. He was leaning at a tilt, clutching his chest. His gun hung limply from his right hand. "Are you all right?"

"I'll live," he said, oddly quiet. "Take care of Staci."

Cavanaugh saw the young girl tied to the chair. Taking Travis's pocketknife, she carefully cut the ropes that bound Staci to the chair and cut the gag off her mouth.

She planned to ask the girl how she was, but she never had a chance. Before she could speak, Staci leaped out of her chair and ran to Travis. She wrapped her arms around his waist and hugged tightly.

"He's hurt," Staci said.

"Travis," Cavanaugh said, "no more excuses. You're going directly to the hospital. Do not pass Go. Do not—"

She froze when she noticed Dan's body lying motionless on the floor.

She approached slowly, dearly afraid of what she might find. "You . . . shot him."

"Believe me, he deserved it," Travis replied. "I'll explain everything later."

"But—you shot him. I mean—you pulled the trigger."

The corners of Travis's lips tugged upward. "Yeah. Yeah, I guess I did." He threw one arm around Staci and the other around Cavanaugh. "Come on. Let's go to Denny's or something. I'd like the two of you to get to know one another. We'll let Henderson buy, as soon as he finishes cleaning up here."

Cavanaugh went along with him, but her eyes jackknifed to the body on the floor. Dan's body was splattered with red.

Red paint.

# TUESDAY

*May 14*

# 76

### 4 : 3 0 P.M.

"And so, ladies and gentlemen of the jury, despite what you may think of my client Alberto Moroconi, despite the desperate flight that interrupted this trial, and despite the great sympathy you and I share for Mary Ann McKenzie, the fact remains that the prosecution has not proven his guilt beyond a reasonable doubt."

Travis leaned against the jury rail. "The prosecution has failed to come forward with any positive identification linking Mr. Moroconi to this crime. They have not even proven he was in the neighborhood, much less that he was one of the vile perpetrators who tortured and abused Mary Ann McKenzie. With as little proof as that, can you sentence this man to a lifetime behind bars?

"No doubt about it—a cruel crime has been committed. An injustice. But let us not in our rush for vengeance compound the injustice. That will not help anyone. Indeed, that would only serve to make us as bad as the men who committed this foul deed."

Travis paused, clasped his hands together, and gazed out at the jurors. "There is an old story about a young student and his elderly Oriental master. The master was very old and wise, and it was said that he could answer any question. But the student was young and brash, and he decided that he would trick the master. He captured a small bird and enclosed it in his two hands."

Travis cupped his hands together in demonstration. "The student's plan was this—he would ask the master if the bird was alive or dead. If the master said the bird was dead, he would open his hands and let the creature fly away." Travis opened his hands and spread them across the expanse of the jury box. "But if the master said the bird was alive, then the student would crush his hands together"—Travis clapped his hands together suddenly, startling the jury—"and snuff out the poor creature's life.

"And so the student went to his master, the tiny creature cupped between his palms, and he said, 'Master, I hold a small bird. Is the bird alive or dead?'

"And the master looked directly into his student's eyes and said, 'My son, the bird is in your hands.' "

Travis made eye contact with each of the jurors. "Ladies and gentlemen of the jury, Alberto Moroconi is in your hands."

He held their gaze for an extended moment, then returned to counsel table.

After Judge Hagedorn dismissed the jury, Travis left Moroconi with a bailiff and strolled to the back of the courtroom. Cavanaugh was waiting for him.

"Now that the trial's over, am I permitted to smooch with opposing counsel?"

"I think that's in the Rules of Professional Conduct somewhere."

His lips met hers for a long, sweet moment. "How did I do?" he asked.

"Great, as always. You won the case."

"Don't jinx it. Let's wait until the jury returns before we declare a winner."

"Unnecessary. I know how it will come out. We had a flimsy case and you tore it apart. Moroconi may be vile, but he didn't commit this crime."

Travis nodded. "What has your boss decided to do about Dan?"

"The grand jury handed down the indictments this afternoon. Sixteen counts. Against him and Kramer and Mario."

Even now, weeks after Travis confronted Dan, he still couldn't shake his lingering sorrow. The man he had known so long and so well, the man he considered his mentor and hero, had met a pitiful end. "Should come as quite a blow to him."

"Well, he's had several severe blows lately. Including one involving red paint."

"I heard it took him a week to get it all off."

"You heard right. I can't believe he passed out when you fired that multistrike gun."

"Well, he was already quivering in his shoes, and the gun packs a pretty good punch at close range. Who's handling Dan's case?"

"I don't know. Not me. They're planning to use me as their star witness."

"What about me? I'm available."

"They're not ruling you out. But you've gotten a ton of bad press lately, and even if it's all retracted, they're afraid you'll be a suspect witness. Plus, your close relationship with Dan, and the money you've accepted from him over the years, would just give opposing counsel grist for cross-examination. If they can make it stick without you, they will."

Travis felt a hand slap down on his shoulder. The blow sent a spike of pain through his patched rib. Even now, it provided a powerful reminder of all he had been through.

It was Curran. He looked very different in his seersucker suit and tie. No infrared goggles. No Puukko knife strapped to his chest. "You actually went through with it, Byrne. I can't believe it."

"I had no choice."

"After all I did for you. You actually got Moroconi off the hook."

"There's no proof he committed this crime, Curran. I thought you hired a PI to track down the men who really attacked your sister."

"I did. But that's no reason to let this scumbag off the hook."

"Hey, I resent that." Moroconi was standing behind him, grinning from ear to ear. "I was innocent."

They both ignored him. "I was appointed to represent him," Travis explained, "and I had a moral obligation to do so to the best of my ability."

"Lawyer talk. Fancy words to hide behind."

"Well . . ." Over his shoulder, Travis saw Special Agent Henderson entering the courtroom. Brad Blaisdell, the U.S. Attorney, was standing beside him. They were having an animated conversation.

"Congratulations, Travis," Henderson said. "Brad tells me it looks like an acquittal will be forthcoming."

"That's right," Moroconi said. "So call off your FBI goons. I'm free to go."

"Well, not exactly. Brad?"

Blaisdell slapped a piece of paper into Moroconi's hands. "Mr. Moroconi, you're under arrest."

"Arrest? *Again?* For what?"

"First degree murder. Frank Howard. The guard you killed during your escape."

"There were no witnesses. That was self-defense!"

Blaisdell ignored him. "Plus the hit-and-run murder of one Eugene Hardcastle during your spree through the West End. Plus the attempted murder of Jack Gable."

"Says who?" He glared at Travis. "You're my attorney. You can't testify against me!"

"He's not going to testify against you," Blaisdell said. He pointed his finger at Cavanaugh. "She is."

Cavanaugh smiled pleasantly. "Told you that you shouldn't have hurt Jack."

"But—but—" Moroconi sputtered. "What about at the West End? She wasn't even fuckin' *there!*"

"We're going to get Kramer to testify against you there. We've offered to reduce his sentence if he talks. Say, from roughly twenty thousand years to only ten thousand years. I think he'll go for it. He doesn't seem to care for you much. And by the way, the second guard, the one who survived, will testify about your jailbreak. Sergeants."

Two uniformed officers grabbed Moroconi by both arms. "Byrne, you son of a bitch! You're my mouthpiece! Do something!"

Travis shook his head. "Sorry, Al. I only signed on for one case. My duties are officially terminated. Have a good day."

The sergeants dragged Moroconi out of the courtroom, kicking and screaming the whole way.

Travis looked pointedly at Curran. "Good enough?"

Curran slowly nodded his head. "Good enough."

Travis turned his attention to Blaisdell. "I understand you and your staff are going to be busy."

"True. We're putting together airtight cases against Holyfield and Kramer and Catuara. Even if we don't get the death penalty, we'll get life against Kramer. He'll die in prison. Parole boards never let anyone connected with the mob out."

"And what about the rest of the mob? The ones you don't have behind bars?"

Henderson and Blaisdell exchanged a concerned look. "That presents a problem," Henderson said. "Apparently as soon as you left his place, Mario contacted some of his mob buddies in Chicago. Some of the other Elcon officers have disappeared; we don't know what they're planning. We hope to track them down someday, but . . ."

"What he's trying to say," Blaisdell explained, "is that we have to assume the mob will attempt to exact some kind of retribution.

That's the way the Outfit works. Since Cavanaugh is going to testify against two of their own, and her testimony is likely to blow
apart this whole Elcon operation . . ."

"She's going to be a top-drawer mob target," Travis said, com-
pleting his sentence. He pondered for a moment. "Is Mario still in
the grand-jury room?"

Blaisdell nodded. "He should be with his attorney waiting to be
taken back into custody."

"Can I see him?"

"Why on earth would—"

"Can I see him?"

Blaisdell glanced at Cavanaugh, then shrugged. "Be my guest."

Travis crossed the hall and walked downstairs to the grand-jury
room. After brief conversations with the federal marshal on guard
and Mario's attorney, he entered the small witness waiting room.

Mario Catuara was obviously surprised to see him. "Byrne?
What the hell are you doing here?"

Travis stood in front of Mario. Although a chair was available,
he didn't sit. "I have a question for you, and I want it answered.
Understand?"

Mario had lost weight since Travis had seen him last. Ironically,
instead of making him look healthier, it made him seem tired,
spent. "Suit yourself."

"Am I a marked man?"

Mario pursed his lips but did not answer.

"Answer me, Mario. And no bullshit."

Mario licked his lips, then slowly began to speak. "After
Moroconi tried to kill me, I panicked. I called my . . . business associates in Chicago. I told them everything. The general consen-
sus was that you knew too much about us."

"And Cavanaugh?"

Mario nodded grimly.

"Call them off, Mario."

He spread his arms helplessly. "Once the wheels are set in motion . . ."

"You owe me, Mario. I saved your worthless life. More than once."

"Still, I—"

"I thought your organization prided itself on honor. I thought you paid your debts."

"I'm sorry, but—"

"And if you don't, I'm going public with my account of how you acted like a sniveling coward and revealed mob secrets to Moroconi. You violated the *Omerta*, Mario. The blood oath of secrecy. And I understand the penalty for that is somewhat severe."

Mario sighed. "Even if I did everything I possibly could, it would be months before . . . before it would be wise for you to appear in public."

"That's fine. Just take care of it."

"And you'll keep your story to yourself?"

"I will."

Mario bowed his head slightly. "You have my word."

Travis returned to the courtroom upstairs. Cavanaugh, Blaisdell, and Henderson were still talking. "Have you worked out a deal for Cavanaugh yet?"

"I'm prepared to offer her full-scale, round-the-clock protection until the trials are completed," Henderson said. "And afterward I'll take her into the Witness Relocation Program. This is a totally revamped program. Heightened security. Bureau 99 has an entirely new staff. Janicek and his clique have been expunged. And," he added significantly, "we're going to burn all the lists."

Travis glanced at Cavanaugh. She must have seen this coming; she remained calm. "For how long?"

"As long as necessary. It's just a precautionary measure. After this all blows over, if we determine that there's no continuing danger, she can come out of hiding. If she wants. Think of it as an extended vacation."

Travis nodded. She would be safe until Mario got his dogs back in the kennel. But . . .

Cavanaugh seemed to be reading Travis's mind. "Can I bring my friend Travis undercover with me?"

"Is he going to testify?" Henderson asked.

"Not if we can avoid it," Blaisdell replied.

Cavanaugh stepped forward and took Henderson's hand. "Please," she said quietly.

"Well," Henderson said, clearing his throat, "FBI policy wouldn't permit you to bring a *friend.* But you could certainly bring your husband. . . ."

# SATURDAY

## *June 29*

# 77

## 6 : 45 P.M.

Travis arranged the firewood, the leaves, and the scrap paper in a proper campfire formation, then waited patiently. The instant Cavanaugh turned her back, he whipped out a lighter and started the fire.

Cheating? True. But despite being a Boy Scout for five years, he had never managed to get the hang of that rubbing-two-sticks-together routine. Working with a flint was even more difficult. It had been such a pleasant, peaceful four days out at Robbers' Cave; he didn't want to spoil it with petty aggravations.

"Hey, you got the fire started," Cavanaugh said. She sat down and snuggled next to him. "Congratulations."

"It was nothing." At least he couldn't be called a liar.

She grinned. "You're my hero."

"Don't be silly. It's easy, Cav—" He closed his eyes. "I mean, Daisy."

"Takes some getting used to, doesn't it? Harvey," she added.

"Yeah. But I'll get it down."

"No rush. We have lots of time." She put her arms around him.

"I feel great. My blood pressure and ulcer are under control, and I've dropped ten pounds. Despite your cooking." He smiled. "You miss your job?"

"Nah. You?"

"Not much. Miss your friends?"

She hugged him tightly. "Not when I'm with you."

He returned her embrace. "Ditto."

"Is Mary Jo still fishing?" she asked.

"I certainly hope so. This fire is ready to cook, and I for one am tired of canned beans." He pulled Cavanaugh to her feet. "Let's check on her."

They walked hand in hand to the bank of the lake, only a few hundred feet from their campsite. Staci was standing near the edge, bracing herself against a tree. Both hands were clenched tightly to her fishing pole.

"Look!" Travis said. "I think she's actually caught something this time!"

"Of course I've caught something!" Staci shouted. "He's a gigantic rainbow trout—the biggest I've ever seen. I've been trying to reel him in for ten minutes."

Travis ran up behind her. "You should have called for help."

"I've *been* yelling for help, but you two were probably too busy making moony eyes at each other to notice."

"Is that so?" Travis waved his hands dramatically over the edge of the bank. "Now watch this. I'm going to make the fish jump into my lap."

*"No more magic tricks!"* Cavanaugh and Staci shouted in unison.

Cowed, Travis braced himself behind Staci and grabbed the fishing pole. Cavanaugh stood behind him, reaching under his arms to add her support. As the sun dipped below the horizon, they were all pulling together, laughing and shouting, a newborn family frolicking under assumed names.

## ACKNOWLEDGMENTS

Once again, I want to thank those who have made me seem much more knowledgeable than I really am: Trey Matheny, for his extensive telecommunications background and the first-person tour of WilTel switching facilities; Arlene Joplin, for everything you ever wanted to know about federal criminal law but felt stupid asking; Dave Johnson, for his insights on police procedure and the criminal community; Gail Benedict, for whipping my manuscripts into shape and putting up with endless confusing revisions; F.W. "Steve" Stephenson, for his unwavering support; and my wife, Kirsten, for virtually everything else.

**William Bernhardt** is a partner and trial attorney at the Hall, Estill law firm in Tulsa, Oklahoma. Mr. Bernhardt's efforts in providing legal services to the poor and elderly and his work with teenagers interested in law resulted in his receipt of the Oklahoma Bar Association's Award for Outstanding Service to the Public. In 1993, the American Bar Association's *Barrister* magazine named him one of the top twenty young lawyers in the nation.

Mr. Bernhardt made his debut as a novelist with *Primary Justice*, and he has since completed five other novels: *The Code of Buddyhood*, *Blind Justice*, *Deadly Justice*, *Perfect Justice*, and now, *Double Jeopardy*.

He lives in Tulsa with his wife, Kirsten, and their children, Harry and Alice.